Praise for LINDS...

Dreamstrider:

"Livia's a very appealing protagonist . . . [who] will engage readers and leave them rooting for her to succeed."
—*School Library Journal*

"The imagery of dreams and nightmares is unusual and vivid, and a web of romances and arranged marriages among the spies adds emotion and intensity."
—*Kirkus Reviews*

Sekret:

★ "[A] smart and fresh supernatural take on the spy novel."
—*Publishers Weekly*, STARRED REVIEW

"Smith's debut novel not only captivates through its fearsomely stubborn main character but also through its intriguing setting. . . . Will keep teen readers on the edge of their seats and primed for more." —*VOYA*

"The teen is a vivacious, clever character with a voice full of spellbinding imagery and wit. Smith mesmerizes readers with sprints and twists in the plot."
—*School Library Journal*

"Cold War espionage smoothly blended with psychic romance." —*Kirkus Reviews*

Skandal:

"The author's elegant, occasionally poetic prose serves as a refreshing contrast to the unrelentingly swift plot."
—*School Library Journal*

"Well-paced action and mystery for an appealing heroine, complete with Cold War attitudes." —*Kirkus Reviews*

DREAM STRIDER

LINDSAY SMITH

SQUARE
FISH

ROARING BROOK PRESS
New York

For Dahlia, Ellen, and Leah,

who always push me to chase my dreams

(and add more kissing scenes)

SQUARE
FISH

An Imprint of Macmillan
175 Fifth Avenue, New York, NY 10010
fiercereads.com

Library of Congress Cataloging-in-Publication Data

Smith, Lindsay, 1984–
    Dreamstrider / Lindsay Smith.
        pages cm
    Summary: "Livia can enter other people's bodies through their dreams,
an ability that makes her an invaluable and dangerous spy for her kingdom."—
Provided by publisher.
    ISBN 978-1-250-09070-6 (paperback)   ISBN 978-1-62672-043-5 (ebook)
    [1. Dreams—Fiction.   2. Fantasy.]   I. Title.
PZ7.S65435Dr 2015
[Fic]—dc23

                                                                2015011848

Originally published in the United States by Roaring Brook Press
First Square Fish Edition: 2016
Book designed by Elizabeth H. Clark
Square Fish logo designed by Filomena Tuosto

1 3 5 7 9 10 8 6 4 2

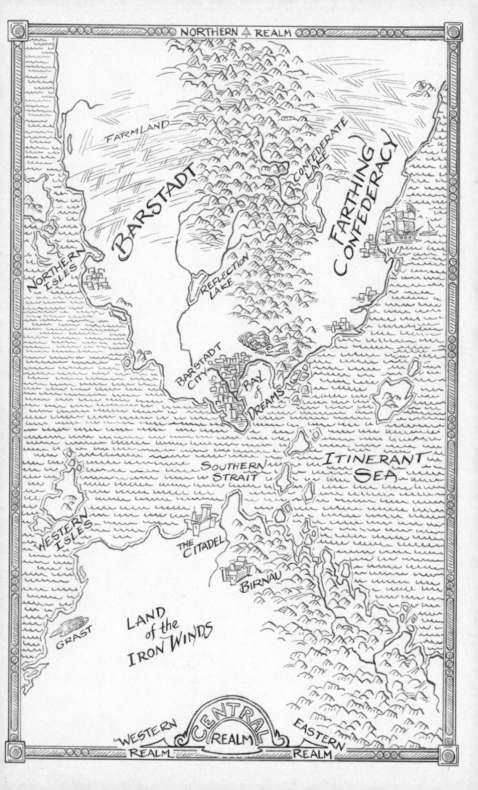

Prologue

I always dreamed too big, too bright, too much. Every night, in the dank corners of the tunnels, the knobby spines of other tunnelers digging into my own, the Dreamer filled my head with promises of a better life. A life of sunlight and beauty—a place where I'd have purpose, and I could serve the Dreamer and his faithful people in the Barstadt Empire. He filled my head with hope.

But hope might as well be poison to a tunneler like me. We're not meant to become anything more than what we are: the unseen, unheard hands that carry out the menial tasks for Barstadt's dazzling daytime world. Hope seeped into my bones and weighed them down. For who wants to scrub at grime, sink her hands into painful limewater, and pocket away crumbs, day after day? Not when her nightly dreams hint at a life of real beds and warm stews as she defends Barstadt from nightmares and the enemies at its borders. I was poisoned with such dreams, and I had no way to flush them out.

Then Professor Albrecht Hesse offered me the antidote.

My tunnel's ganglord rented me to the university for cleaning duties, but in Professor Hesse, I found a friend. He knew so much about the Dreamer, and Hesse was more than happy to teach me, chatting with me throughout the night while he monitored his experiments and I tidied his lecture rooms. I was bursting with questions about the Dreamer and the meaning of my dreams, but the more Hesse taught me of the sleeping world, the more I realized I knew nothing of the waking one. Soon I begged him to teach me to read and to write, to explain the history and politics not only of our home, the Barstadt Empire, but also its colonies and other neighbors in the Central Realms. But dreams—it always came back to my dreams, where I earned glory and fortune protecting Barstadt from pirates, enemy armies, gang leaders, monsters, and any other evil my sleeping mind conjured up.

"You dream so vividly—far more than my jaded students," Hesse told me one evening, while he read over my meager attempts at recording my dreams and I rushed to finish my cleaning tasks. "A gift like this should not be wasted." He offered me a chair. "How would you like to learn to make your dreams come true?"

As if there were any answer I could give but a desperate yes.

Hesse pulled a red leather journal from his desk drawer and sketched a girl sleeping in a city. "Every night when you sleep, you dream in the world of shallow dreams." He drew a trail like a tether from her down into a forested land. "But there is a shared dreamworld, as well, for the Dreamer's most faithful.

2

That world is called Oneiros. It exists in perpetuity, watched over by the Dreamer. The souls of the Dreamer's most devout can enter Oneiros, bound to their bodies by a slender cord."

I was bound by a thousand ropes in those days. Paying tithes to the tunnel enforcers and turning over most of my earnings to the gangs. Hunting for crumbs to feed myself and my half brothers and sisters. Enduring the cruel scrape of my mother's nails as she stared through me and begged me to bring her another wad of Lullaby resin to let her sink into dreamless sleep.

"I can take you to Oneiros, if you like." Hesse pulled two vials from his laboratory stand and held one out to me. "The world of your dreams."

I considered all the ropes that bound me to this world, but it was my dreams that decided for me. Perhaps Oneiros could make them feel more real. Perhaps in Oneiros, I could find a way to make them so.

I took the vial.

• ◦ ● ——————— ● ——————— ● ◦ •

One minute, I was sitting in Hesse's study, and the next, I was tugged away, like the lurch of sudden sleep. Sunlight surrounded me, golden liquid sunlight dripping down my skin. To a girl from the tunnels, that sunlight I'd rarely glimpsed in the real world convinced me I'd do whatever it took to make this my life.

I ran first, sprinting across the vivid jade grass, over flowers that twinkled as though their petals were made of jewels. But my feet were weightless—I stretched my legs and leaped in great bounds until I was flying, arms wide, soaring into the fresh, clean air. A vast quilted land unfolded beneath me—fields and forests and whitewashed stone cottages. Mountains loomed in the distance, and in a valley to my right spread a city with a central spire. Trailing behind me, more felt than seen, was that golden tether from Hesse's sketch. But this rope didn't try to restrain me—it only kept me whole.

As I flew toward the spire in the sparkling city, I recognized the two golden posts at its crown, thrust skyward: they represented the Dreamer's Embrace, guiding his faithful toward their dreams. I landed atop the crown and, as I scanned the beautiful world around me, tears stung my eyes. For the first time in my life, my dreams seemed within reach.

In a soft gust of air, Professor Hesse landed beside me. "What do you think, Livia?" he asked.

I blinked away the tears as I turned to answer him. "I think I like it better than the real world."

Hesse smiled, but it looked forced. "So do I."

· ·•· ———— • ———— ·•· ·

We entered Oneiros rarely, at first. Hesse taught me how to navigate it only after all my work was done and we were sure my gang masters wouldn't find out. But I hungered for the dream-world with an ache that deadened everything around me, and Hesse was only too happy to indulge my pleading for another journey, while the dust thickened along the university's baseboards and the floors dulled with grime. At the end of each trip to Oneiros, I hurried back to the tunnel entrance, too many chores left undone.

But one night, I lingered in Oneiros after Hesse departed to tend to his work, and I returned to the waking world much later than usual; thin tendrils of sunlight were already stretching across his office windows. In a panic I grabbed my cleaning rags—I'd be punished by the gang lieutenant if I wasn't at the tunnel entrance before sunrise. Just as I was about to hurdle out of Hesse's office, though, I was stopped short by the sharp sounds of an argument in the next room.

"—but you said yourself she isn't ready. I don't think it's worth upsetting the gangs over one little tunneler."

"She's clumsy and careless, I admit. Stunted by life in the tunnels. But she's learning. She's not ready yet, but she's the best prospect I have," I heard Professor Hesse say. "I can't keep her from her duties to the gangs much longer. Someone's bound to complain. We have to choose now."

My breath ached in my lungs. Clumsy, careless, stunted— Hesse had always showed me nothing but kindness.

"I don't suppose you could hire her directly from them? Give you more time to see whether she's really suited to our work?" the other voice asked. "We can't give her this kind of power over the sleeping if there's a chance we could lose her back to the gangs."

"No, if we ascribe too much value to her, it'll attract the gang leader's interest. I prefer we give her temporary papers—purchase her outright, and if she demonstrates her worth, then maybe when she's older we can grant her her freedom," Hesse said.

"*If* she demonstrates her worth," the other man echoed.

I spun away from the door, squeezing my eyes shut. I'd never heard Hesse speak this way before—so callously, with none of the patience and kindness I was used to from him. I knew my life was worth less as a tunneler, but to hear him, of all people, speak of me like a belonging—the way the gang lieutenants spoke of me—

"Hey, it's all right. You can't take them too seriously."

I nearly leaped out of my skin at the sound of the voice. A boy perched on top of Hesse's desk, chin propped on his fist. He was only a few years older than me, dressed in the impeccable suit of a young aristocrat, but with a wry smile that belied his formal clothes.

"I'm Brandt," he said, looking me right in the eye. Dark blond hair thatched his tawny face, hanging into his eyes without diminishing their intensity.

I forced myself to look away. "I'm—I'm not supposed to be talking to you." I shrank back from him, pressing against the wooden door.

Brandt hopped off the table and stepped toward me. He moved with an ease I could only dream of—confident and unhurried. "It's okay. I know all about you—your secret's safe. Hesse says you're an incredible dreamer." He held out one hand to me. "That he can barely keep up with you in the dreamworld."

I started to reach for Brandt's hand, then thought better of it and pulled myself to my feet. "You've been to Oneiros, too?"

"Are you kidding? I'm no good at dreams. My skills lie elsewhere." Brandt plucked a piece of parchment off Hesse's desk and began folding it as he talked. "I can lift the mustache right off a constable, though, and persuade a banker to give away all his coins."

"You can't either," I said, crossing my arms.

Brandt smiled at me, lopsided. "Well, maybe not yet, but it's good to have dreams."

He finished folding the blank sheet into a paper sculpture of a lily. I scowled at him as he held it out to me. "What are you doing here?" I asked.

"We're going to work together. Hasn't Hesse told you? He's got big plans for you."

I stared, something tightening in my gut. "For me? But . . . why?"

"Because you're special." Brandt tilted his head. "There's no one else who can do what you do."

"I—I'm afraid you're mistaken." I backed toward the door, twisting the cleaning rag in my hands. "I'm just a tunneler. And I have to get back underground."

Brandt took another step toward me. "But what about your dreams?"

I froze. My dreams stirred inside me, restless, unable to stretch their wings.

"I heard you have dreams of doing great deeds for the

Dreamer and Barstadt," Brandt said. I turned around to face him. "Is it true?" His expression softened, open and warm. "Because I don't dream like that, but I'd love to hear about them."

For all his ease, the tunneler in me was suspicious. I didn't survive in the tunnels without suspicion in my bones. "Why? What can you give me in exchange?"

He tilted his head. "Well, I can show you what you need to know about the Ministry."

"The Ministry?" I asked.

But then the door swung open, and Professor Hesse and another gentleman stormed into the office. Brandt tensed, snapping to attention like a soldier, but Hesse went straight toward me and clutched me by both shoulders.

"Livia. You told me once that you wished you could be free of the gangs." Hesse's face tightened as he studied me. "Is that still what you want?"

I stared back, trying to reconcile the callous man I'd just overheard with the kindly Hesse I'd always known. Which one was the truth? "Of course it is."

"You'll have to work hard," he said. "Not for the gangs, but for Barstadt. For the Dreamer himself. Are you willing to do that?"

My heartbeat throbbed in my ears. Barstadt was a land of growth, of achievement, of expansion. How could a malnourished little girl possibly embody those things? Yet the Dreamer hinted at greatness for me. For all of Barstadt. "I am."

Hesse nodded, glancing over his shoulder toward the other man. "Good, good. Livia, this is Minister Durst from the

Ministry of Affairs. He's going to purchase citizenship papers for you."

I swayed backward. "My papers? But I—" My head spun; I felt my knees buckling beneath me. "You mean I'm going to be free? I don't have to live in the tunnels any longer?"

Minister Durst pursed his lips. "Not quite. The Ministry of Affairs will retain the papers for safekeeping until you're old enough to determine your own fate. But you'll be free of your masters in the tunnels, and we'll take charge of your training along with Hesse." He tugged at his coat lapels. "It's quite an honor to work for the Ministry. And we are honored to have someone with your potential."

"But what *is* the Ministry?" I asked.

The minister turned toward Hesse. "I thought you'd taught her the most basic of—"

"We're the Emperor's secret police," Brandt said, words spilling from him eagerly. "We keep tabs on the aristocrats and the gangs, disrupt criminal activities, conduct spy work abroad . . . I mean, I haven't done any of that *yet*, but I will." He grinned at me again, that wide gas-lit smile. "We can learn together."

"Spy work?" But if Hesse thought I was clumsy, slow-witted, daft . . . "I'm not sure I'm cut out to be a spy."

Hesse snorted. "Don't be foolish, child. What you offer is somewhat different."

Brandt stepped forward. "Anyone can be a spy," he said. "But no one can use the dreamworld like you can. What you're going to do is something much better than basic spy work."

"No. I'm afraid you're all mistaken. I'm just a tunneler.

And—and I really need to return." I looked down, face burning, and found the crumpled paper lily in my hand.

Hesse's grip eased on my shoulders. "But, Livia, you can be so much more. I'm going to teach you how." Hesse smiled then—a real smile, the sort I only ever saw from him when we were in Oneiros. "I'm going to teach you to dreamstride."

Part One

DREAMS

Chapter One

'll never get used to those first few moments of dreamstriding, when I open my host's eyes and look down at my own body crumpled before me. Today, it's in the hay of a stable hundreds of fathoms from home: fear tightens my jaw even in sleep, honey curls spill over my ruddy, freckled shoulders, and my chest flutters with shallow breaths I no longer control. I want nothing more than to burrow back into my shed skin.

But before I can return to myself, Brandt and I have a mission to complete. Everything depends on me and my skill.

While the Ministry employs dozens of spies like Brandt, each better trained and with sharper reflexes than me, when the mission is this critical, I'm the one person they can't afford not to use. I've endangered lives with my clumsiness, blown informants' covers with my slow wits, but this cursed gift forever guarantees me a spot on the team. Yet I wish anyone else could have been given this skill. It pulled me from the sewage-laced tunnels I was born to and gave me a purpose, the life I'd longed for, but the weight of failure hangs heavy on my soul. I wish I could give this gift to someone more deserving.

But there is no one else. I call myself a dreamstrider because there are no other dreamstriders to protest.

While my body sleeps, I inhabit the body of General Cold Sun, a top military commander in Barstadt's neighboring kingdom across the southern strait. The Land of the Iron Winds. Our sources report that the Land of the Iron Winds is preparing to attack Barstadt, but we've not been able to gather proof or plans. And so this is what all of Hesse's research into the dreamworld led to: while the general's consciousness sleeps in Oneiros, I can fill his skin, walking and talking as if I'm him.

At first, Cold Sun's skin hangs awkwardly around my soul like a wet shift, impossible to shrug into place. His joints move all wrong, like he's a crude marionette, and I'm not used to seeing the world from his height—the tops of doorframes loom dangerously close, and I have a view of the cowlicked crown of Brandt's head. But slowly, I adjust. I steal into the gaps between his heartbeats and the rhythm of his breath. I ease into the general's muscles, his bones, his very marrow. For the next few hours, while the mothwood smoke we piped into his carriage keeps his consciousness dormant in Oneiros, his body is mine.

"Oh! Livia! Why, I can hardly tell a difference." Brandt grins up at me as he wriggles into the valet's outfit.

I try to twist General Cold Sun's face into a scowl, but it quickly breaks into a grin. "A flattering look for me, don't you think?" My words grate through the general's vocal cords like coarse sand. I help Brandt scatter hay over my abandoned body,

14

covering up that cold, vacant face, as well as the unconscious general's valet, whose clothes Brandt's now wearing. "Let's find out what the Commandant's planning."

Brandt leads us from the stables, and in only a few paces, his confidence melts into the guise of the meek, hunched little man-servant we'd drugged inside the general's carriage. Unlike me, he can become someone else without leaving himself behind. But this is what it means to dreamstride—this is the freedom Hesse promised me. I hold the tether from General Cold Sun's body. So long as I hold that tether, my soul can control his body in the waking world while his soul slumbers harmlessly in the dreamworld.

As we round the stables, Brandt halts with a sharp inhale. A towering fortress of black metal juts from the earth before us, turrets like claws raking through the rust-hued sky. We've reached the Citadel, the seat of power for the Commandant—the supreme commander, general, and for all intents and purposes, god—of the Land of the Iron Winds. It smells sharp like a smith's furnace, molten and a little bit like blood.

"Now to see if our spies were lying to us or not," Brandt says. Foreigners are barred from entering the Land, and all subjects are forbidden from leaving. Everything we know about the Citadel and the Commandant was smuggled out of the Land at great cost. Entering it terrifies me, but Brandt is electrified. He was born for this—the chase, the subterfuge, the danger. I can almost see the plans spinning like a weaver's loom in his mind. I have no such gift. If I were in control of my own stomach, I'd probably be emptying it right now.

The Citadel's front entrance is cut into the vertical ridges of the fortress, a heavy portcullis raised over it, with guards on either side. They shift their weight as we approach, halberds swinging from hand to hand like great pendulums. The glowing doorway behind them casts their faces in shadow and stretches their horned-helmet silhouettes across the slate path.

"Compatriots," the first guard barks. "Speak to the winds so the trees may filter the truth of your words."

I barely manage to conceal a shudder. We've studied the reports about the speaking style of the Land of the Iron Winds, but it still gives me chills. "I present General Cold Sun, whose loyalty to the Commandant no winds can erode." Brandt's Iron Winds accent is flawless—airy as a loaf of Kruger's bread and duller than dirt. He keeps his eyes on the ground and his hands clasped before him.

"That is for the Iron Winds to decide," the guard says. I can't read his expression—in part because of the failing light, and in part because our Ministry instructors stressed that a general should not make eye contact with a mere guard. "The Commandant is expecting you. Please proceed."

My racing thoughts echo through the general's hollow body as we cross the threshold, and I sense it in Brandt as well. In each of our missions, we reach a moment when we've bound ourselves to the whims of fate, and the only way out is to survive whatever lies ahead. I used to think Brandt and I functioned best in this moment—our strengths harmonizing, his hand ready to catch mine in our intricate waltz that has foiled gang leaders and corrupt aristocrats. But since the Stargazer Incident, I can only pray that we work so well this evening. I know Brandt can play his part. But the question is, can I play mine?

The portcullis slams down, and a locking system clicks and whirs into place behind us. As we pass through the hall, I glance up at the vaulted ceiling paneled with thousands of mirrors, all throwing back the reflection of General Cold Sun with Brandt beside him. I can see other figures, too, lurking in the corners—the tufted hats of hidden guards, tucked behind the corridor's ribs.

Focus, Livia. One misstep and I'll get Brandt killed, and my soul trapped in Oneiros, far away from my body's tether—and the Nightmare Wastes are a deadly prospect I'd rather not dwell on. Brandt raises his head, breaking character just long enough to give me an encouraging nod. It's time.

Now I have to figure out where in the nightmares we're supposed to go.

I cast my thoughts back into the forests of Oneiros. When I am in another's body, my consciousness straddles two worlds; my subject, however, stays asleep in the dreamworld. General Cold Sun's consciousness threads through the woods in the form of a calm, cool stream. As long as he stays asleep, his body is vacant enough for me to occupy. But to find the information we need, I'll have to disturb his slumber. I can't press too deep into his memories—I have to let them trickle out naturally. I've practiced this countless times. I can get away with small ripples—he'll remember the glimpses of wakefulness as only a hazy memory—but every disturbance will tug at his consciousness and risk waking him up.

17

If the general wakes up, he can cast me out of his body, leaving my soul untethered in Oneiros. And if that happens . . . I say a quick prayer to the Dreamer to protect me and dangle my fingertips in the stream.

General Cold Sun's thoughts trickle past me, chaotic, like the illogical knotted yarn of a mind on the edge of sleep. I sink my hand deeper into the stream and spread my fingertips wide. I have to sift through the thoughts and bring them to order.

I channel General Cold Sun's consciousness and let his deeply ingrained habits take over. His instinct is to charge down the hallway before us, and I follow his lead: he remains oblivious of the guards, paying no mind to the strange bared-teeth sharp corners and polished black stone of the Citadel. With Cold Sun's guidance, I stride with purpose straight for the compound's heart, focused only on the Commandant himself.

"Come," I bark. The voice from the general's mouth startles me, harsher than I'd intended. Brandt falls into step behind me. My feet—General Cold Sun's feet—know the way, and his thoughts lap at my fingertips to guide me.

Our journey through the Citadel coils on itself like the roots of a tree. I quickly lose my sense of direction, but the general's instincts seem to be carrying us along the right path. We approach a suite of guards flanking double doors.

I clear my throat, waiting for them to open the door. Brandt fidgets beside me. I glance toward him, about to scowl, until I realize he's trying to prompt me. Oh, yes—they want the passphrase. I dip deeper into the general's stream of thoughts within Oneiros to coax the passphrase from him. The water runs faster

18

the deeper I sink into it. "You shelter the Commandant as a roof shelters us from snow," I say.

"But even roofs can collapse, General. We shall never fall." The captain of the guard snaps his boots together and stands aside.

The heavy doors creak open.

Thick shadows fill the hall before us, punctured only by wrought iron chandeliers, their chains twisted around columns like vines. The smell of cold metal washes over us. At the far end of the chamber, on a raised platform, a figure sits bathed in candlelight. We stride toward him in near-darkness. No, not one figure—two, but the second springs away from the first and disappears down the platform in a flurry of sparkling gems. Sapphires, diamonds, flecks of silver.

Brandt and I glance at each other, my suspicion mirrored on his face for only a moment before he resumes his role. Was that a Barstadter who just slipped away? Our aristocrats stud their faces with jewels, cultivating elaborate, swirling designs on their forehead, cheeks, and throat as they accumulate power and wealth. Perhaps we aren't the only Barstadters in the Land of the Iron Winds after all. The very thought chills me through.

We're too far away to make out the Commandant's face, but we know what to expect from our informants' sketches and smuggled bits of artwork: cut-glass cheekbones and a pointed, gaunt jaw. Yet when we reach the base of the platform, we find a soft-faced man not five years my senior. I flinch, struggling to keep the general calm despite my shock. This young man with the faintest tuft of a goatee on his bone-pale chin can't possibly be the same Commandant who's ruled the Land of the Iron Winds since he seized power thirty years ago and enforced the Iron Winds code of strength and victory at all costs. My mind churns over the possibilities—maybe he overthrew the previous Commandant, or maybe he's the first Commandant's son.

Whatever the case, we've been trained to lure information from the wrong man.

"General," he says in an uneven tone. "You walk against the wind, but you do not fall."

General Cold Sun's pulse starts to canter. Not falling to the wind sounds like a good thing, but the Commandant is looking at me like there's something I should do. Am I supposed to be kneeling? I glance toward Brandt. He's not urging me to kneel, so I stand as tall as I can and try to remember our training. I've rehearsed for this moment even if the Commandant's identity has changed.

"I shall never fall with the Iron Winds at my back," I say. The general's voice ricochets through the rows of columns, then echoes back toward us in the dead air. The Commandant stands unmoving, unblinking, and panic cinches tight around me. What have I done? Everything in me wants to abandon the mission and flee, but I force myself to hold the general's breath and wait for a response.

Slowly, the young Commandant smiles, then charges down the stairs to grip my hands in his own. "You are early," he says before giving both my hands a hearty shake with his. He's much shorter than Cold Sun and pudgy in the midsection. No, this is certainly not the old, gaunt Commandant.

"I did not wish to keep my Commandant waiting when victory is so close," I say. The Commandant lifts his eyebrows for a fraction of a moment—have I misspoken again? We were told the old Commandant demanded complete and utter subservience at every turn, but maybe this Commandant distrusts excessive posturing. My head hurts just considering the possibilities. These personality games are Brandt's realm. I know his instincts won't fail us; that boy could talk our way out of the grips of Nightmare himself. But Brandt can't pose as the general for me.

The Commandant holds one arm out to his side. "Come, then. Let us waste no more time."

I climb the dais on wobbly legs. The barrel-chested General Cold Sun must weigh three times what my body does, and though walking usually works out the kinks, stairs are another matter entirely. Sweat builds under the general's armpits; in Oneiros, the stream is flowing faster now. I pray to the Dreamer that Cold Sun's slumber will hold.

The Commandant escorts me to a low wooden table at one end of the platform, where a scroll painted in shades of brown and black is weighted down across its surface. It takes me a moment to recognize the design as a map of the Itinerant Sea, where it swoops up the western edge of the Land of the Iron Winds and sneaks through the narrow strait that separates the Land from the Barstadt Empire in the north. Black iron figurines in the shapes of horses' heads, pikemen, war vessels, and cannons line up along the Commandant's edge of the table.

I lean forward, scarcely able to contain the excitement

skittering through me. It was all worth it—my uncertain dream-striding, the outrageous expense in smuggling us into the Citadel, our months of preparation to infiltrate the Iron Winds' culture. Because our informants were right.

The Land of the Iron Winds is preparing to invade Barstadt—and I'm looking at the battle plans.

The Commandant shuttles three of the war vessels to a port city on the western shore. I squint to make out the stylized lettering of the city's name. Grast. "The Second Fleet will await your troops in Grast in one month's time," the Commandant says. "Will they be ready by then?"

Were this the older Commandant we'd prepared for, I would know it's not a question at all, but an order, unless I fancy getting Cold Sun's head conveniently detached from his body for him while he sleeps. This Commandant, however, seems more casual than the man described in our reports. Nonetheless, I'd rather err on the side of caution. I suspect one doesn't become Commandant without an explosive blend of shrewdness and egomania.

"Whatever the Iron Winds . . ." I glance toward Brandt, but he's looking through the living space on the other side of the dais, searching for additional clues while the Commandant's focus is on me. I cast about for a suitably formal word. "Demands."

The Commandant nods. "And what of the battle preparations I proposed?"

A spicy curse springs to my tongue—well, the general's—but I stop from voicing it. I knew I'd have to sink deeper into the general's thoughts sooner or later, and this is far too important not to take the risk.

In Oneiros, I dip my bare feet into the stream and settle them into the loose dirt at the bottom. Suddenly a cloud passes over the sun, flooding the forest with darkness. The birds cease their chatter. Am I interfering too much with Cold Sun's thoughts? I fight to rein in my panic. *Focus, Livia,* I remind myself. *Direct the stream and nothing more.* The battle preparations. How did the Commandant send them to Cold Sun? By raven, by horseback messenger? *Hurry, General, yield your secrets. Awaken just enough to provide the answer.*

The stream churns, frantic, agitated by my probing. *Elite squadrons,* it cries. *Troops from the west.* But the water is leaping up, crashing against the banks—I've pushed too far; I'm letting him wake too much. He'll remember this conversation as more than just a hazy dream. I need to hurry and leave the Citadel before he wakes up completely.

"We shall have two of the elite squadrons prepared for Barstadt City's dockside gates." I'm rushing through the answers I gathered from the general's thoughts. "And the ground troops will arrive from the west." *Please, Dreamer, don't let him awaken.* But then another thought of the general's reaches his lips before I can stop it—"You're not seriously considering the mystic's proposal, are you?"

Brandt's back is to me, but I see him pause, hands withdrawing from whatever he'd been reaching for. The Land of the Iron Winds is supposed to be stern, revering subservience to the Commandant above all else. Nothing in our research indicates

23

they are given over to mysticism about anything but the Commandant's supremacy.

"That isn't your concern," the Commandant says. "If his aid ensures our victory, then I must seize such an opportunity." But the Commandant's gaze lingers on the heart of the Land of the Iron Winds map, a hatchmarked patch of earth labeled only as "Quarry."

The general leans forward with a determination I'm not controlling. "It's madness, you know." The stream rushes faster now, threatening to sweep me under, as his thoughts pour out of his mouth before I can rein them in. "We should leave the dreamworld to the Barstadters who understand it. We have no right to meddle in metaphysical gibberish—"

"You think I don't know that?" the Commandant hisses. "But the mystic has shown us proof of what he can do. If he can pull *that* off with the entire fleet, then Barstadt's navy won't stand a chance."

I strain to get ahead of Cold Sun's thoughts—I could take advantage of this outburst of information by asking the Commandant what exactly he means to pull off—but the general purses his lips, squashing my words down.

The Commandant's eyes take on a glassy sheen as he continues. "The mystic's dream interpretations are too uncanny. His messages from my father . . ." My mind whirs. Does he mean the old Commandant? Perhaps he's not dead after all, or else this mystic is pulling off quite the con. "And he foretells a great victory for us, atop the spine of a mighty warbeast. The

Barstadt Empire shall tremble and bow under our fearsome gale!"

Is the warbeast some new weapon the Iron Winds has designed? Dreamer curse their allegorical speech for muddling it all up! I want to poke further at that thought, but General Cold Sun steers the conversation, my grip on his consciousness slipping once more. "This mystic is a charlatan, preying on us. I've never known you to be one for superstition. It doesn't behoove your father's philosophy: man as god, Commandant as controller of the Winds of Fate. Strength and victory above all."

The Commandant's hand trembles; his fingers dance across the sharp edge of a tiny ship's sail. "I fear if we don't give him what he wants, he will turn the warbeast's power on us."

The general's shoulders tense; I want to learn more about this mystic, but Cold Sun is on the verge of waking. I lift one foot out of the stream in Oneiros, trying to let him settle back into sleep, and let his thoughts wash over my other foot. *Barstadters. Agents. Traitors,* they say. "And what of our agents within Barstadt City's walls?"

The Commandant swishes his hand, as if the question was beneath him, but he betrays himself with a glance over his shoulder, toward where the jewel-spangled figure disappeared. "Yes, yes, they will carry out their tasks. You needn't worry about them."

But my efforts to ease back from Cold Sun's consciousness didn't work. Within Oneiros, the stream is bubbling, rising, heating up, threatening to boil over. I'm out of time.

I try to move Cold Sun's arms to signal Brandt, but the general's body fights against me. I'm getting squeezed out as his consciousness tries to return. In Oneiros, steam pours off the water as it rises from its banks, sharp and acidic against the dark earth. There's no doubt he can sense me now. I splash back onto the forest floor, but it's not enough. The stream turns red—molten.

"Commandant—" General Cold Sun speaks freely now. "I fear that I am—We may have been—"

Brandt rushes forward from the shadows, the perfect portrait of the concerned valet. "General, we must return to our carriage. Take you to a physicker." He casts a glance toward the Commandant. "I'm afraid our fortress has not been spared the latest fever coursing upon the winds."

Dreamer, bless Brandt and his calm, quick mind. Red lava oozes from the stream in Oneiros, turning the trees into columns of fire. The general's instincts war against mine; even as I fight to stride down the long corridor leading out of the Citadel, he tries to turn the other way. Bile tickles the back of my throat—it's more his now—and dimly, I feel Brandt's hand gripping our elbow.

The Commandant is shouting at us, but I can only hear the shapes of his words, not their substance. We must be violating twelve different social customs right now, but whatever punishment the Commandant has in mind for us is nothing compared to the danger that awaits me in Oneiros if I can't get back to my body in time.

My vision blurs as if an earthquake is jostling my sight away from the general's eyes. He's forcing me out. I'm adrift in Oneiros, bait for the hungering void that I dare not tempt. The Nightmare Wastes feed on fear and doubt; they swallow up souls that are lost from their bodies, and forever trap them in emptiness. I have to cling to the general, keep control of my soul until we reach my body—

Until I can—

Rest your head, and join us in eternal rest . . .

The Wastes reach out for me like the embrace of winter frost. *Come,* they beckon. *Forget these worlds. Forget your dreams and your life that can't compare.* A simple request, as insistent as sleep tugging at my eyelids. *You needn't struggle any longer. Surrender, and suffer no more.*

"Livia, please, stay with me," Brandt pleads as he guides me through the Citadel. Then he says, softer, "Dreamer, please show us the way . . ."

The Wastes chuff at me like wolves checking their prey. Their tug is so strong, stronger than it's ever been before. Where once the Wastes whispered behind my back, they now seem to have surrounded me, their urges twisting around my limbs like rope. *You'll only fail again. Surrender to us, pay the price for your weakness . . .* It tempts me more than it ever has before.

Hay, I smell hay and the tang of manure flooding General Cold Sun's nose. *Please, Dreamer, protect me for just a moment longer.* I can't feel the general's feet or his hands; I don't know if we're close enough yet for my soul in Oneiros to seize the

27

tether to my own body. His consciousness presses in on me like all-consuming flames. And still I cling to his body. I can't be cast out, open to the Wastes.

Then I catch a glimpse through Cold Sun's eyes—I want to weep at the sight of me, crumpled in the stall. I take a deep mental breath and prepare to seize my body's tether to return to myself. Just a bit closer.

But the general's body swings around, and he turns on Brandt, his thoughts crackling like flames. *No!* I try to scream at Brandt, because I'm not certain we're close enough for me to seize the lead to pull me back into my body.

Cold Sun is awake and forcing me out.

"What is the meaning of this—"

Brandt cocks his fist, swings it at us—

And everything goes black.

Chapter Two

‒ • • ———————◆———————— • • ‒

I'm swimming through blackness with the scent of blood heavy in my nose. The general is unconscious again after Brandt's blow, but now my soul is completely out of his body, vulnerable to the Wastes. They call to me like rocky cliffs, begging for fresh meat dashed across their faces. *Disappoint your friends no longer . . . Surrender to emptiness . . .*

Visions dance before my eyes—some memories, some not—of my life back in Barstadt. The way the other Ministry operatives fall silent and move to another room whenever I'm around. The Incident, with the crackle of flame and scent of charred meat hanging thick in the air. A glimpse of my mother's milky eyes, roving the tunnels in search of help that never comes. Other illusions appear, too, of failures I fear are yet to come—Brandt, his throat slit by a gang leader's blade when I've botched yet another operation. And always, always, the fear of Brandt disappearing into his other life, the life of aristocratic dinners and alliance building, a world I can never know.

"Livia." Brandt's voice pierces the veil of whispers and sorrow. "Livia!"

I reach, desperate, scrabbling, for the lead that will pull me back into my body. Almost close enough . . . I can see my body's tether dangling down into Oneiros now that we've moved closer to my body in the real world. I fight against the Wastes for just another second—

You'll destroy him—

Brandt. They're right. I'm only going to cause him harm—

"Livia!" Brandt calls.

I bump into the tether, take hold, and *snap.* I plunge into myself and awaken with a gasp.

"Livia!" Brandt seizes me by the shoulders—my shoulders, with my hair draped over them, crusted with hay. He brushes his fingers along the side of my face as a pent-up breath escapes his lips. "Are you all right?"

I flow back into my body a little more with each hammering of my frantic heart. I try to grip his forearm, but my fingers flop against his elbow. My skin feels scrubbed raw; everything is too loud, too smelling, too feeling.

"Water," I wheeze.

Brandt fumbles a waterskin free from his belt and holds it to my lips. The sweet, cool water is just what I need, though my mouth isn't working right yet and half of it sloshes down my chin. I drink my fill, then slowly, carefully bring myself to my legs, tottering like a foal.

"You're safe," he promises me, but I know him too well. He's stern-faced and matter-of-fact, but I see the white rimming his too-wide eyes. His fingertips linger against my cheek. "Will you be all right on your own?"

I manage a nod. "I just . . . need a moment to come back to myself."

"I can buy you a moment." He tucks a stray curl back from my face, then stands up. "I'll fetch the carriage and give the general and his valet another dose to make sure they *stay* asleep."

I can't stop shaking, though I don't know whether it's from cold or panic. The Commandant's guards are surely coming for us, but he shouldn't know what I really am, what I was doing. No one beyond the Emperor, Professor Hesse, and those I work with in the Ministry of Affairs know about dreamstriding. I study the unconscious general's chin, where a nice welt is forming, courtesy of Brandt. *Please, Dreamer, don't let him remember Brandt's face.*

By the time Brandt returns, I've adjusted well enough that I can help him wrestle the slumbering general and his valet into the coach. No thunder of boots approaching the stables yet, but we're out of time. Brandt helps me climb to the driver's bench, and steers us away from the Citadel.

We sit side by side for our trek back to the port village across the splintered, barren earth. Feeling has returned to my legs and arms, but my nose and fingers are still numb as though I'm intoxicated. I'm grateful for the casual riding breeches and blouse I wear in my coach-driver disguise; I haven't the wherewithal to sit up like the proper lady I'm usually forced to play.

Neither of us dares speak until we meet with our contacts at the oceanfront town—two coachmen and a physicker, all native

Iron Winders, all of them desperate for the bags of grain we promised them in exchange for their cooperation. The Ministry had authorized us to pay these associates in gold, but we learned quickly how little value Iron Winders ascribe to things they can't put in their growling stomachs.

"He was having an audience with the Commandant," Brandt tells the physicker, coaching him for when General Cold Sun awakens. "He felt faint, became violent. You're certain it was a migraine. He had to be knocked unconscious so he would not harm himself or others." Brandt gestures to the general's rosy welt. "Give him clues—help him remember. Whatever oddness he remembers, assure him it is a side effect of the migraine."

The physicker nods, eyebrows raised but unquestioning. Brandt has that effect on people when we're on a mission. We make our way down the stairs carved into the ocean cliffs to where our catboat waits, guarded by more bribed Iron Winders.

Once we're safely aboard with the sail rigged, and the Land of the Iron Winds is a sullen gray speck at our backs, Brandt joins me on the catboat's bench and tilts his head back, letting the setting sun spill across his freckled cheeks. He's calm now; there's none of his usual radiance from the thrill of a successful mission, or his grim determination when things go wrong. "I'm sorry," I say, settling in beside him. "For getting us into that mess. I'd be lost without your quick thinking."

"Nonsense." He tips his head forward and smiles at me. "There wouldn't have been a mission if not for you. And then where would we be?"

I clench my teeth, but make myself smile back. "Staring down a fleet of Iron Winds ships, from the sound of it."

"And we know all about it thanks to *you*."

Brandt wouldn't understand what went wrong in Oneiros, but I can't help wondering what more we'd have learned if I'd been a more skillful dreamstrider; if I could have manipulated General Cold Sun more subtly. I wonder if Brandt would be so impressed if he knew how little I really achieved.

He closes his eyes for a moment before he speaks again. "You know, the Dreamer gave me dreams of you last night."

Perhaps to a Farthinger, or anyone unfamiliar with Barstadt ways, such a statement would unsettle or even allure. I'm told other nations find it rude to speak of dreams—that all but the dreamer finds them insufferably dull. But in Barstadt our dreams are sacred, and we share them as readily as we'd share a greeting or a comment on the weather. In the northern isles, I hear they only worship in great halls, surrounded by their gods; Barstadters worship in every street and parlor and corner shop when we speak of the dregs of night.

"You were an oak tree," Brandt says, "surrounded by moth-wood in a field—"

"An oak tree?" I laugh, and pinch at my scrawny forearm.

He grins and nudges me with his shoulder. "I'm serious. Your roots went all the way into Oneiros, just like the mothwood that grew around you. The dreamworld nourished you. You glowed and glowed in the forest, filled with a light from the Dreamer himself."

Maybe he thinks it is a sweet reaffirmation of my talents as a dreamstrider, but I know the truth—I'd nearly succumbed to the siren call of the Nightmare Wastes. They'd been so much more insistent than I've ever found them before. I've always been able to shrug them off, but this time, they'd gotten their hooks into me.

Reading the scowl on my face, Brandt's smile dims and he edges toward me until our knees touch. "Liv." His gaze holds mine. "Are you feeling all right?"

I break his gaze and lean into the wind, letting it toss my curls around. Something to make me feel alive, solid, real—far from the bodiless soul who nearly got gobbled up by the Wastes. "I pushed too hard, is all." I'm about to say *I'll know better next time*, but I suspect I said exactly that after the Incident.

"Our mission's complete. We learned what we needed to know and escaped without giving ourselves away." He laughs to himself—still the goofy young spy in training I met eight years ago. It makes me want to laugh, too. "When we get back, why don't you ask Professor Hesse to help you work on your dreamstriding technique?"

My innards are all knotted up. I hate keeping things from Brandt, but maybe I'm only imagining the Nightmare Wastes' new strength. Memories of their frosty reach prick at my thoughts again, and the sun is too low to bake the chill away.

Brandt studies me with those thunderstorm eyes. "Liv?" he repeats. "Is there something else?" That mischievous glint in his gaze always sees through me.

"I'm just . . ." I glance out to sea, but the sun is fast slipping into the waves. "I wish we could have gotten more information, that's all. That I could have done more."

"Well, this isn't like breaking up street gangs and gambling dens." He rests one hand on my knee; heat rises on my face, making me grateful for the twilight. "Of course it's difficult. Maybe we could've both been better prepared, but we found out the Iron Winds' plans, didn't we?"

But it's not my lack of training. Doesn't he know this? I may be the only dreamstrider, but I'm a sorry excuse for one. Dreamer knows how hard I try; how often I sink into the cleansing pools of his temples and pray for a little more grace and cleverness. I pray that someday I'll be worthy of my gift.

This has not been such a day.

"You're right. I just . . . wish I could do more," I say. "Think on my feet like you, or even—"

"We each have our gifts. And I always believe in you." *Even when the others don't*, I imagine him thinking.

I force myself to lean back and shrug. "I'm more concerned about the Barstadter. Did you get a closer look at her?" I ask.

He nods, letting his golden mop of hair scatter across his brow. "She'd gone to a sitting parlor back behind the dais. She was watching me while you and the Commandant discussed the battle plans, so I couldn't look around nearly as much as I would've liked. There wasn't enough light for me to see her clearly, but she's definitely from Barstadt—she wore the facial jewels. Silver and sapphire."

I wince. "I was afraid of that. Could you make out the design?"

"Not very well, but we can consult the House registries when we get back to the Ministry. Make a list of which Houses use blue and silver in their heraldry, and suss her out from there."

He's restless, fidgeting like there's more he wants to say. Whenever he's not playing a role, he's terrible at keeping his emotions in check, like the real Brandt he'd been hiding has to come spilling out. The real Brandt—he's always first to smile, first to laugh; first to share his dreams with me and even his fears. This is the Brandt I can't help but love, in the locked-up corners of my mind.

But he is also Master Brandt Strassbourg, the future lord of House Strassbourg. The Ministry is only a playground for him—his father figures it no more dangerous than turning him loose on the gambling houses and ale halls where all the other lords-in-waiting bide their coin and time. One day he'll claim his title and a bride, and leave me and the Ministry behind. All I can do is cherish my time with him until that day.

Brandt pats my knee, then hoists himself down to the bottom of the boat. "I imagine we'll have another busy day tomorrow, following up on these leads. I'm going to get some rest."

"Dreamer carry you into slumber in his golden embrace," I say automatically, though it looks like Brandt's already well on his way. I smile as he rumbles with a snore.

I love him, probably more than I have even dared admit to myself, but I can't keep relying on him—he won't always be there to pluck me out of a tense situation or salve my wounds.

The waves catch starlight in their peaks, and the salty air clears my nostrils and my mind as we cross the channel that separates Barstadt from the Land of the Iron Winds. For thirty years, it's been enough to keep the uneasy peace between Barstadt's superior navy and the ground-based forces of the Iron Winds as the latter pushed deeper south into their own continent. But now they're setting their sights northward toward our empire, and one of our own is helping them. I can't lose myself in thoughts of Brandt. We've only uncovered the first piece of the Commandant's puzzle—our work has merely begun.

· • ———— • ———— • ·

Though our dreams are sacred, they are flimsy things, changing colors with the lighting and shifting to match our mood. Sometimes they slip under the bed as soon as I wake, and other times they hang over me throughout the day like a threatening storm. I've dreamed enough to know that sometimes there is no sense to their form, and sometimes they are truer than the real world could ever be.

The Dreamer's priests say dreams are messages from the Dreamer himself: visions and orders and warnings. I cannot say if this is true. Still, the priests will interpret them for a donation to the temple; shadier folk will give you a different spin for coin. Debates over their interpretation fuel the parlors and ale halls each night as surely as Barstadt ale itself.

Some dreams, though, even a Barstadter won't share. Our nightmares—the dreams that frighten us in our very souls—we keep to ourselves.

I had such a dream that night aboard the gently rocking ship.

I don't dare tell Brandt about it, so I only say I dreamed of the sea. But in truth, I dreamed I was a great bird circling Barstadt City's harbor. At first I thought I must be a seagull, for the briny air tasted like home and I craved slimy fish scales between my beak. But then I spied a girl on the docks, her limp body spilled across the planks like honey. My cravings changed, and I knew I wanted to pick at her flesh. I swooped down to peck at her—

The face that stared back at me, lifeless, was my own.

I have to return to my body, I managed to realize somewhere in my tiny bird brain. *Before the Nightmare Wastes find me.* I reached for my body's tether to try to leap back inside, but I couldn't fit into myself—my body made no room for my soul.

That's when I realized I was inhabiting no mere bird, but a winged monster of rotting meat. Agony rolled off me like a foul stench, eager to envelop the body on the docks. I was of two minds: the first knowingly trapped in this monster, but the second filled with blind hunger and rage.

And just as I started to cry, fearing I would lose my soul forever inside this beast, the eyes on my human body opened, and it jerked upward, animated once more.

But it wasn't my soul that was inside.

Chapter Three

The Dreamer must have blessed our voyage; it should have taken us a full day to return to Barstadt City, but the Itinerant Winds grease our course the whole way, and we reach the capital's main harbor shortly after dawn. We pull in the sail, and our catboat drifts silently against the stream of fishing boats setting out to make their daily haul. Barstadt City engulfs the harbor with its craggy hills, buildings crammed onto them in muddled shades of cream crowned with steep black slate roofs. True to Barstadt weather, darkening rainclouds hang woolly in the sky, but I don't mind. They're as much a part of home to me as the Emperor's palace to our right, and the distant towers of Banhopf University to our left. I don't look to the eastern mountains, but I know what looms there, as dreary and constant as the clouds: Nightmare's ragged bones.

I never like looking at that reptilian skeleton on the mountainside, so massive we can see it all the way from the docks. But after my brush with the Nightmare Wastes yesterday,

I dread it even more. The Dreamer slew Nightmare and scattered his heart's shards to the three corners of the realms, I remind myself firmly; the Wastes are only remnants. The Dreamer wouldn't let them devour me, just like he didn't let Nightmare bring further harm to Barstadt all those centuries ago.

Brandt offers me a hand out of the catboat. "Back to proper gowns for you and frock coats for me, eh?" he asks, gesturing to our carriage driver costumes.

"Well, the comfort was nice while it lasted."

The comfort isn't all I'm surrendering, though, by being back inside the Empire. Brandt will slip back into his role as House Strassbourg's heir, and away from me. I can't help but wonder if each mission we embark on will be our last together. Still, if I smell anything like Brandt—sweat and sea and exhaustion, all baked too long in the sun—then I welcome our return, if only for the opportunity to use the Ministry of Affairs's indoor plumbing for a bath.

"Master Strassbourg," the guard greets Brandt as we reach the Ministry's gates. Then his gaze slides to me, and he offers me a stiff nod. "Uh, miss." He looks back to Brandt. "Minister Durst has requested a full debriefing as soon as you've made yourselves presentable."

A tide of panic rises in my gut. Ever since my testimony following the Incident, each meeting with Durst feels like another interrogation. One more mistake, and I fear he'll tear up my temporary citizenship papers and dump me at the nearest tunnel entrance.

Brandt catches my expression before I have a chance to rein

it in. His hand darts toward mine, quick as a lash, and he squeezes my fingers. "I'll present the minister with what we found. There's no need for you to go as well, Liv."

But the guard shakes his head. "The minister requested you both."

Brandt's mouth pops open, but I square my shoulders and answer before he can. "Then I guess I'd better wash up."

I scrub away the Land of the Iron Winds from my skin and the crust of salt from my scalp, permitting myself a few minutes of peace before we plunge into the work ahead of us. Preventing war, capturing a traitor—Brandt and I can catch corrupt merchants all day long, but this is far more dangerous work. My face stares back at me from my vanity mirror, looking even younger than my nineteen years. Fresh, ruddy, and too soft to save a nation. I hope the Dreamer knows what he's doing, entrusting this task to me.

"I'm so glad you're back," my maid Sora tells me as she lays out a fresh gown and chemise. "Vera's been staying in the barracks the past few nights to avoid her family again, and it's been just dreadful."

I tense at that name—Vera Orban has got reasons to doubt me more than almost anyone else in the Ministry—but I mask it with a grin. "Sending you on a million errands?"

"Cider and parchment and a whole basket of pastries from Kruger's! I don't know how she stays so slim with an appetite like that."

"I'm sure being such a pain in everyone's arse is grueling labor," I say. Sora reaches for my hairbrush, but I grab it first and set to work disentangling my damp hair. "How are you otherwise?" My eyes catch hers in the mirror. "The tunnels aren't troubling you, are they?"

Sora's gaze drops away from mine. She's only a sliver of a girl, her hair the color of a candle's flame and as flimsy to boot. She hasn't the strength to deceive, I think, and that bodes poorly for any tunneler. "N-no, miss. They're all right."

"Please don't lie to me. What is it, tithes? Here—this should more than cover you for the month." I scoot a jewelry box stuffed with trinkets toward her.

"Oh, Miss Livia, I couldn't possibly—"

"Nonsense. Keep the tunnel bullies at bay, and soon enough, we'll get you proper papers, all right?"

She smiles; even at fourteen, her doe lashes and fine bones mark her as easy tunnel prey. I see too much of my former emaciated self in her. If I can help even one tunneler escape as I did, then I'll have served the Dreamer well.

"I'll do my best, miss."

Edina Alizard pokes her head into my room, her dark curls pinned up and draped so that they perfectly frame her deep brown face. I notice Sora tensing at the sight of her. "Ah! Miss Livia! You're back. I'll take that to mean my assets in the Land of the Iron Winds did their jobs."

"They smuggled us right to the Citadel's front door with no trouble at all." It was what happened in Oneiros that has me shaken. "Thank you for that."

Edina smiles warmly. I want to believe Edina actually likes

me, but she's the sort of person who can find virtue in even the most savage gang enforcer. "Do you know if Brandt's around?" she asks.

"He is, but we're meeting with the minister shortly. Shall I give him a message?"

She tilts her head, contemplating. "Not to worry, I'll catch him later. Best of luck with the minister."

Sora shakes her head, watching Edina depart. "I'll never understand how as nice a girl as her could have such a wretched father. The Writ of Emancipation went up for a vote again yesterday." Her lip curls back.

I pause, hairbrush stuck in a knot of my curls. For years, the aristocrats' council has contemplated a number of writs designed at granting full citizenship to the tunnelers. And for just as many years, they've found countless reasons not to grant them. "I wager it didn't pass."

Sora makes a retching sound deep in her throat. "All thanks to Lord Alizard."

"Of course he's going to block it," I say. "Look at all the money he makes, keeping the gangs in his back pocket. His livelihood depends on keeping the tunnelers out of proper society."

"It's just not fair. Hardly anyone manages to escape." She crosses her arms. "Some of the tunnelers over in the Bayside branch are talking about storming the next aristocrats' convention. Force them to look at us, hear us out."

My heart twists for her—for all the tunnelers. I can barely

make use of the gift that allowed me to leave the tunnels. But I can't admit that to her. "Be careful. You don't want to jeopardize your work with the Ministry."

"Nonsense. My friend says we have to rub their noses in the truth of us, of what they've done to us. That even if we don't go as far as the Destroyers did, we can't stay quiet." She shakes her head. "I—I'm sorry, Miss Livia. I don't mean to get you in trouble by talking this way."

I grip her hand and give it a sharp squeeze. "No, Sora. I'm only sorry that I can't be of more help. If there were anything I could do to help you get your citizenship papers—"

"Sure. I know you'd help me if you could. But don't worry. I've got . . ." I watch her chew at her lip through the mirror. "Options." She drops into a curtsey. "I'll send word to the minister you're on your way."

Fear pricks at me like frost, but I force myself to my feet. Like when Brandt and I cross the threshold into the heart of an operation: the only way out is through. I pray for the Dreamer to make me strong for whatever lies ahead.

The Minister of Affairs, Petran Durst, is a wiry man, his hair ashy against ruddy, high cheeks and his goatee pinched to a point from years of stroking it while in deep thought. He's already pacing his office when Brandt and I enter; he looks up at us as if he can't remember who we are for a moment before finding his composure.

"Brandt. Livia." If any of his fury at me has returned, he's hiding it well. "I need your report on the Iron Winds right away. It may aid us with another issue that's arisen."

"Yes, sir. The situation with the Land of the Iron Winds is worse than we feared." I take a deep breath. "The Commandant is planning to invade through the harbor, and we think Barstadt aristocrats are helping him from within the city."

Brandt steps forward. "We'll write a full report with the battle plan details tonight, but we need to act now. Alert the Emperor and the Admiralty. They're planning a direct attack on Barstadt City. And the Commandant seems to be building toward some sort of new . . . weaponry."

"A direct attack? And a new weapon to empower them?" He blinks a few times, like clearing something away. "I—yes. I'll need all the details, but your full report will have to wait. I need Livia to—"

"Wait?" Brandt cries. "Beg pardon, Minister, but Barstadt City is in imminent danger. I'm not sure what could possibly trump that."

"A delegation from Farthing's secret police is here," the Minister says, his tone bladed. "The Emperor just authorized an information-sharing agreement with the Farthing Confederacy. It would seem we aren't the only ones concerned about the Commandant's recent aggression. Several Farthing ships have been chased through the straits by well-armed Iron Winds naval vessels. The Farthing Confederacy is spooked, and they don't scare easily. They've decided to offer us their wealth of intelligence in exchange for Barstadt's superior naval protection, should the Commandant attack either of our nations. Which sounds very likely, based on your report."

Farthing, willing to share intelligence with Barstadt? The

Barstadt Empire's relationship with Farthing has always been a tenuous one, which I suppose is the best that can be hoped for when dealing with a nation of pirates, privateers, and merchants known for their ruthlessness. We don't try to absorb them into our Empire, and they mostly leave our ships alone, turning their efforts to the north and east in the Farthing Sea to pick over the Eastern Realms' ships instead. But I suppose the threat of invasion by the Commandant's overwhelming numbers is enough to make them swallow their isolationist pride. Their military is skilled, but unequipped to repel the sheer number of the Commandant's forces.

"The Emperor's already agreed to their terms," Durst says, "and your information only adds to the urgency. The Minister of War is making all the necessary preparations to shield both our nations from an attack." Durst holds up his hands. "But I need someone working with the Farthing envoys to ensure they give us their full cooperation—and that we don't give them any more information than we absolutely must."

Brandt looks at me. With that darkness in his eyes, I fear I know what he's about to say. "Do they know about Livia's . . . ability?"

A chilly perspiration plasters my dress to my skin. Alliance or not, I don't want anyone else to know about dreamstriding.

Durst puffs out his cheeks, the shadows under his eyes dark as bruises. "Not to our knowledge, no." He swallows, and the apple in his throat bobs anxiously. "But the Farthingers are a wily bunch. I personally only trust them as far as I can toss them."

I nod. Some tunnelers used to speak of the Farthing Confederacy like a fairy-tale land, an idyll world far from the rigid hierarchy of Barstadt, populated by pirates and entrepreneurs. With enough wits, Farthingers may scrabble their way into wealth for a time, but there's always another waiting to scrabble over them.

Minister Durst clasps his hands together. "We haven't much time to waste if we're to foil the Commandant, so I've asked the Farthingers to meet with us now for an initial debriefing. Then we can set to work stopping the Commandant's plans."

Brandt ruffles the fringe of soft hair that hangs over his brows. "But who will act as our representative? You're not going to reveal our identities to them, are you?"

Minister Durst wrings his hands like he's trying to scrub something from them. "Yes, as for that . . ." He glances at me. "I can't risk exposing both of you as Ministry operatives to the Farthing team, so only one of you will serve as our official representative through all of this."

Brandt steps forward, fire in his eyes. "Let it be me, then. We have to keep Livia secret."

I shake my head. "Brandt's the better operative—we have to preserve his identity. Besides, any time I work in the field, I'm not actually me. It makes more sense for them to work with me, and not find out what you look like."

Brandt's expression darkens. "Livia, please. These people aren't our friends, even if they are our allies. If they were to learn the truth about you—"

"No, Livia is absolutely correct," Minister Durst says. "If they know Livia's appearance, it won't hinder her missions. But if they know what you look like, Master Strassbourg, all your future missions will be compromised. Who knows what the future may bring—our current alliance with Farthing is never a guarantee." Again, he looks at me, but his gaze is reluctant, and I know he's only picking the lesser of two poor choices. "I can't take that risk."

"With all due respect, Minister—Livia's far more important to the Ministry than I, and she's never had proper field training. And if anything were to happen to her—"

"Yes, Master Strassbourg, that's why I'm assigning you and Jornisander to shadow her meetings with the Farthingers from afar. Will that allay your fears?"

Of course, the future may also bring a better-trained dreamstrider than I to the Ministry. Hesse is always searching for another, and when he finds one, what use will my clumsy attempts be? I see this hope in the minister's razor-thin smile. Despite my gift, I could still be replaced.

Brandt eases back on his heels, though the muscles in his neck are still taut. "It's something, yes."

I relax somewhat, too. Jorn the Destroyer started his career in the tunnels as Stargazer gang muscle, but since he joined the Ministry, he's proven himself an invaluable asset. He knows how to work connections throughout the tunnels and the gangs, and his days in the tunnel brawling rings certainly proved his skill at breaking noses in new and interesting ways, should the occasion require.

"Glad to hear it." The minister's gaze casts about his office. "Brandt, you're welcome to watch our meeting from the observation room."

"As you wish, Minister." Brandt pries open the door to what I thought was an ordinary armoire in one corner of the minister's office and disappears in a flurry of coats.

"It's a trick looking glass," Minister Durst says, pointing to the gilded mirror on the wall beside the armoire. "Brandt can see us, but we can't see him. I have a little study set up back there so he can take notes."

I glance toward the glass and give Brandt a feeble smile.

"Livia, you'll be posing as one of my secretaries for the duration of this alliance. Silke Grundtag—that's your name now."

I wrinkle my nose at the awful pseudonym. "Yes, Minister." I check my pale yellow gown, flocked with burgundy roses hedged by soft blue stripes. It should suffice for the role of secretary, though I've none of Brandt's skills at subterfuge.

"Excellent. Don't attest to firsthand knowledge of anything they ask you about—just claim you've read it in our operatives' reports. And if you have any doubt whatsoever as to whether you should share something, wait for me to say it first."

My first time portraying myself, instead of someone else. I look in the mirror. Everything in me screams that I'm not ready for this new venture, that it's another opportunity to fail, but my country needs me. The Dreamer must have seen something in me worth my gift. I'll try to believe it, too.

Minister Durst yanks a velvet rope along the wall beside his desk and a bell rings deep within the Ministry's bowels. After a few moments, a set of doors swing open, and Durst's head secretary ushers in a man and a woman in brazen garb.

The woman wears leather breeches, leather boots, even a leather girder over her black silk tunic. Two empty holsters hang at either side of her hips, most likely one for a dagger and the other for a revolver; she must have surrendered her weapons when she entered the Ministry. Curling hair an unnatural shade of scarlet drapes her face, hanging down past her not insubstantial breasts. Like most Farthingers, her skin is amber and dusty from a life lived beneath pine trees and winter clouds and overcast seas. Barstadt weather is only somewhat milder, but our skin is much darker and earthier.

The man is only a few years older than I am, but he carries himself with the bravado of Brandt's most arrogant personae. His well-muscled rib cage is hoisted high; his dark eyes sparkle beneath curly raven locks, mussed as if he's just stepped off a Farthing flotilla. I'm not nearly as quick at reading people as Brandt is, but he instantly strikes me as the sort of man who thinks himself three steps ahead of anyone he encounters.

"A pleasure, Minister Durst," the man says, jabbing his hand toward the minister to shake, though the motion is as forceful as a punch. "I'm Marez Tanin, and this is my associate, Kriza Avard."

Kriza inclines her head toward the minister as he and Marez shake. I keep my hands folded behind my back and my face lowered like a good, obeisant little secretary. If the minister chooses not to introduce me, all the better.

"Please," the minister says, "have a seat. May I offer you

drinks?" He strides toward a polished array of bottles and tumblers near his desk, but Marez and Kriza shake their heads and continue to stand, legs spread in Vs and arms behind their backs. Their faces tilt upward, defiant, proud. "Very well, don't mind me." The minister pours himself two thumbs from his favorite bottle of brandy.

"You do not ask your secretary to fetch your drinks for you?" Kriza asks, eyeing me sideways. I suppress a grimace. Have I already spoiled our ruse?

"My secretary has other matters to attend to," Minister Durst says coolly. I can see he's flustered, too, in the heat rash rising on his neck, but thankfully he's facing them dead on.

The man, Marez, steps forward. "All right, Minister, you promised to share the details your source knows regarding the Commandant's battle plans. Will you finally deign to regale us? Did your dreams deem today auspicious enough for you to share?" He looks at Kriza, and they share a brittle laugh. "Your councils and ministries have already picked our agreement to death like rabid dogs over a kill. I think it's time we heard this report."

Minister Durst nods toward me. "Silke, my dear? Summarize the operatives' reports from their expedition into the Land of the Iron Winds last month—the details of the Commandant's battle plans."

Of course, he means Brandt's and my expedition *yesterday*. He must have told the Farthingers that we'd already confirmed similar information to what they shared. I'm shaking as I bow low and clear my throat. I wish I could say it was part of my act as the nervous secretary, but I am no Brandt. "They were able to glimpse battle plans drawn up by the Commandant and General Cold Sun that indicated a direct attack on Barstadt City, via the harbor."

Minister Durst nods, his gaze somewhere beyond my shoulder. Neither of the Farthingers reveal any surprise or concern. Their gaze is far too flinty for my comfort.

"Based on the arrangement of troops, we believe that the Commandant has secured assistance from someone on the inside—someone within Barstadt City," I continue, though I omit that the traitor is likely an aristocratic woman.

"That's a very interesting assessment," Marez says, turning toward me with a strange glint in his gaze. "How would you characterize the potential traitor?"

I glance toward Minister Durst; he gives me a slight nod to continue. "Well, the reports indicate—"

"No, I'm not asking about reports." Marez takes a step toward me, dark eyes glinting. "I'm asking for *your* opinion."

My whole body is trembling like pickled jelly. I imagine Brandt on the other side of the false mirror; I try to summon the quick wit he would use in this situation. But nothing comes. "Well." I smooth down the skirts of my gown, then force myself to look at the Farthingers. "It could be an aristocrat, dissatisfied with their station and aspiring toward the throne. Or it could be a disgruntled crime boss looking to strike back at the Empire for some transgression."

Marez holds my gaze with an iron grip. I feel as if he could slice through my flimsy role in an instant, if he so wished; the prospect puts ice in my veins, even as my face heats from his stare.

"That's very astute of you," Marez says at last, breaking the gaze. I slump forward as he turns to Durst, still playing with that curl. "I wonder if your secretary isn't cut out for fieldwork herself someday. Or is it against imperial code to send women out as spies?"

"We prefer to avoid subjecting our ladies to the dangers of fieldwork, except when absolutely necessary," Durst replies.

"That's a pity. There's so much more to our work than playing a harlot for a bit of pillow talk." Kriza steps toward me and brushes my hair back from my shoulder. Dreamer, but these Farthingers are bold! "I expect you're made of more steel than your minister would give you credit for."

I grit my teeth. "I'm perfectly happy with my duties as they are." But Marez is smiling at me as if in approval, and warmth surges up my spine.

"Your secretary is correct about the potential traitors within your city walls." Marez turns back to Minister Durst. "We heard scattered reports indicating similar activity, though you must understand I cannot fully reveal how we came across this knowledge."

"Of course," Durst says coolly.

"Someone who owns a vessel in these docks"—Marez gestures at the map of the Central Realms on the wall, pinpointing an aristocratic harbor in our city's bay—"has been making voyages to the Land of the Iron Winds. They take great pains to conceal their comings and goings, but our ships have tracked their route."

I risk a glance toward Brandt's mirror, though I see only myself in it and the backs of the Farthingers. I'm certain he's thinking the same thing I am. We can check the registry for the docks and compare it to the master list of House colors in the records hall. It's tenuous, but if only one House decorates themselves in sapphire and silver and also docks their boats at the same harbor . . .

Marez studies the map a moment more before turning back to us. "With your permission, Minister, we'd like to monitor the docks, probe the dockworkers, ask around at the provisioning shops to learn who might be behind these voyages to the Land."

"Of course," the minister says, "provided you allow us to send a Barstadt representative to accompany you."

Marez's gaze rakes over me again. "Why not your secretary?"

"Perfect," Minister Durst says. "As long as you don't demand any work of a delicate nature from her."

"But, Minister—" I say before Kriza speaks over me.

"And we've already met her, so you needn't divulge the identities of any of your other operatives to us." Her smile is toothy as a shark's. "We're in the same business as you, Minister. We understand how it works."

Minister Durst forces himself to return the smile. "Consider her to be at your disposal for the remainder of our agreement, unless my duties for her take precedence."

Marez turns toward me. "Meet us at the Crescent Docks at first light tomorrow morning, then, Miss . . . uh . . ."

"Grundtag." I grit out the word like sand between my teeth. "Silke Grundtag."

"Silke," Marez repeats, and it certainly sounds as smooth as silk from him. "Well then. I suppose you lot have your work cut out for you, finding our traitors and planning to stop a war. We may have a good army, but we bow to your navy's discipline, and at this time of year, our ships are too far to the north and east to recall in time." Marez seems to be speaking only to me, his dark eyes skewering me in place. I duck my head—must play the unimportant secretary—and wait for Minister Durst.

"What else can we do to accommodate your team?" the Minister asks.

Kriza pipes up; through a loose curl of hair, I can tell that Marez is still focused on me. "We'll send word back to the Confederate Council, of course. However, we'd like to work alongside your Ministry of War to counter the Commandant's fleet. If we can foil the first step of their plan here, in Barstadt, then we can ensure the Commandant won't press onward to Farthing."

"As you please. You know how to reach us if you learn anything more." Minister Durst strides toward the door, far more eagerly than he ought, and holds it open for them.

"Likewise," Marez mutters. "Likewise." He bends down to adjust a strap on his sea boots—then straightens, a fine-wrought stiletto nestled in his palm.

Minister Durst yelps, dashing to the far side of his desk; I fall back, expecting Brandt to come charging out of the armoire.

"What is the meaning of this?" Durst demands. "I asked you to surrender your weapons before—"

"Oh, do relax." Marez rolls his eyes; with a practiced twist of his wrist, the stiletto flips around so he's holding it delicately by the blade, extending the hilt toward me. "You Barstadters are sure a jumpy lot. Come, Miss Grundtag."

I step toward him, padding softly, the way I used to approach the gang enforcers in the tunnels. Hands where they could see them. No sudden movements. Marez bobs the stiletto at me; I grip it with unsteady fingers.

"To defend yourself—just in case," he says. "The folks we'll be surveilling tomorrow are rather unsavory sorts, and I'd like you to be prepared." He smiles and bows low while backing toward the door, where Kriza's waiting.

But as I turn the blade over in my hands, I wonder whether the gangs and crooks at the docks are the ones I should really fear.

Chapter Four

I'm used to the abrupt silence that surrounds me in the Ministry's living quarters, thick as weeds, but after all that's happened in the past day, I've no patience for it. I have to prepare myself to deal with the Farthingers while the minister prepares us for a possible war. Yet I haven't a clue how to work as myself in the field; maybe Brandt can help me with that. I snatch a bowl of stew from the mess hall and hurry away to meet him. Don't give the other operatives a chance to meet my gaze; to question me or question the Ministry in silence for keeping me on after what I let happen to our informant during the Incident.

But then I find myself wondering how it might feel to meet those looks. To conjure up the Farthing man's penetrating stare, the one I'd been so certain could part through my own ruse. Marez seems like the sort of man to use flattery and intimidation in equal parts—whatever is required to claim what he wants. He flattered me with his questions, but they felt a little like a velvet leash, guiding me exactly where he wanted me to go. Then again, maybe I am trying too hard to play the clever spy; maybe

I'm inventing conspiracies where none exist. I shake my head and keep my eyes down. I shouldn't be so eager to prove my worth to the Farthing man—but for reasons I don't quite understand, he seems to see potential in me.

The warmth starts to leach away from the bowl of stew I carry. It isn't the freshest meal, but it's fathoms beyond the watery broth and rotted root cellar cullings we ate in the tunnels (when we were fortunate enough to eat at all). Where's Brandt gone off to now? He usually joins me in the barracks parlor, but it's empty save a tunneler dusting the bookshelves; I wander toward the men's quarters next.

Finally I hear Brandt's distinctive laugh—round, unchained, and unabashed—and hasten my step. I turn the corner, ready to call out to him, but his back is to me, and he's deep in conversation with the other young aristocratic men. "What was I to do?" he says through fits of laughter. "I couldn't very well refuse the Empress her tea service, even if she had sneezed in it to rival a summer squall!"

The other boys howl and clap him on the shoulder. "That reminds me of when my parents had me courting the House Addel daughter. She eats like she's putting on a puppet show in her mouth . . ."

I cross the corridor on silent, slippered feet. Brandt's real life is one of chummy, wealthy friends and society balls and courting dinners and carefree country rides. His work with me is like a hobby. I know that—I feel it daily, chafing at me. How can I blame him for choosing his destined life over the Ministry's work?

Sora finishes her tasks later in the evening, and, perhaps taking pity on me, challenges me to a round of Stacks in the sitting room. The rest of the Ministry is silent now, concerned with preparations for repelling the Commandant's fleet. But I've an early morning ahead of me, and if I'm to hold my own around the Farthingers, I'll need my rest.

⁘ ─────── ● ─────── ⁘

"What about that man?" I ask, squinting through the feeble morning light. "His load looks awfully heavy."

Marez follows my gaze across the Crescent Docks to where a man dressed in drab shades of gray and brown struggles to haul the contents of a horse cart onto a sleek single-masted flute. "Heavy, certainly. Enough provisions for a month at sea, if not more. But tell me, Silke, how far a journey do you think it is to the Land of the Iron Winds from here?"

A day, if the Dreamer and the winds favor you—that's how it was for Brandt's and my mission.

But instead I say, "A week, maybe, if the Dreamer favors? I don't know much about sailing, apologies." I twist one curl around my finger for added effect. I've seen Vera do it on missions before, when she wishes to play dumb, and it usually seems to work. Not that Vera would be thrilled to find me copying her techniques.

Kriza snorts. "More like a day. Do you even know how to read a map—"

But Marez silences her with a raised hand. "What does the

Dreamer have to do with it?" His tone is light, but I sense darkness at its corners, like a dream threatening to twist into a nightmare. "None of the Farthing privateers pray to your Dreamer, and they sail the seas just fine."

"It's just a saying." I lean against the wooden railing that overlooks the docks. The Dreamer blessed me with dreamstriding, but sometimes I wonder if that was a lifetime's cache of good fortune used up all at once. "The man could still be bound for the Iron Winds," I continue, eager to change the subject. "If he means to sell some of his supplies—"

But Marez won't let it drop. "You Barstadters are a strange lot." His mouth twists into something between a smile and sneer. "Your emperor's always ready to act when it comes to gobbling up new islands to the west, but when it comes to taking responsibility for what you've wrought, it's all, oh, the Dreamer wills this, the Dreamer wills that."

Anger flashes through me like grease on a flame. "If you'd rather not accept our help, then Farthing is welcome to stand against the Commandant alone. Have fun wrangling your bloody pirates into a unified navy—"

He rumbles with full-bodied laughter. "Such righteousness! Kriza, I like this one." A proper smile settles on his face; it rubs away the hardened edges, revealing a young man not much older than me. "And here I thought it was Farthing who was doing your empire the favor. But if you'd rather pray to your Dreamer to save you . . ."

"The Dreamer rarely has a direct influence on our world. Instead, he encourages us and guides us through our dreams. It's still our duty to act." I pull my shawl tighter around my shoulders. "For instance, last night, I dreamed—"

I clamp my mouth shut, realizing only too late that perhaps I shouldn't be sharing my dreams with these foreigners who Minister Durst only trusts as far as he can toss them. But they're both looking at me now, the vultures, faces positively glowing at the prospect of hearing more religious blather from a foolish Barstadter.

Marez leans in close, propping his arms on the railing beside me. I catch a whiff of his clean leather gear and something spicy underneath it. "Do tell, little secretary. How is the Dreamer guiding you right now?"

For the thousandth time this morning, I wish Brandt were here to tell me what to do. That I could've asked him for a primer last night in handling myself in the field. Something unsettles me about Marez, like he sees me as an experiment for him to poke and prod. Is it better to tell the truth now that I've brought it up, and risk exposing something of my real identity, or tell a lie to protect myself, and risk being caught lying? Brandt shared a real nightmare of his when we infiltrated the Dreamless den last summer—it worked well enough for him then. But that wasn't for a long-term identity like this one is.

I decide to opt for the truth, for now. "I dreamt I was standing in a great room—like an armory—and I had to select what to wear. Against one wall were elegant ball gowns, in every shade and style. Another wall, plated suits and leather armor and halberds and daggers and all manner of battle garb. Then on the third wall were the gauzy robes, like they wear at the Dreamer's temples—the high priests. And—and the final wall—the rags and scraps like the tunnelers wear."

Marez chews at his lower lip, studying me with that stare like a spear. My cheeks start to burn; I made the wrong choice in telling them about my dream. Now that I've spoken it aloud, I can see plainly how the dream could be an allegory for dreamstriding—always donning different roles when I don others' skin. But surely they don't see it that way—to them it might just as easily be an allegory for spycraft.

"Well?" Kriza asks, impatience thinning her tone. "Which one did you choose?"

I glance back out across the docks. "I woke up before I could pick one."

She makes a deep guttural sound. "Bloody Barstadters and their dreams."

But Marez keeps watching me. I can feel the heat of his stare like I'm standing too close to a hearth. "Will you permit me to try my amateur hand at dream interpretation? Isn't that what you Barstadters love to do?"

I grin in spite of myself. "One of our three claims to fame. Dreaming, politicking, and drinking ale."

"Well, as I've no skill for the second and it's too early for the last . . ." He laces his fingers together, then stretches them out, knuckles cracking, as if he's preparing for a brawl. "I think you're confronted with a choice. You're stuck in a secretary's role now, but there are so many other options available to you, though each brings with it a danger."

"Not a bad first attempt," I say.

He wags one finger at me. "Ah, but maybe the roles aren't what they all seem. The fine dresses, for instance—you might think it's entry into a life of balls and social calls, but you might find it as confining as the tunneler's rags."

My throat tightens; memories of life in the tunnels prick my thoughts. "Perhaps."

"Or maybe—" Marez snaps his fingers. "Or maybe they're actually all part of the same choice. Maybe you're meant to be more than just a secretary to the Ministry—maybe you're meant to be an operative for them, stealing secrets, advancing the Empire, all that excitement. And these are some of the disguises available to you."

"Or maybe you should leave the boring dreams to the Barstadters and pay attention to the docks," Kriza says.

Marez grins like a boy whose hand's been swatted away from the dessert tray. "Come now, I'm just having a bit of fun playing the devil's advocate." He tilts his head toward me. "I always forget. Do you Barstadters believe in a devil? Out in the western realms, they have a whole pantheon of them."

An icy breeze whips around us, raking like nails across my exposed skin. His question steers my gaze toward the mountain peaks in the east; try as I might, I can't help but look at the ancient bones strung across the high mountain ridge, the massive ribs on the mountainside curled like the rusted bars of a cage. The Nightmare Wastes' words echo in my mind; soft as silk, they slither around me until they tighten into a knot. In my pocket, I let my fingers graze the hilt of the stiletto Marez gave me.

"No." I shove off the railing and turn away. "We believe in Nightmare."

"Nightmare." Marez snorts. "Are you certain your priests didn't make up the story of Nightmare? Surely the bones on the mountainside are just that—bones of some ancient creature, long extinct. They're only trying to scare you into behaving with the stories."

I narrow my eyes at him. "They aren't just stories. Nightmare tried to turn the real world into a Nightmare realm. He escaped the confines of the dreamworld and sowed chaos and destruction across Barstadt." He's a fool if he thinks Nightmare is only an old legend. I've felt the chill of the Wastes against the soul. I've heard their taunting words. But Marez strikes me far less as a fool, and more someone only too glad to play one for whatever purpose he requires.

The smirk on Marez's face has faded, though; his eyes narrow as he looks back toward the mountainside. "Then how was he stopped?"

"The Dreamer reached through to our world and slew him. He shattered Nightmare's heart, and scattered it to the far corners of the realms so he could never rise again."

Marez falls silent for a moment. "Never is an awfully strong word," he says at last.

Chapter Five

We find no further leads at the docks to indicate who amongst the aristocracy might be taking surreptitious voyages to the Land of the Iron Winds. It's just as well; my mind is snagged on what Marez said about the roles in my dream not being what they seem, and I find myself impatient to finish up. Though the average Barstadter doesn't yet know it, a war is coming, and I'm anxious to do whatever I can to help us fend off the Commandant's force.

"Liv! Glad I caught you," Brandt says just as I'm returning to the Ministry. "Fancy a trip to Kruger's?"

"I'm not much in the mood for pastries. I don't suppose you had better luck looking up Houses in the archives?"

"No luck there, but I've got something even better. While we're out, we're going to meet with One-Eyed Freddy."

Ever since Brandt, undercover, bailed Freddy out of a bad situation with the Bayside gang, Freddy has been one of Brandt's favorite informants. Showering someone with favors and attention until you can irrevocably trap them in your debt is a trick straight from Brandt's rules of spycraft. The fourth rule: anyone you could describe as "your newest and dearest friend" is anything but.

Still, it's not such a bad arrangement for Freddy. He used to be addicted to Lullaby—a nasty resin used in many of the tunnel gangs' Dreamless dens. It induces sleep free of dreams, both good and bad, thereby sealing the mind against the Dreamer's nightly messages. But it perforates the brain all the while, until the users are nothing but a lacework of their former selves. It might shush whatever nightmares haunt their sleep, but it smothers everything else about them, as well.

I've seen the Lullaby addicts before, scattered through the darkest parts of the tunnels. My mother used it quite often. The Dreamless, they're called—they collapse in filthy cots and Lullaby themselves into interminable stretches of slumber, neither living nor dreaming. Nightmares prey, not on blood or flesh, but on joy, on dreams of a better tomorrow. The Emperor outlawed the resin years ago; the Dreamer's priests swear its use is the greatest possible sin. Better to turn to the pricey services of the temple Shapers, who can tug the threads of one's dreams according to the Dreamer's will (so they claim) and keep them from upsetting the recipient. But the impoverished Lullaby users are far beyond caring about the law, or the Dreamer. All they want is to shut out the world both inside their heads and out. They just long to forget.

The heady rush of sugar in the air at Kruger's Pastry Shop is enough to make me forget about traitors and resin and wars for just a few minutes. As soon as we depart with our paper sacks crammed with confections and make our way to the meeting point, Brandt's positively skipping up and down the winding streets of Barstadt City beside me. Normally, I'd worry he'd draw attention to us, but what's the harm? The only souls we pass are merchants, and the occasional social aspirant with a gem or two set in the center of her brow. They pay us no mind.

"What has you in such a fine mood?" I ask. "Something Freddy has for us?"

"What, you don't want it to be a surprise?" He throws an arm around my shoulders, pulling me close, until a gentleman passing us on the sidewalk squints and frowns at us for our impropriety. We share a guilty grin and pull apart; Brandt makes an exaggerated show of tugging down his frock coat like a proper aristocrat. But it's this Brandt I cherish the most—the clever spy and carefree overgrown boy, not the duty-bound blue blood fumbling to put up a respectable façade that never fits him quite right.

"All right, fine. I know who our traitor is," Brandt says under his breath. I widen my eyes, but he hurries to correct himself. "Rather, I've narrowed it down to two choices. Five major Houses have blue and silver livery, but only two of them own any craft capable of making the voyage across the strait."

"That's splendid!" I exclaim, but we've reached the alleyway, and someone hisses at us from the nearby alley's mouth. Brandt does a quick scan of the street to ensure no one's watching us, then we slip into the shadows of the alley.

"Freddy!" Brandt fishes a sweet roll out of his bag. "How about a treat for my favorite songbird?"

"Shh, shh, keep it down!" Freddy rubs at his empty eye socket while his good eye watches the street. "I looked into the two Houses you named in your message."

"And?" Brandt asks, biting into his roll.

Freddy squints at us. "They both got ties to the gangs. No surprise there. But House Twyne, trust me, you don't wanna mess with them. They deal with the Stargazers and plenty of other nasty sorts besides." Freddy cringes. "I wouldn't cross any business partner of theirs, personally. The Stargazer boss is a madman, blood-crazed. I heard he ate his own lieutenant once for betraying him—made an example of him. Serious bad news."

I look away, shame calcifying inside me. Brandt and I know the frightful vengeance of the Stargazer boss all too well, but Brandt keeps his expression loose. "Sounds like a dumb story the Stargazers themselves made up. You can't believe everything you hear, Freddy. Good thing you got friends like us watching out for you."

Freddy crinkles his nose. "Sure. You're a real pal. I risk my neck for you—"

"House Twyne," Brandt says, steering him back. "Suppose someone wanted a closer look at their records. Something that might prove they're tangled up with the Stargazers."

Freddy shrugs. "Okay, it's your skin. Your best bet is probably inside Twyne Manor itself—the Lady doesn't trust the banks, keeps all her accountants on retainer. She's got some fancy ball comin' up—masquerade for the Summer's Retreat. She's not hirin' any tunnelers to work it, though, so good luck getting inside without an invitation."

"I'm sure we'll manage." Brandt stretches, exaggerated, a cascade of coins tinkling somewhere inside his clothing. "Well, Freddy, I wish I could say you've been helpful, but—"

"Wait, wait." Freddy grips Brandt's wrist. "I—I heard a rumor this morning that Jorn the Destroyer was lurkin' around the Crescent Docks. Is it true?" Freddy stares hard at us. "Jornisander's working for the Ministry?"

I exchange a glance with Brandt. The minister assigned Jorn to shadow me with the Farthingers, but only as long as he took his usual precautions to disguise himself. If his former gang, the Stargazers, caught wind of him so close to their tunnels . . .

Brandt shrugs and takes another bite of pastry. "Would you want me telling whoever asks that you're working for us?"

"Come on, don't be that way." Freddy looks from Brandt to me, but we keep our faces neutral. "Look. You didn't hear it from me, but . . ." Freddy sighs. "Not everyone thinks Jorn's a stool pigeon, despite what the Stargazers say. And I'm not just saying it 'cause I'm one myself. Some folks think he did a lot of good. He really put some fear in the big bosses."

I rock back on my heels. Jorn had tried to organize the tunnelers to fight for the Writ of Emancipation before, though the Incident, and my failure, unraveled his efforts. "And some folks think Jorn's methods were no better than the bosses'," Brandt says. "What's your point?"

Freddy glances toward the alley's mouth. "My point is . . .

Jorn or no, the Destroyers are carrying on with what he started, and depending how this whole Writ of Emancipation vote goes, they may be about to get a lot louder."

Sora had hinted as much, too. As if the Commandant weren't enough of a threat to Barstadt's peace, the tunnelers are threatening an uprising, as well. Brandt grins and tosses Freddy the coin purse. "Now, that's the sort of gossip I need from you. Keep me posted, will you?"

"Will do," Freddy says, and checks the alley's mouth again. "I gotta scramble. Looks like the constables are making another sweep."

Sure enough, as soon as Brandt and I step back onto the boulevard, a constable approaches us and signals for us to display our citizenship papers. Brandt flips his open with the well-practiced ease of an aristocrat, but I have to dig around in my pockets for a bit to find the weathered temporary papers the Ministry issued me so many years ago. Just a scrap with a seal and a signature—all that separates me from the tunneler life I once knew.

Once we're safely away from Kruger's bakery and One-Eyed Freddy, I glance at Brandt. "So some of Jorn's old Destroyer compatriots are still fighting for the Writ?" I ask. "Do you think it stands a chance after all?"

Brandt presses his lips into a thin line. "As much as I'd like to think so, I'm afraid the Stargazers have shattered the Destroyers' movement. Tunnelers rely on the gangs too much to oppose them effectively, and even if they could stand up to them, why would Lord Alizard pay them any mind? There are too many crooked aristocrats."

"Like Lady Twyne. Do you think she's our traitor? What should we do next?"

"I'll speak to Edina about piecing together a mission plan and present it to the minister. I say we infiltrate that party at Twyne Manor and see what muck we can rake—unless your new Farthinger friends have a better idea." He rolls his eyes. "Dreamer bless, that Marez is mighty full of himself, isn't he?"

I keep my gaze squarely on the cobblestones surging upward before us. "Nothing wrong with that, if he's earned it."

"We'll see how good their information shakes out to be." Brandt clicks his teeth. "I'm still not pleased that Durst has you working with them. If they ever suspect what you're capable of—"

"Trust me." I snort. "They've nothing but contempt for dreams." Kriza, anyway. Marez was intrigued this morning, but I feel like keeping that to myself. "I'm being careful."

Brandt scans the street—the quiet merchant houses ahead of us, and the crowded market behind, the traders' patter ringing out. "I know you are. That Marez may be full of himself, but you know, he may have a good point about you."

"What? About me making a good field operative?" I scoff and look away, though I feel my cheeks heating, recalling the way his gaze seemed to seize me up by the collar and refuse to let me go. "I don't know. I think maybe he's just . . . testing me, something of the sort. You of all people should know—"

"He's right about your instincts. You haven't been properly trained, is all. I can talk to Minister Durst about it, see if we can't arrange for some basic operative training for you." Brandt smiles, crooked and genuine. "I know you'll catch on quickly."

We come to the end of the residential row, passing a steep bridge that crosses into a pocket of municipal buildings—a constabulary, an office for the Ministry of Colonial Management, and, unlabeled and unknown to most Barstadters, the Ministry of Affairs. But my thoughts run to the tunnel entrance far beneath the bridge, just one of the dozens of networks that crisscross the earth below Barstadt City proper. Brandt may think I can learn, but Durst still holds my temporary citizenship papers. He's trusting me to keep an eye on the Farthingers now, but one more mistake, and he will cast me back to the tunnels for good.

"I'm not sure we have time for training," I say, steering myself away from that unpleasant line of thought. "I'm sure the Farthingers will give me ample practice in the field."

"Make a game of it, then," Brandt says with a grin. "They're here to protect Farthing, but I've no doubt they intend to gather some information on Barstadt in the process. See what they're a little too interested in."

"Aye, Professor." I nudge him with a grin of my own.

We reach the heavily guarded entrance to the barracks, fenced in by a prickly wrought iron gate. I march up to the guardsman, who knows us both so well by now that we rarely have to produce our papers, but Brandt lingers back.

"Well?" I ask Brandt. "I think we're overdue for another Stacks tournament. I'll wager you for your spare pinwheel there." I gesture toward his bag of pastries.

But then Brandt, my best friend, fades away; what he becomes instead is the aristocrat Brandt. From the tight skin around his eyes and the weary quirk at one corner of his lips, I can see it's his least favorite role. He looks away from me while he talks, as if he's reciting something he's rehearsed. "Actually, I'm staying at my family's estate tonight. We're having guests for dinner."

I arch one brow. "Ones you're not fond of, I take it."

He takes a deep breath. "It's another potential marriage contract." He says it so quickly it takes me a few moments to parse out his words. "Father's not going to take no for an answer much longer. The dowries are too large, and the families involved, too influential."

I don't hear the rest of his words, because I am a little girl curled up in a remote alcove of the tunnels, her fist clenched around a tithe that could save her life if she's found. But she only wants the echoing silence of her deep-earth home. Silence too loud to permit footsteps or running water or painful words to break it apart. The silence of true loneliness—of true independence, where trusting no one and feeling nothing is the only way to never get hurt.

"Oh," I hear myself say, as if I'm my own dreamstriding victim, speaking from my subconscious. Then, before I can stop myself, "Who is she?"

That seems to ease some of the tension from Brandt; his

shoulders slump again and he musters a weak smile. "Edina Alizard."

The blood drains from my face. Of course it would be Edina—clever, kind Edina, who keeps the Ministry's operations running smoothly and treats everyone like an old friend.

"She's a good person, Liv. I like that we already know each other—if you could have seen the awkward dinners I've had to sit through with other prospects . . ." He tries to laugh, but stops himself, and frowns instead. "It helps that she works for the Ministry—she understands the truth of my work, and I don't have to lie. I like that she has ambitions of her own, too. Most of the girls my father's picked are the sort who frump about the Cloister of Roses, gossiping and visiting the dress shops."

Yes, Edina is perfectly charming, witty, and amiable—all the things I'm not. Though all she really needs to satisfy Brandt's father is aristocratic blood. My jealousy is a thorny thing, scratching at my skin from inside.

I always knew this day would come; I can't keep my dearest friend forever. And that's all he is to me, I remind myself sternly—my partner, my accomplice, my best friend. He can never be anything more.

"What about her father?" I ask. The words come too easily, spilling out of me like loose grain. "One of the dirtiest aristocrats of them all."

Brandt winces, pastry bag crumpling in his fist. "Yes, yes, I'm aware . . ."

But those thorns are scratching, scratching. "I mean, if

you think it's wise to spend time around someone who'd happily toss you to the wolves if he knew the real nature of your work—"

"Livia!" Brandt cries. "I know what her father's like. She does, too. Obviously she doesn't agree with his deeds, or she wouldn't be working for the Ministry, trying to undo the harm her father's criminal friends cause. But we can't just change the very fabric of Barstadt society. The Houses have to marry, alliances must be forged, the Empire must carry on. We . . ." He hesitates. "We all have our roles to play." Brant's gaze reels out, casting somewhere far beyond me. "If I have to marry to fulfill my duties to House Strassbourg, then better I wed someone who understands me, who shares my passion for serving Barstadt."

What does that matter? I want to scream at him. He's already promised his father—once he weds, he'll quit the Ministry and take his place managing House Strassbourg's affairs. And then he'll be expected to produce heirs, and attend the Imperial Court . . . That's the way with aristocrats and their obligations. As soon as one's met—as soon as one knot's untied—two more pull tight.

I shift my weight, bag of pastries hanging limp at my side. "Well . . . have a lovely night," I finally say.

"You too, Liv." He shoves his hands in his pockets and heads off.

I look back toward the guard station, but as I try to imagine the evening that awaits me—dinner alone in my room, reading in the records room or the library, staring wistfully out the window while I avoid the other operatives' sour looks—I can't bring myself to walk through the gates. The sunlight will last for a few hours more. I check my bag of pastries—still a few honeycakes left, Professor Hesse's favorite—and set off toward the university. If I can't do anything more to protect the waking world from the coming war, then maybe I can look to the dreaming one.

Banhopf University looms in the backdrop of the municipal district, its muted tile buildings crammed every which way on the hillside. Though Barstadt buildings already tend toward the tall and narrow, the university takes the style to new extremes—each subject of study has its own tower, thrusting skyward like a beacon of knowledge and power (according to the professors) or like a gauntlet of interminable staircases (to the tunnelers who must clean the place).

I once called Banhopf home, but that's too misleading—it was my home like a mansion might be home to a rat. At night, while tending to my cleaning duties, I watched, and I fettered away crumbs; I scrubbed and dusted and mopped and fetched professors their food; but when the candelabras were lit and the classrooms filled, my job was to scurry into the labyrinth of tunnels underground and not interfere with Banhopf's lofty pursuits.

But I belong on these manicured lawns now, striding with confidence in a lady's dress, not hunchbacked in a corridor after hours, scrubbing marble until it glints with my dour reflection. The scholars glance at me sideways, but they're deep in discussions of philosophy or math or dream interpretation with their peers, all of them flapping about in black velvet robes like flight-less birds. I keep my shoulders tossed back. I belong.

Rather than mount the trek toward Hesse's office high up in the Theosophy Tower, I decide to check his laboratory first, where he conducts all his experiments, blending his religious scholarship and research with the latest advances in modern scientific knowledge. More often than not, this means training priests of the Dreamer in accessing Oneiros and shaping the dreamworld and dreams. Sometimes, though, Hesse's mad hypotheses about the interplay of body, soul, and dreams results in something like dreamstriding. A scientifically sound theory just waiting for someone like me to come along and prove it true.

As I weave through the honeycomb corridors, I pass a young boy polishing the marble flooring, his hands and knees knobby and red from the effort. I reach into the bag of pastries and fish out a tartlet, then set it atop the nearest bookshelf. I remember the rules. The cleaning boy could lose his job if anyone saw me give it to him directly.

I slip into the back of Hesse's laboratory, but I needn't have worried about disturbing a lecture; Hesse and two students are out cold in their cots. The sounds of Hesse's snores crowd out any other possible noise. I find the timepiece Hesse uses for his exercises—they've still some twenty minutes left in Oneiros. My muscles itch; it feels strange to be surrounded by people lost in Oneiros and just stand by. Both of the students look like typical Banhopf boys, soft-muscled, well-dressed, and without the ashy complexion of a sun-starved tunneler; both show the beginnings of jewel markings set into their foreheads and cheeks. More than likely, they're seeking either priesthood or a fancy scroll with the Banhopf University imprint to hang in their mansion.

I sit at an empty desk, drum my fingers for a few minutes, then can't stand it anymore. I'm going to join them.

In Hesse's vast array of potions and substances, only two are crucial for dreamstriding—mothwood smoke, to send a sleeping soul into Oneiros, and dreamwort brew to send an awake one down. The Dreamer's most devout priests can enter Oneiros without any alchemical assistance; Hesse was the first to find the dreamwort shortcut, and its existence is still something of a state secret. Oneiros is only for the Dreamer's chosen, the High Priest says, not a playground for the masses. Well, a priest I'm not, but even the High Priest grudgingly tolerates my work in service to Barstadt. I only wish I could feel more certain the Dreamer blesses what I do in his name.

The dreamwort brew burns down my throat; I barely make it to an empty cot before Oneiros pulls me in.

I awake in a field of wildflowers, their pink and purple blooms waist high and bursting with wonderful scents. I'm wearing comfortable trousers and a loose blouse; no trim, tailored dresses hampering my movement. Behind me, Hesse is lecturing his students, every word bright and eager as the afternoon sunlight around us. How nice it is to stay tethered to my body inside Oneiros for once—to not have to hunt for my target, or to fear the prowling Wastes. I gather a fistful of wildflowers and bask in the dreamworld. In the distance, I can see some of the Shapers' homes. In addition to weaving dreams, the Shapers can alter the landscape of Oneiros and remake it however they please. Here they've used their gift to fill Oneiros with their hearts' desires: homes and sculptures and other creations that let them claim a corner of eternity for themselves.

"Tomorrow, we'll conduct a few more Shaping experiments, but good work for today, gentlemen." Hesse waves to me from across the field. "Go ahead and explore until the chime rings in the waking world," he tells his students, then he starts wading through the flowers toward me.

"Afternoon, Professor." I wrap my arms around him for a tight embrace. "It's been too long."

"The Ministry's keeping you busy?" he asks. Dreamworld Hesse looks a few decades younger than the actual one, but they're more or less the same—trimmed beard, a face etched by age, and hands as thick as bear paws. A gentle giant, most of the time, but a lively debate about the Dreamer always stokes the fire in his veins.

"Busy enough." My smile fades. "I was actually hoping to get your opinion on something. I've been having some . . . difficulty."

Something always shifts in Hesse's face when I mention any trouble with dreamstriding—like a gas lamp's been turned down. He'd never say as much, but he must regret that I'm not the perfect instrument for the Dreamer that he'd imagined in his lab. "Of course. What seems to be the matter?"

Everything, I think, my heart twisting. I glance toward his students, but they're absorbed in the favorite pastime of any dreamer—trying to fly. "On my last mission, when I was trying to get back to my body . . . the Wastes." A chill courses through me. "They felt stronger. Much stronger—I'm sure of it."

Hesse's face screws shut like the lid of a jar. "My dear Livia, that's not possible. Nightmare is dead. The Wastes can't become any more powerful than they already are. The Dreamer wouldn't permit it. You believe that, don't you?"

Of course I believe in the Dreamer—wasn't my ability to dreamstride proof enough of that? And yet all his priests and most devout followers speak of a presence that fills them, a voice that speaks to them, guiding them with more than mere dreams. The Dreamer never speaks to me, never shows himself to me with anything other than my half-formed gift.

Hesse touches his fingertips to his sternum. "The Dreamer speaks to us of truth, and realizing our dreams. But Nightmare—" Hesse taps his temple. "Nightmare is the doubt and fear and surrender that keep us from making our dreams come true."

"But the Wastes are getting stronger. I'm sure of it." I hold up one hand. "And please, don't tell me I imagined it, or that I just have to try harder to fend them off. This wasn't like the usual challenge they pose. I know what I felt and heard. It was real." My voice shatters on that last. "They were real, in here."

Distantly, I hear a chime; not in Oneiros, but in the real world. The timepiece Professor Hesse sets to keep his students from missing their next class. Time to return to the real world. The echo of the bell rings though my flesh while the dreamworld crumbles away.

I lurch out of the cot in Hesse's laboratory as Hesse and his two students do the same. While Hesse bids them farewell, I hang in the back of the room; they stagger around as if drunk, readjusting to their weighty real bodies after their adventures soaring through Oneiros. Hesse's toothy smile is broad as ever while he speaks to them, but as soon as he closes and latches the laboratory door behind them, he turns to me with a weary frown. He looks older—so much older now than his dream-world self. More than just age has put those deep furrows in his face and that anxious tension in his mouth. It twists at my heart to see him this way.

Hesse rubs at his eyes. "The Wastes are only a shadow of Nightmare's former self. The lingering darkness that couldn't be cleansed away. If they were growing stronger, then . . ."

I wrap my arms tightly around me. "Then it would mean Nightmare isn't completely dead."

Hesse's head shakes back and forth, as if he's trying to convince himself. "But he can't be. No. It would mean—No, Livia, you must be mistaken."

I want so badly to believe him. All the priests say Nightmare is long dead; that the Dreamer slew him to save Barstadt. But I remember the tug of the Wastes, the whispers as soft as silk against my skin, so convincing and cold. I remember, too, how Hesse didn't tell me the full truth about the Wastes until I'd successfully entered his assistant's body for the first time—that he'd told me if I heard any strange voices, just to ignore them, and focus on getting into my target's body or my own as quickly as possible. Only after did I learn what danger I'd been in. Hesse has deceived me about the Wastes with half-truths before, but I have no one else to ask for help.

I turn away from Hesse and busy myself with tidying up his lab tools—flasks and vials and a dirty mortar and pestle. There's comfort in such labor, I suppose; I doubt I'll ever lose the compulsion for it. "Are you still searching for another dreamstrider?" I ask, refusing to look at him as I do so.

"Livia." His footsteps draw closer. "I'm—I'm pausing my experiments to reevaluate my efforts. Readjust my criteria." His hand shakes as he reaches for his glasses, perched on a shelf. "I've made some errors, misjudged some factors—"

My fist clenches around the neck of a glass bottle. "You're 'reevaluating'? Does the Minister know that?" I want to feel relieved, but only a cold hollow aches in me. "He must be awfully disappointed there are no new prospects in the works. The Ministry would love to be rid of me once and for all."

"And what if I did find another?" Hesse asks. "What would become of you?" He lifts one eyebrow. "Have you even earned your citizenship papers yet? At least this way, your position is secure."

In the tunnels, I could never let myself cry—tears are a weakness, luring predators as surely as lost souls in Oneiros lure the Wastes. I force myself to think on other things until they subside, and nothing forces the tears away like hardening myself against their source. The Ministry can take my papers away, but I refuse to go back to the tunnels, to be a slave to the gangs and their will.

I could flee Barstadt. For the first time, that possibility nestles in my heart like a warm ember. Seek out work in Barstadt's colonies, perhaps. If Brandt leaves the Ministry, if Hesse gives up his work, then there's little left for me here. If the Dreamer never answers my call, why should I continue to serve him?

"I'd be all right. I'd find something, I'm sure." I step back from the laboratory table—everything in proper order. "Thank you for hearing me out, Professor." I drop into a curtsey without meeting his gaze. "I'd best return to the barracks."

"Livia, please. Listen, I—I need you to do something for me," Hesse says.

I've spent my life doing favors for Hesse—earning him endless accolades and funding for his search for more Dreamstriders while I struggle and fail. But I'm done for now. I'm already out the door.

Scholars and students flap about the Banhopf campus in their velvet robes; across the city, at the Strassbourg Manor, Brandt is dining with Lady Alizard, probably discussing politics or the latest opera. The Ministry's spies and Barstadt's countless crime lords spin their dangerous stratagems while the tunnelers clean up behind them. And glistening in the moonlight, Nightmare's bones watch over it all.

At last, I think I grasp the message of last night's dream. I belong to none of Barstadt's worlds, and I'll never inhabit any of them as fully as I want. Even in my own body, I'm an impostor.

Chapter Six

"This mission should be fairly straightforward." Brandt tugs at the collar of his velvet coat, trying to get it to lay properly. "Far less dangerous than our last one."

I bat his hands away from the collar and refold it for him so it lies flush. He smiles at me through the mirror, but the tension in his shoulders remains. He's resplendent in the coppery velvet suit, shimmering either brown or fiery red depending which way the light strikes it; paired with the fox mask on his dresser, he'll fit right in with the crowd at House Twyne's Summer's Retreat masquerade ball we're infiltrating tonight.

"Isn't Lady Twyne the Emperor's cousin?" I ask. "Do you really think she's capable of treason? Of plotting with the Commandant?"

Brandt brushes back his bangs from his forehead, but they fall right back into place. "Of all the Houses with silver and sapphire colors, House Twyne certainly fits the profile. Her arguments with the Emperor are infamous, and she's always got her claws in one shady deal or another. Including with the Stargazers, if you believe One-Eyed Freddy. I want to find her records and see what we can learn from them." He gives his reflection one quick nod, then extends an arm to me. "Shall we?"

We look ridiculous side by side—him in his elegant costume and me in my servant's garb. He's attending the masquerade as a minor aristocrat, but I need to fade into the background. My best disguises are as someone whose disappearance for an hour or two won't be noticed. But for a few more minutes, at least, we're still Brandt and Livia. I take his arm and he ushers me toward the Ministry stables. "How will we know what to look for in her records?"

"I'll chat up Lady Twyne's good friends, needle them for juicy tidbits. Indications that some of her dealings aren't above board. I'd like to use you to pry Lady Twyne in person, in the guise of someone she trusts."

"Pry her?" I ask. "I can try, but luring someone to admit to treason isn't easy. Especially without knowing what my dream-striding host may hold over her."

"I know it makes you nervous, Liv, but our other teammate should be able to help you—"

That draws me up short. "Someone else is coming with us?"

Brandt releases my arm. "Well . . . yes, Edina and the minister thought . . ."

"Nightmare's teeth, could you two be any slower?" Vera charges toward us, in a billowing cloud of deep orange silk. Terror pins me in place. Instinctively, I find my gaze drawn to her right arm, but she's covered it in a velvet glove that reaches all the way to the middle of her bicep; a tuft of tulle conceals the rest of her right shoulder. Her deep brown curls spring around her face as she glowers right at me. "The ball's going to be half over by the time we get there."

I haven't worked with Vera since the Incident, and for good reason. Her hand shoots out—I cringe recalling the sight of the puckered, mottled skin beneath that glove—and she snatches me by the wrist and yanks me toward the carriage.

"One false move on this mission," Vera whispers in my ear, voice sweet as syrup, "and I'll have your intestines for my corset lacings." Her lips stretch from ear to ear in an unnatural smile as she pats me on the shoulder. "Let's have a pleasant time tonight, shall we?"

Twyne Manor rears up from the hills of northeast Barstadt City like a glowing fortress. Even in the Cloister of Roses, where most of the older Houses keep estates, it manages to outdo its peers. The whole house is built from strange alabaster stones shipped over from the Northern Realms that soak up sunlight during the day, then leak it throughout the night in a subtle shimmer that could be a trick of the moonlight if you didn't know to look for it.

The doorman announces the masked Vera and Brandt using some pompous fake names dredged up by the Ministry. Sweeping string music washes over us as we plunge into the great hall, fighting our way through dreamsilk gowns plump as cream puffs. The women buried inside them all wear masks—some don cat's ears, or bird plumage, or more elaborate headwear, but it all manages to reveal a hint of kohl-smudged eyelids, sparkling facial gems, or perfectly stained lips. The men wear masks picked to flatter their stiff-cut suits (some much tighter than they ought to be). Brandt strides away to join the ranks of younger unmarried men his age at the other side of the room. In the center of the dance floor, younger couples place their palms together for slow polonaises.

I keep waiting for Vera to clue me in on her plan, but the deeper we wade into the swirling mass of dancers, the more I suspect she's intentionally keeping me in the dark. "What should I be doing?" I hiss at her after fighting my way around yet another masked reveler.

"Shutting up and letting me do my job," she snaps back. "Like a good little servant girl."

Vera plucks a handful of cheese cubes from a server's tray and shoves her way into the nearest gaggle of gossipers. I cling to her backside, always in the shadows.

"Can you believe the gall of Lord Alizard, challenging the Writ? I was certain it would pass," one girl says, soft brown coif toddling with each syllable.

"Nonsense, it's only the work of overemotional busybodies. Our very society is founded on order; we can't go upsetting it . . ."

"Besides, my head butler tells me a bunch of violent vigilantes—calling themselves the Destroyers, something vulgar like that—tried organizing the tunnels, fighting for rights from their gang lords and such, but it was short-lived. In the end, the gang lords themselves ran them off."

Jorn. I clench my teeth until the pain throbs in my jaw.

"I hear the tunnelers have to eat their own children for want of any food!"

"Well then, that's all the proof I need that they're savages deserving of their plight. Why emancipate them? Leave them where they're most useful."

Vera opens her mouth while still chewing on her chunk of cheese. "What's Lady Twyne's opinion on the Writ?"

The girls closest to Vera lean away and wrinkle their noses. "All the shady deals she makes? Of course she's a fan of keeping the tunnelers where they belong. You won't find her pitying the lower classes like House Yorgen does."

"Oh, really?" Vera stuffs another cheese cube into her mouth. "What kind of shady deals?"

Vera manages to drive off the rest of the girls but for the pair of sisters (House Tidwell, they later introduce themselves) whose love for gossip outweighs their demand for decorum. Vera sends me to fetch a flute of champagne for her while she needles them for further juicy gossip about Lady Twyne.

At the serving table, I pause to search for Brandt's coppery fox mask, but it's too crowded. The ladies' coifs tower over me. The false starlights dangling from the ceiling of the vast ballroom are too sharp. The tart, too-sweet scent of pastries and sausage and sugary bread is making me dizzy. Everyone's chattering all around me. I've no talent for navigating crowds like this; I do much better somewhere quiet, dark, cramped like a tunnel nook. Somewhere I can curl up and sift through the sounds around me for an approaching threat . . .

I feel wooden paneling against my back. I've backed myself into the corner of the grand staircase, just as I used to wedge myself into the tunnel crannies. From here, I have a clear view of the mezzanine, where Lady Twyne hovers over the whole proceedings, like some bird of prey. She's nearing forty, only a few years younger than her cousin, the Emperor, but the faint web of lines across her face only adds to her royal beauty. Dark curls are piled atop her head, and her angular brows assess with diamond-tipped precision everything in her gaze. An elaborate network of sapphires and silver nodules set into her face and throat add the final ornamentation to her, dazzling like the night sky.

Could she really betray her country? Her cousin? I can't fathom a good reason for any of it, but I've met enough aristocrats like her to know they operate under different constraints than the rest of us. Is there a greater wealth she hopes to gain by working with the Commandant, even more power that she craves? I can't feign camaraderie, not the way Brandt can; he feeds their outrageous beliefs back to them, even if it appalls him on the inside, in order to win their trust.

I step toward the edge of the dance floor and search for Brandt. A band of hired tumblers shoves past me, festooned as various woodland creatures, complete with velvety masks. I dart out of their way, but the wolf glances back at me, head cocked, before continuing to the dance floor with his companions. I quickly duck my head and let a stray wisp of hair shield my face.

"I say there, girl, my drink has been dry for far too long. Fetch me a fresh one, won't you?"

I whirl around, but it's only Brandt, grinning at me from behind his fox face. "Of course, my lord." I bow low.

As I stand back up, he lurches toward me, staggering as if drunk, and grips me by the shoulder. A thrill strums down my spine as he leans in close to my ear. "The Farthing woman is here. Kriza? She's dressed like a phoenix. Probably best if she doesn't see you."

His fingers trail across my wrist as he hands his empty glass to me, blazing a path of sudden warmth. I catch his gaze for a brief moment—comfortable and playful—but he's already turning back into the clever spy, the unattainable son of House Strassbourg. I nod to let him know I understand and then scurry back toward the serving tables.

"There you are, girl." Vera throws an arm over my shoulder. "My shoes are dreadfully in need of re-lacing. I don't know what you were thinking earlier. Come, let's set them right."

I accompany her to a low bench set into an alcove and, Dreamer curse, she actually hoists up her skirt for me to re-lace her heels! "I think you and Brandt are enjoying these roles a bit too much," I mutter as I tug the lacing extra tight.

She smirks and unearths a fan from her cleavage. "Please. I joined the Ministry to *escape* these endless balls. But I think I have an opening for you." Vera tosses her glossy brown curls over her bare shoulder and adjusts the iridescent feather trim of her gown. "The elder Tidwell girl is already half a punch bowl in, and she let slip that the Lady Twyne—the *unmarried* Lady, might I add—has a daughter hidden away in the upstairs apartments."

"And?" I ask, my throat tightening.

Vera rolls her eyes. "And she sounds like a perfect target for you to get more information from Lady Twyne."

"A child?" I squeak, trying to keep my voice down. "I can't use a little girl."

"Why not?"

"It just feels . . . wrong, somehow." But my conversation with Professor Hesse about the whispers of the Nightmare Wastes looms in my mind like a behemoth. Am I really afraid of dreamstriding into a child's mind? Or is it dreamstriding itself that I now dread?

"Will you do it or not? I can't think of a better opportunity to gain access to the Lady or her private rooms."

I shove her feet out of my lap and stand up. I can't keep fearing the Wastes. "Fine. I'll try it."

"Excellent!" Vera flashes me a false grin. "I'll go fetch Brandt."

We return to the main hall. Some of the alchemical starlight globes have winked out, and strange shadows play across the masked dancers' faces, lending them a ghoulish quality. I look for Kriza's phoenix costume, but Vera's is the only fiery dress I can see.

The wolf-headed tumbler circles around me again, on the prowl. I lower my head—I can't look too alert. I'm meant to be invisible here.

Vera spots Brandt and bustles through the sea of silk, out of sync with the slow, plodding gavotte. "Follow my lead," she whispers. Apparently she's not one for drawn-out seductions: she throws both arms around Brandt's neck and latches her lips onto his. I shudder, my knees locking underneath me. The gavotte is far too syrupy to keep time with my pounding heart.

But who am I to feel envy? Brandt is my dearest friend, but I'll never be more to him than some weapon in the armory he must guard. He's aristocracy through and through, born to continue its bloodline.

"I said to follow me," Vera hisses at me. I open my eyes in time to see her bob past, Brandt in a vise grip beside her. I count to three as they start up the curling marble staircase, then trail after them.

"Tumblers! They have tumblers!" Vera laughs at a nonexistent joke between them; Brandt weaves from side to side of the upstairs hall as if intoxicated. We reach the top of the stairs and cross the threshold into the northern wing of the house.

"My deepest apologies." A butler charges toward them. "Guests are not permitted in this hallway. If you wish a private room, we have made several available on the third floor—"

"Nonsense, my good man. We won't be but a minute." Brandt stands up straight, blocking the butler while Vera uncurls from around him and starts rattling doorknobs along the hall. Brandt keeps himself wedged between the butler and Vera, arguing vehemently, until Vera finally settles on a room and stumbles inside.

"My lady!" The butler edges around Brandt. "You are forbidden from these rooms!"

Vera catches my eye, and the drunken façade vanishes long enough for her to glower at me. Bloody dreams, she wants me

to follow her, but I don't know her cues like I know Brandt's . . .
I scurry to catch up.

The intoxicated slurry returns to her face, and she laughs,
high and piercing. "Of course we can. You're just an old fuddy-
duddy! Did you dream of . . . of watching a pot boil? That
sounds like the Dreamer's idea of folks like you!"

Somehow, Brandt manages to lure the butler into the room,
hemming him in with Vera. I trail them inside and slam the
door shut.

The butler lurches for Vera. She takes a swing at him, all pre-
tense of aristocracy gone. He staggers backward into Brandt,
who's ready and waiting with a kerchief soaked with the smoke
from burning mothwood. The butler thrashes against him for
only a few seconds before falling limp.

"Dreams of death," Vera mutters to me. "You don't have the
slightest clue how to be a spy. It'd be easier to just drag you in
here already unconscious."

"No, it'd be easier if you told me your plan in advance,"
I retort.

But Vera and Brandt are already stripping away the excessive components of their costumes as they stride to the opposite side of the sitting room. Vera throws open the next set of
doors to the little girl's bedroom. Shrieks flood from the room
as Brandt and I peer through the doorway, masked by shadows.

A nurse, wild-eyed and shaking, coils around a tiny figure
on the mattress. "What do you want? Please don't hurt her! She's
done nothing wrong!"

"Shh, shh. Everything will be just fine." Vera opens up her handbag, lights a censer of mothwood, rolls it on the floor and slinks back out, closing the door behind her.

"They'll remember seeing us," Brandt chides her. "You should have pumped it under the door."

"They were already panicked by the disturbance. Let's just get on with it." She rolls her eyes in my general direction.

After a few seconds more, we tie scarves around our faces and open the bedroom door. Brandt and I move as we always do into a new room—him sweeping to the left and me to the right, though Vera traipses right down the middle. Both the girl and her maid slump against one another in the center of the bed. Without the maid coiled around her like a constrictor, I can see the girl's face now. It blazes through me like a shock.

"Cursed dreams." I swallow hard. "I think we've found our traitor, all right."

A native Barstadter is always easy to pick out of a crowd— our skin ranges from light to deep brown, and our hair, from dark blond like Brandt's, through redder shades, up to the dark brown of sunbaked earth like Vera's. Coal-black hair and skin the color of birch trees—those are the signs of someone from the Land of the Iron Winds. But despite the solitary sapphire set into the girl's forehead, a mark of Barstadt nobility, the girl's dark hair and creamy skin mark her as just that.

Chapter Seven

"Nightmare's bones," Brandt swears. "Looks like Twyne is doing far more than just working with the Commandant."

We stare at the little girl, eyes screwed tightly shut in deep, engrossing sleep. Even at five years of age, she bears the harsh countenance of her father's lineage, only somewhat softened by youthful chub. "And for several years," Vera says. She rolls her eyes skyward. "Dreamer, might've been nice if you could've given us a warning."

"The Dreamer guides us as he feels necessary." I pull the pendant vial of dreamwort out from between my breasts and flip open the lid. "Let's hope he guides us toward more clues of what Lady Twyne's involved in."

Vera fiddles with the lacing on her ball gown, exposing the lacework of scars along her right shoulder and arm. "I'll pose as the maid. Brandt, get the butler's outfit."

I brace myself for the foul rotten-apple taste of the dreamwort elixir and gulp it down. Dimly, I feel the mattress soften my fall before I lose all sensation.

I stand on the beach of Oneiros, chilly waves lapping at my ankles. I charge along the coast and approach elaborate seaside villas that part through the ocean mist, eerie in their seeming emptiness. I have a limited amount of time to slip my leash and claim a new body before the Nightmare Wastes catch my scent. After my brush with them in the Land of the Iron Winds, I'm not about to underestimate their strength.

I stumble past another experimental Shaper's creation—the beached husk of a ship, its exposed side torn through, as if it were a great insect's molted shell burst open. I try not to wonder why it looks like something broke free as I circle around the bow and plunge into the forests beyond. The little girl's soul has to be close by, given our proximity in the real world, and I'm reaching the end of my tether . . . A stretch, like fibers fraying, and then—*snap*. My soul tears free from my body.

Stop running from your fears. You can surrender, find eternal rest . . .

My breath falters. They've already found me.

The Nightmare Wastes' call threads through the trees like a delicate wind. Delicate, but insistent—my soul flutters on the breeze. They're blowing me off course, pulling a snare around me with those velvet words.

They will never forgive you. Isn't it better to let go? Why suffer their disappointment a moment more? Surrender now, and never feel their hatred again.

Dreamer, but it's hard to fight. Before, the Nightmare Wastes were only a gnat buzzing around me as I sought my host—irritating but escapable. Now I feel a great undertow gripping me, pulling me toward surrender. But I can't, I can't, I have to fight. Brandt needs me. The Empire of Barstadt needs me.

But they would rather it be anyone else.

Professor Hesse taught me to cleave to my purpose when the Wastes called my name, but they've never been so strong. I grab at a nearby branch and brace myself against it.

Surrender, foolish girl. There is nothing more you can do. Why fight?

Tears needle at my eyes. The sting of the Wastes' cold hardens around my skin. I don't know how much longer I can resist them.

But then I catch sight of it: the little girl's consciousness, dangling gossamer-thin between two sapling branches—a spiderweb. It seems a fitting representation for her here, brought into Oneiros by the mothwood smoke. Her thoughts are more delicate than the adults I usually seek; I must brush against them tenderly to keep from tearing them to shreds. I take hold of the little girl's tether and slip into her body.

Why bother, Livia? the Wastes cry out. *You'll only fail them once more—*

We open our eyes.

Weak, watery shapes in cream and shadowy blue. It takes a moment to bring the world into focus. Brandt's already donned the butler's uniform and is busy wedging an arm into an armoire. Blearily, I recognize it as my own.

"Ah, there you are." He shoves the armoire door shut with

his back. I hope my fingers were out of the way. "Might want to figure out your name before we get any further."

"Good point." The girl's voice is fluid; I can't seem to hold it down. I lean back into her spiderweb thoughts, her fleeting dreams. "Martine."

"All right, Martine. Ready to make a scene?" Brandt asks.

I don't feel at all ready, but with Brandt supporting me, I'm far better off. "Let's."

We charge out into the sitting room. As soon as Brandt's checked the restraints on the unconscious butler, I run from the bedroom suite. "Mommy! Mommy!" I shriek, tearing down the hallway and onto the grand staircase. Martine's instincts tweak at me and I correct myself. "Maman! Maman!"

Brandt and Vera, in guise, chase after me and silence me halfway down the twisting stairs. Few party revelers look up, unable to hear us over the waltz, but we've achieved our desired effect. Lady Sindra Twyne rears up from her chair, glaring icicles at Vera and Brandt. She excuses herself from the ruby-flecked aristocrat with whom she'd been chatting and cuts a murderous path through the dance floor.

"Bring her to my rooms," Lady Twyne hisses at Vera without turning to look at her, and keeps climbing the stairs past us, as if to deny all relations. Is this how poor Martine lives her entire life? Locked away with a nursemaid, forbidden from ever being seen on her mother's arm? My heart aches for this little girl, even as I tangle up her spidersilk thoughts for my own nefarious purposes.

98

Lady Twyne ushers me into her grand suites on the mansion's top floor and closes Vera and Brandt out in the hallway. Her sitting room is lined in the same exposed alabaster as the exterior, emitting a sun-kissed, pale glow. Ferns soften the harsh cutstone edges, and gauzes in a variety of dyes crest the slender floor-to-ceiling windows.

"Come, darling. Sit in Mummy's lap." She nestles on a divan and billows her skirt around her. I toddle forward, still unsteady on such tiny legs, but the uncertainty feels appropriate for this delicate child. Lady Twyne throws her arms wide and hoists me into her lap.

"Maman, I had bad dreams." I burrow my face into her bosom, trying to recall how I behaved with my own mother in the tunnels. But my mother was more like a ghost or a shadow to me than any solid figure.

Lady Twyne ruffles Martine's thick bird's nest of black hair. "Nonsense, dearie. Remember what we always say? The Dreamer is just a fairy tale; we can control our own dreams. Our destiny. Nightmare gives us the power to make it so."

I suppress the shudder that wriggles into Martine's delicate bones. Words of a traitor, indeed. How can she say such heresy? "But, Maman, this dream was different. It was about . . . Daddy." I'm flailing here, completely fabricating this tale, not looking into Martine's thoughts at all. I'm afraid of pushing too hard against her delicate young mind. Better to make a mistake. As little time as I suspect the lady spends with her daughter, she surely won't know the difference.

Lady Twyne's face hardens, like a great iron portcullis has been lowered between us. "Now, my little dove. I've asked you never to speak of him."

I've struck a nerve. Perfect. "But Daddy talks to me in my dreams. He says he's the ocean and he's going to flood Barstadt." The tremble in Martine's voice isn't faked. "It's scary, Maman. I don't want Daddy to drown us."

Lady Twyne's gaze pierces me for a moment, then she glances toward the door.

"Maman?" I ask. "Is it real?" I'm pressing her hard, I know, but if I remember my half siblings correctly, one can never overestimate the persistence of children.

Her expression is difficult to read. When she furrows her brow, the furrows only change the whorls of gemstones nestled in her skin; their twinkling masks her true intent. In her eyes, though, something dark smolders. Like she's seeing straight through the disguise I've donned of her daughter to who I really am: small, clueless, and terrified.

"Soon, you won't have to worry about what happens to Barstadt," is all she says. She hoists me out of her lap and pushes me toward the door.

I cringe. No. We can't have put in all this effort for nothing more than that cryptic hint. I must push harder. I cannot be afraid.

The spiderweb thoughts of Martine glisten in the moonlight. The tidbit I need to trip up Lady Twyne clings to them somewhere—it must. But where? How can I skim it off the surface?

And then it hits me—every spiderweb has a spider.

I flutter against the web like the tiniest gnat, too small to tear apart the strands. Martine's thoughts and dreams drip past me like dewdrops: her mother's face; playing in her room with only her nursemaid to keep her company. She dreams of soaring, arms spread high above the Barstadt harbor, weaving through the towers of Banhopf University and the Dreamer's temple spires. She dreams of a true family.

And this dream lures out just the thought I need—the tempestuous, unmeditated, unfiltered reaction that only children can call forth. Martine blurts it out with no need for my help:

"You're a liar! A filthy liar, and I wish you were dead!"

Lady Twyne rears back as if stung. Success. My consciousness warms with a twinge of pride for little Martine. Some of us spend our whole lives without standing up to our bullies, after all. I wish I had such gall.

"How dare you speak to me in such a way," Lady Twyne says, with a voice slick as frost. But her hands shake; she tucks them into the folds of her skirt.

"You promised me that after my fifth birthday I could see Daddy," I continue, Martine's thoughts flowing effortlessly through me. "Are you going to keep your promise, or break it like all the others? I don't want to stay locked up *forever.*"

Lady Twyne lurches toward me, dropping into a crouch. Her face, jagged as the cliffs, loses all calm, all beauty as she speaks. "Listen to me, darling. Life is about to become very dangerous for us." Her tone could curdle the freshest cream. "I promise, your father's people are coming for us very soon. I'll be Empress, and we won't have to hide anymore. The nightmares will be ours to command."

I fight down my surging panic. We've gotten our confirmation that Twyne is working with the Commandant, but I need to know if there's anything Twyne can tell me about the Land of the Iron Winds' battle plans. "How soon?" I ask.

"Another month, perhaps, and then we'll all be together. You'll have a lovely new throne all your own, and you'll never have to hide again." She pinches the bridge of her nose and takes a deep breath. "You must keep that a secret, though, love. Can you do that for me? You can't even tell your nurse, else I won't let you meet Father, I swear it."

I hang my head in what I hope is an appropriately sullen fashion. "I promise, Maman."

"Good. See that you keep your word." A sneer mars her painted lips. "The nightmares are not kind to those who betray them."

Chapter Eight

"**N**o." Minister Durst shakes his head with the desperation of a condemned man. "It's simply not possible. You—surely you misheard."

I clench my hands into tight little fists, wishing for something solid to hold on to. "Lady Twyne's threat was perfectly clear. Whether or not she's capable of doing what she claims, she seems intent on seeing Barstadt destroyed, and thinks that she can use Nightmare to do it."

"But she's working with the Commandant as well." Durst looks from Vera to Brandt to me, his scowl deepening. "So she's a traitor to the Empire and the Dreamer both."

"Is it possible Nightmare is the warbeast the Commandant mentioned?" I ask, though an icy fist closes around my heart at the mere thought. "That he was working with someone who believed they could bring Nightmare back?" It shouldn't be possible. The Dreamer can't let it be so. But the way Lady Twyne spoke didn't sound like mere wishful thinking.

Vera gives me a disgusted look. "Bring Nightmare back to

life? Are you joking? Even if that were possible—which it can't be, the Dreamer wouldn't allow it—how would he even know about the shards, know where to find them—"

"Anything is *possible*, Vera," Edina says, though her tone is much softer than usual. "Even defying the Dreamer's will."

"Oh, as if you know anything about defying someone," Vera huffs.

Brandt steps forward, shoulders thrust back. His frock coat is rumpled; the collar I'd turned down for him has ridden back up. "If there's a whole underground movement of Nightmare worshippers, it's our duty to expose them for their heresy. Someone must be leading them. I don't know how the Land of the Iron Winds plays into it, but they must be based here—in Barstadt." He tightens one hand into a fist. "I'll start with the temples in the seamier parts of town. Look for disillusioned priests—"

"That's rather hasty, don't you think?" Edina asks with a tiny frown. "One ranting aristocrat is hardly an indicator of a deeper conspiracy. Lady Twyne may very well be working with the Commandant alone. Why upset the priesthood?"

"We're just trying to get answers! The sooner we can stop Twyne and her allies, the better," Brandt says.

I nod at Brandt. "If someone's found a way to bring Nightmare back to life, we have to stop them immediately."

"Then we should approach the priests as allies, not charge in accusing them of conspiring against the Dreamer himself," Edina says. "We might need their aid to stop Lady Twyne.

They're suspicious of . . . our usage of the dreamworld"—Edina's gaze darts toward me—"as it is. We want them to trust us, and that means presenting them with hard proof."

Vera's laughter slices through the room. "Oh, that's rich, coming from you of all people." I cringe; Vera's always been short with Edina, but tonight, she's in rare form. Vera flops into a chair with a crackle of stiff satin. "As if anyone would trust you again!"

"Enough," Edina snaps. "Let's focus on what we do know—it's more than enough to keep us busy. Lady Twyne is conspiring against the Emperor with the Commandant."

"*Precisely*," Vera says, "so let's just *arrest* her and be done with it—" Then her face turns deep scarlet; she narrows her eyes at Edina. "Wait. You're trying to trick me into agreeing with you."

Edina sighs. "It isn't a trick."

"If we arrest Lady Twyne right now," Brandt says, talking over them both, "then her allies will vanish, like a mirage. I'd rather we let her continue to operate for a bit longer, and see where it leads us."

"Brandt is right. Let the rats continue to scurry. We'll put a stop to it before they can do any damage." Minister Durst finishes the drink he'd been nursing, straightens his own coat, and runs his fingers through his bed-mussed hair. "I must report this to the Emperor, however. In the meantime, I want the rest of you hunting for anyone who might be working with Twyne."

"I can do some legwork in the Cloister of Roses. Find out her closest associates," Vera says.

Brandt nods. "And I'll look into her business ventures. My informant mentioned she'd dealt with the Stargazers before."

Edina steps forward, tapping her pen against her teeth. "I'll pull records of Lady Twyne's business dealings."

I say nothing, for I'm not expected to know how to help. Only to wait for the next order to arrive.

"Good, good." Durst rubs his goatee. "See if she's been talking any heresy to her friends—any of this Nightmare business. Someone must know—"

"Minister Durst." Durst's oldest secretary slips into the room, eyes red with sleep deprivation. "The Farthing representatives are here to see you."

Durst groans. "What the nightmares do they want? It's not even dawn yet. Tell them it'll have to wait, and ready me a carriage for the Imperial Palace."

The secretary's jaw quivers. "They *insist* it is of the utmost urgency, Minister."

Durst looks toward me as if for clarification, but I shrug my shoulders. "Last I knew, they were hunting down leads at the docks," I say.

"Five minutes." Durst pinches the bridge of his nose. "And get that carriage ready." The secretary bows and scurries out the door. "Vera, Brandt, track down those leads. Edina, pull those financial records you mentioned. Livia, stay here to meet with the Farthingers."

I bite down on my lower lip and smooth the skirts of the shift I'd donned after we'd left the ball. *Dreamer, give me strength to serve your people well.*

The secretary ushers in Marez and Kriza, both of them dressed head to toe in dark clothing, with kohl smeared around their eyes. Marez's gaze finds me immediately, and he grins briefly, as if he and I share a secret. I catch myself returning the smile before I force my expression blank.

"Minister Durst." Marez drops into a deep bow. "Or am I supposed to kneel to one of your rank? I find Barstadt's endless social customs so confusing."

Durst folds his arms across his chest. "Just tell me what you've found."

"One of the ship captains we were watching at the docks," Kriza says, "had the most fascinating conversation with us."

"You went to the docks again without Silke's accompaniment?" Durst steps toward her. "Our agreement was—"

"Yes, believe me, we know the terms, but when we visited the Ministry this afternoon, we were told Silke was indisposed," Marez says. Of course I was—I was preparing to infiltrate Twyne's ball.

"We're more interested in results than protocol," Kriza says. "So, yes, we continued our investigation."

Marez plucks a small dagger from his belt and slides the blade's tip under his fingernail, cleaning it. Minister Durst opens his mouth again to protest the weapon, but Marez speaks too loudly. "Turns out, this ship captain's been making short trips up and down the coast, strictly off the log books, on behalf of one of your aristocrats."

Durst's frown deepens. "Did he tell you which one?"

"Eventually." Kriza smirks. "After some persuading."

I tighten my jaw; I'd rather not find out what sort of persuading Kriza is capable of.

Marez finishes with the nails of one hand and moves to the next. "Lady Sindra Twyne. Anyone you're familiar with?"

Durst keeps his calm, but my lungs are burning from trying not to cry out. "I know of her, yes." Durst shifts his weight. "She's first cousin to the Emperor."

"Well, she appears to be searching for something. According to this captain, every few weeks she'd come to him with a set of coordinates, and he'd carry a small entourage of her thugs to the location. Fortunately for us, he kept a record of everywhere she sent him. We've just come from her estate, where the records in her office confirmed it." Kriza pulls a battered scroll from her pocket. I'm relieved we rushed back to the Ministry after interrogating Lady Twyne instead of heading for her office as well—we might have crossed paths with the Farthingers. "Don't suppose the pattern means anything to you?"

She unfolds the scroll on Durst's desk and we all crowd around it—a map of the Central Realms, riddled with circles, some of them with crosses through them and some not. They speckle along the coast of Barstadt, mainly, but some are inside the city, some deep into the Land of the Iron Winds, and even a few in Farthing's territories.

"What about the ones in the city?" I ask.

Marez nods at me. "Excellent question. Apparently, those are locations of some of the fences she employs to off-load illicit goods—whatever it is she's buying and trading, her associates do their business there. He helpfully provided us with a list of their names."

"We're thinking we should pay them some visits next," Kriza says.

"Tomorrow," I say, blood pumping loud in my ears. Brandt's right—we have to find out what Twyne is up to, whatever she means to do, and stop it.

Marez looks at me with an eyebrow raised. "Eager to get back into the field, are you, little secretary?" His smile spreads like a stain. "Tomorrow is too soon, in case Lady Twyne notices anything amiss in her office. We don't want to raise any suspicions. But don't worry. We'll go after them in due time."

After the Farthingers leave, Durst turns toward me, red-rimmed eyes narrowed. "Did you happen to notice the Farthingers at Twyne's soiree tonight?" he asks. His tone is calm enough, but I suspect there's a warning below the surface.

"Brandt spotted Kriza at the ball, but I never crossed paths with her, I swear it. We were careful." Yet my voice shakes; I'm not sure whether I'm trying to convince Minister Durst or myself. "Both our hunts brought us to Lady Twyne. As far as I'm concerned, that only further cements her guilt—not just of conspiring with the Commandant, but of actively aiding his invasion."

Durst forces a tight nod. "Get some rest, Livia. I suspect we all will have long days ahead of us."

I stagger into bed as the first rays of sun peek over the mountains in the east. Foul dreams find me, but whether they are portents or dormant memories stirred up by my fear, I can't say. A wolf stalks me in slow, loping circles. I often dream of wolves beyond the tree line in the forests of Oneiros, but this one seems like a human in costume, like the tumbler we saw at the masquerade ball.

I follow the wolf through the forest, feeling drawn toward some unspoken goal. Before I even see it, I feel its call in my bones: Nightmare's Spine. It looks just like it does in the waking world: the vertebrae hang fifty feet in the air, suspended on ribs wider than a man, large enough to encase the entire Ministry of Affairs building within its great rib cage. Birds wheel around the spine's peaks, but even they know better than to land.

I see the massive skull from behind. I never want to see its shape, to know the face of Nightmare. Yet in this dream, I am drawn toward the skull's front like the face of a flower to sunlight. Drums are beating in my ears, in time with my own heartbeat: Nightmare's shattered heart, made whole once more.

No, I try to scream, but my words turn to ash in my mouth. I have to stop it. Nightmare cannot rise again.

I've always held control in my dreams—if not of the dream's contents, then at least over my emotions and reactions to whatever horrors I face. But when Nightmare's skull turns toward me, panic seizes me in a stranglehold. Rotten skin, like fish scales hammered onto diseased flesh, drips from the desiccated jawbone of the massive reptilian beast—Nightmare made manifest. My mind is screaming. My body revolts. I open my mouth to shriek, but my voice is like a nest of wasps inside my throat, buzzing around furiously but never breaking free so someone can hear.

Finally my legs obey me. I run. I have to reach the Ministry building, though I don't know what support it can offer me if Nightmare's shattered heart is whole once more. I run down the slope of Nightmare's Spine, sailing over jagged rocks and fractured cliffs long since collapsed. I need the Dreamer to save me, but the Dreamer is silent as always.

I burst through the Ministry doors and launch straight into the records hall. This dream again—the one where I'm searching for knowledge forever beyond my grasp. Nightmare, Nightmare. I scour the endless shelves. Who could do such a thing? Where did they find the shards? I have to stop it, and somehow, I feel certain I will find the answer in here, in a red leather journal. I flip through file after file, from waterlogged shipping manifests to coded transmissions to fragile, frantic maps scrawled in the field centuries before, which crumble in my hands. In the dream, my quest to find the truth of the Nightmare fragments makes sense; it is the most important thing that I could do.

And like all dreams, it dissolves at last, without resolution. I awaken tangled in sweat-slicked sheets with nothing but broken questions and the throb of dread in the back of my mind.

Chapter Nine

⋯ • ▪ ───────◆▶───────── • ▪ ⋯

Over the next several days, Brandt infiltrates a half-dozen temples, and Vera attends endless tea parties and formal dinners in search of leads on Twyne's associates, but they turn up nothing further. Minister Durst, Marez, and Kriza are busy readying the city's defenses and coaching the Barstadt navy on the Commandant's plans we had found in the Citadel. They're stymied, however, by a rash of tunneler protests, calling for the Writ to pass; one group even manages to break into the Imperial Palace through the tunnels before the palace guards subdue them and order those tunnels sealed. I know they just want their citizenship—access to respectable work and living quarters, not the indentured servitude of tunnel life—but I worry for the tunnelers. For how the aristocrats might lash out in fear.

No such excitement for me. I dig through the archives with Edina, play Stacks with Sora, and wait—for there's nothing more I can do, even as my dreams taunt me with the horrible possibility that Nightmare is returning to life. But there's not much I can do in Oneiros without a hint of whom I could use to gain the knowledge we need. I dream of returning to the archives at night, searching for answers, but in dreams and in the waking world, I have no proof. I have no clues. Finally, when I can take it no longer, I decide to try Professor Hesse once more, despite how our last conversation went.

As I wind the interminable stairs of the Theosophy Tower, I wrack my mind for a new joke to tell Professor Hesse—anything to ease the bad blood between us after our last conversation. The cheesier, the better. Brandt had found one for me on a recent mission—what was it? A corrupt constable and the Dreamer's High Priest walk into an alehouse . . .

Hesse's office door on the twelfth floor is shut. I'd already checked the lab, but it was locked. Perhaps he's deep in a fresh thesis. I test the handle: unlocked, but the door fights me as I lean into it. "Professor Hesse?" I call timidly, once more feeling very much the naïve little girl I'd been when Hesse and I first met. "I've brought more honeycakes from Kruger's."

The office floods me with the stink of mildew and sweat as soon as I open the door, as if I've unsealed a tomb. Tears spring to my eyes, and I bury my nose and mouth in the crook of my arm as I enter, leaving the door open to air out the room.

"I told you I don't want any cleaning," Hesse growls from somewhere behind a pulpit of manuscripts, books, scrolls. Then I see one eye flicker toward me. "Oh. Livia. I'm sorry, I didn't mean . . ."

I scramble over the stacked trays of half-eaten bread crusts and chicken bones buzzing with flies that guard the doorway like a moat. "Dreamer bless, what's happened to you?"

Hesse is swaddled in a patchy blanket on the window seat, staring down at the main plaza. The closer I draw toward him, the more overpowering his stench becomes. An overflowing chamber pot languishes beside him; his usually shiny white hair hangs in clumps about his face. I pull a kerchief from my sleeve and press it to my nose. When we spoke just a few weeks past, yes, I'd noticed a fog of weariness around him—a tremor in his voice and a world-weary scent. But this is extreme. Has he even bathed since we last spoke?

I throw open the window; the sunlight bursts free into the room, no longer suppressed by the grimy diamond-patterned glass. Professor Hesse flinches and leans away from the light. "I wish you wouldn't do that," he says, but his voice is thinner than a tunneler's broth, and I can barely hear him.

"What's the matter with you?" I ask once I've taken a deep gulp of the outside air. Even after his wife's death, Hesse never stopped teaching, never halted his research. I scan the mad scribbles of paper he has accumulated on his desk, like he was searching for something.

Professor Hesse tilts his head back against the stone wall. "It's all my fault. I should have destroyed it. No lock is good enough. Shouldn't have researched it in the first place."

A shudder tears through me as I wipe the dust and grime away from his bookshelves. Surely he doesn't mean the dreamstriding theorem. Me. My nails dig into the rag in my palm, and

I scrub furiously. He gave me a new life when he unlocked the secret to dreamstriding. How can he regret that?

I dig through his reams of papers. I'm still cleaning for him—I will probably spend my life cleaning up after this man, tunneler or no—but I'll make damned sure he knows how unhappy I am about it. Great clouds of dust swirl around me as I sort, shake, stack.

I fight to keep my voice contained, like the meek, silent servant I once was. "You know what my life was like when I met you. Before you dared to give me a chance. Would you have me surrender everything we've discovered and the far better life I live now?"

"What? No, no. But I shouldn't have forced you into this life. Maybe I saved you from far worse, but my motives were . . ." He cracks. "Impure."

A chill down my spine momentarily slows my frenzy. He can't possibly mean that. That word brings to mind what happened to some of the other maids my age when they were assigned to cleaning professor's offices. Professor Hesse never closed the office door, never reached for me, never even bore a dark sliver in his eye that I've seen in other professors. He gave me a new life—what could possibly be impure about that?

"You told me you dreamed so strongly. How could I resist that? The perfect test subject for my greatest theorem yet. And you were so tiny . . . no one would miss you if my experiments went wrong."

Professor Hesse collapses into a dry sob. It sounds like the air rushing from a corpse's lungs as its body constricts. But

I am frozen in place. Not by what he has said—for it's true, all of it. My father disappeared into the Dreamless dens, or so I'm told; my mother had energy only for tunneler work and crumpled into her pallet each night long before my siblings or half siblings were fed. No one to miss me, indeed. No one but those endless hungry mouths, with no one to hear their cries.

No, it's his tone that troubles me. I was only a scrawny little wisp who loved to help him dissect dreams; I'd assumed I was his very first test subject for dreamstriding. But his description of me sounds too much like the Hesse who turned me over to the Ministry so long ago, like he was presenting them with a new toy. I'd forgotten how cold Hesse could sound—the detached scientist Hesse, who'd attack an experiment from every possible direction until it yielded a result.

"Professor." My throat clenches tight. "What are you saying?"

"I've done terrible things, Livia. Why do you bother with me? I never should have created those formulas, never hunted for a dreamstrider . . . I could have spared so many deaths. I fear now even more deaths will come."

"Deaths?" I cry, panic rising in me like a tide. Surely he isn't speaking about the Incident. "What do you mean? I'm here—I'm alive."

"No, Livia. You're the only one to *survive*."

The room spins around me. "No." My hands had been tidying, unconscious, a bone-deep reflex, but I drop the stack of papers I'd been about to move. "No. What do you mean?"

He keeps staring out the window. "You know what the Wastes are capable of."

They say it was easy to get lost in your dreams in the days before Nightmare was destroyed—that you could slip too far into Oneiros in your sleep and get devoured by the Wastes. It's why the priests forbade anyone but themselves and a few professors like Hesse from entering Oneiros. So many died. They succumbed to their deepest fears and darkest regrets, and Nightmare's minions preyed on their pain until their souls were devoured. But it's safer now—the only real danger comes from severing that tie to your body, like I do when I dreamstride.

"They—they died trying to dreamstride?" Even now I can hear the chatter of the Nightmare Wastes, snaring like hooks into my skin. "But you—but you never told me—" I swallow down the bile that burns in the back of my throat. "You sent them to their deaths!"

His fingers trace the lead lining his window panes. "Most did quit after the first hint of danger from the Nightmare Wastes. A few others accused me of trying to resurrect Nightmare himself—that another theorem I was working on . . ." He stops himself, finger trembling against the glass, then hangs his head. "But those who pushed on, who took that leap from their bodies . . . Every last one of them . . . dead."

I ball my hands into fists. Rage is useless to me; there's nowhere for it to go. "Why wouldn't you tell me? Why let me think no one had ever reached that stage?"

"Because I didn't want you to be afraid."

He squeezes his eyes shut and rocks back and forth on the sill for a few moments; I fear that I've lost him. I'd always feared that age would claim him before he could help me escape the tunneler life, but guilt looks to have a head start, crushing him slowly like the heavy slabs of stone the people of the northern islands once used to crush their criminals. Finally, he rears up his head.

The great Albrecht Hesse, esteemed professor of theosophy, renowned scholar of dream interpretation and manipulation, and, for those initiated into the Ministry of Affairs, creator of dreamstriding. Dreamstriding had been nothing but a formula on a page before he met me, a jumble of variables boiled down from decades of study—not with the reverent hands-off fervor of the Dreamer's priests, but the relentless prodding and scraping and measuring of a scientist. He knew, mathematically, it could be done, and didn't give a damn what the priests said.

But he could not do it himself. He told me it was because he was too old, and his mind too inflexible to allow him to succeed at dreamstriding. But now I wonder if it was his fear of death, a conviction that he was too important to lose. Only one damned foolish little girl managed to dreamstride—because she didn't know enough to be terrified of what this man asked.

"How could you?" But I already know. Research was more intoxicating than any drink to him, and each of my tiny successes fed his ego like nothing else could. We both knew I should be capable of more, though—digging further into a subject's mind and using that access more fully. It was there, in his formulas, backed by reams of published articles and sealed Ministry reports. Hesse had envisioned a whole squadron of dreamstriders, actively spotting threats to the Empire by searching others' dreams and using their bodies to gather information. Instead, there was me and my rudimentary grasp of dreamstriding.

I'd spent my whole training wondering why I couldn't do more with my gift. I'd never stopped to think what would have become of me had I been even an ounce weaker.

"So many lies I've told. To protect Barstadt—that was always my goal—but it's too much. Lies about dreamstriding. About Nightmare's death. About the Dreamer himself—"

"About the Dreamer?" I take a step closer to him. "What are you talking about?"

"You all put so much faith in him, but he's powerless. It's just a great lie, keeping Barstadt in its sway."

"The Dreamer isn't powerless." My skin tingles; anger flares up inside of me. "He gave me the gift of dreamstriding. He slew Nightmare to protect us."

But Hesse just snorts. "Sure he did. It's all too much," he continues, as if the dam has broken, and now the truth is gushing forth. "I never should have gone down this road, and now I'll pay for it. I wish I could destroy it all. The theorems, the equations, the ritual. Livia." He twitches. "You have to destroy it. Find the key and destroy my research. You know where it is, Livia." His stare bores straight through me. "My work has to stop. No one can know the truth of what I've found."

"What work has to stop? What research do you want me to destroy? Dreamstriding?" But as I move one stack of papers and clear a space on his writing desk, the question dissolves on my tongue. A hardened chunk of something wrapped up in wax

119

paper is stuck to the desktop. Its cloying scent had been masked until now under the stench of his squalor and despair. I peel back the wrappings, but I already know what I'll find.

Lullaby. The Dreamless resin. It's already partially worn down.

"You have to forgive yourself," I tell Hesse, rewrapping the sticky wad of resin. "And tell Minister Durst the truth. We need you, now especially." I hesitate, lowering my head. "I need you." *To protect me against Minister Durst,* I think, if nothing else.

I scurry over to the window—even with wax paper between the stuff and my skin, I don't want to touch it for long—but as I lean over Hesse to lob it outside, he snatches my wrist. Our eyes meet. He pries my fingers apart with a strength I've never seen from him and takes the ball of filth from me.

I grit my teeth. Within a minute of using Lullaby, he'll collapse into dreamless sleep, and I'll lose him again. He's shut me out, and there's nothing I can do to stop it.

"You're better than this," I say. "You've created incredible things—the Dreamer has given you an incredible mind. Why are you throwing it away?"

"Please. Destroy my work." He rubs the sticky mass against his gums and sinks back against the windowsill, eyes lidding as sleep reaches for him. "If you value this life I've given you, then make sure it ends with you."

Chapter Ten

Marez tosses back the rest of his ale and slams it onto the tabletop with the other emptied steins. "Ahh. Just what I was thirsting for." His elbow knocks into my ribs. "Fun. You could stand having some."

"We're working," I reply, folding my arms across my chest. We're supposed to be finding out what business the ale hall owner had with Lady Twyne, but Marez and Kriza insisted we grab a round to lend credence to our presence. My throat is rubbed raw from having to shout over the din of the ale hall, and we're no closer to uncovering Lady Twyne's plans. "Do you always conduct investigations while inebriated?"

For all the ales he and Kriza have downed, Marez's gaze is as sharp as broken glass. I can feel his mind whirring like clock gears, his eyes darting about, his ears homing on every sound. His nose grazes my ear as he leans in to make himself heard. "I'm not inebriated. And as for fun and work—I always prefer to combine the two."

I'm grateful for the poorly lit ale hall, for whenever I blush, my face seems to radiate heat like a well-fed furnace. "I'm afraid we don't have that luxury right now."

"No? More's the pity, my dear." He smirks at me. "In Farthing, we can *always* make time to enjoy ourselves."

My skin tingles at his words. I work my jaw, searching for an appropriate response, but before I can cobble one together, Marez leaps up onto the bench, and joins Kriza and the other patrons in a fresh round of drinking songs. I slump forward with a mighty exhale.

Stouts, porters, and saisons shower down on me from all directions as the grating, oomphing melody rings through the ale hall. "Well, I see there's one bit of Barstadt culture you Farthingers don't hate," I say. Not that he can hear me over the lyrics detailing a northern farmer's daughter and her bountiful virtues (among other bountiful things). After several more verses, some of the singers reach their limit, and tumble off the benches; the song collapses similarly. Finally, the Farthingers plop down on either side of me.

"I don't hate everything about Barstadt," Marez says.

"Just most?"

Marez slings an arm around my shoulder, crashing into me like a drunkard, but his words are frightfully sober. "The problem with Barstadt," he says, "is its obsession with *order*." The hand around my shoulder trails down my back, sending a fresh flush to my face. "Everything must be so prim and proper. So rigid."

I sit up straighter and shy away from his touch. "It's—it's good for there to be an order to things," I stammer. "It keeps us honest. Allows us to focus on fulfilling the Dreamer's messages."

"You call it honest, the structure of Barstadt society?" He laughs—harsh, rimed in frost. "Only fully fledged citizens can live and work on the proper streets, while those deemed unfit for society are forced down into the tunnels. The rats of the city, herded this way and that by crooked gang leaders who know how to trade their tunneler subjects for a coin, any way they please. It's slavery."

"Slavery has been abolished in the Barstadt Empire for over three hundred years—"

"Really? You could have fooled me." He cups my chin in one hand and turns my head toward the doors. "Look around you. This hall was built by tunnelers, it's cleaned by tunnelers, and the whole thing is orchestrated by a vast network of criminals, the go-betweens for the right proper citizens and the sad, forgotten wretches."

Anger churns fierce inside me; his touch burns on my chin. He knows nothing of what it's like to be a tunneler. The cycle of violence in the gangs, the tunnelers' lack of citizenship—they are all broken, yes. But the Dreamer will show us the best path to resolve these issues. He must. We must trust in him and his plan—I can't imagine any other way.

"And what of Farthing?" I ask. "Are you telling me that a confederation of pirates, smugglers, foresters, and more is free of all criminal elements? You're nothing but a bunch of crooks. Your whole nation is founded on crookedness."

"It's not a crime if it isn't illegal," he replies with a twist on his lips. "We watch out for our own. No aristocratic inbreds telling us what to do. Everyone does their part for the confederacy because they *want* to be a part of it."

What of the Dreamer's plans? I want to ask, but I doubt Marez cares much about those. I can't imagine the Dreamer leading us away from Barstadt, his chosen land.

But neither do I hear the Dreamer asking me to stay.

Marez shakes his head. "You really must learn to loosen up, enjoy the small pleasures in life. If you ever have a chance to visit Farthing, take it, little secretary. You're sure to learn a lot more about enjoying yourself."

I try to imagine what it would be like for me in Farthing, or anywhere but here—not being indebted to Professor Hesse or the Ministry of Affairs. Not relying on my paltry skills as the dreamstrider to spare me from returning to tunneler life. Freedom to pursue whatever best suits me. Feeling like I belonged.

But it's a fleeting fancy—these Farthingers are no more my people than Brandt and his aristocrat friends. He's picking through my weaknesses with the same skill I'm certain those nimble fingers of his can pick locks. I lean away from Marez and hope the dark hall is hiding my blush. Tonight, I'm doubly glad it's Jorn shadowing me, and not Brandt.

"Kriza? I think it's time." Marez glances over my head at her. She's singing and flailing around with the best of them, but as soon as their eyes lock, she goes cold with determination. A shiver runs through me. Even Brandt isn't that talented an actor.

Kriza hops off the bench and wraps an arm around my shoulder. "Hey, girlie, let's you and I visit the pissin' room and have a chat, hm?" She's slurring her words, staggering around. If I hadn't seen her eyes seconds before, I'd swear she was three tankards past sane. I try not to let the prickle of fear under my skin rise to the surface. Let the professionals do their work.

We burst into Kriza's "pissin' room"—the chamber, as we call it in polite circles—and she hooks a chair under the door handle. The stench of ammonia and the weak bouquets of flowers that attempt to conceal it bring tears to my eyes.

"Ye gods, it's worse than I imagined." Kriza pulls the paisley-patterned scarf from her hair and ties it around her mouth. "Ain't you stuffy imperials ever heard of plumbing?"

"It gets clogged down here by the docks, but you get used to it," I say in a pinched, nauseated voice that indicates otherwise.

Kriza hops onto the long wooden bench. I gasp as her foot edges dangerously close to one of the holes that open onto the sewer far below. But she's as nimble as a squirrel, finding purchase on a sconce to hoist herself higher along the wall, then swinging her elbow into the giant wooden slats of the ventilation opening overhead. Brandt once told me that the ventilators in ale halls are the sole thing standing between a chamber full of ammonia, lit candles, and a massive explosion, and I've no interest in finding that out for myself.

"Do you need an engraved invitation?" Kriza asks me. "Come on." She wriggles her way up the ventilation slot, and I hear her stomp onto the roof of the chamber.

Dreamer, protect me. The acrid stench of human waste floods my senses, reminding me what awaits me if I fall. I've no desire to take a dive into that particular pond. Once, I evaded a gang enforcer by clinging to the stone wall that dropped down to sewers far below, praying he wouldn't believe I'd been so foolish to drop down into that waste. Maybe I still have some of that strength. I reach for the wall sconce and prepare to swing myself up. *Come on, Livia. Focus.*

The door handle rattles, jostling the chair to no avail. "Hey! Who's in there? Let us in!" someone shouts from the other side of the door. My mother once warned me never to come between a bladder full of ale and a chamber, no matter how much more cleaning I had to do. I take a deep breath. I can't lose my concentration. *Pretend you're dreamstriding, Livia, and make your body work with you.*

"Come on, now, I can't hold it much longer!" another man yells. The chair groans as the mob on the other side throws its collective weight against the door. Now or never. I lunge for the sconce and swing a slippered foot into its crook. Pure determination carries me upward through the ventilation hole, and I brace my arms on the topside of the roof, my lower half dangling through the opening. Kriza stares down at me, hands on her hips.

I kick my legs, trying but failing to haul them onto the roof with the rest of me. "A little help?"

She presses her lips into a thin line, eyeing me like a worn bit of clothing she'll soon have to throw out, then braces both her thick hands on my forearm, and yanks me up. Not a moment too soon, either. As my feet clear the lip of the hole, I hear the chair in the chamber splinter, and the mob clambers inside.

Kriza takes off running along the angled roof before I have so much as a chance to catch my breath.

"Wait! Won't they know we're up here?" I call after her.

She rolls her eyes. "I'd love to see any of those drunkards try to follow us. Come."

I pad across the sloping slate roof and join her at a corner of the building. Like most buildings in Barstadt City, the ale hall is a tall and narrow pale structure with high, dark roofs that come to awkward points. Rooms jut out in a labyrinth of stacked floors.

"We should find the records we need in the manager's office—up there." Kriza points to the third floor. "Tall enough to sit on top of the main hall, with mirrors cut through the floor so they can watch for trouble."

"And we're heading for the office?" I ask.

She nods, her bloodred hair loose and wild around her face, free from her scarf. "We'll see what tales their shipping logs tell." Kriza hoists herself onto the roof of the second-story room beneath the office window.

"And we're taking the outside route why?" I flail and flop around a few times before finally joining her on the next roof.

"Coz it's far more fun!" She flattens against the outer wall beside the window. "Marez should be starting that riot for us right . . . about . . . now."

"Riot?" I screech.

"To draw the owner out of his office." She rolls her eyes. "I would expect anyone in the Minister of Affairs' service to know such basic tradecraft."

"I mostly deal with paperwork, and—"

Kriza whips around to face me, her eyes deadly cold, like a viper. "Marez clearly sees something in your skills that I'm missing, and our nations' agreement requires us to bring you along. But if you're going to get in the way of our investigation—"

"Sorry," I whisper. What else can I say?

She nods. "Stay close. Follow me inside. Move like I move; step where I step."

I remain pinned against the wall while she busies herself prying the office window open. After a quick peek around the curtains, she shimmies through. *Dreamer have mercy on my poor, misguided soul.* I plunge in after her. I take care to place my feet only on the same floorboards she does as we move into the center of the office.

Kriza throws open a massive leather-bound ledger on the manager's desk and flips through it a page at a time, scanning each one briefly for indications of what Lady Twyne was using the fence for. I raise one eyebrow and await further orders. "Check the room for hidden compartments," she says after a prolonged silence. "Walls, desks, drawers, floorboards . . . It's all right to make noise, but be quick about it."

I nod like I know what she's talking about and do my best to imitate Brandt and Vera whenever they search a room. I knock against walls, press on chair rails and crown moldings, tap on the floor. I've no idea what I'm listening for, but Kriza seems satisfied enough with my efforts to leave me be while she continues to pore over the manager's records.

"This looks promising," I say. I swing open a hinged painting of the turbulent Itinerant Sea to reveal the front of an iron safe. Kriza glances up, tilts her head at it for a moment, then crinkles her nose.

"You really *are* a secretary, aren't you?" She smirks. "The ale hall's manager likely makes regular payments to the many criminal groups in your fair city. He'll only be keeping worthless Imperial notes in there. Any of the real proceeds—like those from his smuggling operations—will be hidden elsewhere."

"Imperial notes aren't worthless," I mutter, but I continue my quest. Fixed to the underside of the desk is a lewd sketch of a naked lady in what I'm quite certain is an anatomically impossible position. I drop it on the desk and shuffle a mass of papers over it.

Kriza pulls a small notepad from her blouse—where she found space in her ale-wench clothes, I can only hazard a guess—and jots something down, but she offers up no clues, and I ask no questions.

My foot catches on an uneven floorboard beneath the northern hand-woven tribal rug. I toss the rug back, and the floorboard pulls away cleanly in my hand.

Kriza peers over the ledger at me. "Anything useful?"

"Looks like a stash of papers." I pull out a tightly rolled scroll and unfurl it. "A map. I'm not sure of where." I sort through the stash. "A list of figures. They look like dates perhaps, and then some sort of shorthand . . . And what's this?"

A gem winks at me from the bottom of the hollow. It's an

amethyst, but a particularly ugly one, shot through with a milky crack and caked in grime. It warms my fingertips as I pick it up; maybe the hollow rests atop a gas line. I glance around the office, looking for gas lamps.

"Let me see." She shoves me out of the way and scoops up the contents of the concealed stash, scarcely glancing at the gemstone before wrapping it in a paper scrap. "I'll ask your minister if there's any significance." She studies the roll of papers hidden beneath where the amethyst rested. "Mm. Shipping records. We'll review these with your minister." She stuffs them all down her shirt and nods at me—about all the approval I'll get from her, I suppose. "Anything else?"

I turn up some false citizenship papers (a poor job, really; I've worked the streets with Brandt enough to recognize bad fakes when I see them) and a stack of Imperial notes that must have been set aside in case a hasty escape was needed. I think for a moment about pocketing the bills. It's only slightly more than the monthly pay the minister sets aside for my living expenses—I live in the barracks free of charge—but this kind of money would feed a family of tunnelers for the rest of their lives. It's the kind of money that might, just might, buy them the type of citizenship papers that could actually pass for the real thing, opening the door to working in the ale halls, or the merchant shops, and maybe even renting a room in a tenement someday.

My fingers twitch, thinking of the paltry savings I've set aside with Brandt's creditor. This one stack of bills would nearly double it. I could easily buy my citizenship papers—no longer be owned by the Ministry. Or a lab rat that Hesse would have gladly sacrificed in his pursuit of greater knowledge and power.

No. I wedge the floorboard back into place. These Farthingers may see no problems with their moral flexibility, but I have the Dreamer to answer to. I can't stoop to theft, no matter what scum I'd be stealing from.

Kriza finishes sifting through the ledgers and moves to a strange set of binoculars jutting out of the wall. "Pretty common invention back in Farthing—they show what's happening down in the ale hall, thanks to an elaborate set of angled mirrors," she explains, noting my expression. "Mm, looks like the riot's still going strong, but I wager that pond-scum manager'll be back up here to secure his money soon. Let's be on our way."

I follow her out the window. The smell outside has changed sharply; instead of the distant chamber stink and the scent of hay from the stables next door, there's something harsh and warm in the air. I pause, sniffing again. As I recognize the scent, my stomach drops.

Fire.

"Was burning down the ale hall always part of the plan?" I charge after Kriza as she effortlessly hops down to the alleyway below.

She merely shrugs. "And why not? We've no more use for it. We found the information we needed. Now everything will burn, and they'll have no idea that we even took the records."

I stomp after her through the narrow alley. "But all the people in there! Innocents—and the manager's money, whether it goes to the crime rings or not—"

"Innocents? Oh, please. An hour ago in the ale hall, you looked like you'd set fire to them yourself, given the chance."

"It's one thing to be annoyed, quite another to risk their lives!"

"I'm not sure you realize what is at stake here, little secretary." Kriza stops at a junction in the alley and faces me with sharp, dangerous eyes. "Both our countries' existences, our lives—*everyone's* lives. If some poor drunkard can't find his way to those gaping barn doors in time, then that's a small price to pay."

"I'm not sure it's for you to decide," I say under my breath, but my words are lost in the crackle of catching flames.

Chapter Eleven

Barstadt City is riddled with temples to the Dreamer in every possible shape and style, from spires encased in solid gold, where the aristocrats cleanse themselves and pray, to makeshift huts wedged into alleyways. I only visited the latter as a tunneler, while aboveground Barstadt slept, and I still prefer them for their silence, their emptiness. It took only one trip to the Banhopf University temple with Professor Hesse to learn that the ostentatious, chatty temples where everyone splashes and babbles about their dreams all at once, as though they were comparing mansion décor, were not for me.

My favorite temple is a small, windowless fort just off the main harbor, quiet as a crypt and almost as cold, where they pump seawater in for the cleansing pool. With the strange dreams I've been having, and my unsettling conversations with Professor Hesse and Marez, I need somewhere I can untangle those images without interference—just me and the Dreamer, like a soothing hand steering me along toward the right path. The pool's salty tang flares my nostrils as soon as I step through the carved bronze doors into the dank sanctuary. A priest in training helps me into a loose white shift after I press a few coins into her palm, and another priest, a dream interpreter with an onyx eye set into his brow, approaches to offer his opinion on whatever dreams have visited me of late. But I cross my arms and bow to him—a polite decline. These eerie dreams are for me alone.

Sometimes, the temple priests recognize me—the frequent trespasser on the sacred grounds of Oneiros. The strongest priests split their time between this world and Oneiros. They might work as Shapers, altering the dreamworld to suit their needs and easing or interpreting their clients' dreams, or they may serve as guardians ushering home the souls of lost dreamers who've slipped into the shared world. They once held Nightmare's minions at bay and would do it gladly again. The priests' work is noble. Sanctioned. The High Priest, who knows of Hesse's work, resents my presence in Oneiros and questions whether it serves all of Barstadt.

Fortunately, no one here today knows me for the intruder I am. No scoldings or resentful stares.

Once barefoot, I slip into the reflecting pool. The water is cool, but not bitingly so; I stride farther into the pool as quickly as I dare until the water reaches my breasts and the white shift billows around me like a jellyfish. Waves slap against the granite sides of the pool. I close my eyes and focus on the sounds of water, on the whispers of candles guttering in their stands, as I recite an old nighttime prayer.

Bury your fears, and bury them deep
Where they shan't find you while you sleep
The Dreamer has locked the Nightmares away
But only your hopes can keep them at bay.

No one is safe from a lesser nightmare or a frightful dream, from replaying moments of regret or guilt or doubt while he or she sleeps. The Dreamer cannot save us from fear. All he can offer us is the assurance of glorious moments not yet lived.

How many will never see their better dreams come true because they sought to dreamstride? Just how many died before Hesse found me? The cold water stings my skin, making it contract like scaled armor, but I welcome the pain.

Dreamer. Why did you give me this gift? Why did so many others have to die where I was allowed to succeed?

The water kisses my arms. The salty sea mingles with soft incense and the smell of damp stone. I sift through my jumbled thoughts for the Dreamer's calm voice, the reassurances the priests claim to hear, but I do not find it.

Sometimes I wonder if it is a curse that someone as insignificant as me should carry this great duty. But I want to serve the Empire. I want to serve you. What do you mean by these strange dreams? Are you only warning me of the endless trials I must face, or will you teach me how to pass them?

The Commandant readies his army while Barstadt and Farthing join forces against him. The tunnelers struggle for emancipation. An aristocrat speaks of raising Nightmare from the dead. Professor Hesse warns of the grave cost of dreamstriding—one I'm not certain I can bear, now that I know of the deaths. And I, the sole dreamstrider, the Ministry's dismal disappointment, pine for a boy I can never have and a freedom I can never earn.

I wade deeper into the pool until the water reaches my chin. The Dreamer's monolith stone rises before me, at the far end of the small pool. Carved into the rock above the water, the faceless Dreamer's arms stretch wide; clouds swirl around him as he towers into the heavens, surrounded by fanciful images from dreams. Beneath the water's surface, however, I can just make out the dark silhouette of inlaid onyx representing Nightmare. The Dreamer pins that winged reptilian beast underwater.

The Nightmare Wastes once slurped up untethered souls to feed Nightmare, his black heart feasting on despair and surrender. With Nightmare vanquished, true nightmares prey most easily on only the most miserable spirits, who have allowed their dreams to become prisons of their own making. The burden of guilt and regret, the looming shadows of fear and anxiety, stitch together into frightful beasts while they sleep. They drive people to the Lullaby—even the mighty Professor Hesse.

Show me how to serve you. Show me how to protect my Empire from the Commandant, and from Nightmare.

"Livia."

I whirl around; the splash ricochets through the temple chamber. Brandt stands at the shallow end of the reflection pool. He's never accompanied me to the temple before; he looks more out of place than the time we had to drag a Bootstraps

136

lieutenant out of a brothel. I'm not ready to leave the pool, but something darkens Brandt's soft gray eyes, and a warning trills down my spine. I cross my arms, bow to the monolith, and then wade out of the pool.

"What's the matter?" I ask. "How'd you know to find me here?"

He hangs his head as I climb the steps. Candlelight bounces off the waves, tiling his face with squares of reflected light. "It's a challenging time for you right now. You always come here whenever you're troubled."

He's right; usually, the Dreamer's temples comfort me. So does talking with Brandt, but he's been so busy of late with his other life . . . I cross my arms over my breasts, for modesty's sake; the soaked white gown sticks to me.

"I'm afraid I have bad news," Brandt says, eyes flicking to my face for just a moment. "Professor Hesse . . . The constabulary found his body this morning." Brandt hunches his shoulders. "I'm so sorry, Livia. I know what he meant to you."

My arms fall to my sides. I've searched all morning for the Dreamer's Embrace, and now I ache for arms, any arms, to squeeze me until I stop shaking. My ears ring with the absence of sound. The temple grows darker as my vision narrows, as my ribs knit shut.

Brandt steps toward me, arms raising, reaching for me. The embrace I craved. He wraps me in his warmth, but only for a second, and then he's gone, hands jammed in his pockets and a guilty cast to his face.

Foolish Livia. What more was I hoping for? I force my eyes

shut and curl my hands into fists as my thoughts whirl out of control.

How dare Hesse regret what he'd created, how dare he turn to Lullaby to ease the guilt? He bore the weight of the dead's souls for so long—I don't understand why they'd only begun to trouble him of late. Am I responsible for them, too? But the anger behind my thoughts only curdles into pain, a pain deep in my chest, where Professor Hesse should be. Maybe Hesse was a monster for experimenting on us. Even while he knew it might kill me, he allowed me to be something more than a tunneler. Something more than a piece of property the gang leaders could sell off, something neither seen nor heard unless it pleased the masters to take notice of me. He saved me from far worse work and gave me coin to silence my endless hunger.

But I betrayed them for him. I left my mother to her stupor and the other tunnelers to their plight, changing only my fate, not the whole system that bound us so. The criminal system— that's what Marez called it, and he was right. I took the golden platter of service to the Empire that he offered me and didn't so much as glance back. How could I?

I wander through the uncharted desert of my grief while I shiver and drip on the sacred temple floor. What more could I have done? What should I have left undone? What other secrets did Hesse try to chase from his mind with a smear of resin on his lips? Perhaps I should be crying, but even though I'm trembling, I can't seem to shake a tear free.

"I'm so sorry, Livia." Brandt tucks a wet curl back behind

my ear, and his hand lingers against my cheek. "I wish I knew what to do or say . . ."

I look into those stone-dark eyes. All he needs to do is stay with me—not leave me, like Hesse, to fend for myself in the Ministry. But I can't ask that of him. And he can't give that to me. I lower my gaze.

Brandt's fingers curl against my cheek, and he lowers his face toward mine. The scent of cedar on his well-kept clothes and fire from a tended hearth cut through the chill that surrounds me. I imagine our mouths colliding. A rush of heat and flesh. For a moment, as his fingers tremble, I can almost believe he's imagining it, too. Something to burn away this mournful cold. But then his jaw ripples with a loud swallow, and he leans away.

"We're expected at the constabulary near the university," he says, jamming his hands back into his pockets. The relief is visible in the slope of his shoulders as he backs away. I must have imagined that warmth. He was only trying to give me comfort, and I poisoned it with my selfish needs. "The—the inspector has a few questions for you."

· • •   ━━━━ • ━━━━   • • ·

Heavy autumn rain slashes the streets as Brandt and I turn the final corner to Banhopf University's constabulary post. I'd started to warm up after the chill of the cleansing pool, but now I'm soaked through. Brandt tugs his heavy tweed jacket up over his head and hugs me tight against him with his other arm so he can shield us both. Ordinarily, I would smile at him. I might even blush at his spicy scent, so close to me, and take comfort in our shared warmth. But I recognize the stiff suit Brandt wears beneath his coat, formal and fresh, the sort of thing he wears for his courting dinners at House Strassbourg.

The constable's deputy seats us, sopping wet, in a questioning room. "Aye, I've some questions for you, miss. You've been seen in the deceased's company. But I can't allow you to view the deceased unless you're a family member." He's taller than some horses I've seen; his spike helmet scrapes the low ceiling, dusting his black velvet uniform with flecks of paint.

"Not exactly," I say slowly after looking to Brandt for reassurance. "He was—he was like a father to me."

"I'm afraid you'll have to explain that a bit further, miss. I'm on strict orders only to show him to immediate family."

Strict orders, my arse, I think bitterly. I haven't met a constable yet who can't be convinced to blind-eye his duty for enough coin. A city doesn't grow a gang culture as elaborate as ours without such corruption. Marez's condemnation of Barstadt rings in my mind and rankles my blood. I hated him when he said it, but now I see that he's absolutely right.

"Hesse had no other family." Despair frays my tone. I'll not buy into the corruption if I can help it. "His wife died before I met him, and she never bore him any children . . ." I trail off, finding no shift in the deputy's stony expression, and look to Brandt.

"You say the Ministry's overseeing this case?" Brandt asks, and the deputy nods. "Then consider us part of the case, as well." He pulls a leather folio from inside his breast pocket and drops it onto the table between us. It bears the lacquered red symbol of the Ministry, flecked with enough gemstones to discourage most casual forgers. I glare at Brandt. It's not safe for him to carry such a thing when we're working a mission, obviously, and as a general rule, he should keep his association with the Ministry quiet. But I owe him my thanks.

The deputy bristles—disappointed to have lost out on a bribe, no doubt. "I see. Yes, I see. But I must warn you, young miss, the deceased's current condition might be . . . upsetting to you."

"I can handle it," I say through clenched teeth. "Just tell us what happened."

He grimaces, setting his handlebar mustache twitching. "Very well. At approximately two hours before noon, a constable making his rounds on the university grounds encountered a panicked crowd outside the theosophy building. The deceased had fallen from a twelfth-floor window, apparently under his own power, according to the crowd. He was pronounced dead on the scene. After a thorough investigation, all evidence points to an accidental death."

"And what makes you so sure?" Brandt asks. But I am a thousand leagues away from them. Professor Hesse, propped against the windowsill, moaning like a starving cat. How easy it would have been for him to neglect to reset the window latch. But for all his regrets, an accident somehow feels off. Had this newfound guilt truly eaten at him so? If he felt so ashamed of what he'd done, why was it only surfacing now? It doesn't add up, but I'm missing too many pieces to see how.

"The professor appears to have been alone in his office for some time. The theosophy department's secretary reported no visitors all morning, which rules out all but those wretched tunnelers that scurry around in the early hours," the constable says. I sit up straighter; Brandt's hand tightens around my own. I glance at our interlocking fingers, but remind myself that he's only comforting me. "We found wax paper scraps coated with the Dreamless resin—Lullaby, as it's known on the streets," he continues, oblivious to the rage chafing under my skin. "Do you have any reason to believe the deceased wished to harm himself?"

Hesse's guilt is not mine to tell, I think; but I need to know the truth. I look away from the deputy and take a deep breath. "He had some regrets about past research that had gone awry." Brandt opens his mouth to interrupt me, but I know to stop there. Any information we give this constable on Hesse's research has a good chance of being bought and sold.

The deputy nods and jots a note on his little folio. "Lullaby addicts are often haunted by regrets. If you'd seen what I've seen in the Dreamless dens . . ."

He trails off, and I rankle with bitterness. I don't need to imagine what he's seen. I've seen it myself. The smell is as foul as any tunnel sewer; the Lullabied men and women roll around in their own excrement as they immerse themselves in endless dreamless slumber. As soon as they wake up, their limp, atrophied hands wave for an attendant to bring more resin so they can pass out again. And the men running the dens are every bit as foul: lieutenants for the various gangs who keep the tunnelers in their debt and their shady aristocrat partners over the barrel.

The constable clears his throat. "What about enemies? We can't rule out the tunnelers who tended his office, though it appears no one had done a thorough cleaning for quite some time."

I shake my head. "No. None I can think of. Before he . . . before he became so overwhelmed with grief . . ." I take a deep breath. "He was well loved. He gave people opportunities they wouldn't have otherwise had."

"One final question, miss, then I'll permit you to view the deceased."

If he calls Hesse "the deceased" one more time, I may be forced to punch him. I manage a stiff nod.

"We also found this note buried in the stack of papers in his office. Someone else must have written it to Hesse; it doesn't match any of the writing samples we found in Hesse's office. It's a bit threatening in nature, which concerns us, but again, there were no signs of a struggle, or of anyone entering or exiting the room." The constable clears his throat and smooths out a bit of rumpled parchment before us, covered in a snarled, unfamiliar script.

I am forgotten but not lost.
Surrender the key before it's too late.

I sink, forgetting there's no chair to catch me; Brandt grips my arm firmly to keep me upright. "A *bit* threatening? You call that a *bit* threatening?" he says.

The constable's mustache puffs in consternation. "Black-mailers and extortionists usually give their targets time to make good on their demands before offing them. In any case, we conducted a thorough search of Hesse's office and home, but we found no keys, save those for his home and office. His home bore no signs of forced entry. The floors were covered in dust, as if Hesse had not been home in a long time—any footsteps would have been easy to spot."

I nod, but I'm burning up inside. Who would want to threaten Hesse? And what key could they possibly mean? "I'm sorry, but I'm afraid I know no more about it than you."

The deputy closes his folio and opens the interrogation room door for us. "Let us know if anything comes to you later. Please, right this way."

Our viewing is only half a viewing—Hesse's entire right side is covered with a heavy black sheet, exposing only his left half, his one visible eye rolled back in despair. Though he's tightly packed in a bin of ice at the center of the morgue, I can smell rot already settling in. My stomach twists. How can half this man appear so alive, just like the man who took me in, while the other half lies mangled beyond repair?

Brandt stays at my back, waiting for me to signal that I'm ready. His hands are folded behind him and his head is bowed. How I ache for him to embrace me now, to tell me that life will go on, that Hesse's legacy will endure. That I'll endure.

"He was . . . he'd started using Lullaby," I tell Brandt softly, out of earshot of the constables. "He was upset about things that had happened long ago. To the other people he had tried to train to dreamstride."

Brandt swears under his breath. "Others?" He steps toward

me; places a hand on my shoulder. I melt into his touch. "I didn't know about any others."

My jaw tightens like a screw. "Because they all died. Couldn't get back to their bodies . . ." I close my eyes. "And Hesse had been prepared to lose me the same way."

"No. No." Brandt's fingers uncurl from my shoulder and he rakes them through his hair. "How could he have done that? How could he have knowingly subjected you to that?"

But we both know the answer. I look away.

Brandt's mouth works as he tries to parse out his thoughts. "Even so, it makes no sense. Why is it only troubling him now? Is it something to do with that note?"

"I don't know," I say, "but I'm not sure I trust those constables to find out."

"Well, someone knows." A darkness creeps into Brandt's features, one I recognize all too well. The determination he dons when we're up against a heinous criminal—murderers and pimps and the like. "And I'm going to find out."

Brandt hires a coach to bring us back to the Ministry. The drumming rain on the coach's roof and clatter of wheels over uneven cobbles swells to fill our silent cab. When we pull up to the Ministry gates, Brandt doesn't move to climb out.

His hand finds mine in the darkened cab; our fingers lace together and cling tight. I wish I could keep this moment forever, the warmth of his bare hand against mine, the darkness concealing us from our obligations, from the roles we must play.

Brandt strokes his thumb along the ridge of my knuckles. "I'm sorry, Livia. Truly I am."

"Then stay with me," I whisper.

His face looks ashy against the sullen weather; shadows veil his gaze. His brow furrows, considering. But for too long, he doesn't answer.

"You're wanted back home. I understand." I pull my hand from his. "Go."

"You know I'll do anything it takes to find out what happened. Don't you?" He stares hard at me, intense as lightning. His fingers stay laced in mine. "Do you know that? I'd do anything for you."

But I know he won't do the one thing I want most—surrender his obligations as a son of House Strassbourg. Stay at the Ministry. Stay with me.

I say nothing, and turn and head inside the Ministry gates.

· · • ——— • ——— • · ·

"Message for Silke, Miss Livia," the clerk at the barracks entrance says, perching his glasses on his nose. "From the Farthing liaison. He's asked you to meet him at the Crossed Heart tavern if you've a free moment this evening."

The mere thought of forcing myself to be someone I'm not after all that's happened today exhausts me. Part of me wants to curl up in bed and cry, mourn for Hesse, and feel sorry for myself. But then again, isn't that the best part of playing a role? I needn't be Livia any longer. I can shed Livia and her troubles and her loss, at least for a few hours.

"Thank you," I tell the clerk, and head to my quarters to don my best Silke outfit, with my stiletto hidden in the pockets.

* * *

Marez is in the far corner of the Crossed Heart, a cleaner and smaller tavern than the ale hall I'd last met him in. He's smiling and joking with the serving girl, but as I approach his grin broadens.

"Silke. So glad you could join me." He beckons to the seat across from him at the cramped two-person table. "I hope I'm not keeping you from . . . whatever secretaries do in their free time."

"Visit taverns, mostly." I try on a wry grin for size, and rather like the way it fits. It patches over the ache inside of me.

Marez laughs and shoves a full mug of ale toward me. "Ahh, so you do have a sense of humor after all. I was starting to worry." Then his smile dims, and he hunches forward over the table. "I'm afraid I don't have any exciting news to share with you this time. I merely . . . wished to apologize."

I curl my fingers around the mug's handle and lean back in my chair. "For what?"

"For my behavior on our last—outing together."

Marez tugs at a loose curl over his ear. Is this his "tell," his indication he's about to deceive me? Brandt taught me about tells during our missions in the gaming houses, but I was never any good at spotting them—I overthink the clues, falling into

147

endless spirals of possibilities. Is it a tell, or simply a nervous tic? Is he feigning at one, or both? My head spins just contemplating it. Let me dreamstride any day; let a slumbering mind make these connections for me. This subtle art of spy work is far too intricate a spiderweb for my tastes. I feel as trapped as a fly.

"How do you mean?" I ask coolly.

"I confirmed afterward that no one came to harm in the chaos, but Kriza tells me you were upset about it, and you were absolutely right to be. I should have chosen a more subtle method of conducting our search, one that didn't place any bystanders in danger."

Something in his contrite face—soft lips, dark and downward gaze—reminds me that he's not so much older than I am. Isn't he allowed to make mistakes as well? To misjudge an operation, to mischaracterize a threat. Dreamer knows I've done the same. "Barstadters too often make the mistake of valuing some lives more than others," I say. "I didn't think you were like that."

Marez winces. I've struck a nerve. "You're right. I should have considered the threat not only to the ale hall patrons, but to the tunnelers and servers who could have been harmed as well." He glances up, eyes gleaming like a puppy's. "Am I forgiven?"

I hesitate a moment, then nod. "Apology accepted," I say. "We all err from time to time. The important thing is that we learn from it, yes?"

He lets out his breath. "Precisely, my dear." His finger traces a slow circle around the edge of his mug. "You aren't like other Barstadters, you know." He tilts his head. "Considering the well-being of others."

I narrow my eyes. "The Dreamer teaches compassion for all living things—"

"Yes, yes, I know what the Dreamer *teaches*, but what his students learn is another matter. You think I haven't heard about the tunneler protests, the fight over the Writ of Emancipation? It's my job to know of these things." He grins again. "Tell me, Silke. You've let me interpret your dreams for you. But I wager that I can intuit something about your waking life, too."

"Can you, now?" I fight to keep my tone light—playful, even. But fear is scrabbling at my insides like an animal desperate to escape. What can Marez guess about me? How much does he really know?

He taps one finger against his lips as he looks me over—those eyes of his burning like coals. "Mm, yes. I'm sensing . . . that you weren't always a secretary. You've risen up through the ranks, and feel you have something to prove. It's why you strive so much to appear proper, like at the ale hall, when there's no harm in enjoying yourself."

I feel a sinkhole tugging me into myself, though I try to smile back at him. "I suppose that's fair," I say. "Though I'm enjoying myself now."

He beams. "Well, that's a relief! I'll drink to that." He takes another sip from his mug, then studies me once more. "In fact— bear with me here—I'm going to guess that you started out from a lower social class than the average Ministry employee. A store clerk's daughter. Maybe even . . ." He lowers his voice. "A tunneler."

The thrum of my pulse crowds out all other sound in the

tavern. My mouth tastes like a furnace as I try to respond. "And if I were?" I finally manage to say.

Marez holds my gaze for a second longer, his smile not reaching his eyes. Then he softens and leans back in his seat. "Then I would say you must be very clever and talented indeed, to rise to your current rank." He laughs to himself. "I would be very impressed—more so than I already am."

"Than you already are?" I hear myself echoing. Surely he doesn't mean it—that he wouldn't regard my former life as a shameful mark. Even if I earn my citizenship papers, I know my peers in the Ministry can never forget where I've come from. They can never forget what I represent.

"Despite what Barstadt would have you think," he says, "the only person who can tell you what you are worth is yourself." The lamp overhead gutters, tossing his face briefly into shadow. "Not the Dreamer. Not your dreams. And certainly not some foolish aristocrat, passing judgment from the comfort of his lavish home. A home built and maintained by people far more skilled than he, I might add."

"There's more to Barstadt than our caste," I say, but the words are like muscle memory. I say them from habit, not from my gut.

"Of course, dear Silke. Of course. But it's a person's talent that fascinates me. Not their upbringing. And in the interest of my not being a complete snob about all things Barstadt"— Marez gestures toward a nearby table, where a group of university students are playing an increasingly loud and alcoholic game of Stacks—"I was wondering if you might teach me how this bloody game is played."

"What, you don't play Stacks?" I laugh. The earlier line of conversation settles like sediment; I can't completely forget the fear of discovery I felt as he questioned me, but I won't forget, either, what he made me feel. That I am a person for where I stand now, and not for where I was born. "I thought you sea-faring folk were the masters of gambling games."

"Oh, we have plenty of games. Arm and Leg, the Dead Man's Wake, What the Tide Brought In . . . Problem is, all my Farthing friends have already mastered these games." Marez's eyes glint in the candlelight. "I need a new game I can crush them at."

We both laugh at that, and I take a swig of ale. It scorches all the way down—burns away the dreary rain, Brandt's cold departure, even the mangled corpse of Professor Hesse. I am Silke Grundtag tonight, and Silke's life is a far merrier one than mine. "Make you a deal. I'll teach you to play Stacks, and you teach me to play your Farthing games, so I can crush *my* friends."

Marez juts his hand toward me. "Deal." We shake, his soft skin curling the corners of my smile up even more.

We keep playing and joking until well into the evening; I excuse myself for the night only when a large group of students pay their tab, and wander along the streets with them for a time before cutting back to the Ministry barracks. Only the realization that I'd alerted neither Jorn nor Brandt of my evening plans keeps me from playing for several hours more. I'd been exposed—vulnerable to the Farthing operative, my determination to forget the day's events my only barrier from letting him know the real me.

Yet didn't he see the real Livia? He understood my dreams, he accepted me for my shortcomings in the field, and still he offered me his companionship. He sniffed me out as a former tunneler, and didn't make me feel ashamed. Would a Farthinger forsake his life's work as a spy because his family expected him to quit, expected him to marry? Would he let someone like Minister Durst hold his strings, forcing him to comply or lose his chance at leaving the tunnels once and for all? From what I've seen of Marez, I think Farthingers are far too determined for that. They never let themselves be beholden to anyone and are always in charge of their own fate. I want a fiery certainty like that.

My dreams that night are all jumbled—thoughts tangle together of Hesse and Marez and Brandt, shot through with alcohol. My dreams find me in a memory of the past—Hesse's old office in the university basements, before they flooded and he moved to the twelfth floor. I'm digging through his old storage boxes in the dream, waiting to feel cold metal in the palm of my hand. *Surrender the key,* a voice tells me, echoing the note in Hesse's office, but as soon as I think I've sorted out what it's talking about, I awaken with no more answers than before.

Chapter Twelve

"Thanks to the records Livia and the Farthingers found in the ale hall, we have the proof we need to substantiate Lady Sindra Twyne's treachery and hunt down her associates." Minister Durst props himself against his desk and surveys the small team assembled in his office. "We arrested her last night, and she confessed to her conspiracy. She said she's been working with the Commandant to overthrow the Emperor and conquer parts of Farthing as well. The girl, Martine, is her daughter with the original Commandant, and it is her deepest wish to see our two cultures united, as they are in her daughter's blood."

Vera crinkles her nose. "What a load of rubbish."

"What about Nightmare?" I ask. "Trying to resurrect him?"

Durst shakes his head; the shadows under his eyes look even deeper than usual. "She seemed to know nothing about it. Swore up and down that she didn't even believe in the Dreamer, much less Nightmare. Went on some rant about the Iron Winds as her new religion now—the Commandant as her god and savior of all mankind, and that his forces would be victorious over Barstadt and all the other realms."

My throat constricts; the dark skull of Nightmare from my dreams looms in my mind. "No. No. She told me, when I was her daughter. I'm sure of what she said."

Durst glances at me from the corner of his eyes. "Livia, my dear, I don't doubt what you heard. But our interrogators are quite skilled, and she was more than willing to admit to far more serious things that guaranteed her a death sentence. Without further evidence, we can't make a case for it. It's too impossible to believe that Nightmare could be brought back to life—we have no proof."

Edina Alizard, pen poised over a bound journal, leans forward in her chair. "When do we expect the execution to take place?"

"The Emperor is pushing for this evening." Durst holds his hands up against our protests. "I know, I know. That isn't nearly enough time to pursue further questioning. But he wants a swift example made of her, and she's been quite forthcoming with everything we've asked. We would need an extremely good reason to convince him to delay."

"It just smells off. Like the fish market after Tremmer's month." Brandt wrings his hands in his lap; I press my palm to his knee without thinking, but quickly pull it away. "She's too proud and stubborn to surrender so easily. What's her angle?"

" 'The face of death makes cowards of us all,' " Edina says, then looks down at her notes, cheeks coloring. "Sorry. One of my father's sayings."

Vera had been slumped against the wall farthest from Edina, but at that, she shoves off the wall with a roll of her eyes. "And what does your father say about traitors? I imagine the Alizard family knows all about being promise-breaking little—"

Brandt forces a loud cough, cutting Vera off. "What about this other plan of the Commandant's? With the mystic?" he asks.

Minister Durst pinches his nose. "Again, she's professed an irritatingly convincing ignorance on that front. She claims to know very little at all about the Commandant's plans."

"But she's too smart," Brandt says. "I'm certain there's something more."

"Well, we have agents watching her servants and known associates day and night, but there's no indication a raven's been sent, or anything else."

"Did the Farthingers turn up any other leads in the logs we recovered from the ale house?" I ask. "Beyond confirming her dealings in the Land of the Iron Winds."

"They're still researching it, last we spoke, but nothing solid thus far." Durst sighs. "Enough to give credence to her admission of colluding with the Commandant, but naught else."

There must be some key element we aren't factoring in. She couldn't possibly have conducted this plan for five years or more without assistance from other aristocrats, could she? She'd named no names, assuming all responsibility herself. "There must be others she's protecting," I say, though my voice falters, betraying my uncertainty. "She's speaking freely so that we keep our focus on her, instead of casting a wider net."

"I considered that as well, but she insists she worked alone, with minimal help from sailors and the like to arrange her voyages to the Land. And we've no evidence, no shred of proof this extends any further into Barstadt." Minister Durst leans back against his desk and presses knobby fingers to his temples. "All we have is the word of a traitor against . . . nothing. Absolutely nothing."

Vera groans; Brandt's shoulders tense beside me. Edina's pen taps frantically against her teeth.

I study the minister's map of Barstadt and her neighbors, and Marez's check marks copied onto it. "The maps. Did Marez and Kriza find any links between them and Lady Twyne's trades?"

Minister Durst scoops up a scrap of paper from his desk. "Yes, let me show what our precious alliance has won us. In addition to a hefty bill for damages dealt to the Shanty Ale Hall, we found no records to indicate that the Lady Twyne and the Commandant of the Land of the Iron Winds had smuggled any arms, advance guards, horses, or other elements of war into Barstadt. However, the map you all recovered from the manager's office indicates that the plans for such an operation had been made. The map marked House Twyne's estate at the northeast corner of the city, along Nightmare's Spine, and the archeological site south of Birnau in the Land of the Iron Winds."

"Oh!" Edina exclaims. "We received a report earlier this morning about Birnau. A dispatch from one of our sources inside the Land of the Iron Winds." She flips through her notebook. "Looks like the Commandant has called an emergency meeting with all his generals at Birnau."

Durst scrubs at his goatee. "Interesting. I wonder if the Commandant knows Lady Twyne's been caught."

"If he does, then the meeting might be to formulate a new battle plan," Brandt says.

Vera groans. "Wonderful. Even the average Iron Winder can't get into Birnau—it's sealed up even tighter than the Citadel. Only the Commandant and his trusted advisers and staff are permitted within its walls. How in the nightmares are we supposed to peek inside?"

"I got Brandt and Livia into the Citadel safely," Edina says, with more starch in her tone than usual. "I'm sure I can arrange it."

Vera's head cants to one side with unsettling precision. "Well, we all know how excellently you follow through on arrangements."

"Miss Orban," the minister says, low and slow. After a moment, Vera huffs and slumps back in her chair.

My gaze returns to the marks on the minister's map. Whatever Vera and Edina are bickering about now, I've not been privy to it; and I have other concerns to tend to. Like the pattern of the marks. They're like a constellation, that strange network of slashes spun across the Central Realms. Do they mirror the stars: the Dreamer's Embrace, the Clipper, the Star Ladle, the Questing Swine? I squint but can't summon any sort of pig or outstretched arms from their arrangement.

Minister Durst buries his face in his hands; his ears burn crimson, and his chest heaves as he smothers the anger surely burning through him like a brushfire. "We can't fall behind whatever the Commandant is planning next. As soon as we can make the necessary arrangements, I'm sending you all to Birnau." Minister Durst lowers his hands and sucks in a deep breath. "All four of you."

That snaps Edina and Vera to attention. "What?" they shriek in flawless harmony.

"Brandt, Vera, you're the finest operatives that I can spare right now. As for Edina, I know you handled the logistics to get them into the Land of the Iron Winds last time, but Birnau requires more finesse. I think you're better off managing it in person. And of course I'll need the dreamstrider. We've already tied up too many resources in watching the gates and patrolling the sea for signs of an impending attack. I'll send Jorn with you for security, but it's the best I can offer."

My heart plummets as every eye in the room falls on me. Color rushes to Vera's face, even as it drains from my own. Two words hang amongst us all, denser and ranker than the worst sewer stench. Our shared failure and our overshadowing shame.

Stargazer Incident.

"No," Vera whispers. "No. I'll go with her on trivial missions—fluffy balls and the like—but I don't trust her with something so dangerous."

"Livia?" the minister asks. "Can I trust you to pull your weight?"

I freeze under his gaze. How can I defend myself against her fears? I've earned all of it and more. "You don't need me," I say. "Vera's right. You're safer without me."

Minister Durst presses his lips together. "Were it not for the threat of this mystic, these schemes involving Oneiros itself, then I'd agree. But the Commandant is too paranoid to trust anyone beyond those already in his circle of advisers. I need your skill." I can't blame him for looking so grim. I'd be angry, too, at being backed into such a corner, forced to rely on my skill.

Edina nods, looking down at her notes. "We need Livia. It's our best chance at getting the Commandant to tell us what we need to know."

Vera sputters like she's swallowed turnip juice. "But, Minister, you can't possibly—If it's only a dreamstriding mission for Livia—I mean, she and Brandt met with the Commandant himself without our presence! You don't need me—"

"Yes, but when the Iron Council meets in Birnau, it hosts the Commandant *and* all his deputies," Minister Durst says.

Edina nods. "I need all of us there so we can split up and cast a wide net."

"And we need Livia most of all," Brandt says, far more confidently than I deserve. "She's our best chance at getting right there in the midst of the Commandant and his private conversations. She can go places no one else can." I manage a faint smile his way, though I still ache from how he left me after Hesse's death.

Vera glances from Brandt to me and back, lips twisting. "Ahh. I see." She turns toward Edina. "No, you're absolutely right. Brandt and Livia work so well together."

Oh, Vera's vile tonight! Whatever she imagines is between Brandt and me can never be, and soon, he'll be gone for good. Edina, for her part, looks equanimous as ever, but I'm blushing straight up into my scalp. "What about the Farthingers?" I ask hastily, desperate to take the attention off Vera's comment.

"Don't need to be involved. If you're right and they are a few steps ahead of us on this puzzle, then we're better off letting them rest on their laurels a bit longer." Durst claps his hands together and rubs them, as if wiping the whole affair from his skin. "All right! We'll put a few additional pointed questions to Lady Twyne and see what more we can wring out of her. You'll depart two mornings from now—Edina, can you have all the necessary bribes and logistical arrangements settled by then?"

"Yes, sir," she says.

Brandt leaps to his feet and issues a stiff nod to Durst. "We won't let you down."

Edina moves toward the door, but nearly collides into Vera; the two of them exchange looks that could peel paint. "After you," Edina says.

"Oh, no, I insist," Vera retorts. "I know better than to turn my back to an Alizard."

Poor Jorn. He's going to wonder what grave punishment he's being sent to endure.

"Livia?" Durst asks as the others depart. "A moment, if I may."

Brandt's gaze meets mine, and he gives me a quick nod before leaving. I sink back into my seat, as if my legs have gone to gelatin underneath me.

"I know our time together has been . . . difficult. For both of us." Durst pinches the end of his goatee. "We both believed in Hesse's research, and expected great things to come from it, many of which it simply could not deliver."

Much as I'd like to protest, I can't argue with what he's said. The memory of listening at the door of Hesse's office, overhearing Durst and Hesse argue about bringing me into the Ministry's care is fresh. It had felt like a dream brought to life, leaving my tunneler life behind, but the reality has been much less enchanted.

"I blame myself," he says, "for expecting too much. I believed Hesse was giving me a miracle, but you're only a person; it wasn't fair of me to see you as such. I'm afraid"—his voice cracks—"I expected more of you than was fair of me. Believe me when I say that I wanted more than anyone for you to succeed."

"What exactly are you asking of me, Minister?" I fold my hands into my lap to keep them from trembling. His tone is gentle, but his words sound dangerously close to a dismissal.

He leans over his desk and passes me a stack of papers, folded in half, though ribbons and sealing wax dangle down from inside. "I need you to succeed on this mission—help us prevent the Land of the Iron Winds from invading. If not for Barstadt, then for this. You have to put aside what's happened, Livia. Help us stop the Commandant, and these will be yours."

They're papers—citizenship papers. Papers like these are exorbitantly expensive if one goes through the proper channels, and even more so if greased with bribes. My temporary papers granted me clemency from a lifetime of tunneler serfdom, but Durst always held issuing power over them, and was free to dispose of them—and me—at any time. These papers are the next step—true citizenship, not a temporary grant.

I look from the paper to Durst. "Permanent papers? No provisions?"

"After we've stopped the Commandant, they're yours. Completely. You'll be free to go and do whatever you please if you can see this matter with the Land of the Iron Winds through."

I press the heels of my hands against my eyes. My life, completely mine to control. Half a year ago, I couldn't imagine life away from the Ministry, but knowing now that there's far more of the Central Realms to see than just Barstadt . . .

Whatever I decide, my papers are the beginning of it—of true freedom. I have to earn them, no matter how challenging it proves. "Thank you, Minister." My voice dissolves around me. "I won't let you down."

· ·• ———— •———— •· ·

"Your Farthinger friends left a message for you with the clerk," Sora says when I head back into the barracks. "They'll be by tomorrow morning to fetch you for something."

"Thanks, Sora." I grab my coat. "Feel free to help yourself to the pastries in my room. I need some time to myself tonight."

I climb atop the steep barracks roof, my favorite hiding place, as twilight dusts the turrets of the Imperial Palace on the hill ahead of me. Between Hesse's death, our impending mission back to the Land of the Iron Winds, and Brandt's recent distance, I feel tangled up like a dropped stitch, and I need the crisp autumn air to clear my head. But then I spy the crowd gathering along the sloping square that leads up to the palace, and a fresh wave of nausea washes over me. It's almost time for Twyne's execution, and the roof offers all too clear a view.

The rooftop hatch pops open, and Brandt's head emerges, grinning like a little boy who's just gotten away with something. "I thought I might find you here."

"Are you sure you didn't get lost on the way to another ball?" I'd meant it in jest, but the words come out too harsh. His grin fades so quickly it must have been for show.

He climbs out of the hatch and settles back against the roof. "Now, now, how could any self-respecting aristocrat miss out on . . . all this?" He sweeps one arm toward the square. The jail cart hasn't even arrived yet, but the square is bursting with black-clad Barstadters, from the lower merchants to jewel-encrusted aristocrats seated in private tents. While the din of gossip reaches all the way up to our roof, every single head is turned toward the temporary platform, where the Emperor sits beside a wooden block. "Not even the courting season takes precedence over such a scandal."

I hug my legs to my chest, tucking my chin over my knees. A question lurks on the edge of my tongue, and even though it pains me to ask, I have to know. "Brandt." I glance at him. "Are you still courting Edina?"

"Nightmare's teeth, Liv." He runs both hands through his hair, then curls them into fists, taking long, steadying breaths. "I'm sorry. I just—I wasn't expecting to—I came here to say—" He swallows down hard. "I, ah, I came up here to get away for a few moments, is all. Before we're off on a deadly mission again."

I nod, face still hidden behind my knees. "I wish we didn't have to go back. And with Vera and Edina and Jorn—"

Brandt's smile makes me falter. "You can do this, Liv. I know you. You just can't let your fear get in the way. That's when you get tripped up."

His bangs fall back into place across his tanned forehead, a smooth array of soft browns and heady golds. I reach forward to brush them back, but stop myself short. "I pray to the Dreamer that I'll be strong enough. That I won't be afraid. But . . ." My hand drops to the slate tiles. "It never seems to be enough."

"Maybe it's not for the Dreamer to fix. Maybe he wants you to be strong for yourself."

For myself? I start to laugh. All anyone's ever wanted from me is what I can do for them. Clean for the gangs, earn enough for my mother to buy Lullaby, dreamstride for the Ministry. But perhaps it's time I learned to care for myself. If I can truly earn my freedom, then I can finally do whatever I wish, for me alone.

Brandt unhooks a wineskin from his belt and unfastens its lid. The scent of warm cinnamon and nutmeg spills over us, and I tilt my head back with an indulgent grin.

"Mulled cider," I say, then take another sniff. "And you've spiked it, you devil. What's the occasion?"

"A peace offering. And an apology." He hands me the wineskin, but his fingers catch in my loose curls; he sweeps them back from my shoulders. "I should have been there for you after . . . after we visited the constabulary."

The cider blazes down my throat, but I stiffen at his words, passing the wineskin back to him with a grimace. "You have your obligations. Your duties to your House. I understand."

"No. I want to help you—help serve the professor's memory. The constabulary may not be taking it seriously, but I do." He gulps down the cider as well. "Why was Hesse so overcome with guilt of late? Why now?"

I stare down at the restless crowd in the square. "I thought maybe it was because of what happened to the others who tried to dreamstride." I can barely speak past the lump, hardening like clay, in my throat. "But it doesn't explain why it troubled him recently."

Brandt tightens, a line of muscles standing out along his neck. His eyes sparkle celadon in the dusk. "No. Livia—no. If he knew it could—what it might do to you, to dreamstride, then how could he—"

"I'm only a tunneler, not meant for anything more. Who would have missed me?" I pick at the slate tiles of the roof.

"I would have, for one. You're . . . you're *you*, Livia. You've got smarts, and when you let yourself, you have this determination that I—that inspires me, too. How could anyone not see that?"

I laugh, dry and bitter. "That's why they're all scrambling to go on missions with me, right?"

"Only because Durst doesn't know how to use your properly. I've been doing this for ten years—half my life. And you've the added burden of mastering dreamstriding, on top of it all. Even the Incident—that wasn't your fault. Durst just doesn't know how to use you. It's like asking a fork to do a spoon's duty." Brandt takes another pull from the wineskin.

"If I'm a fork, then I'm a badly dented, tarnished one, a fork no one needs." I wrinkle my nose. "The nicked one you're always slicing the inside of your mouth on—"

"Livia." In an instant, Brandt is looming before me, my cheeks cupped in those strong, broad hands of his. "Don't talk about yourself that way. I know you—I know your good heart, your determination to see things through." His mouth softens, all pinkness and spring thaw. "You're perfect. Nicks and all."

My heart is thundering like galloping hooves. I lean forward, forehead resting against his, his warmth as radiant as the cider in my blood. I need Brandt—I need to see him smile, see him unburdened. The real Brandt, not the one who wears the Ministry's masks or his House's fancy dress. Brandt believes in me in a way no one but the Dreamer ever has.

The crowd roars in the square. Brandt jolts away from me, hands sliding to his hair again; he bites down hard on his lower lip. My chest is heaving; my face must be as red as Brandt's coat right now. But the sight in the square chills me through.

The iron-barred jail cart rolls slowly through the crowd. Even the horse pulling it proceeds with its head down, bloodlust in its eyes, its nostrils aflare. Those closest to the cart press against it, shouting, taunting, hands darting through the cart's bars, reaching for the traitor. Inside the cart, Lady Twyne stands tall, chin jutted high. I think she'd stand that way even if she weren't shackled in place—defiant, looking down her nose at her detractors to the very last.

I snatch the wineskin back from Brandt and draw another mouthful of cider to ward this awful chill from my heart.

"Livia . . ." Brandt twists his head to watch me, but he's turned inward, shoulders hunched, hands in his lap; whatever we'd been about to share, it's gone. The space between us aches like a bruise. "I don't want you to think I—"

"I don't think anything." I let the words fall swift as an ax.

Someone in the crowd manages to catch hold of Lady Twyne's black robes and tugs them free, baring her upper body to all of Barstadt. She doesn't scream or attempt to cover herself, and for a moment I feel embarrassed for her, but then I recall what she meant to do to Barstadt, and my pity stokes into rage.

"Edina and I are to be married," Brandt says, staring down at the crowd.

The world falls out from under me. I lurch forward, and the wineskin tumbles out of my hands, spilling down the slate tiles, and I scrabble for it as I sift through the hundreds of questions in my head all screaming to be heard.

"Oh, Brandt, that's . . . wonderful." I take a deep breath and sink back down on the roof. "Congratulations on your . . ."

My throat closes up around the word. *Betrothal*. Such a heavy little word, the sort of thing one slams onto the table as a wager for the final round of Stacks. I can't say it; I won't. I force myself to grin like a woman possessed, but I can't wear masks like he can.

Despite his placid face, Brandt tightens and flexes his left palm, watching it intently, like he expects it to perform a trick.

"Our parents signed the agreement just this morning. It's—it's the first chance I've had to tell you."

"And why do you need to tell me?" I hear myself say, from somewhere very far away.

"I just . . . thought you'd like to know."

I catch him watching me from the corner of my eye, but I keep my gaze straight ahead. Whatever he thought—whatever I dared to hope—it can't be. I have no right to a son of House Strassbourg. I've lived within the strict confines of Barstadt society this long; I can endure this boundary as well.

I will not acknowledge this fraying in my heart, tearing a little more each day as the distance between Brandt and I grows, stretching its fibers just a little too thin.

"Lord Alizard. Oh, he'll make for an interesting father-in-law." I suppress a snort. "I know you have to quit the Ministry to work for your family, but please tell me you won't be working for him, too."

"Of course I won't." Brandt's mask slips as he grimaces. "Edina and I agree it's best we distance ourselves from whatever vile deals he brokers with the gangs. Edina will manage our household while I work for my father's trading concerns." He shakes his head with a wry half-grin. "Is that why you look so vexed?"

As if I could tell him any other reason. As if I could admit out loud why my heart is aching so, why my mind is a thousand leagues away from this blunted pain I'm feeling. As if there is any other way but distance to survive. I'm watching myself, like my body is just another temporary vessel for my dreamstriding, and I can let it do the work of emotion and pain and speech for me. "As long as you're happy, Brandt, then so am I."

He doesn't answer immediately; instead he squeezes that fist as hard as he can. Veins dance along his exposed forearm—such a lovely olive shade. "Edina is kind—nothing like her father. She's clever, but not in a scheming way. And Edina, well—" Brandt hesitates. "She'd been . . . *involved* with someone before. Some of the Houses are still scandalized about that, but she's done her best to overcome it. I think she truly cares about my happiness. Isn't that what matters? Her father's happy, my family's happy, everyone's at peace. I'll miss working with you— with all of the Ministry—but, well, I know you'll do great things. You don't need me."

I don't have a chance to respond. The drum corps begins its slow, lumbering beat.

The executioner has covered Lady Twyne back up; now she's only a black shadow on the horizon, backlit by a sliver of sun, climbing the platform steps. He stands her before the block and turns her to face the crowd. The Emperor reads her sentence, though he's too far for us to make out much. I catch "treason," "conspiring with," "against the Empire."

"What's going to happen to the little girl?" I ask Brandt. "Martine."

Brandt rubs at his chin. "Lady Twyne's sister is married to the lord of House Kircher. I believe they're going to take her in."

I nod. House Kircher is not the kindest, nor the brightest, but it's better than the streets. Better than leaving her to crawl into the tunnels, never to find her way back out.

The Emperor turns to Lady Twyne, and only because I've seen more of these than I'd like do I know he's asking for her final words. She shouts something, but her voice is swallowed up by great gasps that trickle through the crowd, rushing like water down the hill.

The executioner pulls the hood over her head, snuffing out the dazzle of her facial sapphires, then lays her head onto the block so delicately as if he's nestling a jewel back into its case. The drumbeats hasten. Brandt reaches for my hand, but I'm sitting on it, frozen in place.

The drums speed up, dissolving into uneven, thundering chaos.

The executioner's blade swings up, then down.

The crowd roars.

It is only later that night, as Sora and I play a round of Stacks in the barracks, that the gossip mill reaches us with Twyne's final words: "Awaken into Nightmare."

Part Two

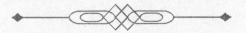

NIGHTMARES

Chapter Thirteen

I dream of citizenship papers, of records, of words blurring together like drops of water into a pond. Once more, I dream of the archives, hunting for anything that can help us in Birnau. But I walk away more confused than when I began.

Rather than sink back into dreamless sleep, I find myself awake within my dream. The Dreamer must be hearing my prayers after all, because even without the vile dreamwort tonic I usually use for dreamstriding, I've wound up in the city at the center of Oneiros. My feet are bare, and I'm dressed in the same ruffly nightgown I'm wearing back in my bed in the barracks, but the night is just the right temperature, and the cobblestones are soft under my soles. I twist through the labyrinthine streets, between buildings towering over me that rise like tidal waves of metal, or erupt like bouquets of glass flowers, or sink into the earth, opening to deep subterranean lands.

Yet the streets are strangely empty this night. I don't pass a single soul as I wander—usually I see at least one or two priests wandering about. Perhaps it's the hum in the air, like the frantic quiver of insects before a storm, that keeps them away. I'm grateful to avoid the priests' suspicious stares—I need the space to think and dream—but their absence itches all the same.

The night sky greets me with millions of winking stars, and the two golden posts of the spire at the center of the city rise up in greeting. They represent the Dreamer's Embrace, holding a golden disc high in the air. I take a deep breath and launch into the sky, and then rush up the height of the spire and land on the disc's upper edge. The dreamworld unfolds in every direction; the city fades into the patchwork pastoral fiefdoms of Shapers' homes. But nothing moves. No birds, no animals, no humans. The night air turns stale and heavy around me.

Something flickers in the forest, a structure with walls that glow amber like a candle's flame. I've seen stone like that before, drinking up the sunlight and leaking it back out. It looks just like Twyne Manor. But it must be coincidence; what dreamshaper wouldn't want a shimmering alabaster castle? Still, the sight of it tugs at me. I ought to surge across the city and into the forest for a closer look, just to put my mind at ease. I ought.

I look away, to the streets beneath me, to gather my resolve.

Now I see others in the streets. At first, they're only shadows, rippling from side to side. The figures swell, rising from the cobblestones like tar oozing up. The sticky black shapes congeal into figures: hunched-over half humans with vile, sightless holes for eyes.

Wings sprout from their disfigured backs. The night sky fades under a rotten cloud of thick, putrid smoke. The ragged creatures circle the spire's base, looping around it like a hungering pack.

A massive shadow falls across me from above.

The creatures take flight, wings fully formed, still circling the spire. The stink of rot floods my nose. I try to will myself airborne but remain pinned to the disc's edge. I try to cry out, but my screams crumble in my mouth. No sound leaves me, and I can't move.

The mob becomes a buzzing black wall of death that cinches closed around me. My chest heaves with agony, as if the weight of all my failures has crashed into me at once. Professor Hesse's empty eye, piercing despite its cloudiness, his fist clenched around some terrible secret that I couldn't be bothered to pry free. My mother's hand reaching for me as I turned away, my bag full of everything I owned. The beasts are closer now, rank breaths heating my face. I reach up to claw them away—

I sit up. I'm back in my barracks bed. My throat burns, as though I've screamed it raw. I claw at my arms, trying to rip off the feeling of beating wings. Is that blood under my nails? Tar? I leap out of bed, and my legs nearly collapse beneath me. *Come on, come on, wake up.* I shake one leg, then the other. Finally, I hobble over to the desk on fuzzy, uncooperative feet, and I crank on the kerosene lamp.

Nothing under my nails, nothing on my arms. I'm all in one

piece, though decidedly sweaty and ragged. I click off the lamp and let the moonlight guide me back to bed.

Dreamer, protect us all. I pray for some time and regulate my breathing, but sleep remains cold and distant, watching me from the far corner of my room.

Chapter Fourteen

"Thank you for meeting me on such short notice." Marez settles onto the lip of the marble fountain at the center of Dreamer's Square. He's gnawing absently on a meat pastry from a market cart and watching a gaggle of bejeweled aristocrats stumble out of the High Temple. "I thought you might benefit from joining me on this questioning. If my source is correct, something far more sinister than we anticipated is afoot."

"How do you mean?" I try tucking one leg under me on the fountain lip, but can't keep my balance that way, so I swap to the other. I'm trying to act calm—Marez has no idea we're undertaking a mission to the Land of the Iron Winds tomorrow morning—but my pulse is galloping.

Marez gulps down the last bite of his roll. "My source claims to know something about the late Lady Twyne. Something to do with those nightmares you all fear so much."

I narrow my eyes; suddenly the cool mist from the fountain at our backs turns chilly on my skin. I still haven't shaken the dread I'd felt in Oneiros last night; that coupled with Lady Twyne's eerie final words about Nightmare makes the hairs on my arms stand on end. "You don't mean to mock us again, do you?"

"Of course not, my dear." His eyes sparkle as he looks right at me. "In fact, I was hoping you could help me make sense of it."

"Then what do you want to know?" I ask, still on my guard.

"Well, all this business about nightmares—how Nightmare has been vanquished, and all that. Clearly people still have bad dreams, or they wouldn't turn to Lullaby."

I cringe inwardly, recalling Hesse, but take care to keep my feelings from my face. "A true believer can fend off a nightmare easily. They're nothing more than our doubts and regrets haunting us. If you can keep the faith, the Dreamer's guidance will shine through." *But the Nightmare Wastes are growing in Oneiros,* I think. "The Lullaby users shouldn't give up on their hopes—if they keep their good dreams close to them, then their bad dreams are powerless."

"Ah, so it's their own fault." He nods, his eyes dark now. "What about the Dreamer? Isn't it his duty to protect them?"

The Dreamer's duty—what do I really know of that? He never answers my calls. But then, I am not as devout as I should be. If the priests are to be believed, I disgrace the Dreamer every time I dreamstride. I don't know if they're right. I'm trying to do right for the Dreamer and for his people—honestly, I am. But the only way I know how is through dreamstriding. If the Dreamer would only let me know that what I'm doing is right, that I'm following the path he's set for me . . . I clench my teeth together and try to force that thought away.

"Maybe they don't trust in him like they should," is all I say.

Marez drums his long, slender fingers against the fountain lip. "Interesting."

A few weeks ago, I'd have been certain this conversation was another game of his; that he was a predator, hunting for my weaknesses. But now I see it's just his nature—to be curious, to seek deeper knowledge of things. He may not trust in the Dreamer like I do, but he seems more respectful. More understanding. He saw me for what I really am, after all—a tunneler—and didn't so much as flinch.

"And what about the dreamworld?" he asks.

"Oneiros?" I say before I think to stop myself. The dreamworld's existence isn't a secret, per se, but no one but the priests are supposed to be able to visit it. It's where they do their work Shaping and soothing others' dreams. A sacred place, meant only for the Dreamer's chosen servants, who understand it in a way the average Barstadter can't.

He nods. If my mention surprises him, he doesn't show it. "I hear common folk occasionally slip into it from their private dreams."

"Rarely," I say. "And it's very dangerous—the priests have to usher them safely back."

"Most curious. Can they have nightmares there, as well?"

A rivulet of sweat rolls down my back, despite the autumn breeze. "Not that I'm aware of," I say. "Nightmare is dead, so his minions are powerless. The Dreamer's priests protect us."

Except for whatever vile threat is festering even now inside Oneiros.

"So it's forbidden to dream badly. But even though your Dreamer slew Nightmare, there are plenty of souls who experience bad dreams."

Yes, bad dreams persist. In the tunnels. The Dreamless dens. They hang over the luckless like a cloud of misery. I say nothing and stand up, straightening my skirts. "Shouldn't we be meeting with your informant now?"

But he plows onward. "I can't help but think that if you bottle those bad feelings up, eventually they have to break free. Like steam from a kettle, you know?" Marez seizes my hand in his. "In Farthing, we believe in balance. Give in to all emotions in turn; accept your baser instincts, lest they tear you up inside." He flips my hand over in his and studies the thick calluses at the base of my fingers from years of scrubbing stone.

I snatch my hand back from him. "Are you saying it's our own fault?"

"I'm only playing the devil's advocate again. I like finding a way to argue for or against whatever suits my needs in the role I'm playing. It's something every successful operative should be able to do." His lips curl into a closed smile. "Let go of your convictions and sink into whatever role you must play."

"Maybe I'm not interested in playing a role," I say.

He arches one brow. "Don't you remember your dream, trying to choose which costume you should don? You're in the wrong country to get away with not playing a role." He stands and shakes the crumbs from his trousers—dark, well-oiled leather. "Today our role is to tolerate all sorts of despicable creatures to find out what we need."

Marez swaggers against the throng of aristocrats pouring from the temple, leaving me to scamper along in his wake. I risk a glance around the square, seeking out Jorn, who trails us from a distance. He gives me a slow nod; I harden my expression and stay close to Marez. At first, I didn't like the way Marez keeps poking and prodding me like I'm an experiment, but now I can see the value in his tips on conducting myself in the field, and his hints of Farthing life. Is he really trying to train me as an operative? Somehow that feels far too altruistic a possibility for their sort of people. He said himself that Farthing is about balance, about give and get.

Yet maybe he really does see something in me the Ministry can't. Brandt said I had a determination in me. Maybe Marez sees it, too—perhaps sees it even more. I swallow as a nervous excitement ripples through me. Maybe Marez's interest in me is about something else entirely. Feeling my face start to burn, I duck my head.

We follow a curving alley off the main square; Marez tosses a glance over his shoulder to make sure I'm with him. His glossy curls look especially lustrous in the early dawn light. "Let's see how right you are about your Dreamer protecting his flock from bad dreams."

He slides up to a doorway set into the alley and raps casually, then purses his fist to his lips, affecting modesty. The door cracks open just long enough for a bloodshot eye to appear, and then it slams closed again. Chains rattle and the door flings wide.

"'E's got cold feet." A burly, aging gang enforcer, swaddled in ratty aristocratic garb, holds the door open for us. "I told 'im you'll pay good for what 'e knows, but 'e's not believin' me."

"I'm sure we can convince him." Marez's pencil-thin smile invites me to reconsider the definition of "convince." My pulse races. I've never taken part in a questioning at the Ministry before. I try to turn my fear into excitement at the unknown, a new adventure.

We duck into a smoky gaming den, where men and a few gap-toothed women huddle around tables that constantly rock back and forth under the force of their Stacks playing. I think I could get drunk off the stink of ale in the air alone. Indulging my delicate secretary role, I clutch both hands to my chest and gasp.

In truth, though, I've seen worse—far worse—in the tunnels. I've lived through worse. Suffering is just a fact of Barstadt life. Could Farthing life really be so much better?

"Apologies that this isn't up to your usual standard, Miss Silke," Marez whispers right into my ear. His lower lip lingers a little too long against my earlobe—or do I imagine it? A thrill runs through me, or maybe it's a shiver.

We follow the enforcer across the gaming floor and duck through a ratty curtain into a hallway. I hold my breath in sudden panic. Please don't let him be leading us to a Dreamless den. I can't face that smell of dark memories, laced with the sweet, seductive Lullaby resin. We drift down the corridor, and I feel it on the air, stale and thick as a wall pushing me back. My mother's distant stare swims before my eyes, begging me to let her sleep a moment longer. Please, please, no.

The lieutenant stops before another doorway and holds up his hand. "Wait here while I get him." I release my superstitious breath. The lieutenant ducks under the curtain, revealing only a slash of the horrors beyond: a full-grown man shriveled down to his skin and bones, rolling upon his hammock in unending sleep.

I flatten against the wall and shut my eyes, trying to clear away the memories of my mother as she succumbed to another night of Lullaby sleep or of Hesse and his final days.

"What's the matter, Silke?" Marez asks, flattening his palm beside my arm against the wall. "Never seen a Dreamless den before?"

The lie rests on the tip of my tongue. I expect Marez to be watching me with haughty indignance, but his face is soft, tinged with sadness. Marez understands my feelings toward my previous life; he didn't try to wave it away like the others in the Ministry do, telling me it's just the way of things, it's how Barstadt's always been. "It's been a long time," I say slowly. "From my life . . . before."

He rests a gentle hand against my forearm, his expression heavy with understanding. "I'm sorry you have to see it again."

"It . . . it shouldn't be this way," I stammer. "The gangs. The Lullaby addiction."

Marez's gaze flicks toward mine. "I thought you believed these people deserve their fates, foundering in Lullaby dreamlessness. That it's their own fault for not believing hard enough."

I shake my head, fighting not to lose my nerve. Dreamer, but it feels freeing to speak this way. "If anyone's to blame, it's the constables and the aristocrats who keep the gangs in business—the diseased backbone of Barstadt. We—we could do better."

"And so you could." He tucks a lock of hair behind my ear. "The gangs fill a need—the need people have to escape their troubled dreams. If there wasn't a demand for it—"

"Fine. So the need for Lullaby is the result of some failing on the Dreamer's part. Is that what you want me to say?"

He cups my chin and tilts my face toward his. "Is that what you think of me, Silke?" It burns where he touches me. *Like he's made of poison,* I think bitterly—but no. That's not right. Like he's made of fire. The fire I need to be a better operative. A better *me.* I want that fire, too.

"I'm not trying to turn you against your beliefs," Marez says. "I just want you to question what you've been taught. You must always think up here." He taps my temple. "Not just with your heart."

"Balance," I say, my voice far breathier than I'd meant.

Marez nods solemnly, lowering his head. I can feel his breath on my face. "Balance."

Balance. The word quivers in my blood like a high, clear note. It has to be better than scrambling my way up the crooked spines of the other tunnelers as I make my escape. Better than Barstadt's obsession to climb ever higher—through marriage, through colonies conquered, through gangs placed under one's control. Better than the pressure to be better, more. To live up to Hesse's impossible theories. To be aristocratic enough for Brandt and the legacy he must grow.

Suddenly, I crave balance, the way little tunneler Livia craved a hot meal. I need it like I need air.

The lieutenant stumbles out of the den, escorting a sooty, rat-faced man with crinkled gray hair. Marez's source—Dreamer only knows where he managed to dig him up. Marez releases me, standing at attention, that sharp glint back in his gaze. I tug at my dress and adopt a similar pose, though my face feels like it's aflame.

"Y'see, Karl? I told you they're nobody to be afraid of. They're gonna treat you real nice," the lieutenant says. He shoves Karl forward. "How about you three head back to the parlor and make yourselves at home?"

Karl looks between Marez and me, tongue worrying at a gap in his teeth. "I want the gold up front."

"Done," Marez says. "And the first round is on me."

Back in the gaming parlor, the lieutenant finds us a booth tucked away from the noisy Stacks tournaments, and fetches us three tumblers of some dreadful grain alcohol. I tuck my hands into my lap and try not to let my skin come into contact with the filthy booth.

Karl downs his drink in one gulp before staring a hole through the table as he speaks. "All right. So my buddy works at the jail down in Imperial Square. Where they kept Lady Twyne, right? And he *swears* there was some scary guy coachin' her about somethin' that didn't make much sense. Bribed my buddy so he could get close to her cell and talk to the lady."

"Well?" Marez asks. "What did they talk about?"

Karl raises his drink, gulps, and then lowers the glass to the table. It rattles against the wood; his arm, still gripping the glass, is shaking. "It—it don't make sense. You know? Crazy stuff, like."

Marez snatches back the pouch of gold and stands up, towering over Karl, who's shrunken down into himself. "Come, Silke. We're leaving."

I glance back at Karl, but he's curled inward, away from whatever he heard from his friend. "But . . ." Karl's jaw works like he wants to protest, but nothing makes its way past his lips. He grimaces and shakes his head.

"This man has nothing for us. I'm sorry to have wasted your time." Marez holds out his hand to me, all hints of his earlier good cheer erased. This is the counterweight to his easy demeanor—the carrot and the stick.

Slowly, I lift myself from the chair and shuffle toward Marez. His hand closes around my shoulder.

"Wait," Karl says. "Just . . . a moment. Wait." He digs the heels of his palms into his temples. "All right, all right, I'll tell you."

Marez runs his tongue over the edge of his teeth. Behind him, I catch Jorn's eyes; anger smolders on his face; he's giving Marez the sort of look he used to reserve for Stargazer lieutenants who compelled him to fight other tunnelers to the death in brawling rings. But I'm not in any danger—Marez must be calling Karl's bluff.

Marez releases my shoulder and returns to his seat, eyes never leaving Karl. I rub my shoulder where Marez had gripped it too hard, and follow them back to the table.

Just a play on Marez's part. Nothing to be nervous about.

"They were babblin' about dreams," Karl says. "She was askin' him to hide her soul in her dreams, something like that. Make her live forever."

I stare at Karl, dumbfounded. Is it even possible to do what he's suggesting? I think back to the building I saw flickering through the trees in Oneiros last night—I'd forgotten about it in my panic to escape those horrible beasts. But if a person *were* capable of preserving her soul inside Oneiros, to continue her treachery even after death . . .

Karl continues to bore through the table with his gaze. Marez, always one for subtlety, merely lifts one brow. "And how reliable is this friend of yours?" Marez asks, words oozing with cloying contempt.

"I . . . he . . . Okay. He works for the Stargazers, okay? And he didn't just overhear the conversation." Karl leans in closer. "The Stargazers boss paid him to bring the guy into the jail so he could talk with Lady Twyne."

The Stargazers—tangled up in more than just shady business dealings with Lady Twyne. I'm suddenly overcome with the urge to throw up. Dreamer, why do the Stargazers have to be involved? Anyone but them.

I look back at him and Karl, and try to summon Brandt's skill for playing roles. "It's frightening to think," I say. I manage a watery smile. "Traitors like Sindra Twyne preserving themselves through dreams?"

Marez lifts his tumbler in a toast. "May your Dreamer protect us from whatever it may mean."

I toast with them, but look to Jorn again. Jorn is not a small mammal; though he's all muscle and hair, I'd wager he weighs more than some ponies. The look on his face, though, at the mention of the Stargazers is like the look of a wolf facing an even larger predator. He may be brave enough to sail into the dark metal heart of the Land of the Iron Winds with us tomorrow, but I don't know if either of us has the stomach to face down Adolphus Retch again.

Not after the Stargazer Incident.

Chapter Fifteen

Jornisander the Destroyer—a name long drenched in blood. A prized fighter in the tunnel brawling rings, where victory only came from total annihilation. The iron fist of the Stargazer gang, protecting the gang leader from enemies real and imagined as he carried out whatever gruesome tasks the leader didn't wish to soil his own hands with.

But Jorn was always more than a hammer and a blade. He saw the way the gangs exacted revenge, extracted payment, exploited tunnelers, all while fattening their own purses and those of the aristocrats who colluded with them. He believed life could be different for himself and all tunnelers. And so he decided to spill some blood of his own.

A murdered gang lieutenant here and there, some aristocrat's accountant found strangled in his sleep—the blood stains spread far, though I can't say anyone mourned their passing. All of his victims were monsters in their own rights—one prostituted tunneler children to vulgar aristocrats; one beat a tunneler woman to death for failing to offer a suitable tithe.

Jorn recruited more disgruntled tunnelers to his cause, and they branched out from random violence into more precision strikes. Some of his allies, too, turned to other means—educating tunnelers, urging them to resist the gangs' demands, fighting for rights and pay and even, most improbably of all, citizenship for all tunnelers. Jorn only set it in motion, but the movement grew far beyond his vengeful killings to protect tunnelers who'd been wronged. Eventually, the Ministry couldn't ignore whatever campaign was taking place. And there was Jorn, right at the source.

The Ministry convinced him to secretly inform to them on the gang leaders and their activities. With Jorn's help, Durst promised, they could root out corruption and exploitation through legal means, and help the Destroyers advance their cause of emancipation for the tunnelers (though, of course, they couldn't support it outright). From the information Jorn passed us, the Ministry dismantled three Dreamless dens, five gambling houses, and an elaborate smuggling scheme that stretched across Barstadt's northern colonies.

Jorn was good at what he did, and while the Ministry knew there were always risks, it was only a matter of time before the Destroyers' successes started to put Jorn in danger. Adolphus Retch, the leader of the Stargazer gang, liked the prestige of keeping a winning brawler like Jorn as his pet, but Jorn wanted to see Retch burn. For Jorn, it was personal, given the countless times Retch had sent Jorn into the brawling ring to kill or be killed with no other options as a born tunneler. But the Ministry had other reasons, too, to bring the Stargazers down—not least of all for the chaos they sowed within the tunnels and without. The Stargazers were, after all, the biggest and cruelest of the gangs; rumors of Retch's evil deeds were whispered like warnings to keep tunnelers and aristocrats alike in their thrall. Durst proposed an extraction when he feared the risk to Jorn was too great—we'd pull Jorn out of the tunnels in a spectacular fashion, make it look like he'd been killed so no one would come looking for him to blame, and grab as much dirt on Retch as we could on the way out. Turn it over to the courts. Use Jorn's detailed testimony to see Retch tried for his crimes.

Durst chose Brandt to helm the mission. Brandt and I had mostly done trifling operations thus far, infiltrating alehouses and the like, but this mission was complicated and needed a dreamstrider. Brandt was certain I was ready to handle something more. Durst agreed to put me on the team, not only for the close access dreamstriding offered into paranoid Retch's inner circle, but, it seemed to me, to convince himself that I'd really lived up to all Hesse had promised about me after all.

This would be the first mistake.

I remember clearly the way I felt, sitting in the briefing room while Brandt reviewed his plans with us. The bright blossom of excitement unfurling within me, of pride, of a sense of rightness within the world. If I served the Dreamer right, I'd help Barstadt. I'd help the case for the Writ of Emancipation. If I could be strong enough, good enough. I believe I could be, at last. That the Dreamer would give me the strength.

Jornisander and Thrum, one of Jorn's fellow vigilantes, met Vera, Brandt, and me at the back entrance of the Stargazers' resin warehouse down by the docks. My eyes bulged at the sight of them—Jorn, larger than life, like a stone carving that should be holding up a colonnade in the Imperial Quarter, and Thrum, nearly as tall, but wide enough to seal shut a tunnel line.

They had already knocked out one of Retch's lieutenant's, Synarius, and they took us to the storage room where they'd stashed his unconscious body. Brandt produced a scarf from his ridiculously dapper vest and feathered it under Synarius's nose. I pulled a face before gulping down my dreamwort elixir, and when I opened Synarius's eyes I found Vera pouring a cloudy liquid, like overskimmed milk, from a pitcher into smaller bottles at the bottom of her cart.

Brandt spread a grimy oilcloth over my body in the corner. "Are we almost ready?"

"Almost." Vera kept one eye on me as she topped off the rest of the jars.

I pulled myself to standing. Too fast, but I was impatient, ready to jump into the action and prove myself. I wasn't used to Synarius's scratchy eyes and legs like coiled springs. And the smell from whatever Vera was pouring—sharp, making my head spin from vicious little fingers that sank into my skin and held tight. Then, as I tried to move, Synarius's feet snagged on the bundles of ropes on the storage room floor—

I caught myself, but when I tripped, I'd splashed the substance Vera had been pouring all over her right arm, her chest, her shoulder. She sucked down a deep breath and proceeded to swear at me as quietly as she could manage.

"I'm sorry, I'm sorry! I'm still gaining my footing!" I snatched a scrap of fabric from her cart, nearly upending the remaining jars of liquid, then started smearing the scrap all over her wet gown.

"Give me that, you imbecile, before you kill us both." She ripped it from my hands—from Synarius's hands. "Do you have any idea what this is?"

"Your—your liquor. That you and Brandt are pretending to sell to Retch." Synarius's voice wasn't equipped for such a meek, shuddering tone.

"And also a highly dangerous, *highly* flammable, *highly un-stable* compound. Lion's milk." She sighed. "Didn't you read the mission brief? We're using it to burn this warehouse to the ground."

"I'm sorry," I whispered again.

Vera opened her mouth to continue the tongue lashing, but Brandt spoke first. "Vera. Are you a part of this team, or not?"

Vera's mouth slowly eased shut.

"Good. Then respect your team members—all of them. We have a job to do." He turned toward me. "Be careful. Take it slow if his body's throwing you off, all right?"

I nod, tension easing away.

Jorn knocked on the storage room door before poking his head inside. "It's time."

Jorn accompanied Brandt and Vera into the main warehouse, where Stargazer lackeys stirred giant vats of the noxious Lullaby resin, while we waited in the storage room for them to carry out their charade. I could smell it from our storage room, mingling with the spilled lion's milk, twitching at Synarius's bulbous nose. Thrum watched me with eyebrows stitched together, like he was waiting for the Synarius he knew and feared to reemerge.

Through the tin walls, I could hear Brandt's voice rising and falling in his easy salesman patter as he wheedled with Retch. Retch was having none of it—I could tell from his truncated responses—but it didn't matter. As long as we had Retch on edge.

Thrum rested a hand on my shoulder. "Are you ready?"

The Ministry of Affairs' reports on Synarius scrolled through my head. His quirks, his hatreds and likes (mostly hatreds), his relationship with Adolphus Retch. They were cousins, after a fashion, and had grown up on the streets together, but Adolphus was always one step ahead, a little nimbler on his feet and crueler in his deal making. I was nervous, but I felt prepared. As prepared as I could reasonably be.

I followed Thrum into the main corridor.

"Boss." Thrum stuck his head into the warehouse, and I caught a glimpse of Brandt, freezing mid-gesture as he bartered with Retch. Dreamer, but he looked so confident—shoulders back, head high, lips curled with satisfaction. I pushed my shoulders back, trying to show even a fraction of his cool. "Synarius is here. Want me to take him to your office?"

Retch nodded. "I've heard enough of these jokers. Let's go."

Jorn's mouth twisted. "Boss, you promised you'd hear out my friends."

Retch's face turned ghastly in the lamplight; for a moment the only sound was of the resin brewers churning the vats with their wooden paddles. "I don't give a damn what I promised you." Retch turned to Brandt. "Look, I couldn't care less about your special brewing method. I wouldn't care if it made me shit gold. Piss off, and if I catch you trying to sell this garbage in my market, I'll hang you from the rafters by your balls."

Jorn squares his shoulders. "But, boss—"

Retch silenced him instantly with a raised eyebrow. "I could swear I just gave you an order. You heard that, didn't you, Synarius?"

I swallowed hard. "Aye, I heard that."

Retch whirled back to Jorn with a knife-blade smile on his lips. "So I did. I worry you've forgotten your place, Jorn. You may be friend to every tunneler, but at the end of the day, you report to me. You belong to me." He shooed Brandt and Vera off. "Get your tunnel rat friends out of here, then join us in the office."

Jorn nodded, curt but confident. We'd counted on Retch to turn him down, of course; but I could see some of Jorn's hatred for Retch dancing in his eyes. He and Thrum could easily have killed this man if they wished. They were both trusted guards; they both had regular access to Retch and plenty of brute strength behind them. But they were only two men, and the Ministry could do so much more to dismantle the gangs, see Retch tried for his crimes, possibly even help them liberate the tunnelers. They wanted to see the Stargazers destroyed.

For a moment I let Synarius's features soften as these thoughts ran through my head. I suppose I'll never know if that was the second mistake.

"What did you think of the girl I sent you last night?" Retch asked, striding past Thrum and me to climb the stairs to his office. "Eh? A fighter, wasn't she?"

"Quite the treat," I said casually, not wanting to dip into Synarius's consciousness.

This, this would be the third mistake.

"All right, all right, all business today, aren't we? About time you took our work seriously." Retch led us into the office, where a skylight afforded him a dazzling view of the stars. My gaze, though, went straight to the safe in the corner as Retch made his way toward it—our final prize. With Retch's logbook, we could dismantle the entire Stargazer gang, bring Retch to justice, out every corrupt aristocrat to ever work with him . . . My heart pounded at the thought. Justice for the tunnelers. For all of Barstadt. And with the corruption ripped out at its roots, the Writ of Emancipation was sure to pass.

The dial spun in Retch's fingers, loud as horse hooves in my heightened senses. A click and the door fell open. *Come on, Brandt.* I flexed Synarius's fingers. *Let's get this over with.*

"No! Damn you! I won't leave without selling a batch to Retch!"

Brandt's screech wafted up the stairs to the office, followed by a fierce clattering, like metal ringing against the copper resin vats. "Boss!" Jorn screeched. "Dammit, boss, come quick!"

Retch charged for the office door. In a blink, I saw the rest of our plan playing out. Retch, rushing down to the main room to see what the commotion was, and protect his prize crop—the Lullaby. Thrum seizing the logbook and hiding it in his substantial coat. Brandt striking the match and tossing it into the cart of lion's milk jars as Jorn pretends to evict him and Vera.

Fire. Chaos. And lots and lots of smoke to cover our movements. Thankfully, the milk was slow-burning enough that everyone could make it out safely, but Retch didn't need to know that. Once the whole warehouse was a pile of ash, there'd be no telling that Jorn and Thrum made it out alive, that the logbook hadn't been incinerated.

But Retch stopped at the office threshold. "Synarius."

Lakes have frozen over for less than that voice. Hearts have stopped for less.

"Want me to reason with 'em?" I asked.

"I was just thinking . . ." Retch tilted his head, unsettlingly calm despite the chaotic noises coming from the warehouse, and peered up through the port window cut into the ceiling of his office, bathing us in starlight. "About the girl I sent you last night."

I felt the apple of Synarius's throat twitching against the collar of his shirt. "Yes? What about her?"

Retch's eyes narrowed into knife slits. "That I didn't send you one."

Thrum's hand flew to his belt, but Retch was too fast. With one quick whistle through the air, Retch's dagger buried itself in Thrum's forehead, all the way to the hilt. Thrum crashed to the wooden floor, rattling the whole warehouse.

"Who are you?" Retch took slow steps toward me. He didn't need to hurry—he already had a fresh dagger in his palm. "You look just like my lieutenant. Sound identical. But you can't be him."

"Please, Adolphus!" I threw up Synarius's hands. Retch circled around me like a wolf; over my shoulder, Brandt, Vera, and Jorn continued to shout and stomp about, oblivious to the situation unfolding in the office. "It's me, Synarius! We've known each other since we were kids!"

"Then you know I will kill you. No matter how close we are."

I leaped for the doorway, stumbling on Synarius's thick legs and crashing to the floor. Retch's knife embedded itself into the doorframe, where my hand had been moments before. I gripped the staircase railing to pull myself up, but he snatched me by Synarius's thick ankles. "Abort!" I screamed. "Abort the mission!"

Then Retch's wooden plank connected with the back of Synarius's head.

Flashes. Blood-smeared images of the warehouse, of Jorn and Brandt and Vera running toward me, still hauling that cart full of lion's milk. Adolphus Retch's ghoulish face glaring down at me like a denizen of Nightmare made flesh. Retch screaming that my whole family would burn, that I'd be fed to his hounds. And that piece of lumber, chasing me as I skidded and rolled down the stairs; connecting with Synarius's thick body, again and again, snapping my bones and slicking my eyesight with blood. I had to get closer to the storage room, where my body lay. If I could drag myself just a little farther—

Dimly I felt the pain bubble through as I forced myself out of Synarius's body and went into Oneiros.

I grabbed the lead back to my body and woke up tangled in

a musty tarp in the storage room, surrounded by screams from the other side of the door as Synarius woke back up to his cousin beating in his skull. I seized a torch from the wall and burst back out of the storage room. "Let's go!" I wheezed. "Now!"

And Vera widened her eyes at me too late as I pitched the torch into the cart of lion's milk jars.

Where the gauzy sleeve of her dress tangled in the wooden slats.

It was Jorn, in the end, who saved all of us. He scooped up Vera even as her dress caught fire and shoved Brandt and me toward the door. Vera screamed as the flames dug deep into her flesh; my last glimpse was of Brandt frantically helping her beat them out. Jorn didn't even look back for Thrum; I think he already knew.

"I'll find you, Jorn. You and all your friends. I'll tear the flesh from you myself! I'll destroy you!"

As Retch turned to stop him, Jorn kicked the cart over, spilling the now-flaming liquid all over the warehouse floor.

Synarius may have been Stargazer scum the same as Retch, but no one deserved to go like that—beaten alive and set aflame. Thrum certainly deserved better. If anyone deserved to die that night, it was Retch himself. But he survived, even if most of the warehouse did not, and he rebuilt the Stargazer empire.

And Jorn, who should have led the investigation into the Stargazers, revealing that he was alive only after we'd built our case and he was no longer in danger of assassination, has instead been relegated to a twilight land. Retch can't go after him without drawing heat from the Ministry, but neither can Jorn operate in Stargazer territory without opening himself to an attack from Retch's men.

Months passed before I could look Vera or Jorn in the eye without seeing those flames, that knife buried to its hilt. Without hearing Vera's screams. Smelling her arm as it cooked. Envisioning all the tunnelers who believed in Jorn that I'd now betrayed. I never looked up in the inquisition; I barely answered Minister Durst's questions. The unspoken truth hung in a fog around us like the stink of lion's milk: were I anyone but the dreamstrider, I'd be back in the tunnels now, begging for scraps of food.

I can never forget where I've come from, where I deserve to be. And I will never forget what it's cost me and everyone who crosses my path. I'd be a fool to think they've forgotten, too.

Chapter Sixteen

"Treatise on the Transference of Matter Between Oneiros and Barstadt." Brandt holds up a battered old folio
with a crease in its center that looks like it was used to
prop up a wobbly chair. "One of Hesse's papers, I take it?"

I settle into the cot, curled on myself like a cat. We're holed
up in one of the berths on board the clipper *Sunrise Siren*. By
tomorrow evening, we'll have transformed it into a standard
Land of the Iron Winds river skimmer, complete with appropriate documentation, flags, and cargo, but until then, I've been
poring over a selection of Professor Hesse's journals. "He willed
them to me. I thought I'd pass the time reading up on them—
see if there's any mention of the—the key in that note."

Brandt grimaces as he leans against the wooden post. "Drat.
I meant to stop by the constabulary before we departed to see
if they'd made any progress on their investigation." He squeezes
his eyes shut. "I'm sorry, Liv. I know I promised to help you.
It's only—there's a rather lot going on . . ."

I suspect he means with his engagement, but I'm in no mood

to dwell on that. "Yes, well, Vera's theatrics of late have been very, uh, distracting . . ."

My feeble attempt at lightheartedness clatters between us. I shrink back into my cot and try to resume reading while Brandt looks over at my box of Hesse's notes.

"There's an awful lot of material here," he says. "Care for some help?"

"By all means. Any reference to the key, or some sort of technique or note that might match up with what Marez's informant told us about Lady Twyne's soul or attempting to resurrect Nightmare."

Brandt flips through the folio with a deepening furrow in his brow. "This could take some time. Shall I see if Edina would help us, too?"

A great pressure weighs down on me. "I, uh . . ." I cast around for a suitable excuse. "I'd hate to trouble Edina with some silly pursuit of mine."

"Silly? Why would she think it silly?" Brandt frowns. "Edina thinks very highly of you. She's told me as much herself."

My chest aches at his words—at the thought of him discussing me with his betrothed. "Well, Vera certainly doesn't think much of her. The way they're at each other's throats."

"Yes, well, Vera has her . . . own reasons for that."

"Because of Edina's father?" I ask.

Brandt works his jaw back and forth; his gaze is intensely focused on Professor Hesse's treatise before him. "I suppose that's part of it."

"But not all of it." I put one finger in the spine of the note-book and tilt it down so Brandt must look at me. "What ever happened between them? I suppose I've never had to work closely with both of them at the same time before. I nearly got Vera burned alive and she doesn't look at me with half as much contempt."

Brandt hesitates a moment, gaze boring into me, then tosses the journal aside with a sigh. "Very well, I suppose it's best you hear it from me." He leans back in his cot. "You know how I told you Edina had been involved with . . . someone before."

"Right," I say. It's my turn to furrow my brow.

Brandt ruffles his bangs, then holds his hand over his face as he speaks. "Well, it was Vera."

"Oh." Then, letting the full weight of his words sink in, "*Ohh*. Right. Because aristocrats aren't as understanding about two women fancying each other as we tunneler folk are."

"That's putting it mildly." Brandt rubs at the side of his jaw as he searches for the right words. "Just as it is the duty of every son and daughter of an aristocratic house to marry, in order to further their family's fortunes, so too is it their sworn duty to produce heirs to advance each House into the next generation."

"So what happened?" I ask.

"Well, this was before Vera joined the Ministry, mind you. She and Edina had debuted at the same social season and be-came fast friends, and then more, but Vera's family would have none of it. They're merchants, you know, and badly wanted Vera to marry a man of higher station in order to elevate their own status. So Vera reacted as you might expect."

"Rashly?" I say.

Brandt grins. "Yes, more or less. She abandoned her family, forsook her inheritance, and joined up with the Ministry instead. When they sought Lord Alizard's blessing, however, he gave Edina an ultimatum: that he'd have Vera killed if Edina didn't end things with her. This is what Edina told me in confidence, mind you—Lord Alizard's shady gang ties are still an open secret amongst political circles." Brandt shakes his head. "So she ended it. But the damage had already been done with Vera's family; and neither of them is willing to stop their work with the Ministry, and Minister Durst has begged them to keep the peace for the Ministry's sake."

My mind whirs. "But if Edina fancies—or fancied—Vera . . ."

Brandt's smile fades, and he sits up straighter. "She—she fancies . . ." His face burns a deep crimson. "Um, she fancies men and women both. I'm—this isn't a sham—"

"Look at you." I laugh. "You can't even *talk* about it without getting flustered. How will you ever survive marriage?"

The truth of my words hangs heavy between us. His marriage to Edina. A whole lifetime with her, away from the Ministry. Away from me. Brandt twists away from me, and I'm sinking, deeper and deeper into the cot.

I don't want to lose Brandt, but perhaps it's already too late. I can't forget how he left me the night after Hesse's death, how his duty was already calling him away when I needed him most.

No matter how skilled of a dreamstrider I become, I can't bring him back to me. I can't keep my friend forever. Perhaps it's time I worry about what comes next.

Brandt reaches for Hesse's journal again. "How about I—let's—let's look for a mention of this key."

"Let's," I say, too loud.

01 Tremmer's Month, 618 AN
35, 36, and 39 are the best batch of recruits thus far—their grasp on their own dreams is uncanny, and 39 has already showed an aptitude for remaining lucid, owing in my mind to his exceptional piety and contrition in the university temple. He correctly described the general layout of the temple at the heart of Oneiros after a fortuitous albeit brief slip out of his shallow dreams; tonight I will give him a sample dosage of dreamwort elixir.

I don't know if I can keep going through with this. I try to put on a brave face for 12, because she has trouble enough trusting in herself. But the weight of my failure is crushing down on me. Souls are surprisingly heavy things.

Subject 12. That must be me. Eleven others died before he reached success through me? I suppress the groan clawing its way up my throat. *Why, Dreamer, why did I deserve to live?* I skim through the next few entries until another one catches my eye, later the same year.

09 Juliar Month, 618 AN

35, 36, and 39 are still progressing in the trials. They are responding positively to the dreamwort potion and have thus far successfully entered Oneiros with it on two occasions each (three for 39), but even 12 was controlling her trips to Oneiros at this stage in the trials. Sadly, she remains the sole bright light in this zealot's folly. I don't want to push them too hard, but against the only dreamstrider I can compare them to, they are already lagging behind. But they've survived Oneiros as it is; this seems proof enough to me they have a chance.

Long discussion with Durst about 12's performance and his desire to produce more dreamstriders to better expand the Ministry's capabilities. He is certain 12 is only the beginning of what can be achieved. 12 proved the concept, but he wants more dreamstriders—skilled ones, experienced ones, instead of clumsy youths. He wants to see what a fully capable dreamstrider can do. I pray to the Dreamer every night that he's right, that I am not giving fuel to Nightmare's remnants, feeding the Wastes without cause.

I fear my research has led me astray once more. The binding ritual, the technique of transference . . . I worry more and more now of what could become of them if the research fell into the wrong hands. Not only for the heresies I've uncovered about Nightmare's death, but for the power in these truths . . .

I lean back, head swirling. The binding ritual? Hesse had never mentioned any such research to me. What is it he was trying to bind? And what did he mean about Nightmare's death?

> Despite his slow progress, 39 has all the makings of
> a skillful dreamstrider, but his earlier piety has been
> replaced by an insatiable quest for power. I will take him
> off the experiments for the rest of the month and see if
> that cools his heels. If he survives what is to come, the
> Ministry will be thrilled. But it is too much to hope for at
> this stage.

So Minister Durst is "satisfied" with me, but was continuing to look for someone better. What sort of someone? A man? An aristocrat? Someone with strength, a strong voice, a keener mind and quicker wit than mine? I can't even refute it. I'm at best an instrument on operations, a somewhat cumbersome tool that must be brought to the site but only performs adequately. But as everyone on this ship knows, I'm a disaster, a liability, the stuck cog in an otherwise fluid device.

Why can't I be more?

"Livia?" Brandt asks, lifting his head. "Did you find something?"

"No." The page blurs before me; I squeeze my eyes shut and try to steady my breathing. "Well . . . yes. Maybe." Calm down, Livia. After a count of three, I open my eyes and am composed once more. "These mentions of Nightmare's remnants. What I've been experiencing in Oneiros of late . . ."

And that horrid dream I had after Lady Twyne's execution. Surely it was a rebel priest, playing a prank on me. Or maybe I was not in Oneiros at all, and only believed myself to be.

"Hmm," Brandt says.

I lift my chin. "*Hmm*." But it stings my heart to jest with him like we always have. I don't know how I will continue like this, acting as if our connection is what it's always been. I force myself to frown.

"This is an odd one," Brandt says, bending back the cover on another treatise. " 'The Echoing Soul: Efforts at Preservation Via Oneiros.' "

I sputter, thinking of what the informant told Marez and me about Lady Twyne. "Go on."

"Joint research by Professor Hesse and an unnamed assistant on whether one's soul can be preserved in Oneiros after death. Their conclusion is that it is possible, but imperfect; they were unable to test it on any live subjects." He wrinkles his nose. "Too speculative for my tastes."

"And yet we hear that Lady Twyne attempted it all the same," I say.

Brandt rubs at his chin as he studies the notes before him. "So if Lady Twyne found a way to preserve her soul inside Oneiros . . ."

"But she couldn't have done it alone." I cast my thoughts back to Marez's and my conversation at the Dreamless den. "She had to have someone helping her. Someone who knew Hesse's research." I suddenly catch myself wishing Marez were here, to help me parse through the informant's tale for further clues, and my face flushes.

Brandt sits up straighter. "One of his students at the university, maybe. Or another professor. I know he kept the dream-striding research a secret, but these other treatises—we don't know how many people know of them."

I wrack my memory for the names and faces of some of Hesse's top students over the years. Two are priests in training at the High Temple now, and a handful more at the other temples throughout the city. Then there are the aristocrats who went back to their families after they completed their studies. None leap out at me as prime suspects to take part in such an awful conspiracy as this.

Edina pokes her head into the cabin. "Ahh, there you two are. The sun's about set. Mind helping out with dinner? Jorn's fished us up a few snapjacks."

Brandt swings his legs over the side of the cot. "As my lady requests." He swirls his arm and sweeps into an exaggerated bow. I stifle a giggle, and Edina regards him with a faint twist on her lips; I feel jealousy's prickle once more.

"Your lady requests fewer theatrics and more actual work. You can gut and dress the fish with Vera," she tells Brandt. "Livia, won't you help me prepare the tartlets?"

I catch Brandt's gaze out of the corner of my eye. "As my lady requests."

Brandt joins Vera and Jorn on deck while Edina and I duck into the mess. She pulls a wad of dough from the storage casks and spreads it out on the counter. "Forgive me if I come off as too harsh," Edina says as she rolls the dough with a pin. "Brandt can have all the fun he likes with his work, but I don't have that luxury. It's no easy feat for us, proving our worth to the Ministry as women."

"Minister Durst's fairer than most I've seen," I say, automatic as a ritual prayer. But I wonder if there's truth to it. I'm sent on countless missions because I'm the dreamstrider, but operatives like Vera are confined largely to parlor chatter and masquerades. Edina's rarely out in the field, instead left to tug at her puppets' strings from far away. She seems to enjoy that work, but if she wanted to be an operative, would Durst even give her the chance?

"He has his moments. I'm honored he's finally given me a chance to accompany you all this time, rather than trying to manage the mission from afar." She shakes her head. "A pity it's now, when I'm preparing to depart the Ministry."

To marry Brandt. I imagine Marez's voice in my head, how he might react to Edina's situation. Doubtless he'd condemn the minister's treatment of women the same way he condemns all the other rules of Barstadt society. Marez enjoys forcing people to confront uncomfortable truths, and I've yet to decide if it's a virtue or a nuisance. I'm certain he'd force me to confront my feelings for Brandt, if he knew. But there's no use, I keep telling myself. I keep rubbing that reassurance until it's raw.

"I know how much you mean to Brandt." Edina's speaking slowly now. "How he hates that he'll have to leave the Ministry. I can't imagine it'll be easy for you, either. But I hope you understand that it's not my choice. His parents, my father—" Edina rips the thin dough in half, and squashes each half into a new wad. "Well, it's for the best. We all must do our part for the Empire."

Not long ago, I would accept this without question. But now my mind is churning on thoughts of the looming war and Nightmare's possible return—of faraway lands and the Dreamer's silence and Hesse's reckless experiments and . . . Marez. Marez, who urged me to question the way things have always been done. To decide for myself.

"Brandt told me what happened to you, before," I say. Edina's shoulders tense. "I know it isn't my business, but . . . perhaps love is worth the risk."

Edina hands me a wad of dough to form into a tartlet. "I once thought so. But this is—it's safer. I'll be content with Brandt. I hope he feels the same about me. No, it isn't the sparks and passion I felt before, but I got burned plenty before, as well."

As if I'd expect anything less from Vera. "I do hope you find happiness," I say, because it sounds like something I ought to say.

"We'll be content. A solid enough life." Edina raises her chin. "But will you be all right?"

Her look—it isn't harsh, but it's unmistakable. She knows what I feel. My earlier confidence that I'd shoved down my feelings for Brandt fades away under that gaze. "I don't know what you mean," I say stiffly.

Edina sighs, and leans over to fix my lumpy tartlet's shape. "All right, Livia. We'll speak on other things. What did you learn in the journals?"

I tell her about Hesse's other research projects—the binding ritual. The Treatise on Transference. But my mind turns over and over on her question. Will I be all right without Brandt? What will I do once my citizenship papers are secured?

I've used my tunneler instincts thus far to survive. For a long time, I thought the ministry was key to my survival. But there's a whole world out there—beyond Barstadt and its colonies, beyond all of the Central Realms. Perhaps there's somewhere where survival won't seem such a struggle to me.

Perhaps, as Marez suggested, it's in Farthing.

Chapter Seventeen

I awaken to a scratching noise, and at first I draw my blanket tight around me, thinking the ship's rats have come out to play. But there's something too rhythmic in the sound, and it's nearby, not deep within the ship's innards. My eyes adjust to the fuzzy gray darkness, and I see light glinting off the whites of Brandt's eyes as he stares at the wooden post where he's scratching patterns with a pocketknife.

I swing my legs over the edge of my cot, ropes creaking, and stand slowly. I'm in loose trousers and a tunic, which must gleam like the moon in this darkness. Brandt's eyes flicker toward me, and I'm sure he's seen me up, but he turns his attention back to his lazy scratches.

I sit down on the floor beside his cot and rest my head against the post, just below where he's carving. He slowly folds up his penknife and lets his fingers dangle over the side of his cot, near my shoulder.

"You're afraid of something," Brandt says after a while. His voice rumbles through me, even though it's soft enough the others shouldn't be able to hear.

I'm afraid of a great many things. Nightmare, and the Commandant, and, most of all, losing Brandt. But I can't be afraid. Like Brandt said, fear is how I ruin a mission—how I don't push hard enough to reach for what we need most. Fear will only get me hurt. I have to build a thick wall between me and Brandt to keep out the pain and fear.

"I'm afraid of whatever is to come." It isn't a lie, but I can't tell him the whole truth. About my feelings for him, or my specific fears of Nightmare and the encroaching Wastes.

"You shouldn't be. You're going to do great works. You're the strongest person I know, Liv—truly. The Iron Winds should think twice about blowing against you."

That elicits a weary smile from me, despite my best efforts to the contrary. I hide it behind my knees. "But I'm not as strong as when I'm with my—my partner," I say.

I want to be angry at him because it's far easier than accepting the truth: that not all of my dreams can come true. That if I'm losing him, it must be because the Dreamer wills it. I can feel it itching under my skin, the delicious righteousness of my anger, carving a path like a whirlwind and smashing all my other feelings for him to bits. But it's not fair. Brandt's only doing his duty; he's done nothing wrong. I can't blame him any more than I could blame a hound for killing a rabbit; he's only done what he, as a son of an aristocratic House, was bred to do. Perhaps it's the Dreamer I should hate.

I love you, Brandt. The words wash ashore in my thoughts as the tide of anger recedes. *I love you, and it's torture to me.*

But what I say is, "Dream with me."

He raises his head up off the cot. "Are you certain?"

I nod. "If Lady Twyne hid her soul in Oneiros, then we should investigate." I finger the silver chain around my neck and fish the vial dangling from it out of my tunic. "If you drink the dreamwort potion, it will put your consciousness in Oneiros while you're fully awake."

He arches one brow at me. "I won't slip out of my body or anything like that?"

I press my lips together. "It's possible, but it's not very likely, unless you've become a dreamstrider yourself. Especially since you'll have the advantage of being fully conscious." I wave my hand at him. "Hesse started me off the same way. I'll be there beside you, I promise."

He taps his tongue to the lip of the uncorked vial and then recoils, lips snarled back. "Nightmare's bones. That's nasty." When I give him a stern look, though, he takes a tentative sip.

I swoop in for the vial as his head hits the pillow, his body stone stiff. I position myself to lie flat on the floor and take a drink of my own.

A flock of crows shrieks and scatters away from us as I open my eyes, blinking away the haze. Without pulling free of my tether, as I usually do, I drag myself to a sitting position and let my loose dress spread around me. I'm resting on soft, loamy

215

earth under a canopy of dark pines. Their tiered, needled skirts surge far overhead into a dull gray sky.

"Brandt?" I call, though not too loud; memories of the horrific beasts last time I visited Oneiros warn me from that.

A groan answers me to my left. He's facedown in a patch of moss, attempting to flop himself onto his back, like a wallowing swine. He looks so ill at ease in his own skin that I have to laugh in spite of myself.

"S'not funny," he mutters through a mouthful of dirt. "You could have at least warned me."

"Sorry." I offer him a hand. "Usually I appear upright."

Brandt brushes dirt and moss away from his prim tweed suit while I survey our surroundings. If I'm not mistaken, this is the forest to the northeast of the city that slowly rises into the mountains. I listen through the trees: the shushing of pine boughs against one another in the breeze, the subdued chatter of birds. No thunderous wings. No stench of decay. Just the moist, earthy scent of the forest and a cool, distant stream.

"We're looking for Professor Hesse's cottage," I tell Brandt, pointing north of the clearing. "I want to know if he left us any clues about the binding ritual. And once we're done there"—I swallow—"we'll investigate the building I saw."

Brandt nods, trotting alongside me as I weave through the pines on a faded trail of tamped-down needles. "Are there people here? Awake ones, I mean."

"They usually stay in the city, but a few priests have homes in the woods, or on the beach, or—anywhere, really. There's a desert to the west, mountains to the north, the sea to our south . . ."

He laughs hoarsely to himself. "You dreamfolk are quite the wild bunch, aren't you?"

I wince, guilt rippling through me. As if I deserve to be lumped in with the Dreamer's true devout. I crunch along in silence, leaving Brandt to stroll wide-eyed.

Professor Hesse's cottage spills out of another clearing in the forest, surrounded by an explosion of flowers: clematis, bougainvillea, roses, chrysanthemum, mothwood blossoms, tulips in every hue. None would grow together in the real world, but here they live side by side, craving no sunlight and demanding no rain. I push aside a sunflower the size of my head to unlatch the wrought iron gate and hold it open for Brandt.

"Madness!" he exclaims. "I love it. It's all mad."

"Wait until you see inside," I say with a grin.

The whitewashed cottage, looking like a two-room affair from the outside, opens up into a cathedral of marble and glass within. A grand promenade cuts down the center of the foyer, a glistening reflecting pool at its heart, then branches off to a colossal five-story library to the right and a quaint rough-hewn kitchen to the left.

"He spent his whole life Shaping it." My voice wavers—but how can I be sad? His dreamworld home brings me closer to his mind and his memories than I ever was in life. The filigree pattern carved into the columns reminds me of his stories of his time studying theosophy amongst Barstadt's northern colonies;

the library is bursting with the spines of all his favorite books on dreams, even those that were ruined when his old office flooded. Remnants of my earlier dream about that office flit through my mind, but I bat them away.

This is Professor Hesse, right here—not the shriveled-up specter of misery in his filthy office, or the careless, restless corpse. I let Brandt wander off, but I'm taking my time, running my fingers over every surface, trying to pay homage to the Professor Hesse who deserves to be memorialized in this way. *I should have come here earlier*, I think, but I wasn't ready before. I'm not completely sure I'm ready now.

"Livia?" Brandt calls from somewhere in the labyrinth of the library. "You need to see this."

I run into the library and wind my way around the gleaming mahogany shelves, though with each passing second they expand into an endless sea of books, Shaped into a massive piece of machinery forever in motion. I can't see Brandt, so I close my eyes and let Brandt's essence guide me—his breathing, thrumming *being* that I would know anywhere. In Oneiros, it calls to me like a lighthouse.

He stands in front of a parquetted wood cabinet, a golden key jutting from its face like a knife.

"A key," I say, the wind rushing out of me. "You don't suppose it's . . . ?"

"Nothing is coincidence in fieldwork." Brandt throws the cabinet door wide.

But it's empty. Three narrow shelves are lined with dust and nothing more. I trace my fingers through the dust and find a square where something must have sat until recently. A box? A book?

"You don't suppose he kept some of his research here, do you? What he asked you to destroy?" Brandt says.

"Seems likely. But then who took it?"

"Odd." Brandts fingertips trace a painted drawing on the back of the cabinet door. It looks like an old star chart. A constellation of bright golden splotches stand out from the tinier flecks along the solid black wood, but I can't decipher their shape.

"Any priest of the Dreamer could have come here." I cast my gaze around the silent, cavernous room. "Do you honestly think one of the Dreamer's faithful would have threatened Hesse, though? The note about the key . . ."

Brandt swings the cabinet door shut. "It's an appalling thought, but anything's possible. You don't know any devious priests, do you?"

"Unscrupulous, maybe, down in Dreamer Square, selling interpretations for absurd amounts." I shake my head. "But those sorts are rarely devout enough to serve as Shapers. This is . . . this is sacred ground. The thought of someone threatening an innocent old man, desecrating his—his memorial—" I choke back my words as a sob wrenches out of me.

Brandt tucks a lock of my hair back behind my ear. His face is serious, but tender; I can't tell if he's wearing a mask or not. Is it easier for him to modulate his appearance in Oneiros, or harder? "Livia. We'll find whoever's done this. Whatever they're after—we won't let them succeed."

He'd said something similar to me, that day after Hesse's death. Yet he left me then all the same. I want to sink into Brandt's touch, however faint it might be. But I must be stronger than that. I'm not here to connive a tender moment out of an engaged man, no matter what I feel for him. My eyes meet his, a liquid shade of smoke with only the dimmest hint of green.

"Let's check on that house you saw," Brandt says, shifting awkwardly.

"Hold on to my hand." We link our fingers together. "Try to forget that you're not supposed to be able to fly."

Within moments, I'm drifting into the air, but Brandt keeps bobbing, raising up for a few seconds only to tug me back down as he recalls he's doing the impossible. "Dreams of death," he mutters. "I don't know how you manage."

I tug hard and send him flying into the air with me, dangling from our joined hands. "You're lucky you're weightless here," I say with a grin. I fly us to the city streets, in part so I can get my bearings before our next destination, but also so I can show Brandt this strange and wonderful landscape. We land on the cobblestones in the heart of the High Priest's Plaza, right before my favorite dreamshaper structure of all: an undulating fortress covered in mosaic tiles of every imaginable color. I can taste its dazzling hues in my mouth like the bubbliest cider.

Brandt spins in a slow circle, a smile lacquered onto his face. "Liv. This is just amazing!"

"A far cry from the dreary black and white of Barstadt City, isn't it?" I smile back.

He fixes his sights on the towering Temple of the Dreamer

beyond us, but as he's staring at its golden disc, a priestess rounds the corner and shoots us a fierce glare. "This isn't a place for you." She charges toward me, her index finger waggling. "It isn't safe."

I raise both my hands. "It's all right. I'm not a lost sleeper—I can handle myself here."

"Only the most devout are allowed in Oneiros. We'll have to usher you back into your own mind—"

"Please! We're doing no harm," I say, but a crowd is gathering around us. Priests and priestesses, assuming all manner of surreal costumes, crowd around us. A hat has manifested in Brandt's hand for him to worry over, which he does vigorously; he looks like he's wringing it out to dry. "Listen." I moisten my suddenly parched lips. "I think Oneiros may be in danger."

"What do you know of it?" An older priest surges forward, his flesh pulled taut like leather around the smooth knobs of his joints. "Did you invite this darkness?"

"So you've seen it, too. We think there's a rogue priest out there, and . . ." I slump forward. "He may have killed Albrecht Hesse."

"Hesse!" The word ricochets through the crowd, hissing and contemptuous.

"Hesse. Hesse! A disgrace to the Dreamer. May Nightmare chew his soul for eternity." The old priest sneers at me—daring me to contradict him.

My face burns. "He only tried to do what was best for Barstadt. Why would the Dreamer give us Oneiros if not to use it to help our people?"

"You call it help, what you do? Stealing others' bodies, tempting the Wastes with your soul? It's a disgrace!"

I stammer, searching for a retort, but Brandt charges toward them. "Hesse and Livia have done more to protect Barstadt than your lot ever will. Hoarding the Dreamer's world all for yourselves? *That's* what's disgraceful."

I cringe as the priests' gasps wash over us. "That's not quite what he meant," I tell them. Even if I've wondered the same. I want to believe the Dreamer has a reason for structuring us this way, but after my last few conversations with Marez, I'm not so sure. I wonder if the Farthinger approach is better—let all those able to succeed do as they please.

"It's exactly what I meant. You treat her like an outsider, but what have you done to preserve this place?" Brant's cheeks burn crimson; the hat he's thoroughly strangled is stretching, long and sinuous.

The lead priest jabs a finger to Brandt's chest. "Hundreds of years ago, we stood against Nightmare. We shaped this all in the Dreamer's name. Is it coincidence that this abomination, this . . ." He flicks his hand up and down the length of me. "This *dreamstrider* arrives in the same age as the winged beasts? Perhaps it's her doing."

I shake my head, even as their hands grasp for my curls, assessing me like they expect me to turn into one of those horrible monsters. "Please, no. I'm looking for the same villains you are—a renegade priest, making false promises to the Commandant—"

"Prove it!" the head priest cries.

"Prove it!" the crowd echoes, their words bouncing back at us from the tops of their buildings, from all around.

"Very well," I say. *Dreamer, I know you're not in the habit of answering my prayers, at least not in any way that's clear to me— but please, Dreamer, show me what I need to see now.* "Come with me and I will."

We surge north, Brandt and I, like a great comet with an icy tail of disbelieving priests in their white shifts. My hands tremble as I search the mountainside. The hulking bones of Nightmare loom on the hill, mirroring the ones in Barstadt City, but I school my eyes away from them as I search for that flicker I'd seen two nights past. There—how such solid stone can look so frail and soft, I'll never know, but I recognize it in an instant. We land on the path.

"Livia?" Brandt asks, hand still tangled in mine. "This isn't what I think it is, is it?"

"An alabaster manor house? A flawless replica of the one in the Cloister of Roses, recently vacated by one Sindra Twyne?"

He grimaces. "That would be the one."

Please, Dreamer, let Marez's informant be wrong.

That high-pitched humming again—fraying at my consciousness as we draw nearer. I feel it tugging me forward, across the steps, toward the entrance . . . The head priest pushes past us when we reach the front door. "What's happened to this building? Is this your doing?"

It takes me a moment, standing perfectly still on the porch, to realize what he's talking about. I sense a tremor in the bowels of Oneiros, an aching like a tunneler's empty gut. Chill that stings from the inside.

"I didn't cause any of this darkness to seep into Oneiros. I'm trying to stop it, same as you." I meet his stare beat for beat, too terrified to blink. The earth rumbles under my feet as if some great beast has rolled over.

"Dreamstrider." His lips pull tight against his teeth. "Denizen of Nightmare."

"You think *I'm* in league with monsters? Which of your Shapers built this place?"

He grips the doorknob, but it rusts away clean in his hand.

We both stagger back as the door creaks inward. The darkness inside Twyne's estate is hungry, threatening; I feel it tugging us toward the door like a living thing. The priest glares at me, takes an uneasy step forward, and pushes it open further. A stench like spoiled meat unleashes on us, hitting me square in the chest like a cruel memory—

And suddenly Brandt and I are gasping for air in the darkened cargo hold of the clipper. I claw at my arms, trying to rake away the fear I felt in Oneiros, before I realize I've left it behind. Brandt's hand gropes for mine; he seizes the silver vial from my hands. "We have to stop it! We can't just leave them there."

I fumble for him in the pitch black of the cargo hold and jerk the vial back. "Brandt, don't!"

"But what about the priest?" He reaches toward me but only succeeds in overturning his cot. He spills across the floor with a horrendous clatter.

"Hexers!" Jorn shrieks, leaping to his feet. He crouches into a fighting stance with flat palms raised before him.

"Great work. You've frightened the nasty Hexers off," I tell Jorn. "Go back to sleep."

Brandt narrows his eyes at me as Jorn crawls back into his cot. "That awful . . . wave. It was like a cloud of fear. I can't even describe it properly. Liv, if that's what I think it is . . ."

Nightmare. I want desperately for him to be wrong—for both of us to be. But I feel the grim slam of terror hitting me, just like that oppressive wall, just like the pounding wings, just like the maddening chants. I can't wish it or dream it away. I only hope the Shapers can find a way to contain it while we seek answers in Birnau.

"Lady Twyne's death is only the beginning, I fear." I swallow hard. "Something evil has been unleashed in Oneiros. We have to reach Birnau in time to stop whatever comes next."

Chapter Eighteen

By the time we enter the River of Bronze Sunsets, the clipper has been thoroughly transformed to a Land of the Iron Winds fishing vessel, complete with a hold stuffed with the anemic fish we managed to scoop up a few hours before dawn. We wear simple, loose tunics and trousers in drab blues and grays, and we've lightened our skin by rubbing talcum powder into it, like Brandt and I did last time in our carriage drivers' costumes. It won't hold up to close scrutiny, but we'll hail the dock patrols outside Birnau from a distance. Entering the City of Sacred Secrets, Birnau, will be another matter entirely.

"Just smile and wave," Brandt coaches us through gritted teeth, as we sail under the high-spanning bridges of the fringe town. "Smile like it's a damned honor to toil away for the Commandant's pleasure."

We dock between two shabby fishing boats, paint long ago peeled from their hulls, and the dock officials busy themselves with confiscating our entire haul for later distribution, as the official line goes. Jorn would stick out for his towering height, but he adjusts, adopting the same stooping hunch of the rest of the villagers. We shuffle through the streets with heads down and ears alert.

In Barstadt, even the tunnelers do not live in poverty such as this. The Land of the Iron Winds' citizens may catch a glimpse of the sun here and there, but there is nowhere else for them to aspire toward. When I was a tunneler, the dream of citizenship papers kept everyone warm at night—someone always had a cousin who knew someone else who'd toiled and saved and bought their way into daylight. We could see somewhere higher than where we were, and dreamed of climbing toward it someday—enough sunlight trickled into the tunnels to fuel our dreams. Here, the Commandant and his generals tower over each town in profiles carved from onyx monoliths, high above everyone else. There is nowhere for them to aspire toward. There is the Commandant, and everyone else, toiling to keep him afloat.

The iron and black glass temple of Birnau glitters on the horizon. It's styled similar to the Citadel, only slightly less ostentatious. Where the Citadel is meant for the Commandant alone, this city is where his favored (though not entirely trusted) councilors, generals, and concubines can be stashed away and called upon when he wishes their company or guidance. It seems no matter what street we follow through the village, we wind up facing that sealed city. While I can't take my eyes off the strange spectacle, the villagers around us take great pains not to look its way. I force myself to follow suit.

Though this village looks designed to support the fishing

industry, we pass no markets, no fishmongers. The buildings are little more than shacks formed from scavenged sheets of lumber nailed together in odd shapes. No one loiters in the streets; they shuffle past in battered boots, big toes sticking out, or no shoes at all.

No, I am mistaken—a pair of eyes glitters in the gap between two huts. I don't dare look for long, but I see a man's silhouette propped against the unsteady wall, watching our group intently from inside a stiff woolen coat. My throat tightens. Have we been marked as outsiders? The reward for information in the Land of the Iron Winds is high, far more valuable to the suffering people than the cost of five strangers' lives.

"Here we are," Edina utters under her breath, "our contact." She leads us down a dirt path between two shacks. An old woman greets her by throwing back the tattered curtain draped over the front of her hut.

"Five's too many," the old woman says. She slips the words into the gaps between the sobs and moans around us, lets them ride the breeze like we aren't even there. Her mouth is mostly pink with swollen gums. What teeth she's kept stand like stubborn gravestones, refusing to surrender to nature's course.

"Well, it's how many we have. So you'll have to get all five of us inside." Brandt matches her cadence flawlessly, like he's throwing the words from a carriage window when he thinks no one's looking. No one can remember our presence here.

She makes a fuss of digging through her scant belongings, all of them some shade of gray or tan or filth. Knitting needles, unevenly spun wool, something that might have once been an apple smuggled in from Dreamer knows where. "Space for two in the fish cart. No more."

"That wasn't our arrangement. What about the guards? Can we replace some of them with our own?" Edina asks. Jorn reaches for the dagger hilts tucked just under his sagging tunic.

"Nah." The word whistles through two crooked teeth. "Use General Sly Fox, maybe. Always too big of an entourage. Easy to slip into their group."

Edina starts to protest, but Brandt nods once, decisively. "We can work with that—promise," he adds, the last to Edina. He turns back to the old woman. "General Sly Fox. When is he due to reach Birnau?"

"She," the woman corrects. "Noon, at the latest. She's got her own chef, concubines. Men, women both. Good for you to disguise as."

"You're changing the plans at the last minute?" Edina asks. "You assured me you'd made arrangements—"

The woman meets her gaze, sharp as a lance. "Only if you want inside Birnau."

"All right," Brandt says. "We'll do it."

"It might not be safe," Edina whispers to him.

Brandt laughs. "Nothing about this is safe. But we have to try, don't we?"

And so we find ourselves in the carriage house on the outskirts of town, the tavern cleaned out in advance of General Sly Fox's arrival, with an air bladder full of mothwood smoke. Once they arrive to shake the road dust from their cloaks and primp for Birnau, Jorn will flood their rooms with smoke. Edina paid the old woman in grain and gold both, but she just shrugged at her, as if neither is of any use to her. She has a point. Gold can't be easily spent in a place like this—where could she have come across it, and what would she buy, anyway? Unlike at the port town, even the grain is of no use this deep into the Land of the Iron Winds. The soil here is cakey and shattered across the top like a broken mirror as far as the eye can see. No grain is stubborn enough to sprout through that.

Hooves tear through the hard crust out front; the main door beneath us opens and finally slams. Dozens of feet pound up the staircase outside our cramped room.

Brandt's hand taps me on the knee; I meet his gaze. *Ready?* he mouths. I think of the darkness we encountered back in Oneiros, and I'm sure he's remembering the same. I force myself to nod back. His smile makes it worth it to try.

Jorn positions the bladder's mouth at the base of the adjoining door and, at Brandt's nod, begins to pump.

Thump, thump, thump. Multiple bodies hit the floor in the other room.

We tie scarves over our mouths and open the door.

"How long do you think you can stay in her skin?" Brandt asks me as we survey our options: the general herself, her sleek black hair twisted in an elaborate braid that meanders across her scalp like a scar. Three courtesans—one man, two women—in perilously revealing garb. A valet, whom I immediately mark as Brandt's likely stand-in. Two bodyguards. One is sure to suit Jorn.

"Three hours at the most. Any longer than that and she's sure to slip out of Oneiros." I swallow. Three hours will barely get us inside Birnau and to the assembly. "If you can keep dosing her with the mothwood, though, I may be able to stretch it."

Vera looks like she could chew through iron. "Have you ever tried it before?"

I give my head a tiny shake, unable to force myself to say no aloud. Vera rolls her eyes; Jorn grunts to himself. "Haven't you cost us enough?" Vera asks. "Don't risk our lives with an experiment."

My face stings as if slapped. She's right, and I know it, but there has to be a way to do this. "Hesse always said it could be done. According to his calculations—"

"But no one's ever done it," Edina says.

"We're short on time," Jorn tells us. He's already donned one inert bodyguard's costume and tied up both bodyguards—one stripped, one not—and is setting to work on the courtesans with Vera.

I look Edina hard in the eye, trying to summon up some of Marez's steel. "I can do it—I have to at least try. If we readminister the mothwood to Sly Fox's body every three hours, and if you can add a few more drops of the dreamwort solution to my body's tongue at the same time, there's no reason we can't make it work."

Edina nods after a heartbeat's hesitation. "We'll bring your body with us, then. Get to work."

"No. Absolutely not," Vera says. "I know you're all right at organizing our missions from afar—"

"You really think I'm all right?" Edina asks, a faint smirk on her lips.

Vera's face turns brilliant red; she folds her arms with a huff. "But it's different in the field. You haven't seen what Livia's like, the poor decisions she makes."

"Firsthand? No. I haven't. But I've read every single one of the reports." Edina grips a fistful of her skirts. "I know that every one of you bears some of the blame for what transpired with the Stargazers. And I *also* know that every one of you, Livia included, has shown remarkable skill at making the best of bad circumstances. I trust you—every one of you. Perhaps you should try doing the same."

I'm dumbstruck by Edina's outburst; I shrink back, desperate to get everyone's attention off me. Brandt's eyebrows are lodged high behind his bangs as he looks from Edina to me—I can't tell if he's impressed or intimidated.

Vera just nudges her toe against the floor, but manages a sharp nod. "Very well," she says icily. "Let's be on our way."

Marez would agree with Edina, I think. He would urge me not to stay shackled to my past. I must be stronger than my fear.

No sooner does the vial touch my lips than I'm plunged into Oneiros, on a mountaintop this time. Snow speckles my hands as I stretch them out before me, but the cold doesn't reach me. The only cold I fear is the cold of the Nightmare Wastes. But I don't have time to fear them. I can't let down my team. Even if Lady Twyne or whomever she worked with has unlocked some horrible way to reawaken Nightmare, surely the Dreamer would put an end to it. He has to.

I cannot spare a thought for it. There's too much to be done now.

The mountains slope downward into the wool of fog. Am I meant to find the general's consciousness down there, somewhere? She should be right here beside me, but all I can see is the meager outline of the mountain range, as if I'm peering through thin vellum. I stagger forward, and the snow crunches beneath me like an avalanche. There'll be no sneaking up on the general's consciousness in these conditions.

I raise one bare foot, willing away my boots, then wiggle my toes into the snow. It parts softly; the snow is soft and powdery around me. Gradually, painstakingly, I make my way perpendicular to the mountain slope.

Then I catch sight of a little burrow, a whisper of a shade darker than the surrounding snow. Two ears peek out of the darkness, tipped in downy coal, on an otherwise snow-colored body. A fox. The wind quiets around me as I concentrate on the fox's breathing, which comes in tiny, fitful breaths, characteristic of exciting dreams filled with giving chase to rabbits across an empty tundra.

My hand trembles as I stretch it out before me and lower it into the den. I must use the gentlest touch imaginable. Can't wake the little kit. My fingertips come to rest on the soft patch between her ears. The fox quivers, as if startled; I hold my breath and pray to the Dreamer she won't awaken. But then she settles against me, welcoming my warmth into her rest.

We open our eyes.

Back in the hotel room, Brandt staggers back from me with a weighty breath. "Bloody dreams, Livia, what took so long? Is everything all right?"

"Sorry. She was a sneaky thing," I tell him, though I'm sure the words sound mushy as porridge. I can't tell, myself. My left ear is nothing but a hollow echo, like the distant chatter of insects outside my window at night. "Oh. She's deaf in one ear."

"Which ear?" Brandt asks, and I motion to the left. "All right. Jorn, always guard her left side. We'll manage, as long as we don't have to orchestrate a terrifying escape route."

The fox twitches in Oneiros, as if recoiling from a bad dream—or memory. I stroke the crest of the fox's head to calm her. *Sleep, sly fox, sleep.* "I'll play it carefully—let's be on our way."

My limp body gets stuffed unceremoniously into the carriage; someone has already dressed it in a courtesan's gown, with a deep slash of exposed skin from my collarbone down between my breasts to my navel, another slit running up one thigh. Vera's dressed in a matching costume, gauze artfully wrapped around her scarred arm, while Edina wears a subtle servant's uniform.

The horses gallop toward the sealed city's gates. None of us dares to speak, or even breathe too deeply, lest we break whatever spell has molded us into the shape of a credible Iron Winds entourage. As the saying in this strange land goes, the winds will surely scatter us like dust for our falseness, our heresy. We will bend and break.

Brandt deals directly with the sealed city's guards, producing papers that he's dug up from Dreamer knows where. I hear something of a scuffle outside the carriage, but finally the guardsman peeks his head inside to find Vera coiled around General Sly Fox like a viper, hands on either of my thighs as she coos nonsense words at me. I offer the guard a stern look as I scratch the fox's ears inside Oneiros.

"So what if we registered more attendants than actually came?" Brandt shouts on the other side of the carriage door. "There's been a nasty round of cloud cough in the east. We didn't think it prudent to bring that into Birnau's walls."

The official jerks his thumb toward my limp body, its head propped against Vera's shoulder. *Its. Its.* I cannot think of it as mine. Even if those are my curling lashes, my honey locks, my scrawny-girl form stuffed in a woman's gown. Vera reaches up and pats its cheek and whispers sweet platitudes into its ear for as long as the official watches.

"She had too much to drink on the long ride. She'll sleep it off," Brandt assures the official.

After another exchange, the official must finally be satisfied, for the carriage lurches forward into a dark tunnel. I hold my breath and continue stroking the fox behind its ears, even as my new body's heart races in anticipation. Is the general afraid? Should I be?

Sunlight sets fire to the inside of the carriage, bathing us in gilded glory. We crowd around the windows. The City of Sealed Secrets is built like a vast stadium, similar to our coliseum for sporting games on the fringe of Barstadt City, with an elaborate dome of mirrors that spin and swirl. The brothy, thin sunlight outside Birnau is magnified, multiplied, sent dazzling throughout the walled world, tumbling onto the elevated ring at the city's heart. Our goal—the assembly hall.

"We'll have to find a safe room just off the assembly ring to stash you," Edina says to me, though she's looking at my body as she speaks. "I'll do what I can to arrange it. Jorn, stay with the general at all times. Brandt and Vera, see what you can learn from the other servants and guests—the gossipier, the better."

Vera for once looks too stunned to mouth back at Edina as she nods. I can't help but agree with what Edina said back on the ship—we could have used a commander like her more often in the field.

We exit the carriage at the grandiose base of the assembly ring. A dozen staircases prop it up like great spikes; we pour into one, clinging together tightly enough to conceal my motionless form in our midst. Brandt wears my vial around his neck and keeps grabbing it, running his thumb over its edge.

Thankfully, the outside corridors of the assembly ring are made of the same labyrinthine, black-ridged metal as the Citadel—full of tucked-away corners where we can conceal ourselves. We pass countless patrols of tam-hatted guards and horn-helmed patrollers, but at the sight of me they bow and scrape the ground with their noses. Irritation flutters in the general's veins, even as my consciousness heaves a relieved sigh that they don't notice the deadweight body in our midst.

"Sly Fox! Always with an eye toward the festivities, I see," a man calls out, wearing the same stiff-collared uniform as me. Another general. I greet him with hands clasped over my heart. "Save room for me later, eh?"

"Of course, General," I mutter, but thankfully Sly Fox's feet agree with me, hurrying us away from him. The fox curls herself into a tight ball, like a fist closing. *Easy. Patience.* I can't risk her waking now.

A gong rumbles through the corridors, setting the whole construction to a gentle sway. *Time for the assembly,* Sly Fox thinks, her mind following well-worn trails of habit. I look to Jorn on my left, and he nods. We split off from Edina, leaving her to nestle in one of the alcoves with my limp form, and Brandt and Vera to strike up idle chatter with other courtiers as they dig for clues.

We twist into the corridor to the general assembly, and I nearly fall back into Jorn.

It's made of glass. The whole structure is suspended across the heart of an iron ring, looking over the sealed city far below. Glass seats rise up in a smaller concentric circle; the assembled generals of the Land of the Iron Winds seat themselves here, with their bodyguards at their backs. And at the very center, towering over everyone on a glass pulpit, sits the younger Commandant.

All right, Sly Fox. Show me the way. I swallow down my fear and head into the ring of chairs. "The Iron Winds will shred their foes with gale force," the Commandant intones as soon as I settle into Sly Fox's seat.

"But the Land of the Iron Winds shall never fall," everyone else answers. I find the words a split second behind them, mumbling them under my breath.

As I watch the Commandant, the fox's pulse quickens under my hand. She's twitching and fighting against an unseen foe in her dreams. Fury heats her soft coat. Nightmare's curse, I can't risk her waking up now. I'll need another dose of mothwood soon. But what has her so agitated? Is it the Commandant's presence?

"I have plucked a most magnificent gem from the Iron Cleft," the Commandant announces. I scour my mind to remember the incomplete map I'd glimpsed in the Citadel. The Iron Cleft is their main mining operation, I think—was it the one the Commandant showed me when I was General Cold Sun? "This gem will allow us to devour our northern enemies. Even as they slaughter our faithful on the executioner's block for the path of righteousness, they feed the warbeast that shall destroy them."

Everyone in the circle mutters assent, but my heart is pounding. What is he talking about? Some magical gem? This land gets stranger and stranger. Maybe it's all a mad bluff. Just another strange addition to the Iron Winds mythos. But the bit about slaughtering the faithful—does he mean Lady Twyne? Surely it can't all have been part of their plan.

"Our agents are working now to put the artifact into place. We set sail in three nights, my children!"

Cheers accompany this announcement—bloodthirsty, primal roars, all around me. My voice joins them, though inside I am terrified. I am these hunters' prey.

I lock eyes with the man seated at the Commandant's right as I wait for the cries to die down—General Cold Sun. There's no way he could recognize me for what I am, but his hard eyes set my teeth on edge all the same.

The Commandant's fist crashes down on the podium. "I will give each of you your marching orders. Do not share them with a soul." He folds his arms at his chest, hands clasped at his heart.

"The Winds of Victory have cleared a path for us, and our allies have foretold our victory in terms we cannot ignore! We shall use their mighty weapon, and the Iron Winds shall blow with ever greater force!"

Mad cheers all around me. But the Commandant jabs both fists into the air, eliciting instant silence. We all lean forward, starving for his next words.

He looks around us, jowls sheened with sweat. "Shred our enemies," he finally intones.

"The Iron Winds blow fiercely," we echo back.

That's it? The other generals are already climbing from their seats, jostling into something resembling a line to take their turn receiving orders from the Commandant. The fox quivers under my palm. *Please don't wake up.* I need another dose of moth-wood smoke, desperately, but if the Iron Winds are setting out in three days for Barstadt, I have to find out their plans.

Brandt rests his hand on my shoulder and leans down to my right ear. "Sly Fox is a demanding woman." He grins. "*Be* the Iron Winds."

Yes. I try to summon that strength, and the fox's fur bristles in response as it stokes my blood like a furnace. My hand, of its own volition—or perhaps of Sly Fox's—reaches for my deaf left ear. I find it, just under the sheath of stark black hair, laced with scars.

I charge straight for the Commandant, parting his flock of black velveteen generals. "You owe me more."

His eyes flash like musket flare. "You do not speak to me this way."

But Sly Fox is eager; in her dreams, she is ready to pounce upon her prey. I open her mouth and let her subconsciousness do the talking.

"My men cleared the Iron Cleft for me. Not you. We tolerated your strange foreigners as they searched for the gem. And now you owe me an explanation."

"Hold your tongue, or I'll claim the rest of your hearing," he hisses. The other generals press forward, carrying us toward the corridor, but I feel Jorn steady as stone at my back.

Sly Fox's eagerness spikes like excitement in my veins. "Meet me in the alcove on the northern face of the ring," I tell him, while in Oneiros I try to keep the fox calm.

Dreamer's mercy, what have we put ourselves in the middle of? I fight upstream through the clamoring generals as they jostle and shout, hungry for their scrap of the feast of war. I have to get to Brandt to administer more mothwood smoke to Sly Fox and the dreamwort elixir to my body. We have to uncover this crazy source of power that the Commandant claims will lead them to victory. If it's even real. *Dreamer, let it be a bluff.*

The fox stirs under my fingertips, on the brink of waking up, as the snowfall around us picks up pace. But it's not me who has alarmed her deep inside Oneiros.

Long, sinuous shadows stretch across the mountain slope, tearing through the fog and snow with the rank stench of death.

Chapter Nineteen

The winged horde radiates with frost. *You'll never stop the plan. Already too late . . . better to rest, surrender to whatever's to come . . .*

I smell these creatures; I see them. I'm not strong enough or devout enough to reshape the dreamworld around me in order to fend them off. We have to run. *Please, Sly Fox, trust me just a little bit longer.*

I scoop the fox into my arms and take off through the snow, now swirling into a blizzard. I'm certain each crunching step will wake her. But what other choice do I have?

"Sly Fox." It's Jorn's voice, slicing through the fog. "General Sly Fox."

I look around the real world. We're standing in the middle of the corridor ring while the other generals and their retinues shove past us. My heart races, or maybe it's Sly Fox's, or both.

"Is something the matter?" Jorn asks, tugging me into the shrouded alcove where Brandt sits beside my body, clasping my hands in his own. Oh, how I wish I could be feeling that with my own skin. Jorn helps me onto the bench and wedges his thick shoulders into the opening to shield us from sight.

"In Oneiros. There's something wrong. Nightmare's monsters are back—"

I choke down a scream as pain shoots through me. Oneiros drags my attention back as an outstretched claw rakes against my bared shoulders. It's not a normal pain, not the union of flesh and a sharp edge, but a lifetime of pain bubbling up from my marrow. My mother, staring lifeless at the wall, because I'm too late for her. Professor Hesse and his eyes, his soul drained out of them. Brandt pulling away from me, fingers slipping from mine as Edina Alizard calls his name. The tunnelers, writhing and swarming around me like rats as they flee a tunnel fire. Some truth, some lies, but they all sting with the same hateful toxin.

Suffering. Pain. Not even in dreams will you find relief. We will hunt you, asleep and awake.

I am alone. My skin aches for him. My wounds bleed for him. I am alone.

Another claw tangles in my hair, tugging at my scalp. I imagine how soothing emptiness would feel, draining away my failures, erasing my dismay. I imagine nothingness, and how that absence might feel. Cold. Static.

No. No. I need warmth—I have to resist.

A golden light grazes my skin. I glance up, looking for its source as it parts the swarm of nightmare beasts. Please, let it be the Dreamer trying to speak to me. Why won't he save me? I'm desperate for his guidance, for his interpretation, for anything

242

he can offer me. A weapon placed in my hands or a prayer or incantation that will make this go away.

But he's silent again. No answer comes.

The beasts have circled me and my sleeping charge, a buzzing noose shrieking into the chill night. They open their beaks, and my will to live on seeps away from me, gray ash floating into the night. I am a dried-out husk of the girl who dared to leave the tunnels, the girl who dared to serve the Emperor, the absent Dreamer himself.

No. A tear slides down my face, burning its way down. There has to be more. I have to see Brandt smile again. I have to give value to Hesse's work. I can be more than just a dreamstrider, an imperfect realization of a perfect dream. If I can weep, if I can still imagine more than this, then I haven't given up yet.

The pain in my scalp shrinks, replaced by the warmth of a distant flame. Brandt, smiling, knowing my next step always. The sun tearing through overcast clouds to warm the city harbor for another day, free of war and invasion and strife. I will not succumb to fear.

I think of the Dreamer's warmth—though I've never heard him speak, my dreams warm me, spurning me to reach beyond myself. I'm warmed by fighting for them, earning them—for myself, and for the Dreamer and the world he made into flesh and dirt and tree. Even if the Dreamer never answers me, even if he never shows his face, my belief in him has kept me strong.

My heart pounds as two images war within me. Devastation and victory: Barstadt overrun and Barstadt standing free.

Slipping back down into that sewage pit while I hid from the gang enforcer, or finding a new foothold.

I leech power back from the monsters, one grain of sand at a time. Their wings smolder and scald as a golden glow erupts from them. The snow sizzles against my skin as I force the dark visions away, refusing to let them get their hooks in me.

Their cries rip across the mountaintop, and I stand alone, shaking and radiant, with a slumbering fox cub in my arms.

I collapse to my knees. Can I really fend them off by clinging to my faith, my memories, even when I don't hear his call? Thousands have died under the crushing weight of Nightmare, choking on that black tar of despair. But those monsters were only a vanguard for darker fears—for Nightmare himself. If Twyne's found a way to awaken Nightmare, there are much greater foes to come.

I open my eyes to find Brandt clutching my hand desperately, his eyes marbled with red.

"Livia. Livia. Where are you? Are you here?"

Two bodies, side by side in the corridors of Birnau. I try to lift Sly Fox's hand, but it's like trying to move with a body made of smoke.

"Now," I wheeze in Sly Fox's voice. "Don't let her wake up—"

Cold metal presses to my mouth and I plunge back into Oneiros.

The mountainside melts away under a luscious, filtered sun. A stream trickles nearby, clotted with chunks of ice; the white fox laps from it with a lazy, groggy tongue. She must have leaped from my arms in that moment when Sly Fox started to wake up. A chorus of birds veils my footsteps through the soft, squishy snow and the moist earth underneath as I approach the fox.

The fox lifts her head, right ear twitching. But I am on her left. I wait for her to turn her head my way. I tilt my head back and forth, just enough for her to know that I'm alive, but slowly enough that she won't see me as a threat. I spot a berry bush nearby, a few red fruits glittering beneath a shell of ice. Slowly, I move toward the bush, pluck the berries, and extend them in my palm.

The fox catches my scent—recognizes me, perhaps. One paw, then the other, stretches toward me, like she's embarrassed to be seen moving toward me but can't fight the urge all the same. Her nose prods at my thumb, at the berries. Close enough.

We open our eyes.

The empty ocean in my left ear tells me where I am before my eyes focus. Something gargantuan buzzes before me, two images and then one. Jorn. As soon as my eyes focus on him, he gives a grunt and moves away from me.

"We need to meet with the Commandant," Jorn says.

I moisten my parched lips and look at Brandt's face, his brow furrowed so deep he could plant wheat in it. "The Commandant's giving marching orders. It's an all-out assault on Barstadt." I'd been so frantic as I fended off the creatures of Nightmare that I'd nearly forgotten. "And he keeps talking about some sort of magical gem, and Sly Fox is acting like she helped him dig it up, but I can't press too deep into her memories. I have to let her spill it out . . ." I press the heels of my palms against my eyes.

"I heard about the gem, too," Vera says, hovering in the mouth of our alcove. "One of the girls was talking about a strange envoy who visits the Commandant; the envoy accompanied the lady with the 'night sky face.'" She crinkles her nose. "Bloody dreams, I wish these people would just say what they mean. Anyhow, the envoy told the Commandant about some mystical stone that he must uncover. As long as he surrendered it to the envoy, the envoy would use it to bless his troops and lead them to victory over the northern mongrels. Meaning us."

I pinch the bridge of Sly Fox's nose. "But who's this envoy? What magical stone? It sounds like another ridiculous myth the Commandants make up, like how he rode a firebird across the land that barfed up gold and grain."

"Yeah, or how he tamed a shark that spit up rubies. Lots of vomiting in the Commandant myths," Brandt says with a wry smile.

"I suppose the 'night sky face' means Lady Twyne—all her gemstones like stars—but we still haven't learned who she was working with. Did any of the courtesans know anything more about the mystic?"

Vera shakes her head. "No one else has heard of him or seen him, I'm afraid. Go on; go see what you can wring out of the Commandant."

In Oneiros, the fox has devoured all the berries in my palm and runs slow circles around my wrist, rubbing back and forth. I don't move, but I scan our surroundings. We're in a totally different time and place from the nightmare creatures' attack. It feels like sheer luck that I fended them off before.

Jorn escorts me in Sly Fox's body to the northern alcove, clinging to my left side the whole way. The clamoring metal, shifting and sliding across articulated joints, of armored guard announces the Commandant. He slips onto the bench opposite me, our knees intertwined, and the guard stand in the alcove opening, blotting out the dancing mirrored sunlight.

"I do not care what my father may have promised you. You will follow my orders now. I owe you no explanation." His directness surprises me—I was expecting more allegories and allusions. I'd planned to employ Brandt's third rule of spycraft—*flattery will get you everywhere*—but now I've no idea how to counter. I scratch Sly Fox behind the ears and let her base instincts take over, a habit too deep to interrupt her sleep.

"You said that I would carry the gem across the sea. I would run the flagship, holding the prize that *I* helped you retrieve." The fox's fur bristles along her spine, but her rage is not for me. She still doesn't see me as an intruder, Dreamer bless.

"*No!*" The Commandant's hand shoots out to shackle my wrist. White rims his irises as he stares at me. I can feel his pulse pounding from here. "We mustn't handle the gem. The envoy alone can touch it. He'll carry it into the mists."

"Into the mists?" I ask, dubious. Something tugs at me in the phrase—something from Hesse's research.

The Commandant frowns. "You don't recall his demonstration?"

In Oneiros, I draw the fox cub closer to me. What thought am I missing? Sly Fox's memories skitter around before settling. A dark chamber in the Citadel. The Commandant sinks into sleep as a man covered head to toe in robes passes a censer of mothwood smoke over the Commandant. The robed man slumps beside him; in the darkness he twitches as if caught in a troubling dream.

Finally, the robed man falls still, one hand raised before him as if in greeting. The candles gutter and something flashes in the air above the robed man like a dancing flame reflecting off a blade. No, Sly Fox realizes. That's precisely what it is—a jeweled sword, taking shape in the mystic's hand.

My choked cry nearly wrenches me out of Oneiros.

Hesse's theory of transference. Hesse didn't just Shape those things in his Oneiros home—he transferred them, passing objects between Oneiros and the real world just as Nightmare did when he escaped the dreamworld to ravage our homeland, centuries back. Is this how Lady Twyne intended to keep her soul alive? By transferring it into Oneiros before her execution?

The Commandant stares at me expectantly. Sly Fox squirms in my arms back in Oneiros, agitated that I pressed her for that memory. She's sure to remember this moment. But I can't fear it. We have to get through this and return to Minister Durst. I open my mouth. "Where is the mystic now?"

The Commandant shakes his head, still unblinking. "He walks the dreamworld, assembling our warbeast. He's no charlatan. We wandered the mists together, and I saw his plan. The gem cannot be carried across the sea. It must travel through the mists to recover its power."

Warbeast. My pulse thuds in my ears. I want to turn and run now, but there's more I need to learn.

Something strange has settled into the Commandant's gaze. "The gem," he whispers to himself. His vise grip on my wrist eases, and he leans back against the bench. His eyes look distant as if he were under a powerful charm—not the sightless stare of a resin user, but enthralled as if he had seen wondrous sights. All the earlier edge is gone from his tone. "It is glorious. It is the whole world contained within my Citadel, and all its subjects working for the glory of the Iron Winds. It is a great metal beast, devouring the countryside and spitting up splendorous cities, factories."

Again with the regurgitation, I think, but I don't feel like laughing anymore.

"And at the beast's core, its pounding heart, is the gem. *My* gem. It burns like lava, and flows through all the joints to fuel the unimpeded progress of the Iron Winds, scorching our enemies. It carries my blood to bind it to my will. My father spoke to me from beyond the grave in my dreams. We spoke of the Iron Winds—of the need for every citizen to pledge themselves to the pursuit of victory. He promised I would find a way to bring the Iron Winds to all the world, and I have found it." His chest heaves. "I've found it."

I have to quiet Sly Fox to say what I need, what I desperately need, for Barstadt. "Show it to me."

But the spell is broken—the Commandant lurches forward, and all softness and wonder in his face calcifies into rage. His eyes narrow until they are two pinpricks of disdain burning at me. "No. The gem is mine. No one else can possibly—" He clenches two fists. "Be grateful I give you a post on the fleet, after the way you disgraced my father in our battle against the western islanders. You will not be amongst the ships that walk the mists to enter the bay."

"But my . . . uh . . . Commandant—"

"Go." He stands, towering over slender Sly Fox, pointing out. "Leave Birnau and ready yourself for battle. Maybe you will find an honorable death on our enemy's shore; it will be more than you deserve."

Jorn seizes me by the elbow and practically drags me back to our waiting party. He doesn't even stop to tell them what's happened, only beckons for us all to follow. My own amber eyes watch me, unmoving, from my body draped around Brandt's shoulder. I cannot meet them.

Only when we are back in the belly of our clipper, our costumes shed, and Sly Fox and her party left in the carriage house to rub their heads and grasp at hazy memories of the day's events, do I dare put a name to the growing dread that's spreading its black, oily, rotten wings within my gut.

"I think I know what this magical 'gem' of the Commandant's is," I say to the assembled team. *Dreamer, save us all.* "It's one of the shards of Nightmare."

Chapter Twenty

Upon our return to Barstadt City, my first impression of the Imperial Palace is that surely the Emperor of Barstadt and its northern colonies, who serves as the King of Barstadt City and the Grand Majestic Admiral of the Barstadt navy, to say nothing of his title as the Dreamer's Most Anointed One, could afford more comfortable chairs than the ones Brandt and I currently occupy. I was suitably awed by the grand terrace that led up to the palace itself; I couldn't help but feel flattered to have earned an audience with the Emperor at last. The white-paneled hallway, traced over in gold leaf and crowned with a majestic dreamscape painted across the high ceiling, looked inviting enough when we were first ushered inside. But now that we've been waiting to deliver our report for three hours, it's all I can bear not to stretch out on the wooden parquet floor.

I've hardly slept since we left the Land of the Iron Winds. I dread what my dreams may bring. If I were to slip into Oneiros, would I find it ravaged once more by Nightmare's minions?

I don't want to know. I fear that I can't summon up the courage to fend off their venom again. And in truth, I don't want to cry out to the Dreamer again and hear only silence, only the beating of nightmarish wings.

But since we staggered off the docks, there's been little time for sleep. We pried Minister Durst from his bed and told him everything, though I think the mere fact that Vera and Edina were too frantic to waste any energy sniping at each other told him quite enough. Durst marched us straight for the palace gates, but soon disappeared into a flurry of meetings and chaos while Brandt and I sit, waiting to provide our account.

"I bet they're not even doing anything in there," Brandt says, eyeing the double doors to the war room, flanked by immobile guards who might as well be topiaries. "Having a Stacks tournament, perhaps."

"Performing a revival of *I Dreamt of You*," I counter.

"Ugh, of all the insufferable operas. Maybe they're brewing ale."

"Watching paint dry."

"Trying on the Empress's entire wardrobe," he says, and we both smile, but there's a hard edge to it. Brandt pulls off his cap and ruffles his bangs, then twists the hat around in his hands. "Liv . . ." I glance over at him, smile fading. His gaze stays fixed, though, on the overwaxed floor. "Whatever Durst asks of us next . . . It might be our last operation together. I want you to know . . ."

Hope stirs cruelly inside me. For just a moment, I dare to let myself believe Brandt might feel what I feel. I lean forward, heart thundering. "Yes?"

"Just . . . know how much I'll always cherish our time together. I—I know you'll do fine without me."

The patter of my pulse dies out. I sink into the hard cushion and look away from him. Foolish, foolish girl. Of course he doesn't feel the same for me that I feel for him. A cleaning girl from the tunnels could never compare with the life of duty and comfort and purpose that awaits him representing House Strassbourg.

"I'll be just fine." I stare past him, unable to meet that deep gray gaze. "Actually, I've been thinking of traveling. Seeing the world beyond Barstadt City."

"Have you now?" Brandt's eyebrows shoot up. "I don't suppose your friend from Farthing has anything to do with this decision, does he?"

Heat washes over my face, but what use is it to deny it? Brandt's surely happier this way—with me carefree and tethered to someone else. I should be happier, too. "I suppose so, yes. Marez has made me realize there's a lot more to the known realms. More ways to live than the Barstadt way. All our elaborate rules, our classes . . ." I shake my head, realizing I'm brushing too hard against the truth. "And anyway, if we stop the invasion, I'll be a free person, so I'd like to savor that for a bit."

Brandt laces his hands together over one knee. "That's—that's wonderful, Liv. It's just—it's really, really fantastic. Really." He grins anew, though there's something too stiff about it. "I'll admit, I'm still loathe to trust a Farthinger, but they've given us good information. You always do what's right. You deserve happiness, even if it is—" That mischievous edge touches his grin. "With a man who spends that much time on his hair."

"Oh, you little demon!" I swat at his shoulder, and we both dissolve into laughter.

But it aches. It aches like the darkest part of winter; like a beautiful dream that can't be made real. Well, he said he trusts my decisions; perhaps it's time I trusted them, too. Stoke the fire within me; try and see new things, new places, until it cauterizes this wound.

The doors fling open wide, crashing into the walls. Minister Durst strides out of them with fists on his hips and his lips curled like he's bit into rotten fruit. "His Majestic Imperial Highness and his war cabinet will see you now."

Out of habit, I look to Brandt for reassurance, but he's already pulled away from me, his gaze fixed on the room ahead.

Emperor Atrophus Weideger IV looks every bit the golden-haired, sun-smooched, boisterous man I expected from his portraits, even if he's somewhat softer around the edges. Professor Hesse told me that as a prince, he used to wrestle on the Imperial Square for sport, and I believe it. His skin, like baked clay, attests to a man accustomed to soaking up every last ray of sunshine our cloudy nation gets. He's eschewed the facial gemstones, save for one solitary ruby in the center of his brow. His belly is primed for a laugh, and even in the face of devastating war, he smiles when he stands up to greet us. He looks so inviting that

I almost reach out to shake his hand, like we're old pals meeting at the alehouse, but thankfully Brandt drops to one knee beside me, so I fall into a curtsey.

"These are the two little pups that infiltrated the Land of the Iron Bloody Winds?" the Emperor asks, turning to Minister Durst. He unleashes just the sort of merry laugh I would expect him to have. "Aren't you a ballsy pair! I need players like you on my polo squadron."

"We only did what was necessary to preserve the Empire," Brandt says to his boots.

"Oh, sure, kiss my arse if you must. You know, I had a dream last night of a great stag and a doe emerging from the northeastern hills. They wore wreaths of gold, glowing as if with the Dreamer's light itself. Are you two such creatures?"

"I . . . I wouldn't presume to imagine myself as being a worthy subject of your dreams, Your Majesty," Brandt stammers. I wrinkle my brow, confused by the Dreamer again. The northeastern hills are where Nightmare's bones reside, along the mountain ridge that borders Farthing. What was he trying to tell the Emperor?

The Emperor laughs and claps us both on our shoulders. "Good answer, my boy! Now, stand up already—let's hear all about your little trip."

The Emperor strokes his curled mustache while Brandt explains the plans we overheard. Only while he's speaking do I notice the Emperor's war cabinet—the assorted priests, admirals, and ministers and their clerks crammed around the war table. They follow Brandt's every word, scribbling notes on ledgers and maps as they contemplate how to repel the Commandant's attack.

Once Brandt reaches the bit about the Commandant and his magical "gem," the admiral nearest to us rolls his eyes, but the Emperor leans torward me, smile gone, thick brows a straight line across his forehead. "You're our dreamstrider I hear so much about, are you not?" he asks me.

"Yes, Your Majesty." I straighten as if pulled up by a string, but embarrassment sprouts on my cheeks. I doubt I want to know what kinds of reports the Emperor has heard about me.

"I thought Hesse was mad to attempt what he did—I still do." The Emperor's eyes gleam in the gaslight. "Teaching a girl from the tunnels to use the most sacred dreamworld for espionage. But any advantage we can get in these trying times . . ." He shakes his head. "What do you make of the Commandant's claims?"

I take a deep breath. The Emperor of Barstadt, of all people, is asking *me* for advice. "If we understand him correctly, Your Majesty, then some party with the ability to shape the dreamworld is colluding with the Land of the Iron Winds. I found evidence in Oneiros of Lady Twyne's involvement, as well. It's terrifying enough to think that someone other than the Dreamer's priests have such a skill manipulating Oneiros. Unless— unless it *is* one of our priests." I swallow. "But the worst is that the criminal appears to possess at least one shard of Nightmare's heart. According to Hesse's research, if they mean to reunite the shards, they'll travel to Nightmare's Spine and restore the heart within his ribs."

"And the only way there is through the city," an admiral interrupts, gesturing to the map spread on the table before them all. Nightmare's Spine snakes between Barstadt and Farthing like a puckered scar, and the massive rib bones that signify Nightmare's Spine lie at the northeastern-most corner of Barstadt City, inaccessible by the Itinerant Sea. "So how in the bloody nightmares do you expect them to break through our naval blockade? I know our army is lacking, and the constabulary's tied up with all the tunneler protests of late, but the Barstadt navy is the best."

I open my mouth, but hesitate, looking to Brandt. Why should the Emperor believe me? As he said himself, I'm just some girl from the tunnels. But Brandt nods, certain, as reassuring as his hand upon my shoulder, holding me firm. *Oh, Professor Hesse. If only you'd known what your research could really do.* "Whoever this . . . criminal is, or whatever they are, they may possess some ability that will allow them to transport physical objects, like the shard, through Oneiros," I say. "They could even use Oneiros as an intermediary place to allow them to travel great distances in the real world quickly, by slipping into Oneiros from one location and coming out into another."

"Albrecht Hesse's theory of transference," Brandt supplies. "We have his research notes on the process."

I nod. "I don't know if they wish to transfer the shard alone, or if they mean to attempt to transfer war machines, troops . . ."

Emperor Weideger balks. "Madness. How could anyone with such power slip from our notice—"

"I'm only telling you what I know is possible, based on

Professor Hesse's research." That his research never quite translates into reality in the way he'd hoped, I'm in no mood to tell the Emperor. I draw a steadying breath. "There is something else Professor Hesse was working on, too. He called it the binding ritual. I don't know exactly what it does, but I think someone killed him trying to get it."

"Binding?" one of the priests asks.

"We've only found references to it in Professor Hesse's other notes, so we're not sure what it's meant to do. It's clear, however, that the Commandant and the late Sindra Twyne were trying to unite the shards of Nightmare's heart. If they've been successful in that task, that might explain the recent disturbances in Oneiros."

"What recent disturbances?" the Emperor asks, cutting his gaze toward his High Priest. The High Priest blanches and glances away.

"The—the recent increase in strength of the Nightmare Wastes, and Nightmare's minions returning to life." I force myself to stand firm. "If Lady Twyne and the Commandant really mean to awaken Nightmare, and the criminal can do just that . . ."

"Madness. Absolute madness." The Emperor harrumphs. "But if Hesse hypothesized it, it may very well be possible. Minister, do we have any word on who this betrayer might be?"

Durst steps forward. "A recent report obtained in conjunction with our Farthing colleagues indicates Lady Twyne employed the services of a mystic—possibly an apostate of the Dreamer's priesthood. The dreamstrider believes he or she may have aided Lady Twyne in preserving her soul inside Oneiros through the transference process."

The High Priest, in his loose white tunic and thick golden yoke, shakes his head furiously. "This is the first I've learned of it myself, Your Imperial Majesty, I assure you."

"Assurances? You want to issue me an assurance?" The Emperor waves his hand. "Assure me that you'll scour our records for any apostates who might be capable of such a thing."

The High Priest drops into a series of bows. "Yes, Your Majesty—"

"And what about these disturbances in Oneiros?" The Emperor rounds on the High Priest in a flash. "When were you planning to bring those to my attention?"

"Your Majesty, it's nothing my dreamshapers can't handle. And"—the High Priest jabs a finger in my direction—"we'd have it all under control without the dreamstrider's meddling!"

"Without the dreamstrider's warning, you'd let Nightmare crumble the world around us. See that it is handled." The Emperor's voice is stretched tighter than a drumhead; gooseflesh lifts on my arms.

"Y-yes, Your Majesty." The High Priest bows again, and scampers to the back of the group to confer with his acolytes.

The Emperor turns back to me, drumming his fingers against his belly, just below a golden pendant set with a glimmering ruby the size of his fist. "Dreamstrider? Lord Strassbourg?" Brandt and I straighten up. "Since my priests are so bloody incompetent at sniffing out traitors in their ranks, I want you two to find this rogue priest for me."

Minister Durst's eyes bulge. "Your Most Divine Majesty, if I may, I think you'll find the dreamstrider's talents lie outside of the realm of conventional fieldwork—"

"Nonsense. I want these two." Like he's picking out pastries at Kruger's. The Emperor leans down toward us, all his bluster channeled into a deadly tone. "Find me this traitor. Now!"

And so we are dimissed. After we're all but shoved out of the war room, a maid with a perpetual case of the shakes treats Brandt and me to tea and cakes in a side parlor. I nibble at the cake, but it is so overpoweringly sugary and laden with rum that my already nervous stomach roils in protest.

"Well," Brandt says, staring at his steaming teacup as if it might hold the solution. "How do you propose we do this?"

I shrug and attempt to sip the tea, but it scalds my lips. I only succeed in dribbling it onto my pale dress. "Minister Durst doesn't believe I *can* do it. Nor should he!"

Brandt shakes his head. "Come now, I know you and I can figure this out together. We always manage, don't we?" He smiles and pops a tartlet into his mouth.

My nervousness starts to thaw at the sight of that grin. "Very well. What are you thinking?"

"What do we know about our would-be traitor?" Brandt holds out one palm to tick things off on his fingers.

"He accompanied Lady Twyne on at least one visit to the Land of the Iron Winds," I say.

"Or she." Brandt leans back in the chair, chewing on the mouthful of cake. "She's trained to access Oneiros, which means she must be a former priestess."

"Or priest. But not necessarily. I'm not a priestess, either."

Brandt groans. "All right, so if whoever it is isn't a priest, he—or she—had to learn to enter Oneiros through some other means. Possibilities?"

"Bribed a priest to teach them? Figured it out on their own?" I swallow hard as I summon a possibility so frightful I can't ignore it. "Learned from Professor Hesse?"

Brandt looks dangerously close to choking on a chunk of frosting. "You said yourself that you're the only one to survive his experiments."

"Yes, his dreamstriding experiments. We don't know which other theosophical professors had access to his research, or who the other subjects might have told about his experiments, despite their sworn oath." The very thought rankles and exhausts me, but I can't ignore the possibility. "And his theories about transference of matter between the dreamworld and the waking one—they weren't just theories. Sly Fox witnessed it, unless it was all a trick. We have Hesse's original research notes on transference, but we need to keep hunting for more details about the binding ritual . . ."

Minister Durst clips down the hallway toward us, his face puckered up, like he really has spent the past five hours kissing the Emperor's arse and is none too thrilled about it. "I don't know what you two are gabbing about, but we have other issues."

"We're talking about how to catch this mystic priest. You wouldn't be about to ask us to defy the Emperor's orders, now, would you, Minister?" Brandt asks coolly.

Durst dabs the sweat from his forehead with a kerchief. His

gaunt cheeks look positively skeletal after so few hours of sleep; deep shadows well under his tightened eyes. "The Farthingers," he says, ignoring Brandt. "The Farthing Confederate Council sent official word to His Imperial Majesty that they were prepared to commit as many forces as necessary to defend Barstadt from the Land of the Iron Winds."

"That's awfully generous," I say. "What do they stand to gain from it?"

"Well, if Barstadt falls to the Iron Winds, then Farthing is sure to be next," Brandt says. "And their naval force is considerably smaller than ours. They command all the confederate privateering ships, but I don't think the Council would have any luck bossing them around. Helping us fend off the Commandant makes sense, even for a people well known for putting themselves first."

Durst nods. "Our good friends from the east, Marez and Kriza, are to oversee an influx of Farthing land troops arriving soon to fortify Barstadt City. Brandt, you can keep hunting for the identity of the rogue priest, but I want you on the Farthingers, Livia. Mind that they don't get too nosy—they're here to help us and not themselves. Understood?"

"The Emperor said . . ." I start, but the glare from Durst shuts my mouth.

"The Emperor doesn't know your limitations as well as I do," Durst says. "The Farthingers, however, have for some reason taken a shine to you. You're of better use to me keeping an eye on them—through any means necessary."

"Understood," I say, voice wavering.

"Glad to hear it. Now, get some rest. I want you meeting the Farthingers tomorrow morning," Durst says. "Dreamer bless."

As the Minister's heels report down the vast hall, I stare at Brandt. "We're letting the Farthing army into the city?"

He shrugs. "It's happened before. In fact, I'm pretty sure they helped defend against Nightmare way back when. Why? What are you thinking?"

"I'm thinking when this is all over, I won't be offended if you spike the celebratory cider."

Chapter Twenty-One

I toss and turn for hours, fighting my immense exhaustion after Birnau and our audience with the Emperor. I dread what might await me in my dreams—or worse, inside Oneiros. But I can't escape slumber's yoke forever. I blink—and then I am gone. I'm flying over Oneiros, and I glimpse the Dreamer's Spire rising out of the city's heart, but then I land inside a shallow dream, one I'm sure to forget on awakening.

In it, I stride through the halls of the Ministry, a sheathed sword banging against my thigh. The Ministry's layout feels foreign, distant to me, in that annoying way of dreams. Some of the day's anger with Minister Durst bubbles up and forms shadows that dart along my path. I find myself at his office, and the night guard—is it nighttime in this dream? There are no windows to guide me—nods at me, permitting me entrance.

The office's contents swirl before me like wreckage strewn along the shore. What am I after? Dream logic demands no answer; I fall to my knees and dig, and dig. The Nightmare shards. There must be more about them. Their locations. Some-one has to know.

And then I find it. The blank page that somehow will un-lock everything in this strange dream.

I clutch it to my chest before I soar, soar away into the night.

"Bad dreams, my lady?" Sora asks, straightening my sheets after she sets my breakfast before me on the desk.

"I've told you, you don't have to call me that." I pinch my eyes shut. "And not bad, just . . . odd."

"Mind if I take a crack at interpreting? My aunt used to work in the Dreamer's Temple. She taught me a thing or two."

I shake my head. "I'm sure it's just my nerves." I start setting my own table before she has a chance to fuss over it.

Sora finishes with the sheets and starts sorting through my wardrobe. "Minister Durst says you're to meet Marez at the southern guard post at noon to plan for the Farthing army's arrival. May I help you get dressed?"

"No need. I can manage." I've never gotten used to having someone dress me. "How've you been, Sora?"

Her cheeks flush, and she lowers the gown she'd been hold-ing up for my approval. "Oh . . . Oh, I've been fine."

I tilt my head. I may have left the tunnels behind, but I've never lost their language, the way we tunnelers hoist our bur-dens around us like saddlebags. "Is something the matter? There isn't—" I narrow my eyes. "You're not in trouble with any of the tunnel enforcers, are you?"

"Oh, certainly not!" She claps both hands over her mouth.

"No, my lady, I never meant to make you think that. It's only that I—Well, it's my gentleman friend, is all." Her usually pallid face now matches her kindling hair. "It's not worth troubling an operative such as yourself with."

I settle onto the settee to drink my tea and drag Professor Hesse's journals into my lap. "You know I'm always happy to help, though, yes? Anything at all."

She backs into the door and nods, barely managing to squeak out a farewell before closing the door behind her.

I shake my head. Only one non-tunneler at Banhopf ever spoke to me as an equal, and that was Professor Hesse. I adored that he did so—so why does my casual talk seem to trouble Sora? I mean to be friendly, but perhaps she finds it improper.

In any case, I've much greater concerns. The first is the Farthing army now sailing across the Itinerant Sea. The second is far more insidious, journeying through Oneiros under the control of a heretic dreamer. When the Farthingers arrive, I'll focus on the first, but until then, I want to search for more clues about the latter. I settle in to read more of Hesse's journals.

7 Balzan's Month, 619 AN

Subject 36 did not awaken from his attempt to dreamstride into 39. I witnessed his fall—he circled 39's consciousness, again and again, but the Wastes pulled at him too fiercely. He was not strong enough to linger in Oneiros.

Had an awful row with 39 afterward. He understands why we cannot offer up a proper funeral pyre—it isn't that—but he is convinced my timidity is leading to needless deaths amongst the candidates' ranks. He speaks of slipping into Oneiros at night and trying to reshape it for himself; he taunts me that he knows the truth of how Nightmare was first slain. But how does he evade the grasp of the Wastes? I cannot stray far from my body at all before they tug at me, and 12 has told me much the same. But then, 39 is now far stronger than she.

His insubordination grows daily. I cannot teach him the final steps of dreamstriding, of grasping another's lead—not until I'm sure he's ready.

So there was someone who could dreamstride like me, or was on the brink of achieving it, anyway. And he was even stronger than me. But 39 must have died like all the others, or Hesse surely would have introduced us. Maybe it was 39's death that triggered the outpouring of guilt, the regret that surrounded him like a hardening crust in his final days.

12 Julisar's Month, 621 AN

Subject 39 is no more.

I must put an end to it—all of it. I cannot have any more deaths on my hands. No more dreamstriding, no more transference, no more preservation of souls. And the binding ritual—the most dangerous of all. I have locked away my notes on the binding ritual where they will be safe. Safe from the Ministry, safe from any other outsiders who might come seeking them. 12, should anything become of me, I have left all my research to you, but the key to my research is something you'll have to find for yourself.

From two years ago—so his death wasn't the trigger for Hesse's guilt after all. I swallow down the lump in my throat. He wanted me to read these journals. But who is he protecting them from? The key—I slump forward as I remember the strange cabinet locked away in Hesse's Oneiros retreat. He didn't lock the notes in our world—he hid them in Oneiros, using transference to take them to the dreamworld from our own.

But it didn't save them.

Someone else found them first. They took his research.

I've failed him again.

• •• ———— • ———— •• •

"What a fine dress to go to war in," Marez says, holding out one gloved hand to hoist me onto the battlements with him. "If nothing else, the Ministry certainly pays its secretaries well, I see."

My face heats as I glance down at the worn velvet frock from my meager Ministry-supplied wardrobe; with its worn patches and stubborn wrinkles, it's certainly nothing any Barstadter would envy. But the Farthingers dress much more simply, with an eye toward utility over appearance. My skirts tangle in my legs as I climb, making me grateful for Marez's hand. I'm beginning to see the value of the Farthingers' style.

"Let's hope it doesn't come to war." I lean against the stone battlements. Their ragged surface is cool and damp from autumn sea spray, and pocked from the endless winds. The traveler's winds move swiftly away from Barstadt this time of year, out through the Itinerant Sea and into the vast ocean to our west—an inauspicious time if ever there was one for the Land of the Iron Winds to declare war. But I suspect the Commandant isn't one to let reason trump a certain poetry and impulsivity.

Marez follows my gaze to the frothy Bay of Dreams. A few brave gulls wheel on the horizon with aching, lonely cries. A massive galleon treads slowly south, to the bay's mouth, but the Imperial docks beneath us buzz with pent-up energy: a navy eager to face a real opponent, rather than their usual duties of capturing undefended northern islands and rapping Farthing pirates on the wrists.

"Better to be prepared than not, isn't it? I'll admit, I was as surprised as you to learn the Confederate Council was going to send peacekeeping forces to help fortify the city," Marez says.

"Why does it surprise you? Are you Farthingers so unaccustomed to showing kindness to your neighbors?"

Marez staggers back, clutching his chest. "Oh, how she wounds me! Believe it or not, we aren't complete strangers to altruism."

"You understand, though, how it appears to an outsider," I say.

"Perhaps, but we are known for our attachments. We aren't strictly out for ourselves." He moves toward me, dark eyes gleaming. "We value balance—give and take. Perhaps I can show you someday."

I turn away from him, face tingling from a flush of heat, but I can't stop thinking about his words. I try to imagine the life I might have in Farthing—tending a business of my own, not beholden to the Ministry or the Emperor or anyone else. Not pining for a boy I could never have because he belongs to another class. Forgetting, at long last, the tunneler life that always hovers behind me like a shadow. Once my citizenship papers are in hand and my life belongs to me, I can find out.

Marez makes a notation in his ledger, eyes the battlement further, then jots something down again. "Am I boring you, Miss Secretary? Your mind appears to be elsewhere."

I shake my head. "Not much sleep to be had in recent days. I'm sure you understand."

"Naturally. They must have you taking notes at all kinds of dreary meetings, don't they? Supply these troops with ten thousand pounds of grain, send three hundred kegs of ale down to this dock . . ."

"Exactly," I say, perhaps too hastily, but he doesn't look up from his scribbling.

"I still say it's a waste." His words gain an edge, struck against flint. "Your mind's too quick for drudge work. Hurry, now, tell me which ship that is that they're loading the cannons onto below us."

"The *Thresher's Harvest*," I say, without even glancing down.

"And if they're loading cannons, what type of offense are they expecting?"

I cast my thoughts back to one of the lessons with Brandt at the Ministry—Durst never required me to learn about military tactics, but Brandt thought it better to train me like any other operative. "One by sea. Close-quarters warfare along the blockade line, I'd wager. If we can sink the Iron Winds fleet in the bay, then we never have to test the defenses we're fortifying here." I gesture to the men hammering metal plating against the dock gates.

Marez grins. "Precisely. You've a tactician's mind locked away in there."

I want to believe him, but the truth is, I divined that battle plan from the little toy ships scattered on the Emperor's war table as much as my lessons with Brandt.

"Now, what about the Commandant's weaponry?" Marez strides down the battlements to assess the harbor from a new angle. We're directly above the dockside armory, and men crawl in and out of it with shields, swords, halberds. The tempered black weaponry makes them look like beetles scampering around from this height. "What do you think we can expect him to bring to bear?"

He tucks the folio into the waistband of his leather trousers and props himself against the battlement, leaning toward me. He's fairer-skinned than Barstadters, but I can see why the Farthing council sent him as their envoy—he could certainly be mistaken for one of us, with those dark, floppy curls and devilish eyes. And that smile—well, one can appreciate a smile like that regardless of homeland.

"The reports we received mentioned war machines," I say,

tenuously, like I'm positioning my feet for an intricate waltz. I don't want to mention Nightmare outright. His eyes betray nothing, so I take the next step. "This may mean siege weaponry, cannons, or some sort of pathetic failed invention, like the Iron Winds are so notorious for producing. We aren't really sure."

He nods and starts to speak, but the wind picks up, snatching the words from him and spraying a curtain of my hair across both our faces. Marez reaches up to disentangle it from my nose and where it's clung to my lips. His fingertip brushes from one corner of my mouth to the other, leaving a trail of cinnamon and stone. I swallow hard. As soon as his hand is gone, I ache for that warmth, like it was the last ember in the hearth.

"But I'm not interested in what the reports say." Marez's expression hardens. "I'm interested in what *you* think."

My pulse crackles like a lightning flash, starting in my heart, surging through my fingers and toes. "I'm, uh . . ." What can I say? That I fear the Commandant and a Dreamer's apostate will awaken Nightmare from the mountaintops? That they'll devastate Barstadt City with a flood of anguish? "I'm still concerned by Lady Twyne's involvement. I think there may be others within the city we've yet to unearth. And what your informant told us at the gaming den—"

His thumb slides behind my ear; his fingers rest gently at the nape of my neck. I freeze, unable to look away, unable to feel anything but his searing heat and the frantic hammering of my own heart. "Actually," Marez says, "I take that back. I'm interested in you. Just you."

I swallow. It sounds so loud in the dense, pulsing silence between us. "But I'm nobody," I say.

"No, Silke." His nose touches mine. "You're everything."

His lips press against mine. The kiss washes over me like a wave, determined to drag me under. I don't even believe it's happening at first, but that velvet mouth quickly convinces me. My lips soften, but then I press back, letting his warmth course through me, tamping down my nerves. Unafraid. Full of fire.

Slowly, he ends the kiss, then presses his forehead against mine. "Apologies, Silke." He's grinning madly; it makes me grin, too. "I couldn't resist."

I'm too stunned to speak. I've never kissed anyone before. I lean back from him, but my spine is already against the stone wall; there's nowhere for me to go. And it's not that I wish to escape him, not at all, only that it isn't proper for me to be seen kissing men in public, especially where anyone could see. No, especially where *Jorn* could see, and then if Jorn were to tell Brandt—

Marez's smile curls back down. "I'm sorry. Have I done something wrong? Should I not have kissed you?"

"Yes—I mean, no—it's just . . ." I stop and take a deep breath, trying to quiet my trembling. "It's just that it isn't done, publicly, here in Barstadt."

Marez laughs and takes a step back. Instantly I feel colder, aching for the warmth we shared just moments ago.

Those clever, clever lips twist again. "Does it matter what Barstadters think?"

"No," I say, my face burning up. "Not in the least," I find

myself answering truthfully. The Ministry doubts me constantly; the Dreamer never heeds my call. Marez is right—I don't need their approval any longer. My chest aches as if I've released a long-held breath.

"Then we are in agreement." He cups my head in his hands and stamps a kiss on my forehead, then turns away from me with a start. "Come."

We link hands, and I chase him up the battlements, past the discolored span of stone where they were repaired after Nightmare's flight over six hundred years ago. Nightmare's Spine surfaces into our view from behind the jagged roofs of the sailors' quarter. Marez clucks his tongue at the sight of it. "What a grim sight to keep right above your city, don't you think? If I were Emperor, I'd have scattered its bones to the four winds."

"They scattered the fragments of his heart," I say. "That was the important part."

Marez tilts his head. From the back, he looks much younger. Is his charismatic, easy nature a mask, just like Brandt's? "You don't speak much of your dreams, for a Barstadter." He looks back at me expectantly.

"I thought you found our chatter about dreams intolerable."

He holds a hand out to me. "Actually, I find Barstadt chatter in general quite insufferable. You, dear Silke, are an exception." His smile flashes, clear and bright in the murky fog. "Come, let's check on how the constabulary's preparations are coming along."

We head north from the harbor. In the constabulary's office, I take a seat while the head constable rattles off a lengthy list of contingency plans to Marez, coupled with improbably high numbers of policemen who have been called in to maintain order in the streets. My guess is he mainly intends to cower behind his desk and let the Farthing army clear the streets, if it comes to that.

I'm trying to pay attention to their conversation, really I am, but the wall behind me beckons, and the chair eases itself around me like an embrace. Keeping my eyelids open seems so unnecessary, so cruel. Memories of Marez's kiss play through my head, interlaced with the turmoil of the past few days and not nearly enough sleep. My thoughts are fuzzy as my lashes flutter against my cheek and—

I'm sprawled in a field of daisies, their leaves a luminous emerald under white lacy petals. The sky overhead sings with crisp azure, and the occasional cloud streaks through in perfect counterpoint harmony. The smell of cool grass surrounds the picnic blanket, and the whispering breeze is just enough to make the world come alive.

A safe, shallow dream, not one in the dreamworld. I look down at the picnic blanket and find Brandt by my side, head propped on his arms folded under him. "Hello, beautiful," he murmurs. His skin glows golden under the sourceless sunlight.

A bowl of berries sits between us. I pluck one up by the stem and let it pop into a juicy symphony in my mouth. Such a strong, glorious taste, with dark notes in all the right places. I reach for another, and then one more.

A hand snatches my wrist, grasping at me from inside the bowl.

"No!" I tip backward on the blanket, but the razor-wire grip is too strong. The hand reaching from the bowl roils like a boiling stew of meat. Many fingers—claws, really—sprout from it, coiling around my wrist and slinking up my arm, growing longer by the second. My skin rips open as I try to pull away.

"Didn't you know?" Brandt asks, still basking in the sun. He closes his eyes with a contented sigh. "This is a nightmare."

I try to scream again, but the sound turns into a swarm of bees, chattering and buzzing as they leave my mouth. My throat swells shut. The hive buzzes inside me; my skin vibrates as they try to break free.

Another arm grows from the bowl, and another. The bowl stretches wide, excreting the horrendous spidery demon that has me in its grasp. The gaping hole left behind reveals what looks like the world of Oneiros below us, its avenues awash with blood.

"Nightmare is awakening," Brandt says, and then settles onto the blanket for a nap.

The spider flings me into the air. Its barbed claws send venom coursing through me as it releases me—venom laced with misery. Mother's empty eyes gush with blood as my half siblings tear chunks from her legs and arms to stuff in their shriveled guts. The Dean of Theosophy, Hesse's boss, traps me in his office while I burnish his trophies. Every ring of his heels on the marble as he approaches is a fresh lance in my heart.

"Silke," the ground coos as it rushes up to greet me. The spider pins me to the earth with one claw and joins the earth's chorus. My legs spill over the edge of the tear in the ground, instantly rimed with frost from the Nightmare Wastes that have overtaken Oneiros far below.

"Silke!"

"Silke!" Marez rattles my shoulders. I jerk forward, nearly falling from my chair in the constabulary.

"Where did it—" I squeeze my eyes shut. No spider beast, no rivers of blood, no cruel Brandt. "I'm sorry. I must have dozed off."

"You poor dear. The Ministry must be working you to the bone in this time of crisis." He offers me his arm. I lean on him as I stand, my limbs still rubbery from sleep. "Let's get you some fresh air."

I can still smell rot from my dream as we exit the constabulary, but I push it from my mind. I focus on the clean scent of afternoon and the sweet gas fumes from freshly lit lamps. Only a nightmare. I'd glimpsed Oneiros in it—but had I really started to slip into the shared dreamworld, or was I only dreaming that, too? On the mountain ridge above us, Nightmare's bones lay strewn like garland, and about as deadly. We're safe for now.

"Anything else we need to assess?" I shift my weight back and forth while I wait for Marez to finish fussing with his leather duster. The minister ordered me to spend as long as necessary with the Farthingers. Part of me thinks I should rush back to the Ministry and help Brandt search for the traitor, but I'm reluctant to be apart from Marez. I swallow, fighting down the nervous flutter in my gut. What comes next for us, now that we've kissed? Another evening playing Stacks, or does he expect more from me? How am I supposed to behave around him now? I try to think of something clever to say, but nothing comes to me.

"Actually, my dear, I've one more trip for us to make, but it'll have to wait until this evening." The faintest hint of red touches his cheeks.

I feel the color drain from my face. "Oh?" I ask, trying to temper the tremor of disappointment in my voice. "What kind of trip?"

Marez's gaze crackles across me like a struck match. "I understand there are tunnels—hundreds and hundreds of them, running beneath Barstadt City. How are you at navigating them?"

My breath quails in my chest. The tunnels are the last place I want to go. "I . . . I know the basics," I say carefully. "Why do you ask?"

"As you'll recall, we were tracking a series of illicit shipments into the city, believing them to be related to Lady Twyne's treason."

I nod, but say nothing. I will not tell him what we found out in Birnau.

"We think we know who is working with her. But we'll need to sneak into the High Temple to catch him."

"Him?" I freeze in place. The rogue priest Brandt and I are seeking. The person capable of stealing Hesse's research and using it to summon Nightmare by reuniting his shards. Is Marez really so close to unmasking the traitor? My heart pounds frantically. As much as I dread returning to the tunnels—that world of fear and powerlessness—I'll do it, if that's what it takes to save Barstadt.

"Yes, him. I got wind of a conspiracy that leads straight into the High Temple." Marez's expression darkens. "And we're going to catch him in the act."

Chapter Twenty-Two

He's found the rogue priest, operating in the Dreamer's High Temple at the very heart of Barstadt. Marez thinks he knows who it is—who Lady Twyne's confederate is. Back at the Ministry, I seek out Brandt to help me peruse the archives in search of more information on the High Priest's acolytes, but he's still off canvassing the acolytes' schools. My heart twists at the thought of Brandt, but the pain feels duller now, more removed. I press one finger to my lips and recall the taste of Marez on them. The way he smelled, all leather and spice. Just like I wish to see the realms beyond Barstadt once I'm free, once this mission is done and my citizenship papers are in hand; it feels good to know I needn't be chained up by my foolish yearning for Brandt.

I poke through the archives for a short time, but the Ministry keeps few records on the priests at the High Temple. Dantrim Jurard was a student of Hesse's, but only for a few months, before joining the priesthood full-time. Evisand Brett—House Brett. It looks like House Brett did make several deals with

House Twyne, but not for several years. I jot down notes on Jurard and Brett both to bring with me on tonight's expedition.

"You're smiling," Sora says as she clears away my dinner tray back in my quarters. "Should I be concerned?"

I touch my lips again, like pressing in a secret, and shake my head. "Not a bit."

Finally, the night thickens, and I dress myself for an evening in the tunnels. I linger at the clerk's desk in the barracks entrance. I know, deep down, that I ought to send word to Jorn, despite Marez's warning. The tunnels are a dangerous place; even my intimate knowledge of them isn't enough to protect us fully. But the threat of a traitor within the Ministry chills me to my core. The desk clerk eyes me with wet, toadish lips, and I shudder, wondering if it could even be him. "Heading out for the evening, miss?" he asks in a syrupy voice.

I shake my head. "Only a brief stroll."

Kriza and Marez meet me at the canal grate that feeds into the Temple Quarter tunnels. Kriza's long, frizzy hair is wrangled into the brimmed bucket cap many tunnelers wear, and she's coiled a length of rope around one shoulder. She studies me for a moment, then hops down onto the ledge with a grunt. "I sure hope you know what you're doing," she says, though I'm not sure if she's addressing me or Marez.

"We're headed for the center of Dreamer's Square." Marez shrugs into a dark, ragged coat. "The maps I found were incomplete, but this looked like the most direct point of entry, yes?"

"It's close enough. I should be able to get us to the High Temple shortly." I study him and Kriza—both of them standing tall, chins jutted up like a dare. "No, no. You have to carry yourself a certain way if you don't want to attract the wrong kind of attention here. Head down, eyes and hands to yourself. Walk on the right side of the tunnels." I hesitate; memories cascade over me like sheets of rain. Most of them are brutal, but each taught me a lesson—all the rules I followed to keep predators away from me and ensure my possessions remained my own. "Don't look too meek, though. Mind your own business, but keep a look about you that says you know where you're going and how to handle yourself if someone gets clever." Brandt's second rule of spy work—anyone showing too much interest in you is probably after something. Conversely, people—especially tunnelers—get suspicious if you look at them too much, and suspicion too easily boils over to violence.

Marez tosses his shoulders back. He's far too handsome for a tunneler. Someone's bound to want to see him sullied.

"Keep one eye in front of you and one behind," I say. "Count the people we pass, and track their footsteps behind you. Watch their shadows across the tunnel walls. You don't want to be caught unawares, especially if they're working in a pack."

Kriza groans. "Is this a bloody underground city, or the Farthing Timberwoods? Should I be on the lookout for bears?"

"Do you want this to go well or don't you?" I snap at her. "Listen, it's something you learn through trial and error. And we don't have room for error tonight. I can't put into words what tells me who I can steal from and who I should avoid. Which darkened tunnel is safer than the next." My voice quavers; tears edge into the corners of my eyes. *Dreamer's mercy, don't let me fall apart in front of them.* "It's instinct. If you live in there long enough, you have it. If you don't, none will mourn you."

I slip through the tunnel grate, and it's like slipping on a familiar old robe. The walls smell of iron and moss and a tangy medicinal scent; the runoff trickles calmly through the channel in the tunnel's center. Marez and Kriza have more difficulty fitting between the bars, because they are not little slips of people, shadows meant to fit through the gaps of respectable life. Tunnelers are brought starving into the world, and too often, starving we go out.

The tunnel slopes upward, following the curve of the hill like a shadow just below the surface. Luminescent paint, usually stolen from a constabulary or an artisan's shop, coats the tunnel's ceiling in a thick strip that casts us in an eerie blue-green glow. Wherever the tunnels branch, the paint is used, too, to mark the new tunnel with an elaborate system of markings. Their meanings rush back to me, like a strong gust from the sea. Circles for entry, spreading like leaves off a tree that approximates the next few branches from a given path. Circles with bars through them to indicate a tunnel collapse, or a wavy line to warn of sewage tracks.

Sometimes, smaller chisel marks warn about what sort of tunnelers make their homes in the alcoves of a given branch. But these are inconsistent and just as likely to lead into a trap as steer you away from harm. I pay them no mind—except when I feel I must. Again, it's something that must be learned by instinct, and explaining it to my companions would be like describing the color of the sky to a blind man.

We march single file up the slope, the thick stone walls swallowing up the dull echoes of our steps. We only cross paths with a few rag-laden maids, their gazes caroming away from mine, until we're almost ready to turn off the main trunk line. A line of tunnelers coming back from work clogs the path as they surrender tithes. "Tithes," I whisper to Marez. "Pass me some coin."

He fumbles in his pockets for a few moments, then distributes coin to Kriza and myself. I barely manage to catch the coin as he overshoots my palm. His eyes aren't used to tracing shapes in the near-dark. The enforcer holds out his sack, and each tunneler drops their tithe inside and shuffles along. That's how it's meant to work, yes. But too many times I've seen an enforcer call someone out for cheating; he could be trying to skim a profit for himself, or to add to his boss's wealth to make himself look better to the gang. There's a rhythm to avoiding getting scammed, of dropping your tithe not too slowly and not too quickly, of staying invisible to the enforcer. I pray I can remember the rhythm.

I'm next. I drop the coin in the sack. Don't make eye contact. The enforcer grunts—shifts his weight, bag jangling with metal and wood. I start to walk away, shoulders taut as I wait for him to call me out. But it doesn't come. He lets Marez through, and then Kriza.

I heave with relief and motion to the Farthingers. "Come on. Stick with me."

A young man appears before me: I hear him in the shuffle of his soles against the stone ledge and the rushing water's echo, warping to accommodate his form. His faint shape emerges from the darkness, revealing lanky, soiled locks of hair and an expression like it was carved into him. Kriza, though, doesn't see him until he, walking on the wrong side, nearly plows into her, and she yelps like a beaten animal.

"I should cut you," he snarls at her, pale fists glowing in the false moonlight from the luminous paint. "What did you steal from me? Huh? Give it up!"

"They're with me. Run home to your enforcers," I tell him.

"And who the nightmares are you?" He leers toward me, all knobby elbows and knees. "I'll cut you both!"

His leather sheath creaks as he pulls a shiv from it, but in a flash I grab his wrist and crack it against the tunnel wall. He twists and jams his heel into my shin. But my boots are thick and drink up the blow.

"I told you to run home," I growl into his ear as I twist his arm further than necessary to keep him immobile.

"Stop it! You're hurting me!" he gurgles through fresh tears. The bluster is gone in an instant, revealing the too-young child beneath. I drop him before I can stop myself—he's only a kid—and he takes off down the nearest branch.

My heart races from the rush of the encounter. I haven't used that kind of force since I joined the Ministry. I whirl on Kriza. "I told you to stay sharp." Really I'm disgusted with myself, for letting the boy go, for how soft I fear I've become. I can defend myself against a little boy, perhaps, but what of gang enforcers? Of rogue priests of the Dreamer?

She rolls her eyes. "One way or another, we could have handled him."

"Him, maybe," is all I say. "There's plenty more like him to come."

I catch sight of Marez's eyes gleaming in the false light. To Kriza, he says, "Listen to Silke. We're on her territory now." Heat flares in my gut. "I didn't know you had that in you," he murmurs into my ear.

We reach the symbol I was looking for, directing us from this branch to the central chamber that spans underneath the Dreamer's Square. I used to visit the shadowy market stalls of the chamber to bargain for scraps of food or fresh rags cut from discarded aristocrats' shifts for my cleaning duties. If the Farthingers can behave themselves, we should be able to traverse the stalls relatively unscathed, but I don't know which gang controls the market; I don't know how its dynamics may have changed.

The secondary tunnel we take brims with ghosts, half people who drift past us with the same vacant stares my mother always wore. A rank, festering odor, like a seeping wound, hits me as the crowd thickens. Am I dreaming again? If ever there was a Nightmare smell, this surely is it. But despite the strange shadows passing us, nothing erupts from the walls; no one turns into a murderous beast.

As we step into the great chamber, I catch the telltale signs of the Harvest Moon gang patrolling the market—full moon tattoos, yellow-and-black scarves wrapped at their biceps. They've never gotten along with the Stargazers, and it's a small relief to see they run this hall. A shriveled woman lounges in front of her stall, following us with her gaze as she polishes a wicked-looking blade. I avert my stare from her, but watch her from the corner of my eye. Her bodyguard leans over her and she whispers something to him.

"Let's move quickly," I say, and weave deftly through the crowd until I lose the meaty bodyguard in the mass. Then I push on even farther into the market, to be sure. Braziers ring the circle, and stubby chandeliers dangle from the arching roof. Not half a league above us, the aristocracy and their servants shuffle between the temple and respectable shops, while down here, the tunnelers barter with goods pinched from aboveground. The stink grows stronger as we wade into the throng of people. "Dreamer's Square is just above us," I mutter to Marez. "Those stairs at the far end lead up to the temple complex."

A stall stuffed with severed chicken legs is to our left. Half-burned candles, no doubt swiped from an aristocrat's house, on the right. One woman up ahead ladles watery, bile-colored broth into a man's cupped hands. But all I smell is rot, seeping up out of the ground, spreading like a tumor through the air all around me.

Marez's hand darts behind him and reappears, a little girl dangling from it, her fingers clenched around a coin pouch. "I'll be keeping that," he tells her, and then shoves her back into the crowd.

"Here—here's the entrance to the Temple," I tell them as we approach the far archway.

"Excellent. I'll scout ahead," Kriza says. She darts through

287

the mob, her bucket hat easily merging into all the rest. I'm on alert, scanning the crowd to make sure we haven't attracted any further attention from the tunnelers. But Marez slides his arm around my waist and pins me to him as we follow in her wake. I glance up at him, smiling, warmth unfurling in my chest.

"I've been thinking about you all day," he murmurs, lips against my ear. It shoots a thrill like lightning up my spine. "I can't wait until we've dealt with the Commandant and are free of our respective obligations."

I'll be freer than he knows—citizenship papers in hand. Brandt out of my life—I needn't see him every day and mourn for what could have been. "What, exactly, do you have in mind?" I let myself melt into his side.

"I think you should see Farthing for yourself." He grins. "I'm more than happy to give you a grand tour, when this is all over." Marez steers us after Kriza into the twisting subbasements of the High Temple. But my mind is racing far away, imagining sailing off with Marez, leaving my troubles behind. "Our land, our libertine ways. See that life needn't be the way Barstadters insist on living it."

"I'm . . ." My throat closes up as we pass another noxious smell. The maze of tunnels and stairs that lead into the High Temple narrow into a shaft running along the complex that drops into the sewage tunnels far below us. "I want it, too. I'll go. Once we've dealt with the Commandant."

Kriza whirls back to face us, a slippery grin on her face. Have I ever seen her smile? Maybe when we were burning down the alehouse. I try to smile back, but the tang of the sewers beneath us is nauseating. How did I ever live with that, day in and out? Marez pressing against me is making me dizzy, and I can barely even focus my gaze.

"Thank you for navigating the tunnels," Kriza purrs. "I'll slip in through the acolytes' quarters and find our traitor. You two stand guard down here."

I nod, scarcely listening, and she vanishes up the narrow, coiled stairs.

Marez and I duck under a low rough-stone doorway that leads to a narrow alcove, and Marez backs me into the wall. My pulse thrums in my ears. The wall is cold and sharp against my back, but Marez feels dangerously warm—soft and inviting. He leans close, eyes gleaming, his muscular form blotting away the chaos of the market. His lips brush against my cheek. "Silke," he says, his breath fierce against my neck. "Come back to Farthing with me."

"I . . . I will," I manage to say, my legs wobbling beneath me. Between the smell and his aggressive heat pressing against me, a nod is about all I can handle. I want to relish this feeling, but the smell is distracting—I try to look back at him, but my eyes water.

"Ever since I met you, I've been dreaming of you," he whispers.

My breath falters. What girl wouldn't be reduced to gelatin at such words? Whose heart could help but race under this man's touch, soulful gaze, and desperate tone? I admit I am lost in the fantasy, the promise of what more he may say and do to me. I am lost.

But not forever.

Perhaps it's the smell. Were it not for that foul stench distracting me, fraying my nerves like overstretched rope, then maybe I could lose myself wholly in Marez's attention, his silky-smooth whispers in my ear. He'd command my every fiber, and I'd be swooning and melting into him. I'm certainly on the brink. His nose traces the edge of mine, and his eyes flutter as he breathes in deep.

But that smell—that smell brings me back to myself. To the Livia who loves Brandt Strassbourg, and dreams of a life serving the Dreamer. When I hung rapt on every word of Brandt's and Hesse's teachings.

Brandt's first rule of spy work, the first thing he ever taught me: there are no coincidences.

"Silke," Marez murmurs in my ear, almost like he believes it could really be my name. "Come away with me."

Second rule: anyone showing too much interest in you is almost certainly doing so for the wrong reasons.

"Your talents are wasted on these people," he purrs, hands closing around my shoulders. "In Farthing, you could be limitless."

Third: flattery will get you everywhere.

"Sail the seas, avoid Barstadt and its foolish constraints." He sighs. "I promise I'll make it worth your while."

Fourth: anyone you could describe as "your newest dearest friend" is anything but.

I twist my head away just as his lips crash against me, hitting my jaw. "Please," I whisper, trapped between him and the stone, between nausea and the shackles of panic. "Please stop."

"Isn't this what you wanted?" he growls. His façade is crumbling. He's tired of this game. I don't have long if I want to escape from this unscathed.

Because the fifth rule is: once they know that *you* know, you are living on borrowed time.

Marez is strong, but I'm experienced. Like evading the gang lieutenants, my size works for me. I dart out of the way of his elbow as it swings for my cheek. I slip to the ground and pop out between his legs.

"What is it?" I cry. "Why are you after me?"

"Your Dreamer is a fool, leading a land of cowards." Marez stalks toward me with an unsettling calm to his gait. "You don't deserve your gift. You'll never seize upon its *true* power."

My gift? I nearly lose my footing as I back away. He knows what I am? But of course he does. He and Kriza both—it's why they've been hounding me, why he's been working so hard to seduce me, to make me feel cherished, revered . . . It's what they've been after this whole time. *Dreamer, I'm such a fool.*

Behind me, far below, I hear the trickle of the sewage canal. If it's set up like the others, then it feeds into a branch tunnel, and hopefully washes out into the trunk line. Brandt taught me to always have an escape in mind, and I'll be damned if I didn't manage to pay attention somehow, despite the stench and Marez's heat.

"What is it you're after?" *Keep him occupied, Livia*—keep him focused on talking so he's not watching you closely.

"Balance," he says in the same tone someone would speak of a religious dream. "What I've long been due. Barstadt has reigned long enough. Your *Dreamer* needs to be deposed, and the Emperor with him. The Barstadt Empire is a bloated, mangled corpse ready to be put out of its misery." His eyes are impossibly dark. I don't know how I ever found that snarl and those eerie shadows on his face attractive. "If that idiot Hesse had surrendered when he had the chance, it wouldn't have come to this. But I'll make better use of you. I serve the *real* savior of our world—myself. And Nightmare will aid me."

Footsteps race toward us from the upper stairwell, and Kriza darkens the doorway. "I've got it," she says. "Come on, we haven't time to waste." Nightmare's breath, the smell is overwhelming. Is it radiating off her?

Marez looks between the two of us. I edge backward, but there's nowhere for me to go, save that sheer drop.

"What did you do?" Kriza shrieks at him. She storms past him and snatches me up by my collar. "What did he tell you?"

Her frothy spit flecks my face, but I'm too overwhelmed with revulsion to care. That stench, that smell that has swallowed me up, it's coming from her—or something on her. Like a body left too long to rot in the sun. Like curdled, rancid milk being poured down my throat. I claw at her hands; it's all I can do not to vomit. Can't they smell it, too? Why aren't they incapacitated, like I am?

"I made a mistake. I thought she was ready to be persuaded, but I misjudged her, all right?" Marez clamps a hand on Kriza's shoulder. "We don't need her gift anymore. We've got what we need to finish the ritual."

She shrugs him off and drags me to the precipice of the canal, gripping me by my collar. Somewhere, the metal tang of sewage finds me under the fog of deathly stench. It's not only water in the canal. But I'd suffer it. I'd endure that, to get away from these traitors and their stink.

"We have to kill her now, or take her with us. Give me the cloth," Kriza says. "I'll knock her out." I scrabble to keep purchase on the ledge with my toes. Loose pebbles give way underneath me, tumbling into the stream below.

"I don't have it," Marez mumbles.

Kriza's hold goes slack, and I nearly slip over the edge. "*What?*"

"I don't have it, all right?" He charges toward us. "The dealer never delivered the next batch, so unless you fancy pilfering some of that, too—"

I've crawled my way out of enough pits and wallowed in enough filth. I never wish to return to a life marked by rags scrubbed until they are threads, a corner of the tunnels claimed, violations successfully avoided. But the tunnels are my native language, whose rules flow in my blood even if I can't explain them. The Imperial architects of the tunnels are my kindred souls. I can trust them above anyone else.

I twist free from Kriza's grip and plummet over the ledge.

Marez shouts above me. Kriza is surely staring openmouthed. They do not hear a splash, but perhaps the stream is too far down. No luminous paint lines the canal's chute; they cannot see the slotted stonework in the near wall, where I cling desperately, like a rider to a spooked horse.

The Farthingers bicker back and forth with furious, blunted words. "Let her die. If she won't work with us, she's of no use to us," Kriza says.

But they don't leave. Footsteps shuffle above, but they're coming closer, not retreating. My arms are burning; my hands form desperate claws against the stone holds. *Dreamer, please, make them leave!*

"You two is spendin' too much time in my alcove," drawls a gravelly voice. "I guess you must be wantin' to make a trade of some kind. What do you think, Bee?"

"I'm thinkin' their lives is a fair trade for their belongings."

Brandt. Brandt! And the other is Jorn. Again I'm grateful we're not in Stargazers territory—Jorn must have guided them safely through the market. Oh, nightmares, whatever they're playing at, let them play it out soon!

"We saw you nickin' from the temple." Jorn again, his slow, heavy speech no less frightening to me than the day I first heard it. "What did you take, girlie?"

More frantic scuffling. "Nothing of importance," Kriza says, her cold tone more flustered than usual. "I'm sure we can work something out . . ."

A flurry of noise. Did Jorn seize them? Did they get away? I can't hold out much longer. My left arm wobbles; my fingers burn as they start to slip.

And then Jorn's head appears over the ledge. I could cry, I'm so relieved to see him, even in his gang flunkie disguise. "Give me your hand," he says.

I pry my fingers from the stone, though their vise grip is the sole thing keeping me here, and I reach for him with my right hand. Jorn's massive palm circles my forearm. He hoists me up and over the ledge in one swift arc, like he's executing a hammer toss, and dumps me in the dirt before a very ragged, soot-smeared Brandt.

"Livia." He pulls me into his embrace.

"Dreamer bless you for all eternity." I'm shaking, clinging to him for dear life; shame skitters through me on spidery legs. "I'm so sorry . . ."

"That was a damned foolish thing to do," Brandt says into my hair, but he doesn't let me go. "Not informing the Ministry you were heading out with them."

My heart is still thudding against my ribs like a trapped rodent. "They told me the Ministry had an informant. And Durst said to keep my eye on them through any means necessary—"

Brandt takes a step back, giving me room to stand up. "Through any means necessary," he says, voice laden. "You certainly took that to heart."

I fold my arms across my chest. "And what do you mean by that, Lord Strassbourg?"

Brandt scoffs. "What do you think I mean? I knew you felt something for that man, but I'd no idea you two had grown *quite* so close. Did you really mean what you said?" he asks. "That you'd run away to Farthing with him?"

"Oh, don't you dare!" I scramble to my feet. "You have

absolutely no room to tell me who I can spend my time with, where I can go—no right . . ."

Brandt winces as if slapped. "What are you talking about?" he asks, far too quietly.

Something about the look on his face snuffs what I'd been about to say. Something warns me that it's not Marez who has him upset. But it's far too late for me to pin false hopes on Brandt once more. "Nothing." I spin from him. "Forget I said a thing. Yes, I meant everything I told him," I add.

But rage quivers through me. How dare he be angry at me, when he's the one getting *married* to someone else? I want to keep pushing back. Make him feel even one ounce of what I feel when I think of him, and what we can never be. Let it sting and burn and leave a scar.

Instead, he looks at the dirty ground, the luminescent paint overhead gilding the side of his face in blue. Jorn clears his throat at the mouth of the alcove. I take a deep breath and try to force the torrent of emotions out of my mind.

"They know I'm the dreamstrider," I say. "They told me there was a traitor in the High Temple, the renegade priest we've been looking for, but it was a ruse." The horrible stench is gone, but my head is pounding, pounding, and my stomach aches with nausea and nerves.

"What were they after down here, then?" Jorn asks. But Brandt's barely listening; his jaw keeps working, like he can't find the right question to ask.

"Kriza stole something from somewhere above us. She was

searching for one of the stairwells that lead up to Dreamer's Square."

"The High Temple of the Dreamer." Jorn nods. "I know the area from when I worked for Retch."

I swallow. "They mentioned working with a dealer, as well—resin, by the sound of it. Whatever they stole, it smelled . . ."

"Smelled?" Brandt asks. "How do you mean?"

"It's nothing. I must have been imagining it." I coil my hair into a loose bun. I lost my hat in the fall toward the canals and somehow shredded the grimy duster as well. The smell—it was like my dreams, or rather, my nightmares. Like the beasts in Oneiros. How could I explain it to them?

"We'd better get back," Jorn says. "If someone recognizes me . . ." Brandt grimaces, but nods. He hunches his shoulders to shelter himself and doesn't cast another glance my way.

I'm far beyond exhausted now; I could fall asleep walking, especially with Jorn at my back, guarding me. I can't face those awful nightmares again. As we weave through the stalls, the breathing tangle of bodies, I scan the aisles for the one thing that can keep me safe from my dreams.

If Nightmare is reawakening, to fall into Oneiros almost certainly means my death.

I spy them on a tray, half-hidden by folded scarves cut from aristocrat's dresses. They're bigger than I remember—hard to pocket on the sly. But I've had practice, more than I care to admit. My fingers are around the wax paper wrapping and back inside my pocket in the time it takes to blink. I scan the teeming crowd to make sure no one's watching me, but the two enforcers nearest us are busy threatening a woman with a baby cradled in her arms.

The rumble reaches us before we leave the mouth of the tunnel. Loose rocks spray from the tunnel's mortar as the earth vibrates. I hurriedly slip through the grate and climb hand over foot to street level. The gas lamp flames dance wildly in their casing, slinging eerie shadows across the street. With Brandt and Jorn behind me, we edge to the alley's end as cheers swell around us—applause and brass instruments and the hammering one, two of thousands of heavy-soled boots and hooves and creaky carts hauling cannons and other equipment.

The Farthing army streams past us, waving and blowing kisses to their Barstadt admirers. And why shouldn't our city greet them as saviors? They are not from the Land of the Iron Winds, our sworn enemies. They have come to supplement, perhaps supplant, our own meager military. To flood our city. To overrun us, as we open our arms to them.

Brandt swears beside me, an extra-filthy curse, and sags against the wall. "So if Marez and Kriza were using us all along to steal something, and gain control of the dreamstrider . . . Then what does their army mean to do?"

Chapter Twenty-Three

Brandt leaves me at my quarters with scarcely a word. He must send an urgent message to Minister Durst and the Emperor, who are still strategizing at the palace, and inform them that our Farthing saviors are not what they seem. A kind way of putting it. Dreamer, but I'm a fool. How could I have believed anyone could feel for me the way Marez claimed to feel? How could I not see his deceit in those wicked eyes, not notice the ploys I've seen Brandt use a dozen times? I wanted so badly to believe I was deserving. Of spy work, of a home, of love—even if not Brandt's.

I sink onto my mattress and stare down the bulge in my coat pocket. I can smell the Lullaby's sickly sweetness from here, an overpowering fruity blow. Darkness surely awaits me tonight, whether in my private dreams—full of taunts and reminders of my failure—or in Oneiros, as Nightmare's minions gather strength under the command of the traitor we've yet to catch. The Lullaby would ensure me a dreamless sleep at least. Do I really dare use it? It's a vile, addictive thing, but it would protect me from those awful monsters in Oneiros. But what if it's my duty to face them, as the dreamstrider?

Dreamstrider. The cursed word sticks under my fingernails, irritating me in slow, subtle ways, but I can't remember why. I can't remember much of anything. My arms feel like they're caked with clay from fighting to cling to the canal wall. My thighs sting from climbing up and down ladders on the battlements all day. My eyelids—my eyelids are weighted with lead. I'm fighting to keep them open, but sleep is winning out. It overcomes me abruptly before I have a chance to decide about the Lullaby. Something within my room clicks. I should check on it. I should lick the Lullaby just this once to keep me safe, and I . . .

I am in the doorway of Brandt's office. His own private office upstairs. Does he have one? In my shallow dreams, it makes sense that he would. As much sense as the ridiculous red velvet coat he's wearing, high-collared and flocked in fuzzy swirls of gold. A silly dream, not a nightmare after all. I'm safe.

He looks at me and waits for me to speak, but something blocks my throat, like I've swallowed my food down the wrong way. "May I help you?" he finally says, voice brittle as glass, and sets down his pen on the blotter.

I start to speak, but rather than words, we converse in song. No discernable lyrics—it's a flighty opera, like the one Vera and I heard at the Imperial Opera House while snooping on a soprano who owed money to the Bayside gang. Our song feels like fine grains of sand rubbing between my fingertips. A very strange dream.

Somehow, I convey to him that I'll take the letter he's writing to Durst to the ravens for him when he's done. Then everything goes fuzzy, like a pure white fur coat I once saw on the Empress. When I snap back to myself, the letter is clenched in my hand—it smells like lemons—and Brandt's hand is on top of mine on the desk.

"Did you love him?" he asks in a turquoise tone. We're no longer singing, though the opera aria plays away behind us. "Is Farthing what you truly want? I won't be angry—I'm sorry for how I behaved in the tunnels. I'm just worried for you—for what Marez might still try to do."

The opera halts; Brandt's lantern dims, and he seems to stand at twice his normal height. Dimly, I feel something shift at my hip, like a jeweled sword sliding into a sheath. The sillier elements of my dream retreat into the shadows, and I'm left with something terrifyingly close to reality. I knew I should have taken the Lullaby. I'm only a little girl playing at emotions I can't grasp.

"I'm not sure of what I felt for him, but it wasn't love. And it was built on lies."

"That doesn't mean what you felt wasn't genuine." Brandt looks away.

"But I know it wasn't love." I take a step toward him, steady and solid. "Because I've always loved you."

He rears back like I've slapped him. The air glows between us, and the office walls become a waterfall. "Livia." When he says my name, it flutters like a feather tickling my skin. "Livia, please . . ."

"I know." I take a step back. "I can't—We can't."

"I—But you—" It's his turn to choke on his words now, and they rise from him like glimmering soap bubbles. I taste the sound of them popping, and it tastes like honey. "I had no idea. I thought you didn't—Livia, I didn't know, and if anything happened to you again—Like what happened today—" He staggers toward me. "Why didn't you tell me this before? Livia, why?"

"Because it can't change anything!" My heart twists—this dream is far too real. But instead of the pain I expected such words would bring, the emotions slowly leak out of me, spiraling away, like I've washed them down the drain.

"But, Livia . . ." Brandt looks at me like I've stabbed him. "You never even acted like—"

I am split in two, one part of me rushing toward him to bury my face in that warm velvet robe, the other steered back by a comforting hand. It feels like Professor Hesse's when he'd guide me gently away from the Dean's office. He was always there to rescue me. What's he rescuing me from now?

The guiding hand wins. I don't know how, but it plucks me up, and we soar, soar over Barstadt City where the Farthing soldiers clump up like curds in the city streets, where Nightmare's bones glint with moonlight, dazzling and fierce.

Nightmare. Nightmare. There is something more I'm being guided to do.

Brandt's letter to the minister falls from my grip as the hand drops me. I drift through the air like a fallen leaf, fluttering onto the empty streets of Barstadt—no, it's Oneiros now. But where

302

are the Dreamer's Shapers, the priests? The cobblestones ring out like cannon fire under my footfalls. Birds should scatter in my wake; dreamers should peer from their carefully constructed dwellings to see what all the noise is.

I stare up at the Dreamer's Spire and suppress a shudder. Last time I was here I was attacked by the Nightmare Wastes, but I don't sense any of their darkness tonight. Normally, I'd pray to the Dreamer to keep me safe, just in case, but I can't seem to think of any words that feel right.

Even if I did pray to him, there'd only be that roar of silence, a desperate vacuum begging to be filled with noise.

I head into the entrance to the Dreamer's Spire, where water flows down one side of a great domed room and then flows back up on the other side. But there is no trickling, no gushing sounds. I circle the chamber and flick my fingers into its stream but feel nothing. The gold-flecked smooth stone dome reminds me of stars peeking through a haze of clouds. It's the perfect setting in which to feel the Dreamer's Embrace, but I feel nothing. I am completely and utterly alone.

There's a depression at the chamber's center—I don't notice it until I almost trip into it. It looks like someone has pried away a golden medallion that was set into the floor, revealing a strange pattern of molded black glass beneath the marble tiles. Four massive gemstones sparkle in specially carved settings in the glass; a channel of molten gold flows around them, webbing them together. I've seen this pattern before—the artwork on the door of Hesse's cabinet. The gems pulse dimly, and something finally punctures the fog of noiselessness.

Whispers.

I kneel down and cup my ear over the gemstones to pick out their words. At first they're too soft, like fingers rustling across silk. Then syllables emerge, bobbing in the streams of sound, but I can't decipher them. I hold my breath, but even my pounding pulse is too loud over the voices.

—in a fiery blaze. Melt their hopes from their bones. Feast upon the marrow of despair and make a cloak of their hides. Nothing tastes so sweet as hopelessness. Drink it in like blood, and poison them with the failures they can't escape—

I leap back from the well as if I've been burned. Panic worms through me and I wheeze, trying desperately to breathe even though I'm certain the air itself will drown me. Nightmare, Nightmare. The shards of Nightmare's heart. Four of them, right in the holiest place in all of Oneiros. And one empty groove in the black glass, where the final shard will go . . .

You will fail them all, but you will not fail me. The gems flash before my eyes, washing away all other sight, as they whisper through the room. *You will bring us the last shard. And thank us for the privilege. My heart will be bound once more.*

A shadowed figure emerges from the darkness, the firelight slithering across her facial gemstones. Lady Twyne. A vicious smile curves her lips. A seeping wound stink floods the temple, turning it into a swamp. My eyesight swims. The water turns to tar, flowing up and down around me like the bars of a cell. I hear something circling my cage, like a pacing animal with long, deadly claws. It growls, low and feral in the back of its throat.

You will bow.

Dreamer, please, I whisper silently. He may ignore me, but I have to try. *If ever there was a time I needed your embrace, it's now. I've fought the Wastes before but I don't know if I have the strength tonight—*

Water splashes across my face, warm and welcome as it cuts through the sulfurous chill of my captors. I gulp down air and sit up in bed. Someone's staring at me—my eyes slowly focus on her flyaway hair and dingy gown.

"I'm sorry." Sora's cheeks are flushed with scarlet; big fat tears cling to her chin. "I'm so sorry, but you wouldn't wake up, I know you said never to wake you unless it's an emergency, but he's gone too far and I had to warn you—"

"What? What's happening?" I blink slowly. My thoughts are packed with gauze. Nothing's making any sense, and my vision is strewn with cast-off images from my dreams.

"The Farthingers." Sora looks away from me. "The invasion's begun."

Chapter Twenty-Four

Brandt stands right behind Sora, glowering at me like I put a toad in his trousers. I can hear boots heavy against the barrack corridors, the distant report of cannon fire on the battlements overhead. "The Farthingers are attacking? What about the Commandant's troops?" I ask.

"They've breached the bay." Brandt clenches his jaw. "Our blockade never even saw them approach. They just—*manifested* inside the harbor."

"No—are you certain?" I ask, springing from bed. But Brandt's expression leaves no room for doubt. "They're using transference. Hesse's theorem—traveling into Oneiros and then back out to cover great distances." I wince. "Must be a damned powerful priest to be able to do that for a whole fleet."

"And we have more immediate problems here," Brandt says. "The Farthingers have confiscated the Ministry for themselves. We tried to burn as many records as we could, but the first place they went was the archives, and now they're rounding up all our operatives."

"Nightmare's teeth. We have to help the other operatives."
My pulse is racing; I scan the quarters for something, anything
we could defend ourselves with. "Are we still safe here in the
barracks? We can lead everyone out."

"We barricaded the doors, but it won't last much longer if
help doesn't arrive." He narrows his eyes. "You sent the message to Durst, right?"

I stare through him as some fragment of a dream drifts past
me. "The message?" Did we have a conversation about this last
night? No, surely I dreamt it. Wait—was Brandt in my dream?
"Are you talking about—You were writing a letter to the
minister. In my dreams."

Brandt's shoulders tighten. "No, I'm not talking about
dreams. I'm talking about your little show at my office. You
were supposed to send the letter to Minister Durst at the
palace to tell him about the Farthingers. Nightmares, this is
perfect." He turns away from me. "If you're going to pretend none of that happened . . . that you didn't say those
things—"

"I'm not pretending! I'm just trying to understand. You mean
that wasn't a dream?"

Something shatters in the corner of the room. We both whip
around to find Sora staring at the broken porcelain ewer at her
feet. Her eyes go wide as eggs, and she begins to tremble as tears
run down her face.

"Sora, darling." I throw my arms around her. "Shh, shh, it's
going to be all right. It was just an accident. We'll worry about it
later." I pet her springy curls. "We need to make our way out of

the Ministry right now. Do you think you can help us through the tunnels?"

"It's not an accident!" she sobs, shoulders heaving under my grasp. "It's all my fault! Please, Miss Livia, don't be angry with me. I was only trying to—to get out of the tunnels, like you did."

I pat her shoulders. "Sora, it's all right. We'll get out of this. But we can't fix it if you don't tell us what's happened."

She pulls back from me and turns her head aside. "He said he loved me. That he'd take me away from here. I was only trying to make a better life for myself. I—I didn't know!"

Brandt rounds on us slowly, eyes hooded. "Who promised you what, Sora?" His voice is deathly, stiflingly still. "What have you done?"

"The—the Farthing man. Marez." She smears a trail of snot onto her sleeve. "He said if I'd let him in the barracks a few nights here and there, bring him up through the tunnels—"

I stagger back from her. My chest aches like someone took a hammer to it, and all I hear in my ears is the ringing of cannon shots.

"You let him into the Ministry? Into the barracks?" Brandt seizes Sora by the collar of her shift. Then, in a wave of revulsion, he lets her go and drives his boot down onto the fragments of porcelain instead. This time, his swears are so vivid I couldn't repeat them if I wanted to.

Sora quakes like a cornered hare, each fresh sob gurgling from her lips with a high-pitched snap. "He couldn't get into the Ministry building proper because of the guards, and there are no tunnel entrances to the main building. He had these rags that smelled like molded parchment . . ."

"Mothwood," I whisper. The word comes from somewhere deep inside of me, an instinctive reaction. But the rest of me is adrift. Mothwood smoke. Marez sending me into the dream-world with mothwood . . .

Sora nods slowly. "I think that's what he called it, yes."

My throat aches like I've been swallowing glass. Marez isn't just a slimy operative. He's a dreamstrider, too.

Hesse's angry, vengeful test subject—subject 39.

I cover my mouth with my hand and will myself not to cry. "Marez is a dreamstrider. He must be. And he's been dream-striding with my body to get the Ministry's secrets." All those strange dreams of digging through the Ministry archives rush back to me now. Searching for more information about the shards of Nightmare's heart. Marez used me in my sleep, when he only needed my identity to grant him access. And when I was awake, he used me, too—like guiding him through the tunnels last night.

Of all people, I should have seen the signs—but I didn't have a clue.

"He promised he'd buy me my citizenship papers," Sora says, scrubbing away her tears. "Promised to take me back to Far-thing. He said he loved me! I had no idea he was after Livia. I swear, I didn't know—"

"Enough." Brandt's every muscle is tightened like a loaded catapult as he cups one hand around my shoulder. "Liv, I know you're in shock . . ." He bites off whatever else he'd been about to say, jaw muscles working. "But we have to leave *now*, before the Farthing army breaches the barracks. If you never sent that letter, then Durst doesn't know that the Farthingers mean us harm—"

Jorn appears in the doorway, a pack slung over his shoulder. "I couldn't get everything you asked," he tells Brandt. "There's too many of them."

"We'll have to make do." Brandt turns back to Sora. "We need you to get us through the tunnels. Then we can talk about your betrayal," he adds, with a fresh edge in his voice.

"Of course." Sora stifles a sob and draws a deep breath. I can see the tunneler in her shine through. While I share Brandt's rage—how dare she, after everything I've done for her? But if I were still in the tunnels, wouldn't I have done the same for a chance to escape? Didn't I believe the same wretched lie from those velvet lips? Disgust is curdling, poisonous and sour, inside of me, and I don't know whether I feel it more for Sora or myself.

No, Marez deserves it most of all.

I snatch up Professor Hesse's journal and shove it into my bag, as well as a handful of tithes. The knowledge of Marez's true identity feels like iron in my boots, weighing me down as I try to keep up with Brandt and Sora through the barracks halls. Hesse never specified what happened to Subject 39—I assumed he'd been consumed by the Nightmare Wastes, or else that he decided the danger was too great and forfeited his claim to power. But the truth seems much crueler, and I wonder if that's what sent the professor into such despair. Marez is a dreamstrider with no regard for the Dreamer or the rules of the dreamworld. A dreamstrider who sought to use his powers against the Dreamer's people instead of for them. Marez told me himself how he craved balance, to seize a power that he no longer felt Barstadt deserved. But is that, too, a lie? How much can I trust the doubts I've had in Barstadt and the Dreamer, knowing he steered me down that path?

What more did he need from me? He can already dreamstride; while I'm sure he would love to deprive Barstadt of my ability, there must have been more to it. He needed me for something specific.

I stop in the middle of the corridor, just outside the laborers' entrance that leads to the Imperial Quarter tunnels beneath the ministry building. "The key." I smack myself on the forehead. "The cabinet in Hesse's Oneiros home—he used my memories to find it in Hesse's old storage room, from after his office flooded. I didn't even remember it myself, but it must have been there, recessed deep in my memories."

Brandt reaches for my hand to pull me into the dark mouth of the tunnels. In the distance, we can hear the dull echoes of shuffling feet. "Marez took what was in that cabinet?"

I steel myself against the cool, damp air as we follow the twisting stairwell deep into the earth. "It must have been the binding ritual. In Oneiros—the gemstones—they said his heart will be bound once more. Nightmare's heart. He has everything he needs to launch an assault on Barstadt with Nightmare's help." My hands flutter uselessly against each other. I can't allow that tremor into my voice for what I have to say next. "Marez is the Commandant's mystic, who promised him a warbeast. Nightmare."

Brandt swears, and Sora wails with a fresh set of tears. But she only allows herself that one outburst. She clamps her jaw shut as we enter the main trunk line that runs beneath the Ministry and Imperial Square. A throng of workers stream in both directions past the enforcers at the tunnel's mouth, joined by more than a few folk who I suspect are refugees like ourselves. I dive my hand into my coat pocket, feeling around for the stash of tithes I keep on me, but instead my fingers brush across the wrapped ball of Lullaby.

A line of escapees and workers snakes down the tunnel, and we shuffle into the flow, heads down, unquestioning. Jorn shuffles alongside me with all the coolness of a caged tiger, though the tunneler instincts in him, too, keep his gaze cast down.

Brandt takes a deep breath. "All right. We can use this. If the Farthingers have free access to the Imperial tunnels—"

"Not free," Sora says. "The tunnels connecting to the palace were sealed after the last protest by the Destroyers. But they do have the gang leaders' support and access to several of the main tunnels."

"So the gang here knew the invasion was coming?" I ask.

"That's my understanding, yes." Sora scowls. "Our gang bosses told us all to report to work as usual, though the Destroyers were hinting they had other plans."

"And we already know one of the gangs supplied them with mothwood smoke. Among other things, most likely." Brandt scowls. "Their dealer must know where Marez and Kriza are stationed."

"So we'll just charge into the gang leader's office and demand to know their whereabouts! That'll go over wondrously," I say.

Sora flinches. Jorn cracks his knuckles. "I can try to reach out to the Destroyers. See if they'd be willing to aid me one last time," he says.

Brandt frowns. "They might just as easily turn you in to Retch for the bounty on all our heads."

"Sora," I ask, looking between her and Jorn. "Which gang has control of the tunnels beneath the Ministry of Affairs these days?"

She bites down hard on her lip and mumbles something, the sound lost in the crunch of gravel underneath our feet.

I draw a deep breath. I cannot lose my temper. I need every ounce of energy I have left to find us a way out of this mess. "I'm sorry. What did you say?" I ask as calmly and as patiently as I can.

"Stargazers," she says again.

Brandt crashes into the person in front of him. I nearly choke on my own tongue. And Jorn, Jorn—he sweeps Sora off her feet and in no time at all is dangling her over the stream of runoff by her ankles.

"We're headed straight into Stargazer territory?" He rattles her like he can shake the truth away.

"Enough!" I cry, tugging at his arm. "It's not as if we have any other options. These tunnels are our only way out. Put her down already!"

Jorn flips her around and plops her right on the edge of the creek. Her arms windmill as she seeks balance. An older man sniffs at us.

The Stargazers will be another matter entirely. And right at the fore of their constellation is Adolphus Retch. The man whose main bodyguard Brandt and I liberated so long ago, at the same exact moment his Lullaby operation burned up at the docks, just after he murdered his lieutenant in cold blood. The man who's promised to kill Jorn if he ever sets foot in Stargazer territory again.

"Well then," Brandt says. He flicks the coin I'd given him as his tithe into the air and catches it. "Let's make the best of it. Any way we could get the Destroyers involved?"

"We just might." Jorn fingers a scar that spans the knuckles of his left hand. We're nearly to the gang lieutenant's post, where he collects each tunneler's tithe. "Do you trust me?" Jorn asks.

No, says the voice in the back of my mind, without hesitation. He may have kept us alive in Birnau, during the Stargazer Incident, and plenty of times between. But this is personal for him.

But Brandt answers for us, chin high, defiant. "I don't see how we have any choice."

314

Chapter Twenty-Five

The new Stargazer headquarters, in a shunted-off portion of the Imperial catacombs, are certainly a step up from Retch's old Bayside tunnel digs. Clearly the Incident didn't set them back for long. Each chamber is more elaborately decorated than the one before, with shimmering golden mosaics and marble sarcophagi and altars ablaze with scented candles, although the scruffy, leather-clad guards do detract from the effect. Jorn binds Brandt's and my hands and gags us, and escorts us through the fifth or so set of guardsmen.

Finally, we reach the wrought iron gates, framed in human skulls and flanked by stacks of femurs. Part of the original Imperial catacombs, or Adolphus's own special touch? I doubt I want to know.

"Well, well, well." A vicious smirk curves the first guard's mouth. "Jornisander the Destroyer. Look at this, boys. I guess these catacombs have ghosts in them after all."

I glance at the second guard, who's watching Jorn like he

might evaporate before his eyes. "Retch told us you were dead, or good as."

"Nah, not dead, though he's about to be. Who let *you* through?" the first guardsman asks. He sizes up Jorn, who, for all his considerable girth, only reaches this man's nose. Does Adolphus breed them or what? If we had an army full of cast-off Stargazer muscle, maybe we wouldn't be cowering under the press of Farthing and the Commandant right now.

"I understand your boss has a bounty on all three of our heads," Jorn says. He spits into the canal and glowers right back at the guard, as if he'd spat in his face. "I'll take my chances that I can spare one with two."

The first guard snorts. "All right, Jornisander. It's your head." He pulls the pins holding the gruesome gate in place, and it swings open under its own grave weight.

The second guard, however, is still staring at Jorn with a twitch to his face. "A lot of folks believed in the Destroyers. A lot of folks gave their lives to continue the work your ilk began," he says, looking Jorn square in the eye. "Was quite a blow to learn you were a stool for the Ministry after all."

"Why give a damn about what I did, or didn't do? The Destroyers were never about me. They were about justice." Jorn shakes his head. "You don't need me to fight for the Writ. To oppose the gangs. If they only fought for me, then they were fools."

The guard puffs up his chest. "They're fighting still. We— they'll win freedom without your help!"

"Good." Jorn grins, though there's no warmth behind it. "As

they should. And they should start with bastards like Retch, who let these Farthing monsters take over *our* city—"

"Shut your bloody mouth," the first guard snaps at Jorn. "How about you wait outside, Tomas? You and I need to have a little chat."

Tomas's cheeks darken. "Y-yes. Sorry."

But Jorn lowers his mouth toward Tomas's ear as we pass, only for a second, before we follow the first guard through the gate.

Adolphus Retch's lair is a vulgar twin to the Emperor's—vaulted ceilings gilded in moss and water stains instead of gold. What it lacks in surface space, it more than makes up for with all the absurdly unnecessary bits of treasure crammed into the slots where the early aristocrats' bones once lay. Glittering golden trinkets, stacks of pottery from the kingdom that preceded the Commandant's Land of the Iron Winds, scrolls depicting Oneiros and Nightmare and the Farthing forests and the Itinerant Sea and the ivory-skinned tribesmen of the north. One sarcophagus has been refashioned as a massive bed, complete with a white-eyed concubine sprawled under a satin sheet. A shudder tears through me as we walk past her; I try not to consider the likelihood of my mother inhabiting some similar Lullaby-pacified fate. I know only that she secured protection for our corner of the tunnels, and I never questioned at what price.

Adolphus Retch, boss of the Stargazer gang, stands up from his jagged throne. He himself could pass for a distant relative to the Emperor, now that I look at him. Shorter and rounder, but with the same fired-clay look of a man who'll down a shot of rye with you one minute and throw you in the bear cage the next. The already lazy smile on his moist lips swells up like a blister as he scans the unbelievable prize that just walked itself through his doors.

"Jornisander the Destroyer! Or is it Betrayer now? My least favorite bodyguard. And what were your names again? Barton and Olga?" He tucks his thumbs into his armpits. "Well, I'm sure they weren't your real names anyhow."

Jorn pushes Brandt and I onto the stairs leading to the altar; without our hands free to catch ourselves, we crumple onto the floor. Jorn's boots are caked with sewage and slough as he treads before us. "When I left your service, I stayed out of the tunnels. Not once did I breach your territory. Call me a deserter if you like, but I've done you no harm."

"No harm?" Retch erupts with laughter. "You mean aside from turning me against my best lieutenant and burning down the entire Stargazer warehouse? And how about the ensuing riot that ran me out of the Dockside tunnels? You're as bloody harmless as a sewer roach, aren't you!"

"And look at you now. King of the Imperial tunnels. Hard to see that as anything but a step up," Jorn says.

"Mm. But you don't know the price I paid for it." Retch's voice is thin as a rapier. I wrestle myself to a sitting position. He wants to speak of prices paid? My blood boils at the thought. He better not dare blame us for what he's done—for selling all of Barstadt to the Farthingers.

"I know something of it." Jorn sounds like he's chewing marble. "Your steady buyers from Farthing, for a start."

"Not your concern," Retch responds, too coolly. He's not

318

rising to the bait. Brandt catches my eye, and I blink to give my consent. Dreamer, bless that boy for always knowing my thoughts! "Oh," Retch continues, "by the way—if you think you're going to trade these two in to clear your bounty, you're going to be very disappointed. Boys?"

Two behemoth guardsmen flank Jorn. They're too swift, even for him. Each snares one of his arms, and they fling him onto his back across a sarcophagus. Adolphus is on him like a scorpion, blade raised over Jorn's sternum to strike.

"You're right. I rebuilt my little chemical fiefdom from scratch. Mothwood and Lullaby—they sell well enough, I suppose, but here's where the real money is to be made."

Brandt's foot hovers in front of him; he rolls it so gently onto the stone floor it's like he's giving it a kiss. The next foot follows suit. Stitch by stitch, he silently rises to standing, without even a pop of his knees. From my view at his back, I see the rope dance free from one wrist—Jorn bound them with a trick knot—and he slips it inside the sleeve of the other.

In the corner behind the guards, a little slip of a shadow glides along the wall, small enough to have been just a flicker in the candle flame.

"Nightmare's bile, they call it on the streets. Dash of used cleansing water and a wicked slurry of poison. You'll feel like you're stewing in Nightmare's gut."

Adolphus swipes the blade down Jorn's chest. A shallow cut, but Jorn's screams rattle the catacombs to their marrow. I don't have time to contemplate why before Brandt flies onto Retch's back, moving in one seamless motion as my unlaced bindings slither to the ground. Brandt hooks his rope bindings around Retch's throat like he's bridling a horse. "Guards!" Retch wheezes.

Tomas storms in, blade drawn. He looks at Retch and Brandt, then at Jorn and the guards holding him. "Is it true?" Tomas asks Retch. "You've let the Farthingers take control?"

"You're just cattle to be sold," Retch says. "What do you care who owns you?"

Tomas lunges at the guard, who drops Jorn and throws up an arm to block the stab. Tomas's dagger flies across the room. But Tomas presses forward. He grapples with the other guard. They tumble to the floor, and with a swift punch, the other guard goes limp, unconscious beneath Tomas.

I run to Jorn's side, but he's flailing his arms like a sail ripped loose. Once I manage to pin his arms down, I see why. The wound itself is mild, but his veins are blackening around it, webbing across his rib cage. "What's happening to him?"

Retch laughs, hoarse and wheezing as Brandt pulls the rope tighter. "He's trapped in his nightmares now."

Jorn jerks, twisting as if trying to evade countless blows. "You can fight them," I plead with him. "Pray to the Dreamer. Think of a reason to fight . . ."

Adolphus cackles, straining against the rope at his throat. "Your Dreamer is a lie. He won't help you. Your doom is coming—I can hear its wings, beating like a heart."

"Don't say another word except to answer our questions." Brandt yanks the rope tighter; Sora scurries around him to bind Retch's hands and legs.

Jorn's eyes roll back into his head. Dreamer's mercy, he's not going to make it. Could I enter his consciousness with him, fight the nightmares for him? I thumb the vial at my throat. I'm running low—we weren't able to grab reserves from the storage room in the main Ministry building before we left. I have to save it for Marez, if I can, but if it means helping Jorn . . .

"First question. What did you supply the Farthing spies with besides mothwood?" Brandt asks, holding firm on the rope.

"Connections." Retch wheezes. "Information."

He pulls tighter. "Too vague. What kind of information?"

"Nothing that's any of your business." Despite his purpling face, Retch manages a vicious grin.

I seize one of the fallen guard's daggers and press the tip against Retch's gut. "Everyone knows how you treat your enemies, and I've seen how you treat your friends. I have no problems plunging this into you if you're not willing to cooperate." I tilt my head to one side with a smile. I've spent too long on the other side of blades like this, from Marez and all the rest—it's time we gained the advantage. "Don't be fooled by my aristocratic friends. I'm from the tunnels. I'm not afraid to fight to survive."

Retch's eyes bulge dangerously from their sockets. "Fine, fine. They were after some artifacts."

"You'll have to do better," Brandt growls. I press the knife harder against his gut.

A raw desperation gurgles in Retch's throat. "All right! They were after Nightmare shards. To reassemble Nightmare's heart. My—my smugglers have been hunting the shards for a while, and—"

"And you *gave* them that information?"

"Who cares? It's just an old myth! Yes!" Retch slurps down a greedy breath. "There are five major ones. Lady Twyne smuggled one in from the northern colonies. The Commandant found one in one of his quarries; one belonged to Farthing pirates, and the fourth was in the monolith in the High Temple."

What Kriza must have stolen last night at the High Temple. My heart sinks.

Brandt presses in. His knee plunges into Retch's back now, grinding him into the corpse dust of the catacomb floors. "And where is the final shard?"

Retch's words are a chopped, minced mess. "I—don't—know!"

The rope squeaks as Brandt pulls it tighter. "You said five *major* ones."

"That's right. Rumor has it some of the aristocrats wear smaller shards in their faces." Retch manages a dry laugh. "Now that they've got the five big ones, the Farthingers were going to . . . 'dream' the shards into Oneiros somehow. Don't ask me how. Once they've re-formed Nightmare's heart in Oneiros, they can resurrect him and bind him to their will. But they need the blood of the Emperor and the Commandant to do it."

"So that's the binding ritual." I groan. My hypothesis was right: they stole the papers from the empty cabinet in Hesse's Oneiros home. The research he wanted me to destroy. "It doesn't just reassemble Nightmare's heart? It gives him control over Nightmare, too?"

"Oh, yes." Retch laughs again. "A mighty weapon at our command. And there's naught you can do."

"Where are the Farthingers?" Brandt asks, digging the rope tighter. "Where are they doing this?"

"Restoration artisan shop. Borders the Palace Square. Not—not far from here."

Brandt nods, satisfied. "Then we can start with that. Sora?"

Sora brings him a mothwood rag, and he shoves it into Retch's mouth. Finally, Retch's horrid noises stop as he falls unconscious, and Brandt sets to work tying him up. "We'll bring him back to the Ministry, once it's safe."

But Jorn's still convulsing, fighting the wretched nightmares. I smell his panic thick in the air; a cold sweat clings to his forehead. "Please," I whisper, stroking his forehead. "Stay with us."

The Lullaby! I plunge my hand into my coat and tear away the wax wrapper. Sugary nausea floods my nose, but I force myself to peel back Jorn's lips and smear the wad of resin against his gums. His eyes cloud over, but his breathing flattens out; he ceases to struggle. He releases short, shallow breaths—stable ones.

"He lied," a woman groans.

The woman in the bed. Dreamer's mercy, I'd forgotten about her. We turn toward her as she dangles one wrist in the air with what must be the sum total of her will. She's slender as a bird, with a halo of knotted blond hair shielding her face from our scrutiny.

"The final shard. I know where it is." She draws a long, slow breath—savoring it, perhaps, as the first breath today that's been truly hers, and not another part of her debt to Adolphus Retch. "The girls who work at the palace whisper about it. It's the ruby in the Emperor's forehead."

"Bloody nightmares. Of course." Brandt bashes his palm against his forehead. "So that'll be their next target. And they have the whole Farthing army at their backs to take the palace."

"We'll stop them." I stand up, letting my fingers unravel from Jorn's, and walk over to the woman. She's sunk back into the mattress with her glossy dove-gray stare, but I take her hand and force her fingers around some heavy gold coins. Once the lieutenants take their cut, it may only buy her a week's worth of meat, but it has to be better than dreamlessly wallowing in this monster's bed.

Sora dunks a rag into an ewer and presses it to Jorn's brow. "Is it all right to wake him up, Liv?"

"No! No." Plucking someone out of a forced dreamless state is always risky. "Damn. We need him to stay here until he wakes up." At least he's in a shallow dream, not vulnerable in Oneiros. I silently hope Nightmare's legions are chasing Retch down in Oneiros as we speak.

Brandt nods. "All right. Sora, you'll stay here. Keep Jorn safe. Livia, let's get to that workshop where the Farthingers set up shop. Maybe we can stop them from transferring the last shard of Nightmare's heart." He joins me at the bedside. "Is there another way out of here?" he asks the woman.

I thought she'd dozed off again, but she slings one arm across her chest. "You can go back out the way you came. Or you can climb the stargazing port."

Of course. Even deep in Barstadt City's forgotten bowels, Adolphus Retch had to have his stars, to remind him of the greatest luxury that no other tunneler can afford—the sky, whenever he wanted it. "We'll climb," I say.

"Behind the throne. Key's on his belt," she says, and her eyes flutter shut.

I press a kiss to Jorn's brow, which has thankfully returned to normal temperature, and cinch his shirt closed over the wound. It's no longer a hungry shade of black but the green of fading bruises. It'll have to be enough.

"Be careful," Sora calls as Brandt unlocks the stargazing tunnel door with a terrific groan and the shudder of countless weights and gears spinning into place.

Without looking back, Brandt and I climb the iron rungs under the pinpricked tunnel's roof of blackening clouds.

Chapter Twenty-Six

We climb several stories, the rusty metal rungs tacky under our palms, and emerge into a narrow courtyard, hemmed in by sloping warehouses and grain silos, all of them doubtless under Stargazer control. It's early morning, not that we can tell it from the thick stormclouds in the sky, tinged with reddish brown. My shoulders are on fire from climbing up the ladder of the narrow shaft, and Brandt looks similarly strained as he scans the buildings around us. "Let's see . . . the warehouse should be this way." I point toward an alley's mouth and we set off.

"So you think Marez's been entering your subconsciousness," Brandt says, words carefully sorted. I don't like this Brandt mask, cool and far-afield, unlike any he's ever worn when speaking to me before.

"It has to be. I've had strange dreams lately, where I'm snooping around the Ministry, and other odd things. And you say our conversation last night was real—"

He cuts me off with a finger to his lips, tilting his head toward the entrance to the alleyway. I don't hear anything but the distant rumble of something—horses, maybe, or siege weaponry rolling through the street.

"They're advancing on the palace?" I ask, but Brandt shushes me again.

He's right. Something in the sound is off—a vibration so faint I nearly lose it in the gaps between my thundering heartbeats. Then it crescendos, vibrating faster and faster. It starts in the earth but roars up into the buildings that crowd around us. A window bursts high overhead, and shards of glass cascade onto our heads. Dirt rattles loose from the building frame.

And then I see that there's blood dribbling down the alleyway, loping back and forth through the cobblestone channels. It's boiling over the channels, sprouting up from the cobblestones into almost-human shapes—

"It's Nightmare's minions." I seize Brandt's hand and yank him in the opposite direction. "They're breaking through from Oneiros!"

We tear through the alleys until we stumble onto the main boulevard, but the nightmares have already taken shape. Winged, featherless birds stride through the streets, talons grasping for Barstadters as they flee, screaming.

One beast scoops up a man in its talons. The man deflates like a waterskin, sobbing and shaking as all color and life drains away from him. The beast, swollen and taller now, casts the body aside.

Misery rolls over us in waves. Brandt's grip on my hand slackens; his face sags like a melting candle. The sadness I feel is a more sinister, angry variety than I'd encountered before, when confronted with these monsters in Oneiros. I imagine striking out at Edina Alizard, slitting her throat, only to have Brandt witness it and turn against me. Rage burns me up from the inside.

"Fight it," I whisper, squeezing Brandt's hand with all the strength I've got. "Think of something good. Something worth fighting for."

And then the earth stills, as though it was only rolling over in its sleep. The terrors turn to smoke mid-stride, like a mirage on the road.

"What happened?" Brandt asks, panting, his hand still taut around my wrist.

"They must be still partially trapped in Oneiros," I say. "That means the final shard hasn't joined the rest."

"But for how long?" he mutters.

We take off and sprint across the square. The artisan's shop that the Farthingers converted into their base of operations is a glassblowing studio, and half-assembled chandeliers, statues, and other oddities pepper the main floor like severed stumps. The forge is extinguished, but a lone guard circles the studio's interior, his unimaginative patrol pattern visibly worn along the otherwise dusty floor. We lurk for a moment behind the spiraling chandeliers before we dart for the staircase when his back is turned. I say a soft prayer to the Dreamer that the stairs don't creak and give us away.

We wait outside the door to the upstairs office, and Brandt mouths a count of three before swinging it wide.

From the gust of the door opening, papers skitter across the surface of the office desk, but nothing else budges. Our eyes adjust to the fuzzy gray dark, and we rove around the space. Brandt instinctively moves right, and I move to the left, back in our familiar pattern. Maps of Barstadt City are smeared across the walls—formal Imperial cartographers' maps and hand-drawn scrawls and tunnel diagrams painted onto pressed boards. There's a map of the Land of the Iron Winds and topographical maps of an archeological dig.

The last map is roughly but delicately, lovingly, rendered on stretched canvas. I recognize it instantly from the golden spire piercing its heart.

Oneiros.

Brandt snatches up a fistful of letters bearing the seal of House Twyne. "I should have known earlier that they were all working together. Bleeding dreams, I knew there was something not right with those Farthingers." I should have known, too, I think, but our shame won't help us now.

Brandt comes to rest beside me before the map of Oneiros, his gaze tracing that soaring spire, its gleaming golden crown. Brandt has never seen Oneiros as it should be—alive with the Dreamer's faithful, not bloodied with Nightmare spawn. But Oneiros is crumbling, and if Marez and Twyne have their way, Barstadt will be next for Nightmare to devour.

"What do you recommend, then?" He groans, slumping into a desk chair. "How can we stop them from resurrecting Nightmare?"

Even as he says it, the truth is under his nails, like a splinter, but he can't acknowledge it, can't pry it out. He's afraid, and I am, too. I would rather swallow the whole sticky wad of Lullaby that weighs down my coat than do what I know we must. I would infiltrate the Commandant's stronghold at the Citadel or Birnau a thousand times if it meant never having to walk the path before me.

I don't have a choice, not really. I am *not* the only dreamstrider in the world.

But I'm the only one who can set this right.

"I'll go back into Oneiros," I say, trying not to choke on the words. "I'll find a way to stop them in there." *Somehow. Dreamer, please help me.* A sob worms into my throat.

"But how?" Brandt asks.

"I don't know. I've tried to live my life in a way that honors the Dreamer. I know I'm not—I haven't been strong enough, clever enough, to feel his embrace. But what other choice do I have but to trust in him right now? Barstadt needs us. They need the Dreamer, and me by his side."

Brandt sits up straight in the chair, and he doesn't have to lift a finger for me to know he's heard something. My thudding heart, my anxious breaths fade into background noise, and my every sense homes in on the muted voices in the workshop below us.

And then boots clatter on the staircase.

Brandt stands, quietly, just as quiet as when he'd prepared to strike at Adolphus Retch. He seizes a map tube lying in the corner, wielding it like a bludgeon, and creeps beside the door.

I'm pinned in place at the center of the room, but at least I serve as a distraction. As bait.

The door opens, and Kriza strides through. She stares straight through me, mouth just beginning to round on a vowel of surprise or a curse. But there's no time for her to finish it. Brandt brings the tubing to bear at the base of her skull, and she crumples forward.

But she doesn't go down without a fight. She rolls onto her back and bends her knees to leap back up, but Brandt forces a mothwood kerchief over her face. I crouch beside her and jam my palm over her mouth and nose to keep it in place. She writhes once, twice, and then uncoils as her mind tumbles into the Nightmare-infested world of Oneiros.

Whatever the nightmares do to her there, she deserves it.

"We'll have to smuggle her out of here. Take her somewhere safe for questioning," Brandt says. He tears through the room, probably in search of rope.

"You can't be serious." I stare up at him from my crouch on the floor. "She's not going to tell us anything. And anyway, what could we do even if she did?" I tug on the cord around my neck and fish out the pendant that carries the vial of dreamwort. "What if I can use Kriza's body?"

He stops, hand falling limply away from the drawer he'd just opened. "Please, Liv. If Oneiros looks anything like those monsters we just faced . . ."

"Do you know a better way?" I ask, nostrils flashing. "I don't see any other choice. If I'm Kriza, then I can approach the

Farthing army officers, learn the specifics of their plans. Maybe send them away from the palace gates. Then you can get my body somewhere safe, and find a way to send word to Minister Durst and the Emperor inside the palace."

Brandt shakes his head, stepping back. "No, Liv, please. I couldn't bear it if you—I mean, when I thought—" His jaw shifts from side to side. "Livia, I have to know. What you said to me last night—" He stares at me, all semblance of masks vanished.

I take a step toward him. I feel now the fire in my veins— the fire he's always stoked in me, the one I refused to acknowledge. "I may have thought it was a dream, but I meant what I said." I'm shaking; why do I fear these words more than Nightmare's spawn? But I have to be strong. I need to tell him the truth. "I love you. I've always loved you. You're like my other mind, my other soul. You always know what's best for me, and I always want to know what's best for you."

Brandt cups my face in his hands. "Dreamer, but I'm such a fool. I thought you couldn't possibly feel what I felt . . . That you saw me as a reckless brother, a boring high-society clod."

"Because it wasn't my place to see you as more!" I cry.

He wraps his arms around my neck. "I'd do anything for you—give up my inheritance, my family's support. I only resisted because I couldn't believe . . ."

My lips find his in the dark room, in silence. They always belonged against mine, working with me as seamlessly as we carry out our missions and conduct our daily lives. He tastes so rich and warm, just like spiked cider, and now I want to gulp it all down. He coaxes me toward him, clinging tighter and tighter to this one thing that we never dared to grasp.

Footsteps on the staircase send us ricocheting apart. Brandt's eyes are wide, and his lips are puffy and flushed, like mine feel. He goads me to act with a nudge of his head. "Who is it?" I call out, trying to make my voice low and smarmy like Kriza's.

"Thought I heard somethin'. You okay up there, miss?"

Nightmare's teeth. I gesture toward Brandt, and we both crouch behind the desk, out of sight of the door. "I'll be right there!" I shout.

"Please be safe," Brandt whispers.

I kiss him again, fierce and hungry, but pull away as he reaches for my cheek. "I love you, Brandt." The moment the words leave my lips, I chug from my vial.

· •• ———— • ———— •• ·

The Nightmare Wastes are eating Oneiros alive. No sooner do I gain footing on the cobblestone of the city streets, than an elaborate filigree castle, someone's life's work and sanctuary, crumples to the ground in a heap of golden lace. A pile of rotting flesh climbs from the rubble, its gaping jaw swinging from left to right.

Kriza. Kriza. Where could she be in this disaster? Somewhere smug, somewhere a little too confident, a little dangerous. I spot the tarnished double-pronged spire and take off at a sprint.

The temple's interior has been transformed into swampland. Humid air slithers around me like a wet scarf, sticking to my

333

skin and making each step through the temple's heart an excruciating slog. Leafless vines reach out for me from the cracks and crevices in the stone, snagging at my hair, snaking up my ankles. I wrap my arms tight around my chest and try not to inhale the filthy miasma of Nightmare as it consumes the temple.

A massive lizard, three sets of spikes running down her back, her snout honed to a needle point, wallows in the murk just beside the elaborate design that contains the Nightmare shards. Teeth spangle the edge of her jaw—honed teeth ready to tear me to shreds. She's Kriza—she has to be. Something in those narrowed, poison-yellow eyes and her slothful stance, too casual to deny her predatory gaze, warns me instantly. She won't stay in the dreamworld for long. It'll take great skill and stealth to merge with that lethal beast.

I slump forward and crawl on my belly, making my way across the marble floor now covered in muck as slowly as I can manage. The lizard's eyes follow me, but she remains motionless, not yet threatened. I enter the swamp alongside her and float. The lizard is right beside me, her pulse as sluggish as the swamp—

We open our eyes.

I stagger forward on Kriza's muscle-clad legs that propel me too far with each step. I'm at the door of the office before I can stop myself. Pain flowers at the base of my skull where Brandt cracked Kriza good with the tube. But I'm not sorry. I hope that somewhere in her sleep, she can feel it still.

I throw open the door just in time to come face-to-face with the guard. His hand grasps for thin air, for the doorknob I've just pried away, and he stares into my eyes—for a second I am certain that he must see through the Kriza skin I've donned. But then he rocks back on his heels and presses against one side of the staircase.

"Sorry. I thought I heard a commotion."

"Just a stuck drawer. Not that it's any of your business," I add, doing my best to adopt Kriza's attitude without having to dip into her thoughts. I can't risk waking that lizard. Not now.

But the guard stands there, watching me like he expects me to perform a miracle, so I make a show of closing the door and ushering him down the stairs. "If the confederate council wanted you involved in our work, they'd have told you," I say.

I exit the warehouse and stare, bleary-eyed, up at the window in the little office. Oh, Brandt. Brandt. Please find a way out of there alive. Please don't leave my body behind.

I touch a finger to my lips, pretending almost for a moment that I can feel his warmth still lingering on this foreign skin, and I set off for the Imperial Palace.

Chapter Twenty-Seven

The Farthing army officers have wasted no time making themselves at home on the verdant palace lawns. The officers' tent encompasses a urinating cherub statue, and soldiers lounge in the rose bushes and tie their tents to the spiky gates. I can see how easily one might think them our saviors, given their jovial smiles and easy chatter with the Barstadt ladies who have come out to ogle them. Even some aristocrats take part, gemstones flashing in the setting sun.

The captain is easy to spot—he's the one splayed out on an armchair under the tent commandeered from Dreamer knows where, flanked by three ladies with different shades of facial gemstones, sloshing steins of ale. A nasty word or twenty lingers on my tongue for these aristocrats who are all too eager to abandon our Emperor as soon as their fortunes look imperiled, but I am not Livia. I am Kriza. I am one of them, or even worse.

The captain nods at me as I stride up the slope but makes no move to stand to greet me. "Don't overexert yourself," I say in the most condescending tone I can muster.

"Did you get what you needed from the Ministry of Affairs?" the captain asks me.

I grimace. "We secured the archives, but the people in the barracks escaped," I bluff, though I hope that it's the truth.

The captain finally sits up at that, nudging one of the taffeta-swathed women off his armrest. "I'll have Colonel Guritz's head. Where did they go?"

Somewhere in the rancid, desecrated Dreamer's spire, the mud is drying against my skin, making a putrid statue of me. It cracks like parched Iron Winds earth as I inch closer to the lizard, but I am slow, so very slow. She flicks her tail; her knife-slash nostrils clench and release. I must become one with the corruption in Oneiros. I must know her thoughts.

"They're not important. Right now, we need access to the palace." My hand shoots forward to indicate it beyond the gates, guarded by nervous-looking and wholly inadequate soldiers. I have to warn the Emperor and Minister Durst about Marez's true aim to resurrect Nightmare. "Where do we stand on that matter, or have you been too busy ingratiating yourself with the locals?"

The captain tugs his uniform down and stands. "Excuse us a moment, ladies."

"Don't forget House Jurard," one of the women, topaz and emerald and a diamond between her brows, purrs as they shuffle out of the tent. I make a mental note not to forget House Jurard, either, if we survive this—to report on how quickly they turned against Barstadt.

The captain tugs his rumpled coat back into place. "We've located some of the periphery tunnels your crime boss mentioned, but I understand that the Emperor has mechanisms for sealing them off in case of invasion. I sent some scouts to see if that's happened, but they haven't reported back yet."

I snort. "Those tunnel folk are like savages. Your scouts were probably stripped of their uniforms and left for dead in an alcove somewhere."

"So we take the tunnels by force." The captain shrugs. "What about using your little"—he swishes his hand—"nightmare demon things?"

In a warehouse several blocks away, I feel my blood boiling. How dare these foreigners treat our city like a toy castle to be razed at their convenience! It takes all my will to swallow down my rage; in the swamp, the lizard's eyes glide slowly to meet mine.

"Too unreliable, without the final shard," I manage to say without spitting on him. "The traitor bitch's spirit or 'echo' or whatever she is will put it in place, but you have to get your sorry arses into the palace and claim it first."

"Can't Commander Marez just dream his way inside?" the captain asks.

I wrack my brain for a plausible excuse. "He's busy trying to transfer the shards. Believe it or not, it takes some effort." I narrow my eyes. "Any other smart questions for me, pet?"

"Well, see if he can't find a way around it anyway. The show he put on earlier this afternoon was rather impressive. I might've soiled my pants if I didn't know those demons running around are on our side."

Nightmare's minions seeping into our world—Marez did

that? Kriza's heartbeat races in answer to my panic. I thought it was only because Nightmare's heart was nearly reassembled. If he's capable of weakening the barrier between dreams and reality like that, then he's far, far stronger than either Professor Hesse or I could have possibly imagined.

"We'll see what we can do," I say tartly. "Meanwhile, find us a more reliable way in. What are you thinking?"

He eyes the palace soldiers through the gates. "We outnumber them, there's no doubt. But if we charge in all at once, if there's too much noise and panic . . . It could get ugly. We could lose our chance to nab the shard."

"Yes," I say, nodding. As if not nabbing the shard is the only downside of chaos and slaughter.

"I think your alternate plan will have to do for now. Is Marez ready to conduct his . . . 'ritual'?"

Hesse's binding ritual. And Marez means to conduct it to bind Nightmare's soul to his will once he has the final shard. But Oneiros jars me from my thoughts: quick as a flash, the lizard that oozed torpor is upon me, pinning me in place in the muck. Darkness wells around my eyes. Within Kriza's body, I feel my insides shredding up. Mud sloshes over my face. I hear footsteps along the grimy temple floor, slow and deliberate, approaching me.

I try to wriggle free, but I'm trapped. The lizard's hot breath snuffles along my throat and in my ear. It won't hurt me, not now. But neither will it let me go.

A shadow falls across me in Oneiros; something sharp prods me in the spine.

And then Kriza's lips coil into a smile, one I'm not controlling. *Dreamer, please, oh, please. Is she waking up? Don't let me be thrust into the Wastes. Don't let the nightmares consume me.*

Kriza faces the captain dead on. My grip is fading. She speaks, far too cognizant, too sinister, though not strong enough to cast me out of her body. "Our plan has already begun."

And from the bottom of the hill, I see someone familiar treading toward us on uncertain limbs. A cautious, frightened girl, with no facial gems, wearing a ratty dress. Her honey curls whip around a plain face, but that smile—that smile does not belong to her. I smother down a scream as she approaches, eyes aglitter with victory.

"Halt, Barstadter," the captain calls to my body.

But my body turns to the captain. "I may be Barstadter by birth, but I assure you, I'm loyal to your side. I'm here to gain access to the palace for you. Marez told me to give you this." My body holds out a signed scrap of paper.

The captain scrutinizes it for a few moments. "The Farthing Confederate Council's seal."

I try to fight against Kriza—I have to stop Marez. My body. I have to stop me. But I can't move, can't regain control of the limbs.

"Deepest apologies. An ally of Marez's is an ally of Farthing's." The captain gestures toward the palace. "The tunnel entrances to the palace are sealed."

"Don't worry," my body says with a vicious sneer I didn't even know my lips could form. "I can always gain audience with the emperor. Oh—and I'm afraid Kriza's not to join us in the palace." It's my voice speaking, but I've never put such venom into my words. "See to it that she doesn't."

My own eyes turn toward me, the briefest of smiles gracing my lips. And then I watch myself slip quietly through the palace gates.

Part Three

DREAMSTRIDER

Chapter Twenty-Eight

"Kriza?" the captain asks, touching my arm. "I believe Commander Tanin has use of you elsewhere."

Tears spring to Kriza's body's eyes, even as her lizard form chuckles at me, holding me captive within Oneiros. What easy prey I am. I force our eyes away from the sight of my body slipping into the palace entrance.

But then a fresh thought rounds on me. If Marez accessed my body, then he must have gone to the warehouse. He must have run into Brandt. Brandt. What happened to him?

Dreamer, please . . .

"I'm sorry. I have to—the warehouse—" I shove past the captain and take off at a dead run for the glassworks shop. Kriza's muscles are built for this, and in no time I'm back at the shop without a drop of sweat to show for my haste.

It's abandoned. The guards are gone. I charge up the stairs toward the office. The door is ajar, the floor is empty—not even Marez's body is there—and the window is busted out, glass flecking the cobblestones below. No Brandt. I spin in circles, certain he must be here somewhere, and Marez's body with him. But nothing.

Nothing but blood dabbling the edges of the shattered glass.

Brandt. I choke on the very thought of his name. The memory of the kiss we shared the last time I saw him turns to poison on my lips. *No.* Did they capture him? Worse? I can't follow that blood trail to its logical conclusion. I can't wander that nightmare path.

In Oneiros, the lizard weighs down on me. She's letting me use Kriza now, relishing my pain as I'm forced to see her victory through her eyes. The swamp on the temple floor rises around us in gurgling fits and starts, the stench of decaying vegetation consuming us. But that terror pales to the one in the gemstone setting at the temple's heart, the one I can feel thrumming in my bones.

The four shards of Nightmare's heart are hungry and eager as their final component draws near. A figure now sits by the setting for the shards, humming a merry opera to herself: the specter of Lady Twyne. Her eyes meet mine; she smirks, eyes gleaming. "There's no use fighting," she says. "It will all be ours—this world and the next."

No. I can't let them win—let Nightmare consume Barstadt in misery and suffering. I have to interrupt their ritual with the Commandant.

If only Brandt were here, he'd know what to do.

I run back out to the street, but can find no trail to follow. Just the lattice of shattered glass. No blood, no obvious path that Brandt might have taken. It hurts, it burns in my lungs like I've breathed in coal smoke, but I have to trust that he got away, that he's found a way to get help. We've always trusted one another, knowing the shape of the other's actions before taking our own, so we never overlap and never overstep.

I think. I trust. I hope.

According to Retch, Marez is binding Nightmare to his will, but needs the Commandant's and the Emperor's blood both. I may not be able to keep him from getting the last shard of Nightmare's heart, but I can keep him from whatever comes next. And I know just who can help me get close to the Commandant.

A sprinkling rain lashes Kriza's cheeks as we soar through the streets of Barstadt. More than once, a Farthing soldier steps forward to challenge me, but when he sees who I am, or at least whose skin I'm wearing, he falls back.

The Barstadters are not so fortunate. Outside the houses and shops, the Barstadt soldiers tell them to stay inside for their own good if the soldiers of the Land of the Iron Winds break through, but as I jog through the ale halls and tenements near the docks, I see they're far less gentle. Here, they make no effort to conceal their true role as our captors.

Finally, I reach my destination, an older but still august quarter populated by senior merchant families on the cusp of breaking into the aristocracy. No wonder Vera ran away from that—with her quick wit and good looks, she was an engraved invitation into the uppermost crust.

When she opens the door to me, she immediately rears back and punches me in the face.

"Nightmare's bones!" I shriek, stumbling backward. "Vera, please! It's Livia!"

"But you're that—Farthing monster!" She pounces on top of me, right there on her parents' porch, ready to strike again.

I throw up my hands to absorb her blows with my forearms, which Kriza's arms seem to do surprisingly well. "Don't be ridiculous! You have to believe me. I know about you and Edina, and how you were pouting up an awful storm while we sailed south—"

"Lying fiend!" she howls.

"And I know you never eat the nuts on your rolls from Kruger's, though you always order the cinnamon nut buns. You always pick them off and give them to me. Or you did, before—before I set you on fire."

She slows mid-swing and stares at me, scrutinizing. "Oh. Well, I suppose it *could* be you," she says, tilting her head to one side. "But I'm not sorry for punching you. I hope it swells up something fierce when that Farthing bitch wakes up."

"Yes, about that . . ." I scramble to my feet, surprised to find myself towering over Vera. "The other Farthinger has my body."

Vera swears. "Come inside." She steps back from the door. "I think we're both going to need some of my parents' cider."

"So those awful rumblings," she says, staring into the depths of her cider mug. "You mean that Nightmare's breaking into our world again?" She looks up at me. "It can't be true, can it? They scattered his heart. But the gems they were hunting . . ."

"They're very close. I'd be surprised if Marez isn't prying the final shard off the Emperor right now." I wince, trying not to imagine what heinous criminal acts are being committed with my body, and take another gulp of hot brew.

"But the Commandant. What role does the Commandant play in all of this?" She shakes her head. "Is he just a convenient excuse for them to occupy Barstadt City?"

"There's more to it than that. The captain was very insistent that the Commandant be brought to them." I shudder as, within Oneiros, the lizard's nails sink deeper into my flesh. The mud has nearly covered my nostrils now. That sword pierces me further—Marez's soul, inhabiting my body. He's squeezing at my mind, trying to press into my thoughts. *No!* I can't let him see what we're planning. I push back, and the shadow retreats, but only by a fraction.

Vera drains her mug and stands. "Well, I wish I knew what to do. I could help you find a new body to occupy, maybe, if you've only got a little while longer left in that one. I've got some supplies still. But I'm done with the Ministry, and all the hypocrites who work for it."

"What are you talking about?" I catch her wrist. "Is this about Edina?"

"It's about more than just some silly tiff," she hisses, snatching her arm from me. "Bad enough that she's going to run off and marry stupid Brandt just to keep her father happy. But the aristocrats, the gangs—they're all interconnected. Maybe they deserve to burn." Vera fluffs her skirts with a *harrumph*. "I wouldn't expect you to understand."

"Oh, you wouldn't, would you?" Now I feel it—fire spreading through my limbs, the heat of my anger and indignation stoking me to courage. "I clawed my way out of the tunnels, thinking, praying there'd be something better on the other side. And you know what I found? Dead bodies, of all the tunnelers and dreamstriders who tried before. The boy I loved, taken from me by the very system I was working to uphold. More bureaucracy and corruption and lies. I wanted to give up, too. Run off to Farthing or some place where I could make my own life."

My words sound odd in Kriza's voice, but I feel stronger, saying them. I feel more in control, not less. I feel more like myself.

"I keep waiting for the Dreamer to show me the right way, but what has waiting gotten me? I'm done waiting. Waiting for Barstadt to change, waiting for the Dreamer to live my life for me. We're the only ones capable of stopping Nightmare right now, and it's up to us to do so. Or do you want to keep on letting others dictate your path?"

Vera slumps back into her seat. "Bloody dreams," she sighs. "When'd you get a clue?" She shakes her head. "Fine. I'll do what I can. But if they awaken Nightmare, then what good are we to stop them?"

I pinch the bridge of Kriza's nose; she's developing a terrible headache, and her left eye is slowly swelling shut. Vera's right about her deserving the black eye, though. I try not to mind the pain too much. "We can infiltrate the Commandant's caravan. I'll take control of the Commandant, and he'll lead me right to Marez to stop the binding ritual."

Vera groans. "Damn it, Livia. Why me? I don't even want to be a bloody operative anymore. I'm ready to marry some disgustingly wealthy suitor and bide my days by spending as much of his money as I can."

"You ran from that before," I say.

"Yes, but that was back when I thought there was more to life. When I thought she was willing to give up her title and inheritance for me, like I gave up my family . . . Ah, well. I was wrong." She touches her forehead, between her eyebrows. "I'm getting a gemstone set there soon. I'll have quite a choice of suitors."

I slump back in the overstuffed armchair. "Please, Vera. If we don't stop Marez, Nightmare will destroy everything—including your plans for a quieter life. I don't stand a chance of infiltrating the Commandant's entourage without you."

She laughs then, a wry smile twisting her lips. "They were quite fond of me when we were in Birnau, weren't they?"

"Yes!" I exclaim, maybe too desperately, but I'm too short on time to butter her up slowly, like Brandt would. "You performed fabulously. We'll sneak into their entourage in no time and follow them straight into the palace and put an end to all of this before they resurrect Nightmare." *And find Brandt,* I think silently, but with an aching heart, I know that must come second.

"Fine. Fine." She rubs her hands together. "What's our plan, then?"

I pause for a moment. "Err . . . well . . . How do you normally piece one together?"

Vera shrugs. "I usually wait for Edina to tell me the plan. When I'm speaking to her, that is."

I force myself to smile. "All right, then let's think what Edina would say. Probably something involving disguises, but with the Ministry under Farthing's control, we can't access their costumes, and—"

Vera clears her throat daintily and glances away from me as her cheeks turn a pretty hue of rose. "I may have a solution for that."

"Wonderful! What is it?"

"Well, I . . ." She grinds her toe into the woven rug. "Edina never said as much, but she seemed rather fond of how the serving girl costume looked on me in Birnau, so I, ah, borrowed a few."

I'm about to fling myself at her to hug her, but I manage to stop myself. "Wait, how do you know she fancied them? I thought you and Edina aren't speaking."

"Oh, we're not. It's to make her feel miserable with guilt and envy, and forget all about marrying Brandt." Vera sits up straighter, grinning at herself.

I shake my head. One should never expect sense from Vera, despite her knack for inspiring brilliance when it's required. "All right. But I'm all out of mothwood rags." I pull the last dried up one from Kriza's pocket.

"I've a solution for that too." Vera stands up. "You're aware of my family's business, aren't you?"

I stare at her blankly.

"Well then. Let me introduce you to our family storerooms."

Vera's family's basement is a maze of alchemical ingredients—dreamwort and mothwood, purifying water, resins for every possible ailment. "All of it honestly obtained, too," she explains as we walk through the shelves, grabbing everything we'll need. "My father prides himself on not doing business with the gangs. Another reason my parents weren't happy about *her.*"

Vera wastes no time setting the mothwood aflame in its tinderbox and stuffing a fine selection of scarves into the upper compartment. While the scarves soak up the smoke, we busy ourselves dressing in courtesan garb. I take care to drape a gauzy veil over my eyes to cover the black eye Vera gave me. This much, at least, seems to be going well.

It's what's transpiring in Oneiros that makes me far more nervous. I'm still pinned in place by the sword. The lizard has rolled off of me and is crouching in the mud, her eyes focused on something out of my field of vision. Lady Twyne, perhaps? What is she doing with the heart shards? Why hasn't Marez pressed into my thoughts again? I try to move my arms, but the mud is congealing around me; the stench holds me down, a living and breathing thing that has taken up the lizard's task. Kriza may be toying with me for now, but soon, very soon, I fear she'll awaken and force me out of her body, and then I'll be lost in the dreamworld. If I don't find a fresh body to inhabit, the Wastes will claim me in no time.

Vera and I rush to the docks, cloaks thrown over us to keep the biting autumn cold from our now very exposed flesh, and stop at the edge of the Farthing squadron guarding the battlement gates. The smell of spent ammunition hangs in the air, drifting in lazy tufts over the harbor. In the distance, I can see the black-shelled warships of the Iron Winds fleet, hulking like beetles, jagged horns overpowering their slender profiles. An ant trail of landing boats spans the distance between them and the docks.

"All right," I mutter from beneath my gauzy drapes. "How do you suggest we pull this off?"

But Vera has already slunk away from me and is shimmying her way down a drain pipe at the lowest point of the battlements. I can do nothing but stare slack-jawed at her as she hops lithely from rivet to rivet, until she pauses to glower back up at me and beckons me with a furious wave of her arm.

Kriza may be stronger than I am, but her dense muscles aren't meant for this work. The drain pipe groans under my weight. I'm better off scaling the stones themselves. I flop my way down the wall in an excruciating dance. For once, I sense a tiny fear in the lizard's pulse. She does not want her body damaged. I smirk, grateful to have the upper hand, if only for one painful moment.

Vera sidles up to a guardsman near the gate's mouth, overseeing the reassembly of some ludicrous black carriage the Commandant's entourage has hauled over on one of the landing boats. When he hunches over a wheel assembly, she places one slippered foot before him; he follows her gauze-swathed tan leg up to its terminus and raises a brow at her.

"The Iron Winds blow, but the Commandant is our windbreak. He shall never fall," she purrs, and reaches out to trail her index finger from his ear down along his chest.

"The Iron Winds have truly blown in a beauty for me," he says with a grin.

I try not to gag.

Vera pouts, jutting out her lower lip. "Unfortunately, I'm promised to the Commandant," she says. "When you're finished with your assembly, could you let us inside?"

The guard hesitates, and Vera takes a step back. Of course they're being cautious; this is a strange land, and they're allied with monsters.

"I'll be sure to tell him who helped us," she says, leaning toward him again. "What's your name? Maybe after we've visited the Commandant . . ."

"Yes. Of course." He snaps at the other soldiers to hurry up their assembly. "Lieutenant Radiant Moon. Don't forget me, sweetheart."

"Oh, I won't," she says, her grin as wide as her face, and the lieutenant helps us into the cab.

We settle onto the cushions, leaving a gap between us for the Commandant. "Dreamer bless, woman. You've got nerves of double-forged steel," I tell Vera.

"I do my best." She winks, but I can't help the tightness in my throat and the twist in my gut. This is a far too delicate and chaotic mission to undertake without my partner. Where can Brandt be? *Please, Dreamer, let him be safe.*

Let him be alive.

"Kriza is not going to be pleasant when she wakes up," I say,

trying to push away my terror. If I can just keep talking . . .
"We'll have to restrain her before I drink the dreamwort."

"Don't worry. I have it all figured out." Vera pats my knee.
Somehow, I'm less than reassured.

The carriage door swings open. The Commandant stares at
us with his little, venomous gaze, until slowly, his cheeks relax.
"The Iron Winds blow favorably today."

"They always favor you, my tamer of breezes," Vera says.

"Let's see how much they favor me," he replies with a smirk.
I suppress a shudder as he climbs in between us. He loops one
arm around my shoulder and the other around Vera's, and she
clings to him as though a fifty-foot chasm just opened underneath her. I grit my teeth. I suppose it wouldn't help our plans
much if I lost Kriza's lunch all over the Commandant right now.

I grimace and stare at the curtained window while the
Commandant's hands rove over Vera. She giggles and playfully
swats at him. Then his hand crawls up my thigh. It may not be
my thigh, but I've no interest in whatever he's looking for. I fish
a kerchief out of Kriza's cleavage, holding my breath as I do so,
and feather it against his shoulder.

"Tell me, my Commandant. Do you think this perfume
smells pretty?" I ask him, and I hold out the kerchief to him.

"Let me see, my dear." He holds it to his nose and takes a
deep breath.

Clunk. His head lolls back against the carriage.

Vera exhales, and her shoulders hunch forward. "Dreamer's
mercy. Took you long enough."

"How close are we to wherever they're taking us?"

She peels back the curtain. "I've no idea. We're not headed to the palace."

In Oneiros, the lizard is smiling, that smug grin so like her human form. I can't wait to leave her stranded.

"We'll sort it out when we arrive. Go ahead and tie me up."

Vera hastily binds my hands—Kriza's hands—together in her lap. "All right, let's get on with it already!" Vera raises the vial to my lips and I plunge back into Oneiros—back into a lightning storm of blood.

Chapter Twenty-Nine

⬥ ⬥ ⬥ ◄◆► ⬥ ⬥ ⬥

The lizard is gone—Kriza must have woken up the moment I fled her body—but the swamp remains inside the temple, pelted by bloody rain. I slosh out of the mud and wheeze for air, but it's thick with rot; it feels like the blood is flooding my lungs. The earth rumbles with a mighty crack, and a chunk of the temple's ceiling crushes the spot where I'd been standing just a moment before.

I reach the lip of the sunken black glass where I'd found the Nightmare shards and suck in my breath. Marez must have already gotten the ruby from the Emperor, and is transferring it now. The fifth shard hasn't finished transferring into Oneiros, but a red orb glows in its setting, brighter and brighter each moment that I look on it.

Lady Twyne appears from the shadows, her eyes sinkholes in her sallow face. Blood drips from her facial gems; three long gashes run the length of one cheek. The first Commandant stands beside her—gaunt, his face sharp with hunger. He must have preserved his soul, too, I realize with a twist in my gut. How long has Marez been working with them?

"It's coming," Lady Twyne croaks in a voice like curdled milk. Her gaze passes through me.

"You won't find my son." The first Commandant's voice carries the same hollow echo. "You're too late."

I can't give up. I have to stop them. But I can't linger here. With the Nightmare Wastes taking such vicious root, my bodiless soul is sure to get eaten up in no time. I can hear wings pounding just outside the temple as Nightmare's minions circle as if for a feast. *Please, Dreamer, though you have not answered me yet, please hear my prayers now: let me find the Commandant swiftly. Let me save your world, and mine.*

A blessed breeze wafts through the temple, cutting through the fetid stale air. I breathe it in, let it cleanse me with its gentle coolness. It tickles my ears and flutters against my soul just playfully enough to let me know it's there. It whispers nonsense as it drifts across my skin.

No. I stand up straighter. It's not nonsense—it's a chant. An affirmation of strength, of power, of blood yielding to iron. The younger Commandant. But of course it is.

I fling my arms out wide and let the breeze dance around me. It snakes through the crevices between my fingers and lifts every hair on my arms and legs. It sighs in response, chattering louder now. I would not have expected the Commandant to appear like this, but I won't complain about one thing going easy for me this time.

We open our eyes.

Kriza screams and lunges for me before I can even see clearly. Without use of her hands, she uses her shoulders to bash into my jaw.

"Guards!" Vera shrieks. She throws herself onto Kriza, as Kriza strains at the bindings with a snarl. "Want me to use the mothwood?"

"No! No, keep it away from her! It's better that she stays here. In the waking world," I rasp.

The carriage clatters to a stop. Someone throws open the door—one of the Commandant's guardsmen. "What's going on in here?"

"Take this one away," I say, thrusting my thumb—the Commandant's thumb—at Kriza. Vera can barely keep her wrangled back. "And be careful—she's a biter."

The two guardsmen exchange glances before reaching for Kriza. She charges one of them, bowling him over, and the other pounces on her, wielding a baton. After a brief scuffle, they've knocked her unconscious once more. Once we're safely away from Kriza's unconscious body, Vera slips the vial back to me. It's far too light—only one more dose left, if that. Without access to the Ministry's supplies, this body is probably my last chance at getting back to my own.

If I can ever find myself again.

"All right. Marez has to meet with the Commandant—with me—to perform the binding ritual. As far as I know, he's still got my body."

"So I need to force him out of it. You. Whoever you bloody are." Vera rolls her eyes. "But how?"

"There's Lullaby in the pocket of my dress—my body's dress," I tell Vera. "It should pull my body's tether out of Oneiros . . . and his consciousness out of my body."

She purses her lips. "But if your body isn't close by for you to take hold of its leash in Oneiros . . . then how will you get back inside it?"

I squeeze my eyes shut. The thought of the Wastes, lapping at my soul, consuming me with despair . . .

But it's a sacrifice I have to be willing to make. All of Barstadt is worth more than my life. My willingness to sacrifice is what makes Barstadt my home instead of Farthing—I'm not purely interested in advancing myself. It's what will give us the advantage we need. "If it has to be done . . . it has to be done."

Vera glowers at me. "Livia. No."

"If that's what we have to do to stop him, then you have to do it, all right?"

Vera gives a curt jut of her chin. It's about all the acquiescence I'll get.

We're in a narrow stone passageway, lit by gas lamps but otherwise unremarkable. Is this near the palace? I don't recognize the scenery, or the sloping cobbles hemmed in by rock instead of buildings. The path appears to have been cleaved straight through the stone, as if by some great ragged claw.

"My Commandant. The mystic awaits you," a guard says

from the mouth of the cleft. "He has taken a new form, but I assure you it won't impact the ritual."

Vera and I climb upward. The slope overlooks the whole of Barstadt City, from the splash of red brick at Banhopf University and the glittering gold of the Imperial Palace to the pointed black slate roofs of everything in between; the sailboat masts tower in the docks, and the Iron Winds fleet floats beyond the horizon.

On the ridge above us, strung out like a child's broken toy, stretch the bones of Nightmare.

The ravine we just climbed through was gouged out of the mountain ridge hundreds of years ago. The sharp, geometric bones of Nightmare's claws beckon me to walk through them like an archway. As we pass to the other side of them, lurking below Nightmare's suspended ribs, I see the Emperor, Minister Durst, the Farthing general, and . . . myself. A thick piece of gauze is wound around Emperor Weideger's forehead, drops of blood beginning to seep through from where Marez must have torn the ruby out. His eyes are glassy, as if he's lost in a dreamless sleep, but he can't be, not entirely—he stands upright and slowly turns his head toward me. Durst and the Farthing general appear much the same way, wearing the looks of men who see Death's shadows crossing over them and are not afraid. Marez has drugged them for whatever's coming next.

"I promise this won't take but a moment," my body says, beckoning us forward. She is smiling in a way I've never felt, smiling with every muscle and bone. The rest of the small group stands rigid, without guards or bindings on their hands.

Only my body's eyes turn to follow me as Vera and I step forward.

The Commandant's breeze whispers across me in Oneiros. It's my sole comfort—everything else has turned rotten. I hear the distant groan of building supports giving way. All the creations of the Dreamer's faithful are shattering into nothingness, sucked up into the Wastes. Lady Twyne stokes the final shard like it's an ember; its glow grows with each passing moment. Her gaze catches mine and she grins. "Use this body all you like," she tells me. "We can't be stopped."

"This is not part of our agreement," the Commandant says through me, addressing Marez in the waking world. "You were to turn over Barstadt City to me."

"Oh, but you wanted your weapon. And I shall deliver it to you. Better still, I shall make it a part of you—and you a part of it." I see my amber eyes twinkle as my lips speak. "It's what your father wanted."

My body lurches toward me in the Commandant on the rocky slope, but a horrendous slurping sound stops it short. The noise ricochets off the mountain walls, off the buildings below us. It gurgles like a dying beast drawing its last breath through shattered lungs. It sounds like death, sucking us all into the darkness of the Wastes.

A black swirl appears at the center of Nightmare's rib cage, rotating with lazy, oily arms. It pulsates, and the sucking noise grows louder as the slimy center of the orb stretches and expands to fill those massive ribs. It belches nauseating rot into the air. I raise my arm to cover my nose.

"It's time," my body says.

Two Farthing soldiers seize the Commandant's wrists, pinning them behind my back. Another pair wrestles Vera to the ground. The Commandant is out of shape, but strength lurks beneath his softness; I struggle against the soldiers, yanking at their arms, but they fend me off with a sharp crack to the temple. The Commandant's vision goes blurry, and briefly, I'm thrown back into Oneiros, nearly dislodged from the Commandant's body.

Lady Twyne stares down at me, a low laugh emerging from her. The constellation of shards pulse, illuminating her face with a sickly glow. I claw my way back into the Commandant. If I can just get close enough to my body in the real world, maybe I can force Marez out of it within Oneiros . . .

The soldiers drag me to where my body stands with its silent companions just beneath the void of Nightmare's heart. Within the dreamworld, the Commandant's breeze turns harsh, ferocious. It fights against me, chattering with wordless anger.

"The blood of each nation to stoke the fires," my voice chants into the falling night. "The blood of each to fill dreamland veins and give new life to the master of this world and those beyond."

My body's hands grasp a silver knife. Marez rakes it across the Emperor's palm, and then holds the Emperor's bleeding hand up to the oily void. "The Dreamer's priests would tell you that the Dreamer slew Nightmare, but it was a lie," Marez continues. "It was the ancestral leaders of the Central Realms who stood against him long ago, using their own power to slay him.

They shed their blood to bind him in death. Now their blood will give him new life."

The truth of the binding ritual—the truth he hinted at about Nightmare's death. The truth even Hesse acknowledged was too dangerous to let loose. The truth he died to protect—that people slew Nightmare, not the Dreamer, and that people can return him as well.

The dark sphere that glows in the center of Nightmare's ribs laps greedily at the blood; it sucks and sucks until the Emperor's face turns the color of old snow. The Emperor falls to his knees and then slumps backward into the rocks.

I choke back a scream. His chest still rises and falls, but for how much longer? There is no time for me to wonder. The Farthing general is next. I hate the blackened glint in my body's eyes, on my face, as Marez uses it to carry out this vile deed. The general, too, crumples, drained and dried, next to His Imperial Majesty.

Marez reaches for me; my body's lips curl back like an animal. "Come, Commandant," it hisses, flecking spittle across the Commandant's chest. "We have an arrangement." My body grips the Commandant by the arms and tugs him forward.

I take a deep breath, filling the Commandant's lungs, leaning into Marez's grip.

"Vera, now!" I shout.

Vera twists her wrist back to break free of her captor at the same moment as I throw all the Commandant's weight to the ground, sending his body and mine both crashing down. Marez briefly loses his grip; as he does so, I dive toward my body, aiming for the pocket with the Lullaby. But Marez is too quick. With a speed I've never been able to demonstrate, he uses my body to block my attack while my feet shove away Vera. She stumbles backward into the snow. My body leaps back up to standing and presses its heel into my—the Commandant's—throat, pinning us to the ground.

"I should have known that was you in there," my body says, tone dripping with Marez's venom. "Sorry to spoil your fun, but I've got a binding ritual to complete."

Marez snaps my fingers. I never was good at snapping, whistling, any of those things—but now I know my body is capable, and the fault is mine alone. Is the power within me to be a better dreamstrider too? Is failure just inside my head? A soldier shuffles forward with a handkerchief. But it's not mothwood—at least, not mothwood alone. Something sweet, sticky, cloying that sticks in your teeth and seeps into your gums. Lullaby.

Marez smears the resin against the Commandant's lips, and his body shudders as the Lullaby works through his blood. I straddle both worlds for a second, hovering over that ravine—and then I'm falling.

The Commandant's breeze dissipates like a halted melody, note by note, and then all at once it's silent. I've completely left the Commandant's body. I crash to the cold temple floor, if it can still be called a temple. Deep fissures snake up the walls, spreading even as I watch them, and the entire building heaves like a diseased lung. It robs the air from me and makes each pounding of my heart feel like cannon fire under my ribs.

I will drown in here. I will drown, or be consumed by the Wastes.

But there isn't even a distinction between the Wastes and the dreamworld now. The Nightmare Wastes have flooded our safe haven and consumed it like a parasite devouring its host.

I need to find a new body to inhabit fast if I want to keep from being devoured myself. I run for the archway of the temple, sliding on mud as I go, crashing into thick sinuous trees and leathery stalks of reeds that snake around my ankles and wrists. I reach the arch and skid to a halt just in time—the cobblestone streets are gone. There is nothing below me but a yawning canyon.

Dreamer. I want to curl into a ball and weep; the Nightmare air is crushing me like the depths of the sea, and through the poisonous haze, I want to let it. *Please, Dreamer. I need the strength to serve your people, your worlds. Please, please help me.*

The only sound I hear is my blood singing through my veins and the distant collapse of the priests' monuments.

I bite down on my fist to keep from crying out. Where is my Dreamer? Where are his golden arms, plunging down from the heavens to snap Nightmare's neck and shatter its heart? But if his priests couldn't summon him, then who am I to think myself worth his time? I'm clearly not as faithful as I ought to be. I only use his world for petty human tasks.

Maybe this is why he doesn't help me. It's people like me—dreamstriders, Professor Hesse, and Marez—who have brought this upon his world. We must pay for our heresy.

The tower quivers; its core expands like massive bellows to draw in a deep breath. The stone of the spire begins to crumble, columns and archways turning into bone—the skeletal dragon form of Nightmare. The binding ritual is complete. Nightmare is Marez's to command. I grip the archway—it's become Nightmare's bones, now—with weary fingers as wings, ragged and torn, unfurl from around the monster's sinuous ribs.

Nightmare's wings stretch wide, and we take flight.

Chapter Thirty

· ·• —————◆————— •· ·

I scream, but the poison air robs the sound from me. The temple and spire have finished transforming into Nightmare; his wings beat out their grim dirge. We soar across Oneiros as it disintegrates beneath us. The earth bucks and ruptures wherever Nightmare's shadow falls; Shapers' homes crumble into the yawning chasms that open up beneath them. With each surge of wings, the stone tower yields into mottled, scaly flesh that drips away, as if from a rotting plague. Three heartbeats thunder through the hallways of the nearly decayed spire—the passages are hollow bones now: one for each nation's leader, subjugated within this demon's veins. Nightmare's head, growing out of the golden prongs, whips around to spy me on its flank—me, the intruder, the bodiless soul. A grinning rictus glimmers around the golden disc, and Nightmare's laughter threatens to shake me free.

A lost soul, still clinging to overripe hope. Nightmare's words rumble inside my head. *Still screaming into the Dreamer's deaf ears.*

I squeeze my eyes shut and flatten myself against Nightmare's flank. My hands sink into the flesh that's growing over Nightmare's bones; I try to pry them out, but I'm sinking, sinking.

Brandt once warned me about quicksand. Be quick, and you will rush to death's open arms; walk slowly and death cannot meet you.

My muscles unclench, but it's hard not to panic as the Nightmare Wastes consume me. Each prickle of the tar shoots another failure through me: Minister Durst's disappointed stare; Professor Hesse's body a limp doll, tumbling to the ground; Brandt's hand slipping from mine. My nightmares. Here, my mother's dead dishwater eyes, as my siblings eat the meat from my bones. Here, the tumbler wolf from Lady Twyne's party, removing its mask to reveal Marez.

Here, the executioner's block; as the winking blade falls, Lady Twyne seizes my severed head up by the hair for all to see.

And there: Brandt. Lifeless and smelling stale. Brandt: his skin like worn velvet as his insides rot away. Brandt in his wedding suit, a Stargazer knife jutting from his ribs. Tunnelers swarm his body like carrion birds, plucking away every last scrap of value.

This is my eternity, hard-earned through my failure. If only I had never left the tunnels. If only I had never dared to dreamstride. If only I had been a better operative for the Ministry. If only I had never dared to fall in love.

But the Dreamer dares us. This is what Hesse meant, I think, when he said his works were inspired by the Dreamer and not an affront to him. We're meant to chase such impossible dreams;

we're meant to bring our nighttime longing to reality through our actions and deeds. The Dreamer fills our heads at night with dreams of what we could become in the day. He does not shape our world. Perhaps what he does is better—he shows us, instead, that the world is ours to shape.

I cringe as another painful memory lances me through, but the blow is lessened, somehow, by my thoughts. This knowledge may bring me pain, but at least I dared.

I dreamed.

The dreamworld is already mine. Nightmare's words smother me, thicker and even more insistent than the Nightmare Wastes. **With your blood, I shall devour your nations and cough up the bones as scraps for those who freed me. Surrender, lost soul. Suffer what you've wrought.**

"No," I whisper. But I'm lost deep within Nightmare's body as he flies across Oneiros, rot and misery sloughing off him like dead skin. I have no body and no path back to the real world. I am trapped in these nightmares, in the brambles of my failure. Still, I whisper it. "No. No."

The last I see of Oneiros are the oozing black monsters consuming every scrap of land. The sky shimmers before us—instead of the brilliant hues of Oneiros, I see Barstadt's muted gray tones through a tear in the atmosphere. The towers of Banhopf University, the sprawling palace grounds, the Dreamer's Bay.

And then we punch through the veil separating Oneiros from the real world. Oneiros's bloody sky bleeds into a star-spattered night as Barstadt City shimmers before my eyes.

Nightmare tosses back his lizard-like head and snaps up a handful of guards in his mossy teeth. I see from within him now, a prisoner behind his eyes as the blood offering of the three nations' leaders swirls around us. Red sprays across the craggy mountain face. My body looks up at us, laughing, un-afraid. And why should Marez be afraid? It's not his body that'll be lost if Nightmare betrays him.

You shut me away; you sink your fears and your doubt into the Nightmare Wastes. I've feasted on your dead, those who failed to dream, but I can hold no more. Agony needs a new home, and this world suits me just fine.

"It's yours, Nightmare," I hear my voice shout. Marez. "A gift from the Farthing Confederacy."

So the Wastes is replete with miserable souls who lost their way, who never claimed the dreams that were theirs, granted by the Dreamer. No wonder they smell of despair and crave the taste of suffering, like an urchin salivating at the thought of steak.

And Nightmare hungers most of all. Will I become another lost soul who failed to dream? Will he gobble my soul up, too? Can I resist? Already I feel his thoughts mingling with mine, his flesh seeping into me; my lungs fill with chilled air that longs for others' demise. I crave and crave to suck the happiness and will from every last being, like marrow from the bone.

I am one with Nightmare as we soar. Our claws tear a rift through merchants' shops. Tunnelers pour from a nearby grate, makeshift weapons brandished. Down another street, Farthing soldiers cower behind their cart as our shadow swallows them up.

Our skin drips across the streets of Barstadt, smoldering and smoking, like acid etching Nightmare's brand into the stone. But out of each brand erupts a new shadowy fiend. They flood the Palace Square in Barstadt City and rake through a clump of constables, drinking up their dreams and hopes. For every soul the monsters absorb, our heart beats louder; our roar swells across the valley, spewing out the stench of hopelessness.

This is all there is, and all there shall be. Feast on the prison bars that slam shut before the eyes of every soul.

But I won't.

I know what it is to crawl the tunnels all day and night, dragging a question behind me like a ball and chain: Why bother? Why fight? Why not curl into that corner and let the gang's favored scrape their hands upon me and seize my every last tithe and crumb?

Because someday I will slip out of the grates and never come back.

Why dreamstride for the Ministry when Minister Durst shrugs his shoulders at my victories, and Vera and Edina bicker, and Brandt questions my every step?

Because someday I will do my country right.

Why long for a boy who lives in a different world, whose life of privilege I can never compare to? Why kiss a boy whose lips have been signed away to another?

Because love is worth more to me than rules.

Why pray to a faceless Dreamer, a set of golden arms on a monolith stone? Why scream louder when he doesn't answer? Why walk his empty lands, night after night, knowing that you will never be faithful enough to earn his greatest gift?

Because maybe my dreams are enough.

Maybe it's not for the Dreamer to make them come true.

Maybe—just maybe—they're for me to turn into reality.

It starts as a humming in my soul, like a summertime insect choir. A warmth unfolds inside me like feathers. Nightmare senses it; his flight falters, and he clips the Banhopf tower, piercing the webbing that keeps him aloft. But he doesn't hear those desperate words quaking through me. It's not the Dreamer's voice. It's not anyone's voice I've ever known.

Except for mine.

Dreamer, I whisper, but it is not a prayer. Dreamer. I am a dreamer, the one who can make all my dreams and hopes and wishes real. We are each our own dreamers. The golden arms reaching down, the faceless figure of mercy.

It's me.

Nightmare screeches. The minions stop falling from him; his skin is evaporating on the furnace of his bones. The monsters look up from their feast, eyes glistening with an eerie reflection.

"We are all dreamers," I whisper. "Your greatest gift, Dreamer, is the gift of hope—and you planted that seed in every last one of us."

Nightmare's mouth is a jagged scar, zigzagging through his siege-engine face. It opens wide to scream, but he can produce no noise. Like in so many of my own nightmares, his throat fails him. His body moves against his will. I plunge my hands through his quicksand skin and into his festering, ill-fitting heart.

And squeeze.

Golden light rushes through me. My arms are engulfed in the Dreamer's resplendence. My resplendence. I burn away the suffering and hate that crusts Nightmare's core like barnacles. I cauterize the rotting flesh so it can drip no more misery onto our world. I am a dreamer, a dreamstrider, and I will keep the embers of hope alive with my glowing embrace.

I squeeze Nightmare's heart and he wails; his monsters cower under the painful cry, their human prey abandoned. His flight wobbles and we dip lower, tossing hulking shadows over the mass of tunnelers who have flooded into the streets. Some wield weapons, sticks, chains—beating back the Farthingers. But we swoop away before I can get a closer look.

Every beat of Nightmare's heart forces my grip tighter. I embrace my own strength that was waiting inside me for me to accept it. I embrace the Dreamer's teachings and every unanswered prayer that forced me to fight on my own.

Because I am the Dreamer—not because I was born with a gift, or because he blessed me with dreamstriding, or anything else. I am the Dreamer because I choose to be, forging my place from my own strange mix of talent and pure luck. Only doubt could stop me—did stop me, for a time.

I squeeze the oily, cold, shriveling heart.

The Dreamer didn't choose me for anything.

I chose to dream.

You cannot stop us. The Nightmare Wastes will fill to bursting with misery and despair. It is your failing as human beings. We will always be ready to drink it up and thrive.

I press my eyes shut and twist my grip on the failing heart. "Then I'll just have to give them hope."

Nightmare crashes against the mountainside, a few leagues north of his first resting place. Every last sinew evaporates under the watchful stars. His heart bursts into a thousand flaming chunks, flinging themselves to the far corners of the world as his body withers away, back to a pile of bones.

But as each element of Nightmare is sucked back into the Wastes, I lose my grip on the real world. I have no body to grasp.

I fade. And fade.

Chapter Thirty-One

I hover on a column of earth inside Oneiros, the land around it collapsed into the nothingness far below. Even in their diminished state, the Wastes call to me. I am a bodiless dreamer, a wanderer, and Oneiros is not inclined to kindness right now. The minions have eroded so much of the dreamshapers' work, and even though I cast them back into the Wastes when I slew Nightmare, the damage has already been done.

My soul aches. Its incorporeal limbs and muscles cry out for rest. I want to cry; I need to purge this exhaustion from me. I'm overwhelmed from the Dreamer's powers rushing through me and the echoes of Nightmare's poisonous thoughts. But I cannot let myself slip into the Wastes forever. I have to carry on.

I don't know what I'm looking for—my own body's manifestation in Oneiros?—but I have to trust that I'll know it when I find it.

I dive from the pillar of earth and soar up instead of down. I feather through the clouds, no longer gorged with blood, and let the mountaintops of Oneiros act like cobblestone streets to lead me home, wherever it may be. My heart sings out as I draw closer—a magnetic reverberation steers me toward my soul.

I have awakened the dreams within me.

My throat catches as I approach an unassuming grove of trees. In their midst lies a cleansing pool, like in the Dreamer's temples. There's no gilded and carved monolith, and no censers to spew out sharp, wintry smells. No priests in white gowns wait to brush my hair and offer up platitudes about my dreams. Only the promise of purification. I've never seen my sleeping form inside Oneiros before, but I feel a familiar tug pulling me toward the pool. It's me. I can cleanse myself, if I only have faith.

But, of course, my pool is not undisturbed. A sword sticks upright from the center of the pool, pinning down the trailing strands of the Emperor's soul and the others whose blood was shed. So Marez takes the more direct approach—not happy to merely brush against his target's thoughts, he instead skewers them and demands they cough up their secrets. No wonder I remember so many of my alleged "dreams" when he stole my skin. I should have caught on earlier.

I grasp the sword by its hilt. It's a pale shade of gold, thick with scrollwork depicting screeching birds of prey. It suits him all too well. I grip the hilt with both hands and yank.

But the sword won't budge.

"Problems?" Marez's voice slithers in my ear, as if he stood just over my shoulder.

Shadows dart around the pool, threading through the trees. The first Commandant and Lady Twyne glide forward. The color is back in her skin, her hair glossy and styled once more. "If we can't have the real world just yet . . ."

". . . then this one will suit us fine," the Commandant says.

I tighten my grip on the sword's hilt, pressing into Marez's consciousness. Colors bleed through, strung across short bursts of sound. Screams, the march of boots. I can almost see through my body's eyes—almost feel the pinch of shoes at my ankles and the rough scarf tied at my throat. Then the sword pulses and throws me back to the edge of the pool.

Marez's easy honey-smooth laugh rings in my ears. "And this body suits me just fine."

"Professor Hesse was a fool, same as all the Dreamer's priests," Marez says. "Who was he to keep the secrets of Oneiros for himself, or one hopelessly broken nation? They should be there for the taking of those bold enough to master them. Oneiros belongs to the dreamstriders, not these pathetic priests."

"You're lying." My voice is fuzzy; I fear it might get lost over the roar of the water as it churns around me. A whirlpool centers on the sword. I flail for purchase, but I am incorporeal. I'm lost to the whims of Oneiros.

"Give up, little girl," Marez growls. "You can't suppress nightmares forever. This is the punishment Barstadt has earned. For centuries, Barstadt has crushed hopes and dreams. Why shouldn't they pay? Barstadt doesn't deserve its power!" Marez laughs.

"That isn't for you to decide." I gasp for air. "Even Barstadt can be changed. The right way—not like this."

"Don't be so certain. When I joined the Dreamer's priesthood, they threw me out for asking uncomfortable questions. Hesse locked me out for rubbing his nose in his own disgrace. But I knew what they refused to acknowledge—Barstadt's weakness. Its failure. It's time to stop hiding from the truth."

"What truth? What is the truth to you?"

"The tunnelers and the Dreamer's priests and men like Hesse are all part of a larger machine. They feed endless death to the Wastes so the Emperor and his chosen few can revel in luxury and sweet dreams."

"And you think the Farthing Confederacy can do a better job?" I cry. "You're no stranger to using people for your needs."

Marez's consciousness turns jagged; the sword's blade hums. "Because I've earned this. I *deserve* control. I understand what you fools refuse to see!"

"We will become the Dreamers," Lady Twyne says from her perch at the pool's lip. "Why merely suggest a path to mortals through their dreams? We can command. Control. We can be gods."

The first Commandant nods. "Look what life is like without a stern god at its helm. Nightmare has nearly destroyed your home for a second time, and your dreamland is in ruins. You are a flock without a shepherd. The Dreamer only suggests, while Nightmare *commands*. This is the way of the Iron Winds—to take by force." The Commandant laughs. "What has the Dreamer ever given you? What have you ever claimed as your own?"

"Nothing," Marez says. The sword throbs with painful heat. "Not even a body to call your own."

A memory of tears stings my cheeks. No. I've come too far for this. I've defeated Nightmare and sent him and his minions back into the Wastes. I can't give up now. But my aching, battered soul cries out for relinquishment. How easy it would be to sink into those purifying waters and let Marez do whatever he likes.

But I have too many dreams left to turn to reality.

"I think we'll take our chances with dreams of what might be," I say.

I sink into the water. It purifies, washing away my fears and doubts. There's no monolith, but I don't need one to pray. I pray to that shard of Dreamer inside of me. I pray for strength. I pray for the rest of my life, because I'm just getting started.

At first, the sword wobbles uncertainly. Maybe it's just rippling with the waves. Distantly, I sense Marez's panic. I plunge underwater and let my curls spread around me like a grasping hand. *Three, two, one.* I surge to the surface.

With a pop, the sword sails high into the air before clattering to the ground beside the pool.

Lady Twyne and the first Commandant—I scan the forest for them, but they've melted into the shadows. Someday soon, I'll have to find them. But—as the insistent *snap* within my soul tells me—right now, I need to claim my body for my own.

I'm shaking as I seize my body's tether and anchor my soul to it. I push against my body like it's an unfamiliar hallway at

night, stubbing my toe and crashing my shoulder against unfamiliar corners. An imperfect host for me in my imperfect
land—a great place to begin once more.

I'm home.

I open my eyes.

Chapter Thirty-Two

⋯ •• ⟨━━━◆━━━⟩ •• ⋯

Brandt crouches over me with a dagger to my throat.

"No!" I shriek. I try to throw my arms up to shield myself, but they're pinned to my sides. "No! Please, it's me! I just fought my way back, I swear to you—"

He staggers up and away; the dagger clatters out of his hand onto the stones beneath us. Stones. Where are we? No stars flitter overhead; no beached bones of Nightmare. What about Vera? The Emperor? Edina?

"Prove it," Brandt says. He's choking; his hands are tight fists jammed against his thighs. "Prove to me you're Livia."

I slump back against the stone. "Your middle name is Germanius, which you utterly despise. You always get the almond croissants at Kruger's, and a butter pie, too, if we've just pulled off a mission. Your birthday is the last day in Tremmer's month, and I bought you a notebook for your last one because you swore you'd write down all our adventures someday. And you're . . . you are . . ."

Now I'm the one choking—weeping big, fat, inexcusably childish tears.

"I love you. I love you so much, Brandt Germanius Strassbourg, and I don't care if you're promised to House Alizard, because I'm not afraid to dream."

Brandt's face has turned ashen, and I can see bruises in the crystal-cut hollows of his cheeks. He reeks of exhaustion and strife. But now, as he leans over me, his smile lights him from the inside.

"Neither am I."

He kisses me like nothing else matters at all. Nightmare, Farthing, Barstadt, the Iron Winds—for this moment, there's only my golden-haired boy nestled in my arms, his warmth burning through me like a fire. This is what I dream of—my best friend, my confidant, my love. He pulls me closer, and I curl against him, both of us moving wordlessly in our own fluency.

"I love you, Brandt," I whisper, gasping for breath against his ear. "I always have."

Brandt nestles his nose into my hair. "I love you, dreamstrider."

Reluctantly, we part. In the distance, a cannon rumbles; thick columns of smoke swirl up from the city beneath us. We're on the foothills of Nightmare's Spine, not far from where Marez enacted the binding ritual. "Brandt," I say, "what exactly happened while I was—was gone?"

Brandt reaches for my hands and faces me, those gray eyes looking right into mine. "Marez found me and your body at the warehouse. He had a squadron of Farthing soldiers with him. I tried to escape out the window, but they caught me and dragged me back to the Stargazer headquarters to lock me up.

"Sora was still there watching over Jorn, and she and I rallied together some of the Destroyers that were amongst Retch's forces. There were too many Farthing soldiers with Marez for the Destroyers to overpower them, so we couldn't keep him from walking off with your body." He flinches and tightens his grip on my hands. "But he left me in the Stargazers' custody, not realizing we'd seized control. Once they left, the Destroyers went to liberate a few of the constabularies."

"The mobs I saw." I nod. "They were pushing back the Farthingers. What about Jorn?"

"One of the Destroyers helped me carry him to safety at a physicker's office the Ministry employs from time to time—the wound is nasty, but the physicker's confident it'll heal up all right now that he's cleaned it. The Destroyers made a deeper push toward the palace, so I went to track you—that is, track Marez to where he was using your body to control Nightmare." Brandt's expression hardens; his jaw clenches tight. "I didn't know how to stop him—and not without taking the risk of hurting you. I thought we were done for—that it was all for naught. But then a golden light poured through Nightmare, through all of his monsters in the streets, burning them up." He smiles. "The Dreamer, Livia. He answered our prayers."

I cup one hand around Brandt's cheek. "Sounds like you answered your own prayers." There'll be time later to explain the truth to him. For now, the warmth of his hand in mine and the glow of dreams realized are all I need.

"I—I suppose so, yes." He smiles, nuzzling my hand. "I can't believe you're safe. I was afraid you were trapped in the dreamworld, or—or worse—"

I cup his face in my palm. "The Dreamer blessed us," I say. "He blessed us all."

We kiss against the backdrop of Nightmare's Spine, above the city still glowing with the proof of the power of dreams.

⁂

"Dreamstrider?" Minister Durst calls. "I believe it's your turn."

Two days after the invasion began, Barstadt's forces have managed to push back the Farthingers and Iron Winders alike, and the Emperor is now listening to our testimonies of what transpired. Brandt gives my hand a sharp squeeze before I stand up.

The Emperor's recuperation room swirls around me—all eyes are on me. I'm surrounded by the commanders of the Barstadt army. They are the men who held off the Commandant's ships in the Bay of Dreams amidst the chaos of the transference. The leaders and spies who fought off our supposed Farthing allies. The soldiers and constables who faced down Nightmare's minions. Who am I to stand amongst them, to profess any sort of knowledge?

But I am the dreamstrider. The Dreamer's chosen, or so they all believe after the way Nightmare disintegrated in a burst of light. Will they believe me now? Can they acknowledge that we were all wrong about our dreams?

I approach the foot of the Emperor's bed. "Your Imperial Majesty." I drop into a practiced curtsey, never taking my eyes from him. "For centuries, the Dreamer's priests have told us that the Dreamer slew Nightmare. Shattered his heart and scattered it to the far corners of the Central Realms so he could never rise again. But they were mistaken. People found those shards. People reassembled his heart, and brought Nightmare back to life. I stood in the Dreamer's temple inside Oneiros—I saw what they had done."

The High Priest's teeth are bared; he looks like he's swallowed something foul. I stare right back at him, unblinking, for a few moments, but when he says nothing, I turn back to the Emperor.

"I, too, am just a person. The Dreamer didn't choose me for anything special. Not for dreamstriding or anything else. I learned to dreamstride because I didn't know that I couldn't. I fought off Nightmare's minions because I had no choice. I thought only the Dreamer could slay Nightmare. But that isn't what the Dreamer wants for us. He doesn't want us to wait for him—he wants us to fulfill our own dreams."

"Heresy," the High Priest cries. "Every sacred text—every account of how Nightmare was first slain—"

"Not every account," I say. "Professor Hesse believed it was humans who first defeated Nightmare—that the blood of the early nations of the Central Realms and all the leaders working together brought him down. And Marez Tanin brought Nightmare back to life in the same way. By using what's within each of us—the Dreamer's gift."

The Emperor scoots higher up on the pillows propping him up. "What do you mean, the Dreamer's gift?"

"The Dreamer is in all of us—it's why he gives us dreams, something to strive for. Because we have the power to reach them. Not to wait for him to reach them for us. It's how I defeated Nightmare." I lift my chin. "I found the Dreamer in me."

The priests huddle to whisper back and forth; the generals and admirals chatter amongst themselves. But the Emperor's gaze holds mine. Slowly, a smile unfolds beneath his mustache. "Thank you, dreamstrider," he says.

We depart, leaving Minister Durst and the other members of the Emperor's war cabinet to discuss Barstadt's next steps. Brandt laces his fingers in mine as we head toward the palace's common rooms.

From down at the end of the long hall, Edina approaches us. I try to untangle my fingers from Brandt's, but he only squeezes me tighter. "Livia. Brandt." She's as polished as ever, standing ramrod straight, hands clasped before her, but a tiny smile parts her lips.

I finally disentangle myself from Brandt and step away so there's some space between us. Edina, however, seems to hardly notice me as she addresses Brandt. "Lord Strassbourg?" she asks, her tone playful. "I cannot thank you and Jornisander enough for your successful capture of the heinous criminal Adolphus Retch."

"I'm grateful Jorn's doing better, as well." Brandt's lips twitch into a grin. "I don't suppose this will help you with your issues with your father, Lady Alizard?"

"Well, I can't bloody well marry *you*." She laughs. "Look at you two. You're just—disgustingly in love with each other."

My heart lurches into my throat. But Brandt's laughing; Edina's laughing, too. "So you've completed the paperwork?" Brandt asks.

Edina nods, grining wider now. "Our marriage contract is formally dissolved."

Brandt slings one arm around my shoulder and kisses my cheek. "My parents are going to be furious!" Brandt cries. "I can't wait."

I glance between the two of them, blinking. "I'm, uh . . . a bit lost."

Edina tilts her head toward me, a dark glint in her expression. "My father will find it quite difficult to threaten me to comply with his wishes once he's imprisoned for gross corruption and conspiracy."

"The proof of which Adolphus Retch has in spades. Along with the numerous records the Ministry is recovering from his office as we speak," Brandt says.

"And—and you're all right with your father going to prison?" I hesitate. "With not marrying Brandt?"

Edina narrows her eyes. "My father threatened to kill Vera if I tried to run off with her. All my life, he's threatened me. I'm sure he'll be right at home with the other criminals." She looks from Brandt to me. "Lord Strassbourg will make a wonderful husband someday, but not to me. We both knew that. And I'm going to be rather occupied with the Aristocrat's Council once I inherit my imprisoned father's seat. I'll continue to serve House Alizard while setting right some of the wrongs my father caused."

I stare at her, sensing my lower jaw starting to droop. "But your father's seat is as one of the council heads. One of the most powerful seats in the Council."

"So it is." Edina smiles again. "I'd say the Writ of Emancipation just might get passed after all."

I take a deep breath as I wrap my arm around Brandt's waist. "I—I don't know how to thank you, Edina. Lady Alizard. Councilwoman—whatever you prefer."

"How about the both of you keep up the good work within the Ministry of Affairs?" she replies. "Professor Hesse left so much research behind—it would be a shame to see nothing come of it. No one knows his work better than you."

"You really think Minister Durst would allow me to do that?"

Edina laughs again. "It's your choice, of course, now that you have your full papers, but you've proved yourself a hundred times over, Livia. You're the dreamstrider. He'll let you do whatever you wish."

Edina departs to consult with Minister Durst, and Brandt takes my arm in his as we make our way through the palace's lower tiers. I keep glancing at him in disbelief, as if he'll vanish from me if I let him out of my sight. He grins and presses a kiss to my temple.

"I'm not going anywhere, dreamstrider. You're stuck with me for all the missions you like."

"I wouldn't mind being stuck with you beyond our missions, as well," I say.

He laughs and pats my hand. "As my lady wishes."

We walk down twisting stone steps toward the Imperial Cleansing Pool. It's more or less on the same level as the dungeons, where our prisoners of war—the younger Commandant, Retch, Marez, Kriza, and the Farthing generals—await trial. Marez is kept dosed with a mild form of Lullaby, to prevent him from accessing Oneiros again.

The palace attendants help me into a soft cotton shift. Brandt settles onto a prayer bench to commune with the Dreamer in his own way as I wade into the cleansing pool's depths. The monolith surges before me, and I smile at the golden arms plunging down to defeat Nightmare. The Dreamer's Embrace.

Dreamer, your gifts are far greater than I ever could have hoped. I'm sorry I've been such a fool, looking for them in the wrong places all this time. I close my eyes and plunge underwater, soaking my hair, then surface again right below the monolith. *I will be a great dreamstrider. I will doubt myself no more, and when you speak, I'll have no choice but to listen.*

I will honor the Dreamer within me.

I plunge underwater once more and push all the air from my lungs. My whole body radiates with warmth despite the cool water; every fiber of my skin stands alert, eager for the wonder of Oneiros as the priests rebuild it, ready for whatever duties this world demands. I let the water surround me, still and cleansing, then surface once more. I honor the Dreamer and my own dreams.

I open my eyes.

Acknowledgments

This story took everything short of black magic rituals and malevolent chanting to wrangle into a booklike shape, and I know better than to embark on my journey into the dark bookish arts alone. *Dreamstrider* would not exist without the aid of some amazing souls:

Leah Raeder and Ellen Goodlett, who cheered this book on from its weird beginnings, bludgeoned away my doubts, and demanded more kissing scenes. You're the best crit partners I could ever dream up.

My brilliant, unflappable agent, Ammi-Joan Paquette, who answers my most banal and most bonkers e-mails with equal amounts of enthusiasm. Thank you so much for finding me.

Katherine Jacobs, my editor and champion, who never shies away from calling me out on my hand waving, but always manages to fall in love with the story I'm trying to write—even if it's not all there yet.

The rest of the Macmillan Children's/Fierce Reads team: Molly Brouillette, publicist extraordinaire; Caitlin Sweeney;

Katie Fee; Lauren Burniac; touring saviors Mary van Akin, Gina Gagliano, Nicole Banholzer, and Ksenia Winnicki (team werewolves unite!); and Elizabeth H. Clark and NastPlas, who gave me this stunning cover I can't stop drooling over.

The Fourteenery, who always temper my bouts of insanity and inspire me to no end. Throw some Os.

The awesome DC YA community-slash-therapy group. You are all so talented and grounded and wonderful. In particular, Jessica Spotswood, Miranda Kenneally, Robin Talley, Caroline Richmond, and Andrea Coulter strike the perfect balance of genius discussion and well-curated cheese boards.

Everyone else who gave me wonderful notes and encouragement on this weird little book: Katie Locke (черная вдова рукописей), Audrey Coulthurst, Suzie Townsend, and Molly Jaffa. Thank you so much for your time and thoughts. My writing career would not exist, either, without the tireless work of Weronika Janczuk, Mandy Hubbard, and Bob Diforio. You are true dreamshapers.

Accountabilibuddy Dahlia Adler, without whom I'd be a sad, unproductive lump. You inspire (and scare) the crap outta me. Let's Knope it up.

Mom and Dad, for the early writing encouragement and the finest word processing technology 1990 had to offer; Grandma, for the grocery bags full of paperbacks; and Cooper, for being my snuggly sheltie writing buddy (and for the keyboard covered in dog hair).

And my husband, Jason, whose endless patience and knack for untangling knotty plots are unmatched. I love our life. I love you.

GOFISH

LINDSAY SMITH

Julie Murphy

What were your hobbies as a kid? What are your hobbies now?
My dad composes musicals, so I was really big into musical theater and classical music performance growing up. I took piano lessons for about fifteen years, but quit once I realized my hands were never going to be big enough to hit those Rachmaninoff power chords. I stuck with the viola, though, and still love to play from time to time.

What was your first job, and what was your "worst" job?
My first job was also my worst job! In high school, I started working for a local internet service provider, first as a web designer, then as tech support when the company changed hands. This was back in the days of dial-up modems—and, oh, how that sound will haunt me for life! I'm a major introvert, and answering phones and dealing with angry customers (who, of course, faulted me personally for their troubles) was a total nightmare. I did get some great stories out of the experience, though, like the woman who called me and started with "I can't talk long, because THEY'RE listening. . . ." Who knows, maybe psychic spies were after her.

What inspired you to create Barstadt, Farthing, and the Land of the Iron Winds?

I had just finished my Master's program in International Relations around the time I was working on *Dreamstrider*, and I loved the freedom the fantasy genre afforded me. I could design whatever kind of geopolitical situation I wanted to suit the story I wanted to tell!

For the Barstadt Empire, I very much wanted to depict a mostly free, mostly benevolent empire that nevertheless faced huge structural issues that held it back from being a truly free society. Mainly I drew from the setup of the Austro-Hungarian Empire, where only certain groups (in Barstadt's case, social classes) were afforded full citizenship and were able to participate in everything the empire had to offer. I also wanted the citizens to have a strong religious connection to their god, and explored how that permeated every aspect of their culture and day-to-day life.

The Land of the Iron Winds, on the other hand, was inspired by various military dictatorships of the twentieth and early twenty-first centuries. Blood-bound cults of personality like the Democratic People's Republic of Korea, scarcity, and "doublespeak" codified speech. I also very much wanted it to feel like it was constantly teetering on the verge of collapse, and so sought to save face by being an aggressor toward bigger and more successful nations like Barstadt. As long as the people believed the government was fighting to protect them, the idea went, then they could endure "temporary" hardships.

And finally, the Farthing Confederacy was inspired by many of the free-wheeling piracy hubs scattered throughout the Caribbean in the 1600s and 1700s. Very attractive because of its liberties and self-starter mentality, but ultimately very cutthroat and demanding.

Deep down, who were you rooting for Livia to end up with: Marez or Brandt?

I always wanted Brandt for Livia in the end! Marez presented a very attractive option for her, to be sure. Not just his physical appearance, but his slickly packaged philosophy of limitless potential. That was very alluring to someone who'd lived with a literal stone ceiling over her head for most of her life. But Brandt wasn't trying to use her or change her. He loved her for who she was, not what she could do for him, and I wanted to show the importance of that kind of unconditional love. Of course, he had his own prejudices and hurdles to overcome to be with her, but that's what I love about writing teen fiction—the characters are ideally suited to learn from their mistakes and grow.

What was the biggest hurdle you had to overcome in writing *Dreamstrider*?

Dreamstrider is very much a book about impostor syndrome, something I was wrestling with personally at the time I was working on it. I first wrote it shortly after selling *Sekret*, my debut novel, and even though I knew full well how hard I'd worked to become a published author, I was plagued with uncertainty and doubt. I felt certain that someone was going to realize I was a total hack and take it all away. So Livia's journey was, in some ways, a pep talk to myself—a reminder that we're all in control of our own fates and capable of so much more than we know.

Of course, *Dreamstrider*, with its clockwork-intricate plot, was *also* the book that made me realize the importance of outlining beforehand. In this case, as an example of what *not* to do. It took a lot of work to get all the plot points arranged just so. Given my love for complex storylines, I'm finding it much easier for me to figure out all those minute details beforehand from now on.

I love secrets! Juicy, awful secrets, the ones that make the fate of the world hang in the balance. I fully embrace my nosiness, and I think it makes me a better writer—I'm always looking for the unstated whats and whys behind every story. And I love spy stories because they're all about trying to pry those secrets free. Sometimes the secrets curl up on themselves like a shell, and other times, they explode catastrophically. Both are fascinating to me.

I think with both *Sekret* and *Dreamstrider*, I wanted to explore different ways countries might attack the problem of finding out their adversaries' plans, especially when magic or enhanced abilities might be at play. In *Sekret*, this took the form of upping the stakes on the paranoia and fear the average Soviet citizen felt, worrying what their government might think if it knew what they really thought. For *Dreamstrider*, though, I wanted to play more with the idea of inspiration and ambition, and how that looks whether it comes from an internal source—our own hopes and dreams—versus an external source, like society or religious inspiration. So even though I included strong psychological elements in these different books, I wanted to attack them from wildly different angles!

I have a tendency, when drafting, to make plots incredibly complicated and intricate, often because as I write, I keep thinking of new branches for the story to take. This makes for lots of work in the revision stage! Recently, though, I've gotten more serious about outlining in greater detail. This allows me to write much faster—because I know exactly where I'm going—but also makes the revision process much less painful.

If you could travel in time, where would you go and what would you do?
Honestly, I'd love to travel forward in time! So many possibilities to see how technology advances, geopolitical struggles play out, and of course, how some of my favorite book series end up. . . . If I were to travel back in time, though, I'd love to see the final days of tsarist Russia, or the Renaissance in Europe, or perhaps Saladin's sultanate of Egypt and Syria. Just listening to people, seeing the sights, and exploring the land would be so cool.

What was your favorite book when you were a kid?
Maybe this reveals too much about my childhood, but my absolute favorite book growing up—in addition to the Nancy Drew books and The Babysitters Club, naturally—was *Slaughterhouse Five* by Kurt Vonnegut. I love how effortlessly Vonnegut tells a story that defies genre. It's got time travel, war criticism, science fiction, personal dramas, military history, and so much more! It really inspired me to be fearless in my writing and never shy away from telling weird tales.

What's your favorite TV show or movie?
I'm absolutely in love with *Fringe*, J. J. Abrams's alternate-universe paranormal/weird-science show. I think it has a great balance between lengthy story arcs and serial story-telling, and all the characters are weird and wonderful (with stellar acting, playing multiple versions of themselves!). I also

love *The Americans* (big surprise), *Buffy the Vampire Slayer*, *Game of Thrones*, *True Detective*, *Psych* (about a *fake* psychic detective), and *Firefly*.

What's the best advice you have ever received about writing?

Finish what you start, even when it gets hard. NaNoWriMo, or National Novel Writing Month, was instrumental in forcing myself to do just that. If I hadn't done NaNo, I don't know if I ever would have finished a book! Only once you've started finishing your stories can you really step back from them and see them from every angle. Then comes the hard part of learning how to fix them.

If you were a superhero, what would your superpower be?

Teleportation! I love seeing the world, but hate the travel time. Wouldn't it be great to pop in to a café on the Adriatic for breakfast, take a morning hike outside of Marrakech, head home to get a few hours of writing, then grab dinner in Tokyo? It would make my morning commute way less painful, too.

SQUARE FISH

REIKO IS FULL OF SO MUCH HATRED THAT
she goes to Japan for the summer to try and find peace.
Instead, Reiko somehow ends up in nineteenth-century
Japan, living as the girl Miyu, who is even more vengeful
than she is. Stranded in another century, will Reiko be
able to face down both her own demons *and* Miyu's?

READ ON FOR AN EXCERPT.

CHAPTER ONE

UNCLE SATORI SAYS MASTERY IS A WELL-WORN PATH.
(At least, that's how my cousin Akiko translated it for me,
though I rarely take her at her word.) If he's right, then I am
mastering a path of hatred, carving it deeper every day like the
scars along my thighs. I wake up with a hatred that gnaws at
me like hunger, and I feed that hatred with Akiko's snores
from the other side of the room. I feed it with the sight of my
megalith suitcase spewed open beside my pallet, still not un-
packed. And with the one unread email clogging my phone's
notifications that I can't bring myself to read.

If I carve a path deep enough, then it will become a trench.
A grave. Carve it deep enough, and I'll never have to climb out.

In the three months since I arrived in Tokyo, I've made a

routine that turns me inside out with exhaustion and keeps my thoughts on their well-worn trail. That's what I came here for—a distraction, something to overload my senses and leave me to my self-devouring mind. No time to think about what came before or whatever might come next. Maybe my parents hoped I'd learn mindfulness here, or obedience, or drive, or at least a goddamned Japanese phrase or two beyond *sumimasen—excuse me, forgive me, please pardon me for all the evil I've done.* But no, all I've accomplished is that I've filtered my raw hate into something potent, clarified, lethal.

I have mastered the path of hatred, and I know now where it ends.

It ends with my revenge.

I leave Uncle Satori's apartment with my anger burning through me like a grease fire. The sidewalks of Shinjuku are clean as ever: gray asphalt and crisp white lines and slender concrete fingers of apartment buildings thrust toward a crystal blue sky. Nothing like Seattle, where we smear our lives and our insides across every surface—yarn bombs knitted around statues and trees and signs, used chewing gum crusted against the Market Theater wall, ripe with our saliva and germs. I think that's what my parents have never understood about our life in America: that we're not meant to keep everything locked inside, preserving a uniform facade for everyone else's benefit. Hideki and I lived our lives in a kind of purgatory, halfway between our parents' stonewalled world and the wild, free-range one our classmates inhabited, never able to stretch out fully in either one.

I feed two 100-yen coins into a vending machine and crack open a hot can of Suntory Boss coffee (*the boss of them all*, I say to myself). Black-clad office workers in modest heels and starched white button-downs join me in an eerie, silent parade—our daily mourning processional. Right on cue, I see my favorite couple, husband and wife, walking side by side, not speaking, not making eye contact, and when we reach the corner, her hand darts toward his for a hasty squeeze before he turns the corner without a word.

I want to scream at them—interrupt our vow of silence. *So do it*, I imagine Chloe would tell me. *Disrupt the status quo. Break free and make everyone know your name.*

But it's not yet time. When I get the guts to do it, it's her name everyone will know. She'll be the one to take the blame.

In the subway station, the train arrives with a polite ding. I've fantasized before about flinging myself in front of it, too fast for the white-gloved train pushers to catch. Clog up a million salarymen's morning commutes. But it's useless to throw myself in front of a train as it pulls into the station, as I've learned from my extensive research. The train's already decelerating, and a lot of cities use recessed track wells now so the average would-be suicide usually survives, albeit with grievous body blows and broken bones. Anyway, I didn't come here with suicide in mind, though if it serves my goal, I won't dismiss it. These fantasies, for now, are part of the dark need for vengeance beating inside of me. My death has to serve a purpose— make someone else suffer even more.

We all shuffle on, sucked inside as if the pristine cars are a massive set of lungs. "Please take care that your typing sounds do not disturb other passengers," the signs implore. I know my black metal playlist is seeping out of my cheap earbuds, but I don't care. The other passengers look away, look down, look anywhere but at me. They don't know I'm a tourist— nothing brands me as American-born except my rudeness. To them, I'm just a disgrace.

I close my eyes and sink into the dark forests and ghost-filled castles of the black metal songs as though they're a sludge, pulling me under. This playlist is all Chloe—it keeps my wounds nice and raw. One night in the summer camp painting studios, when we'd been painting our canvases and each other, she snatched my phone to get us some music and declared my half-assed collection of '70s soft rock and classical piano sonatas to be an unmatched tragedy. "Let me fix this for you," she said. I think part of me believed she meant my life. She taught me how to kiss to the aching chords of

Opeth and the thrashing drums of Cannibal Corpse and Sleater-Kinney's refined rage.

It's been over a year now since she chewed me up and spit me out. A year since I was dumb enough to believe that she (or anyone) could love a fucked-up, forgettable little girl like me. For ten short weeks at the PNW Summer Arts Camp, I was cool. I was hot. I wasn't Saint Isaac's Preparatory Academy's punch line and punching bag. She showed me that all the tangled-up feelings I had for other humans didn't have to stay inside my head. That I could trail love on her skin and smear hate on the canvas in a vicious dance, hot and cold.

The playlist starts over again. The trains get more crowded as we draw closer to the center of Tokyo: schoolgirls in uniform, holding down their pleated skirts to defend against perverts with camera phones, elderly women in quilt coats with bags of groceries, sneer-lipped kids my age punching away at their (respectfully silenced) handheld game consoles.

After Chloe released my carefully maintained feelings, I left camp and returned home to start school, locking them away again. But I didn't forget that summer before my senior year when I was free. And so when we had our first long weekend in the fall, I hopped on a bus down to Portland to see her. Her new girlfriend answered the door.

That's when my Chloe problem really began.